Thomas McNicoll

Essays on English literature

Thomas McNicoll

Essays on English literature

ISBN/EAN: 9783337203108

Printed in Europe, USA, Canada, Australia, Japan

Cover: Foto ©Andreas Hilbeck / pixelio.de

More available books at **www.hansebooks.com**

ESSAYS ON ENGLISH

LITERATURE

❧

BY THOMAS McNICOLL

ALDI

DISCIP.

ANGLVS

LONDON

BASIL MONTAGU PICKERING

196 PICCADILLY

1861

PREFACE.

IF a Preface be only of the nature of an apology, it is better omitted even from the moſt indifferent work. But a few words of explanation may be neceſſary to put the reader in poſſeſſion of ſome facts which have largely influenced and ſhaped the author's plan. In the preſent caſe, it is likely that without a ſtatement of the circumſtances of their origin, the following Eſſays would be judged by too high a ſtandard, and made liable to unfair exceptions. The omiſſion of that ſtatement might alſo ſeem to impeach the author's candour.

It is hoped that many perſons may be led to read this volume to whom its contents will be *entirely new.* **But** *it is right to mention that the majority* **of the** *Effays form part of the author's contributions to* **the** London Quarterly Review; *that the fecond* **and third** *papers, as well as a portion of the firft, have alfo had a place* **in** *our periodical literature; and that only the little apologue* **at** *the end of the volume appears now for* **the firft time.**

The author has no defire to fhift the refponfibility of this reprint, by fuggefting the urgency **of** *friends. The Effays could not have appeared in their prefent form without his confent; and if they fhould be judged unworthy* **of** *that honour,* **he** *will clearly be open to the fufpicion* **of** *entertaining an undue opinion of their ufefulnefs or merit. This inference is fo obvious, that he can lofe nothing by its frank admiffion. The fact is, that he believes* **the critical portions** *of this volume may ftill* **be of fervice in correcting** *fome of the vices of our popular literature; and this belief muft*

*form his apology for retaining certain stric-
tures, as in the Essay on Popular Criticism,
which he would otherwise have chosen to omit.
Most of the remaining papers are discursive
rather than critical; and some of the earliest
in date are not free from a rhetorical em-
phasis of style which belongs to inexperience.
The author has given them a place in this
collection because they harmonize with the
general contents of his volume, and also because,
with all their imperfection, he still holds them
to be substantially just. He will say no more
in their behalf, lest he should be thought to deprecate that free criticism of his own performances which he has never scrupled to exercise
on the works of other men; and so, standing
quite aside, he leaves them to their fortune.*

T. M.

Chelsea, **Feb.** 22, 1861.

CONTENTS.

AUTO-BIOGRAPHIES.

E are affured by philofophers that there
is nothing futile or fuperfluous in the
material world. Even the refufe of
man becomes the refource of Nature,
who weaves her gayeft mantle from the fhreds
he fcatters, and in whofe wonderful economy
there is ufe as well as place for all that we con-
temptuoufly call " rubbifh." Indeed, there is no
end to the intereft and the beauty of many trivial
and offenfive things. Ignorance on the one hand,
and engroffing worldlinefs on the other, are hourly
blinding us to the moft valuable truths enfhrined
in very humble forms, and confirming our habits
of indifference towards a world of common wonders. If our eyes were really open, the moft
common-place of daily objects would affume a
romantic novelty, and invite a more intimate
refearch. With a limited clafs of perfons, this
is actually the cafe,—bleft as they are with an
active intelligence and a fcientific curiofity, and
thefe contributing to induce a conftant habit of

obſervation. This enviable gift—for it is a gift
as well as a habit—acts like a charm in opening
the ſources of a thouſand pleaſures. An eye
practiſed and familiar in the obſervation of nature, and accuſtomed to trace in every object of
comparative inſignificance or doubtful utility ſome
curious phenomenon of its exiſtence—an eye that
ſees relation, and deſign, and even benefit, in
objects which are merely repulſive to the ignorant, can hardly fall upon a ſpot of earth that is
not fruitful in peculiar intereſt. Intelligently
viewed, the very vermin take rank in creation,
and even duſt is recognized as the *detritus* of ſyſte-
matic ſtrata. The rock that is ſo bare and profit-
leſs to the uninformed is to ſuch a man an eloquent
companion; it tells him the hiſtory of its ages,
and reveals to him the ſcars of its experience:
and ſo minutely has the record been preſerved for
our philoſopher, that the guſt of wind blown
many centuries ago has left itſelf a witneſs in the
ſilent rain-drop fallen into a ſlanted bed. In like
manner, while his houſekeeper regards with mingled ſcorn and deteſtation that moſt ogre-like of
inſects, the ſpider, and thinks her broom diſ-
honoured by ſuch contact, he has not diſdained to
obſerve, in that leaſt regarded corner of the houſe,
another diſtinct variety of form, an uninſtructed
but inſpired weaver making his matchleſs web,
and a peculiar type of thoſe predatory habits
which, in a manner immediate or indirect, cauſe
every claſs of beings in its turn to become the
prey of ſome other.

There is an interest similar in kind to this, and like this almost infinitely diversified, in the hourly experience of the observer of human life and manners: there is an analogous charm derived from the study of even the lowest type of character, the slight but sufficient links of cause and consequence in the most unimportant chain of incidents, the mingled tissue of trivial and grotesque and serious passages in a career of the most ordinary kind. But what was merely the pleasure of intelligence in the physical survey is heightened by our human sympathy in the moral : the picturesque becomes intensified into the pathetic; and those vicissitudes of fortune which lead out our curiosity to follow another's course are repeatedly suggesting a possible parallel in our own. It is no subject of wonder, then, that man should have a peculiar and absorbing interest in man, where his intellect and sympathies may expatiate together. If the adventures of an atom, whether historically or philosophically considered, are ready to prove full of profit and delight ; if the life of an insect is found to touch upon and illustrate a thousand natural truths, and furnish a distinctive type of animate existence ; how much more real must our interest be in the most unpromising of human characters, and the obscurest fragment of human story ! The stone recoiling from our careless feet, and the fossil cast up by the miner's shovel, is each a link in the great chain of nature,—is joined inseparably to all that went before and all that is yet to come : you cannot ignore its pre-

fence without grofs injury to the material logic in
which God has embodied and demonftrated his
creative wifdom.   But of man all this is true by
emphafis; and though he fhould be the vileft,
pooreft, and idleft of his race, and lefs miffed from
the courts of life than the dog which kept faithful
watch and ward over his mafter's houfe, as man
he is joined to a far higher economy, and ftamped
with a more Divine fignificance ; nor can he fail
to illuftrate, even in his obfcureft wanderings,
and in his moft humble deeds, the majefty of
fpiritual laws and the myftery of human life.
And, befides thefe indications of a great ideal,
typical of his fpecies, and ever and anon ftruggling to the furface through the wrecks of fome
awful foregone calamity, there is in every man a
feparate individuality of thought and action, each
breathing its peculiar moral.   No two lives run
parallel for an inftant of time : no two hearts are
fynchronous in the pulfations of their hopes and
fears.   Each is the hero of a feparate drama : for
him the earth is as really a ftage prepared as for
the great Protagonift himfelf: for his individual
drama of probation all nature is a ftore-room of
acceffories, and all the tribes of men fubordinate.
And though thefe feveral lives do conftantly in-
terfect and crofs each other, and all traces of
feeble men feem perpetually loft in the footmarks
of the ftrong and leaping, yet if we follow carefully the leaft of thefe defpifed, we fhall find him
to be the central figure of fome imaginable moral
circle, and the hero of a true dramatic unity.

By thefe obfervations we have chofen to introduce the fubject of this paper, becaufe we think
they plainly illuftrate, and largely account for, the
deep invariable intereft fo commonly felt in biographical details, and efpecially in the more full
and accurate revelations of auto-biography. For,
be it obferved, this intereft is, for the moft part,
independent both of greatnefs and virtue in the
hero of the ftory, and even of any unufual fortunes affecting his career. It feems to demand
only, what may be termed *genuinenefs* in the narrative, and *directnefs* in the narrator. Truth, we
might have faid, was neceffary, did we not remember inftances in which exaggerations of every
kind, and even grofs and palpable departures from
veracity, were characteriftic but not mifleading,
and therefore rather enhancing the general fidelity
of portraiture defired,—juft as Falftaff is better
known by his prepofterous falfehoods, than he
could have been by a faithful narrative of the
death of Percy. In all thefe confeffions, however,
we look for a certain opennefs and freedom, and
even a fimplicity of fpeech; but by this laft requirement we are not to be confidered as denouncing thofe affectations which may have
become the fecond nature of the auto-biographer, and fo contribute an important charm,
but as infifting only that the writer reveal himfelf, with real candour, or through fome tranfparent artifice, and that all his cunning and
duplicity, though fo great as to include felf-
deception, *fhall not deceive us.*

After thefe confiderations, we fhall not be
furprifed to find that the plaineft clafs of thefe
writings are commonly the moft interefting ; or
rather, the intereft of them is more ftrictly of the
kind proper to auto-biography. This clafs confifts of memoirs of perfons remarkable for neither
their gifts, nor attainments, nor even extraordinary fortunes. Not always does the life defcribed prefent any novel features to the imagination of the reader, nor is it even neceffary that
either in ftyle or fentiment fhould the narrative
rife above the level of mediocrity. The moral
ftandard of the hero may be contemptible, like
that of Vidocq the French thief-taker ; or his
perfonal hiftory trivial, like that of Lackington
the bookfeller : but in the meaneft fubject of
thefe memoirs, and in the moft ordinary fcenes
depictured from the daily life of man, if there be
only that fincerity in the memorialift which
engages confidence in the narrative, we fhall
find attraction and inftruction in a high degree.
The picture, indeed, may be wanting in the elaboration and fpiritual fuggeftivenefs of a true work
of art ; but it will have the excellence peculiar to
a daguerreotype portrait,—a literal and detailed
truth to nature. Characters may not appear
there in moments of their higheft mood, nor
even true to their better felves ; but their momentary prefentment is caught and preferved for
ever, and neither the tone of attitude nor the fignificance of drefs is loft.

To reconcile the afferted interefts of thefe

loweft fpecimens of auto-biography with the deficiencies attributed to them as a clafs, it may be
neceffary to fpeak of thofe deficiencies in qualified terms. While it is true (for example) that
romantic or important incidents may be entirely
abfent from the ftory, it muft be remembered
that—as our opening analogy fuggefts—the varieties of human circumftances infure, in every
cafe, a real, novel, and peculiar intereft; that as
no two individual faces are alike, fo neither are
any two individual charaǎers, and ftill lefs any
two individual careers. Again: if ability or attainments in any high degree are pronounced
unneceffary on the part of fuch memoir-writer, it
is fimply meant that he need have none fufficient
of itfelf to diftinguifh him,—no talent to command for himfelf the public admiration, and no
fcientific or literary acquirement to furnifh his
book with a topic of intereft extraneous to himfelf. But ability of fome kind he will have:
genius itfelf is, perhaps, more a matter of degree
than a rare and exclufive endowment; and the
humbleft author will ever and anon, in fome
direǎion or another, and in a milder or more
brilliant way, give evidence of the " divinity that
ftirs within him." Befides, there are many fources
of intereft,—fuch as, idiofyncrafy, native mental
bias, or fome moral quality forced into promi-
nence by ftrefs of fortune,—one or other of
which muft appear in the moft ordinary record of
human life. And if the aǎs of men fo widely
differ, and their circumftantial relations are fo

complicate and varied, how diftinct and multiplied muft be their fprings of action! How often fhaded by infirmity the luftre of their moft virtuous deeds! How often their darkeft woof of error fhot with a relieving brightnefs!

But is there no fuch thing as trite or commonplace in thefe confeffions? In the literal tranfcript of real life, rarely. It is true that the writer's moral or general reflections may, from the feeblenefs of his reafon, be trite in the extreme; and an excefs of fuch reflections over matters of fact will render the narrative both tedious and commonplace. All extra-literal matter, if not put in with artift-like, judicious touches, tends to deftroy *vraifemblance*, and caufe endlefs contradictions; for what is that which belongs neither to nature nor to art, but a monftrofity? Inftances of this kind of auto-biography are not infrequent; but they are foon forgotten, or never attain notice. It occafionally happens alfo that a vanity the moft contemptible, becaufe totally unredeemed by anything worthy of mark either in character or experience, induces fome dullard to make public confeffion of his incompetence, and feek to break from the hopelefs obfcurity to which he is appointed; and his felf-laudatory work will, of courfe, be, like himfelf, moft wearifome and weak. But this will never refult from the humble nature of the details, nor even from the unfkilfulnefs of the compiler; for thefe cannot of themfelves produce the *morally abfurd*. Truth, however defultory, will manifeft a beauty of its own ; however difconnected, its parts will finally cohere. Fragments of broken glafs, when thrown into a kaleidofcope, affume the richeft colour and moft regular of fhapes ; and every revolution of the inftrument difpofes them into a new combination, equal in beauty, though diffimilar in figure. And fo the life that is moft trifling and difconnected, and as deftitute of brilliance or arrangement as pieces of pale and fhattered glafs, may affume a picturefque variety, proportioned to the number of the afpects under which it is prefented. Each of us takes the view of another's chequered fortunes through the tube of diftance, whether of fpace or time,—a medium that for the moment fhuts out all obfervation befide, and narrows the attention where it concentrates the light.

Let the reader, if he would be convinced of the inexhauftible fund of entertainment and remark fupplied by human manners and affairs, note down in detail the experiences and obfervations of his life : and, in particular, let him portray the characteriftic features of thofe to whom he once ftood related, or with whom he has been led to affociate ; and omit no fingularity in their hiftory or pofition which may formerly have awakened his own curiofity. Perhaps he may not hitherto have fuppofed his life to have been fruitful either in anecdote or character : but reflection will inftruct him otherwife. Things trivial in themfelves will become fignificant in relation to their confequences ; and perfons of

ordinary ftamp may be remembered and fet forth
by fome occafional fuccefs or felicitous remark.
Did he never cherifh a fecret regret refpecting
father, or fifter, or coufin, or friend, that one
of fuch peculiar ability, or fuch perfect but
fequeftered virtue, fhould be fo little known,—
that in his heart and memory only fhould furvive,
and fo ultimately perifh, a picture of excellencies
quite unique, when blended in a charming individuality ? Among the recollections of his childhood, is he never haunted by fome lovely half-
ideal image of grace and beauty, companion of
his fports? or does no romantic friendfhip of his
boyhood remind him of the time when affection
had all the tendernefs, and more than all the
truth, of paffion ? Did he never meet with elec-
trifying kindnefs in an unlikely quarter? or was
he never fhocked into a momentary mifanthropy
by ingratitude or failing goodnefs ? Have not his
own opinions, taftes, and difpofitions been curi-
oufly influenced and modified by outward circumftances, as well as inward growth ? or the little
current of his own fortunes been diverted by
fome accidental barrier, and had to wear a chan-
nel for itfelf? And were not thefe events, though
roughly thus conjectured by another, attended by
fuch features of novelty and chance-control, that
the detailed ftory would have at once the charm
of fiction and the perfuafivenefs of truth ?

Many books occur to us as furnifhing illuftration of thefe remarks ; but we take—almoft at
random—*The Auto-biography of a Working Man,*

publifhed within the laft few years. If not the
moft recent, neither is it the leaft fuitable for
that purpofe. Unpretending as is this little work,
and confifting of the fimpleft details of private life
and ordinary labours, it juftifies the affertion already
ventured, that neither talent in the writer, nor
intereft in the record, will commonly be found
wanting in works of this kind; that a diftinct
individuality may be expected in the hero-author,
and both variety and unity in the auto-hiftory.
The volume is of goodly dimenfions, and contains the fulleft particulars of a perfonal career
" *by One who has whiftled at the Plough.*" Defpite the unpromifing nature of its title, we doubt
if a more entertaining record of humble life and
honourable induftry was ever penned. It is characterized by an air of manly fincerity and fterling
moral fenfe, and gives evidence of a native tafte
for the good and the beautiful, improved by diligent felf-culture. From the firft page to the laft,
there is no fuch thing as wearying; but, on the
contrary, the reader is led onward by a quiet but
increafing intereft, that makes the time lapfe by
infenfibly. There is throughout the volume, and
efpecially in the earlier chapters, a frefhnefs in
the details, a fimplicity in the characters, and a
modeft dignity in the author's manner, that unite
to enlift our curiofity and fecure our confidence.
The materials furnifhed to the auto-biographer
by the circumftances of his birth and after employments, were poor and unpromifing; but our
readers fhall have fome opportunity for judging.

His father, having occasion for migrating south-
ward from his native village, in the centre of
Scotland, settled as a farm-labourer in the county
of Berwickshire; and there married a blooming
young woman, servant in a farm-house, and
daughter of John Orkney, a working man. Of
these his parents our author was the eleventh and
last child. The poverty of this worthy family
rendered their very existence a struggle; for low
wages and high prices made it a difficult matter
to provide for so large a household; and not all
the industry of a steady and upright father, nor all
the diligence and care of a thrifty, tender mother,
could do more than avert the extreme of desti-
tution. Such were the humble circumstances of
our author's parentage and birth. But no false
shame leads him to speak slightingly, or with
other than dutiful remembrance and affection, of
this period of his childhood and youth. His
reminiscences of peasant-life and early trials,—
including some months of miserable schooling, in
which his unfortunate inferiority of clothes and
general poverty brought upon him the injustice
and contempt of well-dressed lads and servile
pedagogue,—are told with graphic force and in
an admirable spirit. Herding his master's cows
was the employment of many years of his boyhood; and in his relation of that period of his life
occur many anecdotes characteristic of country life
and manners, and passages indicative of the growth
of his own disposition, moral and intellectual.
At] school he is unmercifully thrashed " on the

hands, head, face, neck, fhoulders, back, legs, everywhere," until bliftered : but he difdains to wince. "I fat fullen and in torture all the day, my poor fifter Mary glancing at me from her book ; fhe not crying, but her heart beating as if it would burft for me. When we got out of the fchool to go home, and were away from all the other fcholars on our lonely road to Thriepland Hill, fhe foothed me with kind words, and we cried then, both of us." The character of his father, a rigorous Diffenter of the fect called " Anti-burghers," is not without dignity ; nor that of his mother without a homely fweetnefs : and it is efpecially gratifying to witnefs, in the real noblenefs of thefe humble peafants and their children, an interefting proof that no circum- ftances are in themfelves fo wretched or fo bafe but goodnefs may redeem them from contempt, and even inveft them with moral beauty. The whole career of this auto-biographer, could we fol- low it throughout, would furnifh a continued illuf- tration of the fame truth. Character, working from within outwards, is the great transformer of man- kind, and the fource of true individual diftinction. The bafhful hob-nailed cowherd of this hiftory becomes by accident acquainted with the poetry of Burns, and glows, for the firft time, with an intellectual pleafure. He next covets the loan of Anfon's Voyages, of which he had heard parts ; but only after a fearful ftruggle with his fhame- facednefs does he take courage to afk it : then in the fields, at refting-time, he reads about the brave fhip *Centurion,* and all that befell her. After a while, a brother in England fuggefting that he might join him and become a forefter, it feems defirable that Hutton's " Menfuration " fhould be ftudied :—

" *But where get to Hutton, and how, was the quefion. I had no money of my own, and my mother at that time had none; the cow had not calved, and there was no butter felling to bring in money. Yet I could not ref: if I could not then buy Hutton, I muft fee it. One day, in March, I was driving the harrows, it being the time of fowing the fpring corn, and I thought fo much about becoming a good fcholar, and built fuch caftles in the air, that, tired as I was (and going at the harrows from five in the morning to fix at night, on foft loofe fand, is one of the moft tiring days of work upon a farm), I took off my fhoes, fcraped the earth from them, and out of them, wafhed hands and face, and walked to Dunbar, a diftance of fix miles, to inquire if Hutton's ' Menfuration' was fold there, and, if poffible, to look at it,—to fee with my eyes the actual fhape and fize of the book which was to be the key to my future fortunes. George Miller was in the fhop himfelf, and told me the book was four fhillings. That fum of four fhillings feemed to me to be the moft precious amount of money which ever came out of the Mint: I had it not; nor had I one fhilling; but I had feen the book, and had told George Miller not to fell it to anyone elfe; and fo I walked over the fix miles, large with the thought that it*

would be mine at fartheft when the cow calved,—
perhaps fooner."

The money was raifed, the book bought and
ftudied; but inftead of becoming a forefter in
England, our hero (now fifteen years of age) was
raifed to the dignity of ploughman in his native
place, and drove the moft lively and fprightly pair
of horfes on the farm,—to wit, Nannie and Kate.
We cannot now follow the fubfequent career of
this intelligent and independent man; but it is
replete with intereft and inftruction. His cruel
punifhment when in the regiment of the Scots'
Greys, his manly bearing throughout that painful
affair, and his difdainful refufal to become a mar-
tyr-mendicant for his own profit, are all honourable alike to his morality and good fenfe; and
equally fo, the political moderation with which
he laboured for Reform, the tempered joy with
which he hailed it, and the judgment with which
he reftrained the ardour or condemned the extremes of fiercer Radicals.

If fuch is the auto-biography of common life,
we may proceed with expectation of yet greater
pleafure to the auto-biography of adventure. This
latter clafs of writings, in which the homely
perfonal details of the former appear in connection with extraordinary incidents and foreign
objects, is of a fafcinating character, and was
fhrewdly appreciated by the beft of our earlier
novelifts, Daniel Defoe, who adapted its peculiar

features to the purpofes of fiction. In this form accordingly we are prefented with Robinfon Crufoe,
Moll Flanders, and other popular worthies. The
charm of thefe and fimilar creations of art, which
lies chiefly in the literal portraiture of minuteft
details as well as novel objects, is not ftrictly
belonging to art proper; it is dependent upon
a faculty which is the humbleft that art can
exercife,—the faculty of imitation. Their art,
therefore, is not of the higheft kind, and does not
appeal fo much to the educated mind as the
popular inftinct; not to the imagination, but to
the fenfes and the memory. They are painted
with Dutch fidelity and care; but there is feldom
more than meets the eye : there is no fuggeftion
of the romance of matter, no indication that all
nature is typical. For this reafon the fictitious
narrative has little or no advantage over the true.
The pleafure arifing from a confcious and clever
imitation will hardly compenfate for the abfence
of that vivid intereft which always attaches to a
relation of real perfonal adventures. In the picturefque and quiet parts verifimilitude will be
charming ; but in the more critical incidents of
human ftory, reality would prove enchaining. If
the internal truth of the former approve it to be
genuine, we have this added fatisfaction in the
latter,—that we know it to be authentic.

Eldorado, or Adventures in the Path of Empire,
is the narrative of an ifolated, but remarkable
paffage in its author's life, and, at the fame time,
of the moft ftartling epifode in modern hiftory. It

contains the perſonal experience and obſervation
of an intelligent pilgrim to California, the Eldorado
of the Pacific. If truth ever exceeded the ſtrange-
neſs and romance of fiction, it aſſuredly does ſo
in theſe brilliant pages, which will remain to excite the wonder of remote poſterity, and be cre-
dited only becauſe the marvels they reveal tran-
ſcend the limits of invention. The book is,
beyond compariſon, the ableſt record of an un-
paralleled event. It deſcribes the golden cruſade
of the world,—more picturesque in coſtume, more
diverſified in character, more fertile in hopes, more
beſet with diſcouragements, and more pregnant
with diſappointments, than the boldeſt cruſade of
the age of chivalry. It is ſimple, literal, and unex-
aggerated,—what the author ſaw with his eyes,
and heard with his ears: but it is, nevertheleſs,
grand and aſtoniſhing; for he wandered in a
region alternated with redundant foreſts and im-
meaſurable deſerts, towards rivers girdled by the
golden ſands of Pactolus, and mountains teeming
with the fruit of Aladdin's garden. In this motley
pilgrimage are the repreſentatives of every nation,
converging from all quarters of the globe, journeying in every variety of manner, encountering
every conceivable ſhape of danger, toil, deſti-
tution, and diſeaſe, many hearts ſinking in deſpair,
and many frames exhauſted unto death. Yet all are
not animated by the ignoble luſt of gold. In
theſe innumerable groups may be found a wide
diverſity of motives: from our author, enamoured
of the picturesque in nature, character, and life,

to the moſt covetous of Californian devotees, whoſe dollars are the ſilver ſhrines of the god whom he pronounces great, and who looks out for the painted booths of San Franciſco as eagerly as the Jew for the heights of the City of David, or the Hindoo for the glittering minarets of Benares.

It **would** be difficult to juſtify, by a ſingle brief quotation, ſuch as our ſpace admits, **the** character of varied intereſt aſcribed to theſe **vo-** lumes; but a ſingle extract may ſerve to illuſtrate the author's animated ſtyle, and afford a glimpſe at leaſt **of** his **adventure.** **The** difficulty con- ſiſts in chooſing. **The voyage from** New York to Chagres,—the journey acroſs the Iſthmus,— Panama and **its** ruined churches and waiting emigrants,—the **glorious** coaſting **on** the Pacific ſhores,—and the bewildering, buſtling ſtreets **of** San Franciſco on a firſt arrival,—theſe would each ſupply a page for our purpoſe. Then our author's journey inland,—the mule-back progreſs and camp-life reſtings of his march,—Stockton at noon-day with its glowing ſtreet of tents, ſprung up, like gigantic muſhrooms, almoſt in a night,— the Diggings,—the return to San Franciſco,—the thouſand novel features of that ſtrange city,—ex- curſions here and there and back again,—theſe are a few rough indications of the ſtores from which we are to ſelect a ſample. **We** give the author's memorandum **of the laſt** day of his voyage, and landing **in** California :—

" *At laſt the voyage is drawing to a cloſe. Fifty-*

one days have elapfed fince leaving *New York*, in which time we have, in a manner, coafted both fides of the *North American Continent*, from the parallel of 40° *N.* to its termination, within a few degrees of the *Equator*, over feas once ploughed by the keels of *Columbus* and *Balboa*, of *Grijalva* and *Sebaftian* **Vifcaino**. *All* is excitement on board; the Captain has juft **taken** his noon obfervation. *We are* **running along the** *fhore*, within fix or eight **miles'** diftance; **the** hills are bare and fandy, **but loom** up finely through the deep blue haze. *A brig bound to San Francifco, but fallen off to lee-ward of the harbour, is making a new tack on our left, to come up again.* **The** coaft trends fomewhat more to the weftward, and a **notch or gap** is **at laft** vifible in its lofty outline.

" *An hour* **later; we are in** front **of the** entrance **to** *San Francifco Bay.* *The mountains* **on the** northern fide **are** 3,000 feet in height, and come boldly down **to** the fea. *As the view opens through the fplendid ftrait, three or four miles in width, the ifland rock of Alcatraz appears, gleaming white in the diftance. An inward-bound fhip follows clofe on our wake, urged on by wind and tide. There is a fmall fort perched among the trees on our right, where the ftrait is narroweft; and a glance at* **the** *formation of the hills fhows that this pafs might* **be** *made impregnable as Gibraltar.* *The town is* **ftill** *concealed behind the promontory around which* **the** *Bay turns to the fouthward; but between Alcatraz and the Ifland* **of** *Yerba Buena,* **now** *coming into fight, I can* **fee** *veffels at* **anchor.** *High through* *the vapour in front,* **and thirty miles** *diſtant, riſes the* **Peak** *of Monte* **Diablo, which** *overlooks everything between the Sierra Nevada* **and the ocean.** *On our left opens the Bight of Souſolito, where the* U. S. *pro-peller ' Maſſachuſetts' and ſeveral other* **veſſels are at anchor.**

" At laſt we **are** *through the Golden* **Gate,**—*fit name for ſuch a magnificent portal to the commerce of the Pacific! Yerba Buena Iſland is in front; ſouthward and weſtward opens the renowned har-bour, crowded with the ſhipping of the world, maſt behind* **maſt,** *and* **veſſel behind veſſel,** *the flags of all nations fluttering in the breeze! Around the curving ſhore of the bay,* **and upon the** *ſides* **of three hills which** *riſe* **ſteeply from the water, the middle one** *receding ſo* **as to form a bold amphitheatre, the** *town is planted, and ſeems ſcarcely yet* **to have taken root ;** *for tents, canvas, plank,* **mud, and** *adobe houſes,* **are** *mingled together with the* **leaſt** *apparent attempt at order and durability.* **But I am not yet on** *ſhore.* **The** *gun of the ' Panama' has juſt announced our arrival to the people on land.* **We glide on with the tide,** *paſt the* U. S. *ſhip* 'Ohio,' *and oppoſite the main landing, outſide of the foreſt of maſts. A dozen boats are creeping out to us over the water ; the ſignal is given—the anchor drops—our voyage is over."*

It may **be** thought that as theſe volumes of **Mr.** Bayard Taylor are written **with** practiſed literary ſkill, and derive moreover ſuch unuſual intereſt from the ſcene and ſubject, they cannot fairly be adduced as an average ſpecimen of the

auto-biography of adventure. It muſt be acknowledged, indeed, that in theſe reſpects the book is
ſuperior to moſt of its claſs. Yet, on the other
hand, what is gained in artiſtic finiſh is probably
loſt in homely character and freſhneſs; and perhaps the motley multitudes whom the author
encounters and deſcribes, but barely compenſate
for the breathleſs intereſt of more perſonal fortunes and ſolitary peril. On the whole, therefore,
our choice was not exceptional or extreme; and
we may add that the work was recommended to our
curioſity by its extraordinary ſubject, and to our
courteous preference as the work of an American
author.

The life of Benvenuto Cellini, the Florentine
artiſt, belongs to a compound claſs of hiſtory and
adventure. It has many features of ſingular intereſt, which unite in forming a moſt entertaining
book. The author's character is made up of
curious contradictions. Though a man of taſte
and letters, and engaged in a proſperous career of
art, he ſeems to have been one of the rudeſt
brawlers in an age and city infeſted with bullies
and aſſaſſins. He thought little of planting his
dagger in the nape of his enemy's neck, or forcing
his ſword to the hilt in his enemy's body. The
audacity with which he committed theſe outrages
is coolly reflected in the page upon which he records them. A notion of the ſacredneſs of human
life ſeems never to intrude upon him; and he
wreaks mortal vengeance as much for an inſult-

ing look of one whom he diflikes, as for the
death of a brother perifhing in a ftreet-affray.
With adventures like thefe (including an imprifonment in the caftle of St. Angelo, an efcape thence, and various intrigues), are given
particulars of advancement in his profeffion, and
inftances of his fkill in medalling and fculpture.
The higheft parties in Rome and Florence diftinguifh him by their patronage ; and he appears to
have been entirely at his eafe in his interviews with
Pontiffs, Cardinals, and Grand Dukes. Pope
Clement VII. he feverely lectures for proceeding
in a hafty moment, on hearing of fome murderous attack, to order our worthy goldfmith to
be feized and hanged ; and he intimates, in no
doubtful language, what a remorfeful time of it
His Holinefs muft have had for the remainder
of life, had not Providence defeated his unnatural defign by means of an efcape ! Twice
our author is preferved from death by poifon ;
and times without number (according to his own
ftatement) is he purfued by rancorous and jealous
enemies. Yet his life and interefts feem well-
advanced and guarded both by himfelf and by fortune ; and, admirable artift as he was, his profperity kept pace with his deferts. Throughout
the memoir we have many incidental notices of
artifts and learned men, anecdotes illuftrative of
the age and country, and glimpfes of the ftormy politics and difordered fociety of that moft chequered
era of Italian hiftory. Thefe fcenes and fketches,
which in themfelves have a certain hiftorical im-

portance, are doubly entertaining in their connection with fo vivid a perfonal narrative, in
which the ftory of individual fortunes is thus em-
bellifhed and illuftrated by contemporary lights.

We muft briefly mention, if only to commend,
the *Memoirs of Colonel Hutchinfon, by Lucy, his
Widow,* as remarkable for a combination of all
thofe elements of intereft which pertain to its
clafs. It is not, profeffedly, an auto-biography;
but, as the writer concerns herfelf chiefly with
the fortunes of one who as a hufband fhared
them with herfelf, it is virtually fuch; and the
more fo, as her prominent character and genius have
ftamped upon all her reminifcences and opinions
a powerful individuality. As this work is now
well known, and within the reach of all claffes of
readers, we fhall further characterize it in a few
lines only, intended rather to awaken than fully to
gratify an intereft in its ftory. Lucy, daughter of
Sir Allen Apfley, Lieutenant of the Tower of
London, was born in that famous citadel on the
29th of January, 16$\frac{19}{20}$; was married, at the age
of eighteen, to Mr. (afterwards Colonel) Hutchinfon; and—accompanying and animating his
courfe as a confcientious foldier of the Parlia-
ment, and confoling with her fympathy the retire-
ment in which he lamented the perverfion of
the Commonwealth—was afterwards forward to
fhare, and doomed reluctantly to furvive, his per-
fecution and imprifonment at the Reftoration. It
was then, when her bereavement had left nothing
but a dreary widowhood in profpect, that fhe

chofe rather to look back upon the fellowfhip fhe had enjoyed. Since hope could no longer promife **her a** continuance, memory fhould at leaft cheer her with a rehearfal, of its pleafures; and, if fhe could never more receive or tender the daily counfel and encouragement, it was left her to record the exemplary career of a hufband and a father, a patriot and a Chriftian. The fpirit in which her memorial was thus under- taken and written is worthy of all praife; while the talents which it manifefts, and the high moral **tone** by which it is pervaded, call forth the live- lieft admiration. Her portraitures of public men of that time, with whom her hufband was affo- ciated, or **to** whom he was oppofed, are drawn with confiderable fkill; and, though her repub- lican opinions are no way difguifed, nor her puri- tan fympathies unduly fuppreffed, fhe generoufly admits the noble qualities of a foe, and candidly laments the infincerity of a pretended patriot and friend. She was naturally fufceptible of all truly feminine affections, as well as eminently capable of exercifing the more rigid duties of her fphere; yet, while fhe freely difcourfes of the latter, as more properly becoming the dignity of an Englifh matron, fhe holds the former as for the moft part unworthy of recollection or regard. Thus her work is, perhaps, wanting in due lightnefs and relief. The principal exception is her account, in the commencement, of her hufband's courtfhip **and** their fubfequent marriage. **It is a moft** pleaf- **ing** epifode, full **of** fweetnefs of manner and beauty of character; convincing the mind that their union was a hallowed bond of love and principle, and preluding with cheerful and moſt hopeful ſtrains the more ſerious drama of their wedded life. In the progreſs of that double life, the reader is charmed to obſerve the growing correſpondence of character in wife and huſband: how her gentleneſs and truth inſenſibly modify and ſway his martial bearing; and how his ſoldierly ſenſe of duty and honour gives tone and firmneſs to the mother and the wife. All this accords with the beautiful philoſophy of the poet :—

> " Yet in the long years liker muſt they grow ;
> The man be more of woman, ſhe of man :
>   *   *   *   *   *
> More like the double-natured poet each ;
> Till at the laſt ſhe ſet herſelf to him,
> Like perfect muſic unto noble words."

There is a claſs of auto-biographies which may be called epiſodical. Theſe are concerned with ſome brief or iſolated period in the writer's hiſtory, choſen for the moſt part with reference to its more eventful character, whether of perſonal adventure merely, or of a more public intereſt. To this claſs belong ſome of the moſt faſcinating auto-hiſtories. We could ſcarcely inſtance one more intereſting or improving than the Memoirs of his Impriſonment related by Silvio Pellico. The reader will probably remember that Silvio Pellico is an Italian poet of high repute, and known eſpecially as the author of ſeveral tragedies. In the year 1820 he was arreſted, at Milan, on a charge of confpiring againft the Auftrian government; and he **was confined in the prifon** of that city till the following year. Thence **he was** removed to a room under the burning leads **of Venice; and,** finally, transferred to the fortrefs of **Spielberg,** where he fuffered the ftricteft **durance, till re-** leafed from a protracted torture of ten years **in** the month of Auguft, 1830. Perfonal liberty is the firft blefling of every man. It is that **on** which he depends for the acquirement and enjoy- ment of every other. This much our reafon **teaches; but** the miferies **attendant** on captivity **we** can **only** faintly furmife, **till the experience** of **fuch fufferers as** Silvio Pellico **is** brought **to our** aid. Happy **Britons that we are! We** pine when **the** weather clouds **our fun, or temporary illnefs fhuts us from the air.** But, **if our lot had** been caft under clearer fkies, the beft among **us, and the** moft delicately nurtured, might have found both one and the other barred from his fervice or changed into a curfe; the fun, in its fummer height and ftrength, employed to fcorch his brain, while he found no retreat, till approaching winter fhould warn his tormentors to hurry the wafted human ruin to a more difmal region, affailed alternately by froft and damp. Such was the fate of Silvio Pellico. But phyfical fufferings would naturally be the lighteft in the cafe of fuch a man. Social and mental deprivations, with con- tinued affaults of temptation on his moral being, would form the bittereft ingredients of his mifery. Accordingly, his narrative is of the moft touching

kind. The key-note is pitched in this little fentence : " The waking which follows the firft
night in prifon is horrible." His dreams had not
yet been weaned from home, or fhaped by prifon
objects. The firft cheerful thought of his awaking
moment, that rofe like a grateful exhalation, was
fuddenly condenfed amid the furrounding gloom,
and defcended in tears. His fpirit faw at a glance
the long hopelefs future, as a drowning man fees
the irrevocable paft. He was in the crifis of
his hiftory : the time gone by had never feemed
to him fo bright as now ; the time to come appeared proportionably dark. His foul ftood, as
it were, on the Bridge of Sighs, " a palace and a
prifon on each hand :" *that* he had left, and *this*
he was about to enter. The moft affecting deprivation that he now fuffers is that of fomething
that he may love. More than the cheerful light, or
the fmiling landfcape, or the bufy ftreet ; more
even than the dear liberty to choofe his path and
go whither he pleafes, to lie down upon this funny
fward, or go in and out among that laughing
crowd ;—more painful than the need of thefe is
the aching want he feels of the companionable,—
of fympathetic eyes that he may look into,—of a
voice of kindnefs that he may hear and anfwer.
His home appears to have been a very happy one :
he fpeaks with great tendernefs of father, mother,
brothers, and fifters ; and he has fo much time
now to dwell upon their memory, fo little hope
that he fhall fee them more ! For a while they
occupy his heart almoft to burfting. But the plea-

fure is too full of pain. The heart, firft tortured
by bereavement, is then mercifully benumbed.
Our fenfibilities refufe to be for ever on the
ftretch; and, like tender feelers, they draw fhortly
back, or attach themfelves to the neareft object,
—to the barren rock, if nothing better be at hand.
So it is with this poor prifoner. He looks round
him for a prefent comfort. A friendly gaoler is
now more to him than once the choiceft friend.
How he yearns for the companionfhip of fome
unfortunate prifoner like himfelf! But that which
is moft worthy of our admiration, in this little
memoir, is the fpirit of forgivenefs and humility
by which it is hallowed. The difcipline of Providence, to which the unhappy poet was fubjected,
proved falutary and benign. He returned to his
home a wifer and a better man. This is, clearly,
no excufe for the infliction of fuch mifery as he en-
dured at the hands of a defpotic government; and,
although he has furnifhed us with no means of afcertaining the juftice or otherwife of his fentence,—
wifely abftaining from political allufion, and writing
in the fpirit of a chaftened child of God, rather than
of a martyr to the truth,—there is every reafon to
believe that his trial was arbitrary and unfair, and
his punifhment unneceffarily harfh. No thanks
are due to them that condemned him, though his
mind and heart were both profited by affliction;
though, refolving to bear the injuftice of men, he
humbly acknowledged the juft judgment of God;
though the wrongs which he fuffered in his own
perfon made him more tenderly alive to thofe of

humanity at large. Such improvement, in such circumstances, proves only that he had a noble spirit, and suggests that his errors were venial. The darkness and desertion that made him conscious of a present and supporting God, would doubtless have driven one more feeble and corrupt into utter atheism ; and the personal sorrow that wakened and widened his benevolent sympathies towards all the groaning human race, would have quickened into the bitterest misanthropy any less feeling or more selfish heart.

It is probable that the literary character will ever furnish the most valuable subjects of autobiography. In the personal history of its great teachers the world has long manifested a lively interest ; and it finds new pleasure in contemplating every added instance of immortal excellence cast in a mortal mould. It is gratifying to our natural curiosity to obtain a glimpse of the private relations, fellowships, and frailties of one who has powerfully influenced the public mind, and with whose inner and truer self we have already the profoundest sympathy. The lives, letters, and confessions of great authors engage our affectionate attention as much as if they were our relatives and friends ; for, indeed, our acquaintance with them, through the medium of their works, may be equally intimate and unreserved. It is our sympathy with the inner life of these great men that imparts significance and value to the simplest record of their history. We want some picture of

the home they bleſſed, of the ſociety they adorned,
of the ſpot their eyes continually reſted upon ;
ſome illuſtrations of the love they inſpired, the
reverence they commanded, the characters they
moulded and impreſſed.   Above all, we want the
example of their labour and ſucceſs held up to
encourage and to ſtimulate ; the proceſs of their
greatneſs exhibited to after-generations of aſpiring
youth.   The picture cannot be adequately fur-
niſhed by another : it muſt take ſome form
of auto-hiſtory,—whether narrative, epiſtle, or
journal.

Among memoirs of this claſs, and viewed in
the aſpect juſt indicated, thoſe of Edward Gibbon, the hiſtorian, are full of entertainment and
inſtruction. Relaxing the pompous march of thoſe
ſtately periods by which he has linked together
the antique and mediæval eras, and following, at
more companionable pace, the individual fortunes
of his own career, he furniſhes to the reader alternately the humbleſt and the higheſt ſources of di-
verſion; from time to time adorning domeſtic incident or perſonal trait with the fruit of philoſophic
judgment and profound reſearch, and exhibiting
the ſpectacle of ſelf-culture advancing to ſome of
its moſt magnificent reſults.   To the mere con-
noiſſeur, whoſe object is limited to the enjoyment
of intellectual luxury, the Life and Journals of this
eminent man will be full of intereſt ; but their
chief value will be felt by the determined and
ambitious ſtudent.   They will ſtimulate him to
exertion, and to the utmoſt uſe of his opportu-

nities, in the acquisition of knowledge; inspiring emulation of the patient study, deliberate sacrifice, and unflagging zeal, which were devoted to one purpose; and leading to an appreciation of the power which elicits the triumphs of genius and learning by not disdaining the common lot of labour.

But there is **often** found in literary auto-biographies the pre-eminent charm of style; a charm so subtle and pervading as to fuse the whole narrative into one harmonious and enchanting story, as in the case of Goethe's beautiful work, *Truth and Poetry from my Life*; or else a charm inferior in artistic merit, and more simply biographical, as that of Franklin's auto-biography. Each of these favourite compositions affords a model of literary style, using **that** word in the enlarged sense **of** *entire manner*, which consists in form as well as dress, and results in a beautiful correspondence of sentiment and expression. They are not so widely different in merit as in tone and subject; and although the practical man may prefer the one, and the imaginative reader the other, we are persuaded that true taste and the most cultivated feeling will find equal pleasure in both.

The auto-biographical writings of Goethe are among the most interesting of the literary class. They are comprised in the work already mentioned, *Truth and Poetry from my Life*, in the *Letters from Switzerland and Italy*, and in the several *Journals* and personal memoranda with which his writings abound. The first is a connected narrative, in twenty books, of the incidents and experiences of his childhood and youth. The graceful eafe of its ftyle, which has the effect of a moft pleafing fimplicity, is the refult of perfect art : the whole is the confummate product of a mind matured under the higheft culture. A peculiar charm lies in the grouping, and in individual portraitures—fketches of relatives or literary friends ; in epifodes of confiderable beauty, and dramatic fcenes both highly finifhed and effective. Its greateft defect arifes from the author's moral deficiencies ;—the abfence, for example, of any generous or commanding paffion in his nature, which might have imparted a fubftantive intereft, and furnifhed fomething like an epic clofe, to what is now a fragment merely. Still it is a fragment of almoft incomparable beauty,—cold as marble, but exquifitely moulded and delicately veined. We can hardly wifh it other than it is. Its pages are luminous with intellectual truth, if not with moral wifdom ; and, perhaps, no man has rivalled its author in his eftimate of qualities attaching to men and things around him. Almoft deftitute of prejudices and predilections himfelf, his mental eye detected in a moment the inequality and difproportion implied in the preferences of other men. Their exclufivenefs was a deformity befide the fymmetry of his univerfal tafte ; their definite and limited belief was bigotry and intolerance in the eyes of the catholic worfhipper of truth. But thefe characteriftics are moft prominent in the *Letters from Switzerland and Italy*. In thefe, especially, we fee the objective tendency of his mind. He never fhuts his eyes in order to reflect: he is conftantly demanding fome external object, that he may examine and report upon it. Opinion and theory rife up, unlaboured, in him. He wants more material: this is turned into a thought, and that has taken its place in the mufeum of his mind. Give fomething more into his hand ; for he is mafter of all that he has touched, and is impatiently waiting for more. His powers of affimilation are fo great that matter cannot be fupplied him fo faft as he can refolve it, and tranf-mute it into his fyftem—into bone of fcience or blood of art. And it is this greed of knowledge—this untiring exploration of nature—that makes thefe Letters admirable above others. We begin to hate, like him, mere fentiment and fpeculation: we fee the charm of details as we never did before: we find a hiftory or a hint in every ftony frag-ment of this coloffal world, and take for our motto, *Ex pede Herculem.*

Nothing could more faithfully reflect the cha-racter of Benjamin Franklin than the record he has left us of himfelf. It is really a photographic portraiture, in which none of the fignificant de-tails that compofed his real greatnefs are either omitted or refined away. Herein he appears (as indeed he was) the very type of the Anglo-Saxon character,—the reprefentative of Englifh practical wifdom. In him the influence of race predomi-nates over that of country; the former inftinctively animates his whole nature, the latter is compara-

tively feeble and **acquired**. His character is not
materially biaffed by **the** external or political features of the land of his birth. He is hardly fo
much American as Englifh. As a judicious
patriot, indeed, he promptly and fagacioufly
ferves the community among whom his father's
fortunes caufed him to be thrown ; but he ftands
among the more enthufiaftic fpirits of the Revolution with temper, moderation, and experience,
fuch as unite in Englifh ftatefmanfhip. He was
the Alfred of the tranfatlantic commonwealth ; if
lefs fingle in his glory, and lefs authoritative in his
office, yet endowed with the fame enlightened
fpirit of amelioration, the fame rational defire of
compromife between the ideal and the poffible,
the fame ambition of the wideft ufefulnefs. His
genius is the fublime of common fenfe : his virtue
and happinefs (limited and fecular as they unfortunately were) refult from the fupremacy of his
will, the invariable temperance of his life and
manners, and the practical direction of his purfuits. Separately confidered, his actions are trivial,
and his maxims common-place ; but, in their connection with his fortunes and his philofophy, the
former rife into a pyramid of exemplary fuccefs,
and the latter give laws to a nation's daily life.
His deifm was of fo attractive a kind, and fo recommended by a thoufand perfonal and focial
virtues, that there is reafon to fear that many have
turned with difguft from the nominal Chriftianity
of other men to the worfhip of that indefinite Providence which he acknowledged. All thefe traits

in Franklin, whether of excellency or imperfection, were essentially English in their mode of development. If his masculine intellect scorned the feeble verbosity of French declamation, and his truer taste despised the littleness of French vanity and ambition, so did his temperate judgment condemn the sensuality and egotism of French infidel philosophy. Removed from such a people by the homely character of his greatness, he was as far removed from them in the modest style of his unbelief. In Voltaire we see a fiendish activity against the Revelation which condemned his theories and frowned upon his pleasures; and in Rousseau, a moral blindness and corruption which darkened and tainted his whole moral being, even while he boasted of the unsullied purity of his soul. But in Franklin there is too sincere a love of virtue to allow of scorn towards religion. With piety the most ardent (as that of Whitefield), if he has no sympathy, he has yet no quarrel: he can even admire the eloquence and earnestness of the Preacher; and, giving him credit for the simplest sincerity, he refuses to denounce it as priestcraft and pretence.

No extract from the auto-biography of Franklin could adequately represent its excellence. A brick is proverbially an insufficient sample of a house: it may indicate the strength of the material, but cannot prove the thickness or coherence of its walls; and much less the amplitude of its interior, or the external beauty of its style. In like manner, a passage from the life of Franklin would show the simplicity of its details, and might suggeſt the plainneſs of the whole ſtructure : but we could not infer from it the admirable patience, ſkill, and principle, that ſlowly, but ſecurely, added ſtone to ſtone, and proportioned part to part; that ſacrificed no true advantage or convenience to a mere trick of ſhow; but, ſeeking with directneſs the real objects which the edifice was deſigned to ſerve, reſted ſatisfied that it ſhould owe its beauty to its ſymmetry, and its conſideration to its importance. It is a charming narrative of an exemplary career, calculated to intereſt and improve readers of every claſs. The ſtaple of every man's life conſiſts of ordinary duties and employments ; and, in the proper performance of theſe with a healthy and hopeful perſeverance, every man may derive aſſiſtance, counſel, and encouragement, from the brave New-Englander's career. We are all journeying with him on the level road of life ; but if we would attain ſo far, or obſerve ſo much, or earn the reſt of age ſo well as he, it will behove us to gird up our loins, and, neither running here nor pauſing there, to make conſtant and deliberate progreſs, and hourly to extend the horizon of our knowledge and purſuits.

Totally different in ſubject and in ſtyle are the Memoirs of Chateaubriand, the French peer, author and diplomate, as written by himſelf and bequeathed for poſthumous publication. This work is ſaid to have diſappointed the expectations of his admirers ; and it is certain that the tumultuous ſtate of continental politics has not ſuffered it largely to engage, much lefs entirely to engrofs, that public homage which its author anticipates with fo much affeded indifference. For ourfelves, we have found it, to the full, as eloquent and picturefque as the brilliant writings of Chateaubriand had led us to expect; and if it prefented to our eyes no faultlefs hero, without moral blemifh or mental imperfection, we were neither furprifed nor difappointed by the chequered lights and fhadows. We remembered, moreover, that it was the picture of a Frenchman drawn by himfelf. In his foibles, as in his greatnefs, Chateaubriand was the very type of the national character of France; he was effentially, conftitutionally, habitually *French*. This is not faid to difparage his country, but to characterize himfelf. Neither is the circumftance a rebatement to the intereft of the work before us, but rather its conftant charm; always relieving it from dulnefs, though often at the expenfe of the hero's dignity. To the Englifh reader of thefe Memoirs, accuftomed to the modeft referve of Englifh writers when fpeaking of themfelves, there is fomething repulfive at the firft in the inordinate vanity of their author. The "glory" which he fuppofes himfelf to have acquired is ever prefent with him; haunts him, as he would fay, with a melancholy fplendour; mingles in every group which he defcribes; is with him like a fhadow in the folitude where he invites the world to look in upon him. This fame "glory" ferves him like a gilt pafteboard crown; and ever as he comes before you he feems to fet it down upon

the table, fighing like a paviour, as though it were
maffive with gold, and lined with thorns; and
then, with piteous looks, he implores your com-
paffion for the victim of too much greatnefs. You
find it difficult—when this fcene has been repeated over and over again—to reftrain your difguft at fo much genius and fo little fenfe. You
begin to doubt the reality of his renown, when
you hear it moft luftily fhouted by himfelf, with
a deprecating whine to ferve as echo. You
are ready to afk him if he happens to have his
title and credentials in his pocket. If fo, what
are they? Who made him famous? What proves
his greatnefs? Did he build the pyramids, defign
St. Peter's, or write Paradife Loft? Is he the
Wandering Jew, or Napoleon grown lean and
run to feed? To this he anfwers with an unearthly groan, and ftill fits wringing his hands,
and invoking his remorfelefs " *gloire.*"

Thofe who have read thefe Memoirs will acknowledge that the author's vanity and egotifm
are not overdrawn by us: thofe who have not,
will wonder how fuch moral weaknefs can confift with talent in the writer, patience in the
reader, or intereft in the work. Yet the writer
has talents of a very high order: the reader is
more often prompted to admiration than exercifed
in patience: and the work unites moft of the
characteriftic beauties of auto-biography. The
period of the Memoirs is remarkably comprehenfive, and chequered with fcenes of the moft
ftriking variety and contraft. The individual for-

tunes of the author are coloured, more or lefs, by every public change; yet he conftantly ftands by with graphic pencil, and fketches for our plea-fure. Born under the decline and dotage of the old *régime*, he witneffed fucceffively the Revo-lution, the Confulate, the Empire, the Reftoration, the Revolution of July, 1830; and, before he lapfed into his final fleep, his dying pillow was rocked by the Revolution of February, 1848. Starting from a dilapidated family-manfion in an obfcure part of Brittany, he mingled with cour-tiers at Paris, with Indian favages in the Ame-rican woods and prairies, with poor emigrants at one time, and ambaffadors and princes at another, in the crowded city and fuperb court of London; incurring now the perilous difpleafure of the tyrant Buonaparte, and attracting always the admiration of generous hearts by his chivalric and independent bearing, by his fcorn of char-tered infolence, and by his eloquent fympathy with humanity at large. The ftyle in which the per-fonal and public memoranda of his life are written, is worthy of high praife. It is at once fententious and picturefque; it touches upon falient points with unfailing fkill; and often cryftallizes, in one gem-like fentence, the philofophy of a cha-racter or career. Chateaubriand, like other French authors, will often give an exaggerated importance to trifles; and he is more affected by matters of external fhow, novelty, or coincidence, than an Englifhman of well-trained mind would fuffer him-felf to be. But his manner is attractive when his matter is trivial: he is feldom jejune, and never common-place. His reflections are original, and often profound,—the refult of poetic inftinct, rather than of laborious analyfis. His portraitures are felicitous and ftriking ; his fummary of important events, lucid and fair; his fketches of fcenes, incidents, and interviews, dramatic in the extreme. His narrative is often coloured above nature, detailed beyond literal fact. This is done, we are perfuaded, unconfcioufly. His veracity is above fufpicion. But then his imagination is beyond control. In recalling a converfation that he has taken part in, or a fcene that he has witneffed, he cannot bear that the one fhould be reported in broken or general terms, and the other indif-tinctly given : this muft be a picture, and that a little drama. They are works of art founded upon fact. The truth is there, but not in its literal photographic drefs. It is elaborated for pofterity, to hang in the gallery of his Memoirs for ever.

As an illuftration of the ftyle and fentiment of Chateaubriand, in the graver paffages of this auto-biography, we extract a part of his parallel be-twixt two mighty but diffimilar heroes:—" *Wafh-ington does not, like Napoleon, belong to that clafs of men who affume fuperhuman proportions. Nothing aftonifhing is attached to his perfon : he is not placed on a vaft theatre; he is not engaged in a ftruggle with the moft fkilful captains and the moft powerful monarchs of the age. He does not rufh from Memphis to Vienna, from Cadiz to Mofcow. He defends himfelf with a handful of citizens, in a*

comparatively unknown land, **and in the narrow**
circle of the domeſtic hearth : he **does not wage**
battles which renew the triumphs of **Arbela and**
Pharſalia. *He does not overturn thrones, to* **build**
up others with their ruins ; he does not ſay to the
kings waiting at his gates,—

    ' *Qu'ils ſe font trop* **attendre,** *et qu'Attila s'ennuie.*'

Something **of ſilence ſeems** *to envelope the actions of*
Waſhington. *He acts leiſurely.* *One would ſay,*
he felt himſelf *burdened with the liberty of the*
future, *and that he feared to compromiſe it.* *It is*
not his own deſtinies which this hero of a new ſtamp
bears, but thoſe of his **country :** *he does not permit*
himſelf to ſport with what does not belong **to him.**
But from this profound humility what light **is about**
to burſt forth ! *Seek amidſt the foreſts where the*
ſword of Waſhington flaſhed, *and* **what will you**
find ? *Tombs ?* *No ; a world !* *Waſhington has*
left the United States as the trophy of his field
of battle. . . . . *Buonaparte preſents none of the*
features *of this grave American.* *He wages a*
noiſy ſtruggle **in** *an ancient land ; he wiſhes* **to**
create nothing but his own renown ; he **burdens**
himſelf only with his own fate. *He ſeems* **to be**
aware that his miſſion will be a ſhort one,—that
the torrent which deſcends from ſuch a height will
flow faſt. *He haſtens to enjoy and to abuſe his glory*
as if it were a fleeting youth. *Like the* **gods of**
Homer, he wiſhes to reach the end of the **world in**
four ſteps. **He** *appears in every character ; he*
haſtily inſcribes his name. in the records of all

nations ; he **throws crowns to** *his family and his soldiers ; he* **is** *hafty* **in his** *monuments, his laws, and his victories. Brooding over the world, with one hand he overturns kings,* **with** *the other* **he** *beats down the giant of revolution.* **But,** *in crufh- ing anarchy, he ftifles liberty, and ends* **by** *lofing his own on his laft field of battle.* . . . . . . **Each** *is recompenfed according to his works.* **Wafhington** *raifes a nation to happinefs ; then, laying down his magifterial authority, he finks to reft, beneath his* **own** *roof, amidft the regrets of his countrymen* **and the** *veneration* **of nations.** . . . . . *Buona- parte robs* **a** *nation* **of its independence.** *A depofed Emperor, he is hurried into* **exile,** **where the terror** *of the globe* **he has ravaged does not** *think* **him** *fecurely enough imprifoned under the guardianfhip of the ocean. He expires. This news, publifhed at the gate of the palace in front of which the con- queror caufed fo many funerals* **to** *be proclaimed, neither arrefts* **the** *ftep nor aftonifhes* **the** *mind of the by-paffer.* . . . . *The republic of Wafhington remains ; the empire of Buonaparte is deftroyed. Wafhington and Buonaparte both fprang from the* **bofom of** *democracy. Both born from Liberty, the firft was faithful to her, the fecond betrayed her.''*

The remainder of this famous parallel is in fimilar ftyle ; and the reader's impreffion throughout is, that the author **fpeaks more admiringly** of his brilliant and audacious countryman, **even** when **his** language juftly difcriminates the truer great- nefs of the American patriot. While he praifes the perfonal humility of Wafhington, his praife founds much like pity. He feems **to regret** that fo vivid a glory as his fhould be diffipated over a barren continent, and ftream mildly through all time. He would have regarded him with more wonder and delight, if—inftead of fharing his heroifm and fuccefs with fellow-foldiers and future generations —he had gathered **up** both one and the other into his own **perfon**, exhaufted on himfelf the fruits of a **thoufand** triumphs, and concentrated in his **own** the renown of a thoufand warriors.

In memoirs and confeffions of every clafs the French have a diftinguifhed reputation, and **we** gladly invite attention to another and **more** favourable example of that **fchool.** The *Memoirs of his Youth*, which M. de Lamartine has recently given to the world, are invefted with a romantic beauty of fentiment, perhaps **never** employed with **equal** fuccefs in the delineation of actual life. This little work, indeed, brief and unfinifhed as it is, appears **to** us the moft admirable production of its author, **or the** one moft accordant with the tafte of Englifh readers. It is full of attractions, both for fimple and cultivated minds. The vanity fo offenfively difplayed **in the** Memoirs of Chateaubriand is here prefented in a modified and fimpler form : for although the egotifm of M. de Lamartine is manifefted in a truly national degree, it does **not** lead him to make lofty comparifons between himfelf and the world's moft memorable men, as M. Chateaubriand repeatedly does ; it induces him only

to colour fomewhat too highly the perfonal merits
of his hero, and never to forget how brilliant an
enfemble is due to France and to himfelf.   In other
refpects thefe Memoirs differ from thofe of Chateaubriand.   The ftyle is more elaborate, and the
ftory more developed and connected; and if the
language is more frequently diffufe than fententious, and the fentiment rather poetical than
appropriate, the one is recognized as the fpontaneous medium of the other, and the whole is not
too glowing for the picture of blended actual and
ideal in the auto-biography of a poet's youth.   One
portraiture contained in thofe Memoirs is of exquifite beauty and diftinguifhed merit; it is that
of the author's mother.   The excellence of the
fubject has, in this cafe, admirably feconded the
execution of the artift.   The mere fancy of the
latter could never have fupplied the abfence of
the former: the purely fictitious heroines of the
poet are falfe and feeble in comparifon with this
facred object of memory and love.   But if fuch a
character tranfcended his powers of invention, it
harmonized too well with his own high nature
and fplendid gifts to baffle his depicting powers.
Sure we are that no one can read this affectionate
tribute on the part of M. de Lamartine to a parent dignified by all that is worthy of efteem, and
endeared by qualities that irrefiftibly infpire love,
without reverence and admiration,—a reverence
and admiration that are reflected from the object
to the author, from the pattern virtue of the mother to the devotion and homage of the fon.   This

filial record is of an elaborate length, as well as beauty : the author dwells with fondnefs and delight upon reminifcences fo hallowed, and lingers in the angelic prefence, at once familiar and divine. A fmall portion only of this interefting memorial is all that we can here infert; but it will fuffice to fhow the manner and fpirit of the whole. After defcribing the benevolent vifits and almfgiving to which his pious mother devoted a part of every morning, and in which fhe affociated her young children, the author proceeds :—

" *When all this buftle of the daily occupations was at laft over, when we had dined, when the neighbours, who occafionally came to pay us a vifit, had retired, and when the fhadows of the mountain, ftealing along the little garden, had already wrapped it in the twilight of the clofing day, my mother feparated herfelf from us for a fhort period. She left us either in the little faloon, or in a corner of the garden at fome diftance from her. She at laft took her hour of repofe and meditation, apart and alone. This was the moment which fhe devoted to reflection; when, all her thoughts called home, all the wandering afpirations and feelings of the day turned inwards, fhe communed with God, who formed her fureft folace and fupport. Young as we were, we knew the private hour which fhe referved to herfelf amidft the bufy duties of the day. We moved away inftinctively from the alley of the garden where fhe was wont to walk at this hour, as if we had feared*

to interrupt or to overhear the *mysterious* and confidential outpourings of her **heart to her Creator.** It was a little walk formed of yellow *sand*, **approaching** to a red colour, bordered with *strawberries*, and lined on each *side* by a **row of** fruit-trees which rose no higher than her head. A large clump of hazel-trees terminated the walk on one *side*, **and a** wall on the other. It was the *most deserted* and *sheltered spot of the garden.* It was for this **reason** she preferred it ; for what *she saw* there was within herself, and not in the horizon which bounded her vision. She walked **with a rapid, but** *measured,* **step, like one whose thoughts are busily** occupied, who marches on to a fixed and certain **goal,** and whose enthusiasm rises as he proceeds. **She had** her **head** usually uncovered, her beautiful black **hair half** floating in the breeze, her countenance a little graver than during the rest of the day, sometimes slightly bent towards the ground, sometimes raised to heaven, where the gaze seemed **to** search for the first stars that began to detach themselves from the deep blue of the firmament. **Her arms** were bare from the elbow downwards, her hands sometimes clasped like those of a person engaged in prayer, sometimes at liberty, and plucking absently a rose or a few violet marrows, whose tall stalks sprang up along the margin of the walk. Sometimes her lips were half parted and motionless, sometimes firmly closed and working with a perceptible **movement,** like those of one talking through a dream. . .
. . . . When she issued from this sanctuary of her soul, and returned to us again, her eyes were moist-

*ened, her features even more ferene and fubdued
than ufual. The never-ceafing fmile which fat upon
her graceful lips, wore even a more tender and more
loving expreffion. One would have faid that fhe
had thrown off a burden of fadnefs, or relieved her
mind of a weight of adoration, and that fhe walked
more lightly under her duties during the remainder
of the day."*

Such in her higheft, and fimilar in her fubordinate, relations, was the mother of M. de Lamartine. But the maternal character was that
in which fhe pre-eminently excelled: it appears,
indeed, to have fulfilled in her the meafure of
perfection. Even duly confidering the filial heart
and poetic mind of her memorialift, the reader can
hardly conceive of her as lefs than fully exempli-
fying the virtues of faith and practice, or as failing
in any the fmalleft particular of motherly love
and care. He is not furprifed, therefore, to find
that the childifh fenfibilities of the future poet,
foftered by fo pure and tender a concern, were
rudely fhocked when, at the age of ten years, he left
home for the firft time, and found himfelf joftled
and difregarded in a public fchool,—a ftranger to
the fmalleft kindnefs, and a loathing witnefs of
vulgar and depraved habits. From this rude
fcene he boldly efcaped, returning home, and was
afterwards placed at a fuperior feminary under the
guardianfhip of mild and learned Jefuits. Here,
however, his great ftimulus to fuccefs in ftudy
was the profpect of again joining the family

circle ; and that goal he appears to have attained by abfolutely exhaufting the learning of
his teachers. To his enjoyment of domeftic
happinefs was now added the delightful freedom
of opening intellectual youth.

" *Having returned to Milly a fhort time before
the fall of the leaf, I thought I never could enjoy
fufficiently the torrent of inward happinefs with
which a fenfe of liberty in the abode of my childhood and in the bofom of my family filled my breaft.
It was the conqueft of my age of manhood. My
mother had caufed a little chamber to be prepared
for myfelf alone : it was fituated in an angle of the
houfe, and the window opened into a lovely walk of
hazel-trees. It contained only a bed without cur-
tains, a table, and fome fhelves, fixed againft a
wall, to contain my books. My father had purchafed for me the three articles which ferve to complete the virile robe of an adolefcent,—a watch, a
fowling-piece, and a horfe, as if to notify to me that
henceforth the hours, the plains, and the realms of
fpace, were my own. I took poffeffion of my independence with a rapture which lafted feveral months.
The day was abandoned wholly to the chafe along
with my father, to dreffing my horfe in the ftable,
or to galloping him, with my hand twined in
his mane, through the neighbouring valleys. The
evenings were given up to the fweet intercourfe of
family in the faloon, along with my mother, my
father, and fome friends of the family, or in reading aloud the works of hiftorians and poets. . . . .*

Among these poets, those whom I admire in pre-ference were not the ancients, whose classic pages we had, when too young, moistened with our tears, and with the sweat of our studies. There exhaled from them, when I opened their pages, a sort of pri-son odour of weariness and of constraint which made me shut them again, as a delivered captive hates to look again upon his former chains. But they were those which are not inscribed in the catalogue of works of study,—the modern poets, Italian, English, German, French,—poets whose flesh and blood are our own flesh and blood, who feel, who think, who love, who sing, as we feel, as we think, as we sing, as we love, we the men of modern times; such as Tasso, Dante, Petrarch, Shakespeare, Milton, Cha-teaubriand,—who sang like them?—above all, Ossian, that poet of the vague and undefined, that mist of the imagination, that inarticulate plaint of the Northern Seas, that foam of the waves, that murmur of the shadows, that eddying of the clouds around the tempest-beaten peaks of Scotland, that northern Dante, as grand, as majestic, as supernatural, as the Dante of Florence, and more sensible than he, and who often wrings from his phantoms cries more human and more heart-rending than those of the heroes of Homer."

Afterwards, we have yet further proof of the vivid and lasting impression which the works of Ossian made upon the youthful poet's mind; and we cannot help thinking, that to his inordinate study of the northern bard may be traced the cha-

racteriftic defects both of the poetry and profe of
M. de Lamartine. Thefe defects, as it appears
to us, confift in the fubftitution of the vague for
the definite, and a preference for brilliance of colour over diftinctnefs and truth of outline ; and
are precifely what might be anticipated from the
undue influence of the poems of Offian. It is
true, indeed, that a wide difference diftinguifhes
the earlier and later minftrels ; but it is the difference of diftance, and not of diffimilarity,—the
difference betwixt rude antiquity and modern times,
and betwixt the bleak and mifty north and the
warm and golden fouth. In the one, we have the
fombre genii of a frowning clime and an heroic
age, floating cloud-wife over fcaur and mountain,
and filling up the paufes of the ftorm with an anfwering guft of forrow, as the chorus of the Greek
drama echoes and heightens the mourner's grief;
and in the other, every garden of the funny fouth
is made to glow like Paradife, and every maiden's
walk feems haunted by angelic innocence, and
every youth is a divinity, and all verdure is hope,
and all funfhine heaven. In the creations of
M. de Lamartine there is more variety than in
thofe of Offian, but hardly more of individuality :
perfons they are not fo much as types, nor fub-
ftances fo much as fhadows. They are abftrac-
tions of the poetry of life, rather than living and
concrete examples. And for this reafon, they will
always burn upon the ardent imaginations of the
young, though they may ceafe to gratify the
experienced intellect in riper years. Even the

lovely Graziella, whofe image and hiftory adorn
thefe Memoirs with their choiceft epifode, is
hardly an exception to this rule of typical portraiture. A maiden of Greek defcent and Italian
birth, inheriting the claffic beauty of her anceftors,
and abforbing the attractive glow and foftnefs of
her native clime, we conceive of her as the paragon of youth and beauty;—as the foundling of
dame Fortune, caft upon an ifland rock, adopted
by Nature herfelf, and by her endowed with a
plenitude of gifts and graces that tranfcend the
vulgar and conventional ornaments of life. Yet
it muft be owned that this perfection of charms,
and abfolute fimplicity of manners, make up an
enchanting ideal ; and that it is after all touchingly
human and tenderly feminine. How exquifitely
is the tranfition from girlhood to womanhood indicated on the occafion of her liftening, for the
firft time, to the tale of Paul and Virginia, as it is
brokenly interpreted to the fifherman's family by
the lips of the poet.

"*The young girl felt her heart, till then dormant,
revealed to her, as it were, in the foul of Virginia.
She feemed to have grown fix years older in that
half-hour. The ftorms of paffion had marbled her
forehead, the azure white of her eyes, and her
cheeks. She refembled a calm and fheltered lake, on
which the funfhine, the wind, and the fhade were
ftruggling together for the firft time.*"

But we muft not be feduced into a repetition of
the beautiful ftory of Graziella, or rather into a

poor abridgment of it ; for it muſt ceaſe to charm, if touched by ruder hands than thoſe of its firſt framer, and made leſs or other than it is.

Two Engliſh contemporaries of Chateaubriand and Lamartine had alſo planned a retroſpect of their illuſtrious lives ; but the auto-biographies commenced by Scott and Southey were early interrupted by long delays, and finally broken off by death. We have only a fragment of each, written with a taſte and judgment that make us deeply regret the loſs of that which is unwritten, and of which we ſeem to have been ſo accidentally deprived. In their completed ſtate, they would have been models of auto-biography, uniting the ſimplicity and fidelity of the humbleſt works of the claſs to all that is morally and intellectually noble, to the manly modeſty of true greatneſs, and the felicity of true taſte. Both theſe eminent authors were maſters of a pure Engliſh ſtyle; and, if Scott had an advantage in the humour of character and anecdote, the moral tone and admirable expreſſion of Southey imparted a beautiful clearneſs to the reminiſcences of his youth. The one, from the objective tendency of his mind, enriched his perſonal hiſtory with ſketches of contemporary perſons and external things ; the other, writing more ſubjectively, though ſtill with an obſerving eye and a healthy mind, clothed his narrative of every aſſociation or tranſaction with an elevation of ſentiment and a dignity of language peculiar to himſelf. Sir Walter Scott has found, in his ſon-in-law, an able continuator, worthy of that office : the narrative of Lockhart is, indeed, as excellent a fubftitute for the Poet's auto-biography as the cafe would admit of. But Southey, we conceive, has been lefs fortunate in this refpect : the Memoirs of his Life and Correfpondence, as prepared by his fon, are fo inferior in intereft and merit, as greatly to deepen our regret at the incompletenefs of the fketch which forms its commencement, and which, in a more finifhed ftate,—fupplemented by a felection of the author's beft letters,—would have furnifhed the prefent age, and future times, with an admirable example of literary hiftory. Under the circumftances of this double deprivation, it remains for us to make fome paffing reference to a work lefs exalted, both in merit and pretenfion, but not without an intereft of its own ; and then to conclude this brief fummary, by a notice of the volume which fuggefted it.

An announcement of the *Auto-biography of Leigh Hunt* was full of promife to the lover of modern literature. There is no man of the prefent age to whom the profeffion of letters, adopted (if we may fo exprefs ourfelves) by irrefiftible choice, has proved a more conftant fervice of delight than to him,—a fervice to which, though with variety of fortune but conftancy of love, he has now adhered through half a century,—and none to whofe excurfive genius and companionable teaching the general reader is indebted for fo large a meafure of intellectual paftime. In mufical phrafe, he has always written *con fpirito*. It may,

indeed, have often happened to him, as to more
fortunate authors, that to buckle to his tafk and
bend to the defk, defpite the alluring funfhine and
inviting flowers, involved at firft a little hardfhip
and felf-denial; but once there, he grew happy
and contented. To defcant of freedom in the
meadows, or nature among the mountains, feemed
the next beft thing to a perfonal enjoyment of the
fame. Seated in his quiet ftudy, he became the
literary correfpondent of the reading world; took
down a volume of this poet, or of that effayift,
and, diving into the treafury of his own memory
and fancy, rehearfed the one with a commentary
of dainty thoughts, and fupplemented the other
with the fruits of his own experience. He has
not, indeed, laid claim to the honours of conqueft
over any branch of fcience, or by a fingle production* approved his right to be efteemed one of
the mafters of poetic art; but his tafteful and
congenial expofition of the latter will more than
excufe his æfthetic averfion to the cold *theoria* of
the former. If he is not entitled to a Profeffor-
fhip in the one department, he has been long re-

---

* We have not forgotten the graceful and pathetic *Le-
gend of Florence*, efpecially diftinguifhed by the nervous and
novel rhythm of its verfe, the fweetnefs of its domeftic fentiment, and its general purity and frefhnefs. But we are
not quite fatisfied, that its moral is as unexceptionable as its
ftyle; and, even granting it to be a noble fpecimen of dramatic art, it would hardly be fufficient of itfelf to fecure
a high pofition for its author. On the whole, we look
upon the two large volumes which form *Leigh Hunt's
London Journal*, as the field where his genius has expatiated
to moft advantage; it is that alfo from which he has lately
garnered fome of his moft pleafant lucubrations.

ceived as a Mafter of the Revels in the other. All that wit, humour, imagination, or fancy have provided for human pleafure in chafte but exuberant forms, have been ufhered by his wand of enchantment in a thoufand different mafks, appearing now in fingle, and now in affociated, beauty, and lovely alike in every combination and attitude.

Leigh Hunt has not produced an agreeable hiftory of himfelf. He is generally far more happy when fpeaking of books, or birds, or neighbours, or companions of any kind. His Auto-biography appeared in three volumes, but attracted little notice and lefs commendation. The ftyle is often carelefs and faulty in the extreme ; and the more purely literary portion is not only inferior in ability to his former effays, but is in great part deftitute of novelty to the modern reader. Thus fecond-rate in its material, and unconnected as a whole, it ftands in need of fome friendly indulgence ; but this we are not inclined to withhold. Too evidently it was made to order ; it is a pardonable inftance of book-making. We can eafily conceive the reluctance with which the tafk was undertaken, the diftafte with which it was profecuted day by day, and the diffatisfaction with which it was finally difmiffed out of hand. Hence the feeblenefs of a twice-told tale, the loofenefs of ftyle, and the defectivenefs of plan. Had it been entirely a labour of love, it would not have lacked proportion, unity, and finifh. But other reafons, no doubt, contributed to thefe defects ; for thefe in fome meafure reflect thofe of the

author himfelf,—whofe principles and character
are open to exception on fome ferious points.

But if our hero **proves no hero** after all, like
every other auto-biographer he had at leaft a home,
which may furnifh us fome compenfating glimpfes.
It is commonly faid, that the mothers **of great**
men are themfelves remarkable ; but **did you**
never fufpect, dear reader, that this is but **a very**
partial truth ; that men of very middling, ay, and
thofe of very little, powers, are frequently as
favoured in this refpect **as** the nobleft and the
brighteft ? We cannot **open the** confeffions of
the mereft fcamp, **without being** furprifed with a
lovely picture of maternal excellence, beaming on
the earlieft page, nurfing fome puling infant deftined never to reward fuch love ; taking **her**
higheft pleafure from the faint dawning fmile or
childifh prattle, and her firft anxiety from **the**
innocent and heedlefs confidence of youth, and
never ceafing to be a mother when her boy has
long renounced the name and character of child.
If it be true, in any peculiar and efpecial fenfe,
that " Heaven lies about us in our infancy," can
we doubt who is the angel of our cradle, as well
as the guardian genius of our life ?

It is for the fake of fuch a character that we
give a fketch of the early hiftory of Leigh Hunt.
He was born at the village of Southgate, in
Middlefex, on the **19th of** October, 1784. **His**
parents had not long been fettled in this country,
whither the royalift tendencies of the father—who
was a native of Barbadoes, refident in Philadelphia

—had caufed him to be driven at the commencement of the American Revolution. This father
appears to have been not lefs fingular in his
character than in his fortunes ; indeed, the chequered nature of the latter plainly refulted, in no
fmall degree, from the eccentricity of the former.
Gifted in fome refpects in a remarkable manner,
the want of a ferious purpofe, as well as of a high
religious principle, caufed thefe gifts to be thrown
away upon him : unftable as water, he could not
excel. By change of country, he was fuddenly
metamorphofed from a lawyer into a divine.

"*My mother was to follow my father as foon as
poffible, which fhe was not able to do for many
months. The laft time fhe had feen him, he was a
lawyer and a partifan, going out to meet an infuriated populace. On her arrival in England, fhe
beheld him in a pulpit, a Clergyman, preaching
tranquillity. When my father came over, he found
it impoffible to continue his profeffion as a lawyer.
Some actors who heard him read advifed him to go
on the ftage ; but he was too proud for that, and
went into the Church.*"

He became a popular Preacher of charity fermons, and particularly excelled in the reading
defk. But it is admitted by his fon that he made
a great miftake in adopting the clerical profeffion.
He remained in a falfe pofition for life. Subfe-
quently he became tutor to the nephew of the
Duke of Chandos, Mr. Leigh, and had fome

chance of promotion to a bifhopric; "but his
Weft Indian temperament fpoiled all." Later
ftill he fell firft into debt and then into prifon,
from which place his fon's earlieft recollection of
him dates. He became Unitarian and Univerfal-
ift, and died in the year 1809, aged fifty-feven.
The mother of Leigh Hunt was of a fuperior
character, although the complexion of her life and
fentiments was, from true womanly fympathy,
materially coloured by thofe of her hufband. She
was a native of Philadelphia; and of her relatives
in that city we are told fome pleafing particulars.
She was, at the time of her marriage, "a brunette
with fine eyes, a tall ladylike perfon, and hair
blacker than is feen of Englifh growth.......My
mother had no accomplifhments but the two beft
of all,—a love of nature and a love of books.
Dr. Franklin offered to teach her the guitar; but
fhe was too bafhful to become his pupil. She
regretted this afterwards, partly, no doubt, for
having miffed fo illuftrious a mafter. Her firft
child, who died, was named after him." This
lady, after embarking to join her hufband in
England, encountered a violent and protracted
ftorm, in which fhe is reprefented as behaving with
fingular courage, animating her young children,
and exciting the warmeft admiration of the Captain. Her fon, who fondly memorializes her
goodnefs, appears to have been the youngeft of
her large family, and was born fome years after
her arrival in England. He has no recollection
therefore of his mother's earlieft afpect. The

critical danger of her hufband, on the occafion of his flight from America, had caufed her extreme fright, and fenfibly fhaken her conftitution.

"*The fight of two men fighting in the ftreets would drive her in tears down another road; and I remember, when we lived near the Park, fhe would take me a long circuit out of the way, rather than hazard the fpectacle of the foldiers. Little did fhe think of the timidity with which fhe was then inoculating me, and what difficulties I fhould have when I went to fchool, to fuftain all thofe fine theories, and that unbending refiftance to oppreffion, which fhe inculcated. However, perhaps it turned out ultimately for the beft. One muft feel more than ufual for the fore places of humanity, even to fight properly in their behalf. Never fhall I forget her face as it ufed to appear to me coming up the cloifters, with that weary hang of the head on one fide, and that melancholy fmile.*"

There is more about this excellent woman which we fhould like to quote. We muft content ourfelves, however, with one trait more. She adopted not only the religious, but the republican, creed of her hufband, and, in maintaining the latter, was apt to be rather intolerant. Poor lady! not only can we forgive—we muft even admire—a vehemence fpringing from the force of ftrongeft feminine affections. Her zeal may not, indeed, have been according to knowledge; but, better ftill, it was according to love. To regard the unfortunate partner of her life with paffionate efteem, was a neceffity of her nature, the condition of her life. The affertion of his characteriftic opinions was therefore become **with her a fort of felf**-defence, and the more fo as he feemed to fail in them before the world. To this fubject **fhe would** bring all the inftinctive fkill and tender **fiercenefs** of a woman ; for it was the apology of her own devotion, and that which alone redeemed **her** married life from felf-contempt.

The moft recent auto-biography is that of Thomas **de** Quincey, **known to all** lovers of Englifh literature as **a writer of** fubtle genius and great learning. **It is,** emphatically, the auto-biography of digreffions. To thofe who are familiar with the author's writings, this circumftance will bring no furprife. It is characteriftic of his fruitful and difcurfive mind, and is that to which both the charm and imperfection of his ftyle are mainly due. All Mr. De Quincey's works are diftinguifhed—not to fay, disfigured—by the very large proportion of epifodical matter. Not content with indulging in a copious and ramifying text, this alfo, in its turn, is loaded and enriched by numerous illuftrative notes, often of great value, which hang loofely on the body of the work, like the fcalps in an Indian's wampum-belt. They are the trophies of his vigorous and triumphant genius, gathered from every field of learning. They often encumber the free exercife of his artiftic talents, fo that few of his productions have

any claim to the beauty of form and higheſt ſymmetry: but the reader cannot wiſh them away;
for that would be ſo much loſs, while their preſence
is a welcome ſuperfluity of good. They are a
kind of riches that our judgment might have forbidden us to deſire, but which our avarice will not
ſuffer us to refuſe. They are an unexpeſted, and
even a bewildering, addition to the author's theme;
but our greed of knowledge overcomes the ſtriſt
ſimplicity of taſte, and we take them by the way,
like mouthfuls of a choice collateral ſalad.

But theſe endleſs deviations of Mr. De Quincey are ſtill leſs to be regretted in reference to the
volume of his memoirs. The byways of a country
are always more delightful than the main-road;
and in a memorial retroſpeſt we may be profitably
led to viſit thoſe without wholly loſing ſight of
this. The opening chapter is devoted to the
author's remembrances of childhood, and eſpecially
of a young and gifted ſiſter. There is ſomething
marvellous in Mr. De Quincey's memory of that
early period, as well as in his eloquent deſcriptions
of its affeſtions and its griefs, of its pure and paſſive happineſs, of the unconſcious awe which
inveſts the feeble mind of infancy when ſtanding,
for the firſt time, in the myſterious company of
Death. But the reader of the "Confeſſions" is
familiar with this peculiar power of our author,
and we prefer to quote an inſtance of domeſtic
portraiture.

" This eldeſt brother of mine was, in all reſpeſts,

a remarkable boy. **Haughty** *he was, aspiring, immeasurably active ;* **fertile** *in resources as Robinson Crusoe ; but also* **full of quarrel as** *it is possible to imagine ; and, in default of any other opponent, he would have fastened a quarrel* **upon his own shadow** *for presuming to run before* **him when** *going west- ward in the morning, whereas* **in all** *reason, a shadow, like a dutiful child, ought to keep* **deferen-** *tially in the rear of that majestic substance which* **is** *the author of its existence. Books he detested, one* **and all,** *excepting only such as he happened to write himself. And these* **were not a few.** *On all sub- jects* **known to man, from the '** *Thirty-nine Articles' of our English Church,* **down to pyrotechnics, leger-** *demain, magic, both* **black and white, thaumaturgy,** *and necromancy,* **he** *favoured* **the world** *(which world was the nursery where I lived among my sisters) with his select opinions. On this last subject espe- cially—of necromancy—he was very great ; witness his profound work, though but a fragment, and, unfortunately, long since departed to the bosom of Cinderella, entitled, '* **How to Raise a Ghost ; and when** *you've* **Got him Down, How to Keep him Down.'** *To which work, he assured us, that some most learned and enormous man, whose name was a foot and a half long, had promised him an appendix, which appendix treated of the Red Sea and Solomon's signet-ring, with forms of* **Mittimus** *for ghosts that might be refractory, and, probably, a Riot-Act for any émeute* **amongst ghosts inclined to raise** *barri- cades ;* **since he** *often thrilled our young hearts by supposing the case, (not at all unlikely, he affirmed,)*

*that a federation, a solemn league and conspiracy,
might take place among the infinite generation of
ghosts against the single generation of* **men,** **at one**
*time composing the garrison of earth. The Roman
phrase for expressing that a man had died,* **viz.**
' Abiit ad plures,' ('* He has gone over to the* **ma-**
jority,') my brother explained **to** *us ; and we easily
comprehended* **that any one** *generation of the living
human* **race,** **even if combined,** *and acting in concert,
must be* **in a frightful** *minority by comparison with*
all *the incalculable generations that had trod this
earth before."*

From this point **the author** goes off into **one of**
his digressions of speculation ; but our space forbids us **to** admit the whole of this characteristic
passage.   We should **have liked** to tell the reader
more of this enterprising boy, and **to have enriched**
our page with **a** companion-picture,—that of **a**
younger brother, familiarly called "Pink," strangely
endowed with a feminine sensibility and beauty, in
connection with heroic strength and courage.
But we must forbear.   So far as Mr. de Quincey
has yet proceeded, there is no want of interest in
his reminiscences ; but his style is more faulty
than we had expected to find, and the arrangement
of his story is hardly agreeable to his acknowledged
skill and practice in composition.   One cause of
this defect is due, no doubt, to the fact that some
of the sketches that make up this volume were
written **many** years ago, and at different times,
and **are only** made intelligible in their present form

by repeated reference to the circumſtances of their
firſt appearance.   Of the growth of the author's
mind, under literary influences, we have no
account; and, on the whole, we ſhall form a
better opinion of this work from a firſt impreſſion
than in a critical and ſtudied eſtimate.

In this haſty ſketch of one intereſting branch
of literature, of courſe there is much omitted that
individual readers might expect to find.   Many
ſtandard examples of auto-biography have been
neceſſarily paſſed by ; with many lighter, but not
leſs curious, memoirs,—ſuch as thoſe of that
quaint and plauſible impoſtor, William Lilly, and
that pleaſant and conceited goſſip, Colley Cibber.
The one aſſures us what it is to lie like an alma-
nack-maker ; and the other calls back the faded
beauties of the ſtage, and re-animates their patched
and painted ſmiles.   We have found no ſpace
even for a due conſideration of the laſt and ableſt
of our Engliſh Diariſts,—ſo remarkable for his
reſtleſs energy, his ſanguine ſpirit, his fluctuating
fortunes, and his reſilient hopes ; and ſo unfortunate in wanting the ſuſtained moral temper
requiſite for all great achievements, in art as well
as in affairs.   From this example we might have
enforced the greateſt leſſon which the career of
genius has ſupplied to the preſent age.   But the
painful hiſtory of Benjamin Robert Haydon has
recently been dwelt upon by many of our contemporaries ; and thoſe who have taken it to heart are
not likely to require its freſh recital.

SACRED POETRY; MILTON

AND POLLOK.

IT is, perhaps, not eafy to determine the limits within which facred fubjects may be permitted in modern narrative or epic poetry. Yet the topic is full of intereft, and the limitation a very defirable object of criticifm ; for, even if we fhould fail of fatisfactorily defining the grounds of facred poetry, it cannot but be profitable to afcertain the conditions under which alone they may be occupied, and the manner in which they have been moft fuccefsfully cultivated. The neceffity of checking the prefumption of weak and inexperienced poet-afters, who are even lefs able to inflate the trumpets of the Year of Jubilee than to bend the bow of Ulyffes, is an urgent motive to this end. We cannot ignore the fact, that themes of the moft awful importance, gathered from holy writ, are frequently made the fubject-matter of ambitious poems ; and fuch is the general ftyle of thefe

F

productions that, whenever we meet with the announcement of a facred poem, we now make up our minds for fomething unufually profane. Many of thefe poems, fo-called, are utter failures; and, if we judged from them alone, it might readily be decided that themes fo weighty could not be worthily fuftained in human hands, and that the Chriftian verities are both too ferious and too inflexible for the purpofes of poetic fable. But this eafy decifion of the matter is denied to us : for inftances of the higheft treatment and wideft fuccefs prefent themfelves to the mind; and, though few, they are living and eloquent witneffes for a fpecies of compofition that is rather difhonoured than difcredited by a necropolis of failures. The works of Milton, and even of Pollok, are of themfelves fufficient to fhield from unqualified cenfure the practice of adventuring upon themes fo high and difficult. But too much muft not be prefumed from occafional fuccefs; nor fhould it be forgotten that the inftances adduced may be the very exceptions which are faid to eftablifh, rather than to contradict, a rule. This, indeed, we fufpect to be the cafe. Secular poetry is the rule, and facred poetry the exception. The fuccefs of the mafters juft mentioned was neceffary to juftify their own effays, and cannot avail to excufe the attempts of men lefs naturally gifted, or lefs morally prepared. The undertaking of Milton was full of peril : to have failed either in truth of defign, or in dignity of execution, would have degraded the facred topic of his verfe, and expofed his own weaknefs and prefumption. He had none to fhow the way, when, with daring wing, he penetrated " the palpable obfcure,"—none to pitch the high key-note of his eventful fong, when he effayed " things unattempted yet in profe or rhyme." As he incurred all the danger of the attempt, fo let him receive all the praife of his fuccefs. So, in his degree, with Pollok : to retrace the traverfed *Courfe of Time* was an act no lefs adventurous, and perhaps even more arduous, than to relate the lofs of Paradife. The very triumph of Milton increafed the difficulties of the later bard. To fucceed equally he muft foar as highly, and yet avoid the flaming track which revealed the other's flight. To be worthy of his theme, he muft be equally fublime and fpiritual with his great predeceffor, and yet it was neceffary to be abfolutely original and diftinct. No doubt the temerity of this attempt was barely juftified by the refult, and it will hardly be caufe for wonder if a comparifon of thefe two authors fhould have the effect of marking their very unequal merit. Yet the younger and inferior poet may prove not altogether unworthy of being brought, though only for a moment, into the prefence of his mature and mighty rival; and we are perfuaded that his originality and merit will furvive the ordeal.

It is a remark occurring in the " Table Talk " of Samuel Taylor Coleridge, that the only fubjects proper for epic poetry are either national or mundane. Whether hiftorically or theoretically confidered, this dictum will be found entirely warranted by truth. It is true, historically : Homer, Virgil, and Camoens are authors of great national epics ; Tasso, Milton, and Pollok, of poems either in the widest sense mundane, or of interest commensurate with the extent of Christendom. It is true, theoretically : for the stronger interests of poetry are wholly dependent upon personal or social relations ; and it may be fairly assumed that the cordial attention of a great people is not to be engaged in the most brilliant events in which they have no concern, and with which they have neither natural nor spiritual connection. Strange as it may seem, those human feelings which are most universally experienced, and so might be supposed to have equal sympathy with objects near and remote, require a limited, particular, and intimate bond of fellowship : our hearts, when they most yearn to embrace the world, find the greater necessity to localise their affections and concentrate their love. So, if the poetry of a nation is to be confessedly national and popular, it must be either patriotic or religious—must link itself either with the social pride or the individual faith of its members. This continual predominance of self, or requirement of personal interest, is the necessary condition of our being and identity, and is therefore no way disparaging to human nature. And although it is true that poetry, from the elevation of its tone and the profound humanity of its spirit, is the most calculated of all liberal pursuits to widen our sympathies, and refine the grosser felfifhnefs of our nature; yet experience teaches that fome limited bond of focial or perfonal ties, fome remote or nearer connection with our individual felf, is neceffary for infpiring that cordial preference, and fuftaining that unflagging intereft, which an elaborate poetic narrative demands, and without which it is neither appreciated nor enjoyed, neither gladly undertaken nor frequently refumed.

We are not furprifed to find that Milton, when contemplating a great poem, and anxioufly felecting its theme, fhould be "long choofing and beginning late;" and ftill lefs do we wonder that his choice fhould vacillate, as it did, between our fabulous national hero, King Arthur, and the head of the human family. His ultimate decifion was juftified by the refult; but the reafons which determined his choice are fufficiently obvious and ftrong to enable us to judge how wifely he refolved, both in what he rejected and what he undertook. Had the ftory of King Arthur been more hiftorical in its credit, more national in its character, or of more human intereft in itfelf, it would have furnifhed a fubject of fafe and legitimate intereft to our afpiring poet; and even as it was, we fhould have had to regret to this day, and through all time, the fubftitution of his greater theme, if his genius had proved lefs fuperlative, or his mind been lefs earneftly religious.* But there

---

* This was written before the publication of the *Idylls of the King*. We may now ftill further congratulate ourfelves

cannot remain a doubt, that he was impelled by the force of that high religious genius to fing of the world's great lapfe and wonderful recovery, feeling himfelf to poffefs a moral and intellectual fitnefs for the tafk, and finding only in fo vaft and fpiritual a theme due fcope for the amazing faculties and gifts with which God had endowed him. It is probable that he was yet more fpecially baptized for his great work. He was fuffered to mount above the ordinary watch-tower of a poet's fancy, though ftanding lower than the Pifgah of a Prophet's vifion. He was in fome fort ordained a feer of the glorious paft, though denied an apocalypfe of the ineffable future. This is no more than to affert that what he was called *to* by the appointment of Providence, he was qualified *for* by adequate influence; and that the peculiar facrednefs of his fong was honoured and fuftained by a yet richer infpiration than that which the higheft poets are wont to enjoy. But, in faying this, let us be fairly underftood. In the extraordinary power afcribed to Milton, we do not hold him up to the emulation of fucceeding bards; and it fhould be duly remembered, that he was not fo favoured by reafon either of his fubject or of his invocation-prayer. The mere invocation of the

---

on the final choice of Milton, fince it left the fubject of King Arthur in referve for the prefent Laureate. Mr. Tennyfon is, even as compared with Milton, "of imagination all compact;" and the region of mythic hiftory and allegoric fiction is that in which his genius moves moft freely and fuccefsfully.

Holy Spirit, however folemnly phrafed, cannot be
fuppofed to engage His immediate help and direction in the performance of any work of our vain
imaginations. It is for the moft part the higheft
prefumption of which a poet can be guilty, fo to
addrefs the Divine Being, that the reader is led to
infer that he fecures little fhort of plenary infpiration for the work enfuing; by which abfolute
freedom from error, and confiftence with all
truth, would be guaranteed. This is to make
God anfwerable for our fin and folly; to put the
feal of infallible truth to a tiffue of conceptions
fabricated in a corner of darknefs. Some meaner
mufe, the perfonification of human genius and
knowledge, we may allowably invoke; for, in fo
doing, we exprefs our defire to attain the higheft
meafure of truth and beauty which our limited
faculties permit; beyond this, it is impiety to go.
But in Milton we think we fee a fubordination of
intellectual to moral objects, and an implicit fubjection of heart and mind to the Divine teaching,
which remove his cafe far from that of ordinary
poets. The ftudy of the Hebrew Scriptures had
been the moft earneft employment of his life:
his mind was imbued with a knowledge and love
and reverence of God's word. His life was pure,
his character patriarchal. The habitual temper
of his mind was earneft and devout. There was
no mirth or levity in all his broad, deep foul.
What was little, or merely local, won no attention from him: his mind dwelt only on great
verities and great events. He was, fubftantially,

a faint of the antique Hebrew clafs.   If he re-
fented, it was like Samfon : if he triumphed, it
was like Deborah.   Yet over thefe fterner elements of character was fhed the foftening light of
a better difpenfation, and through them permeated
the tender warmth of a poet's heart.   In recount-
ing the fatal fin of the firft Adam, he already ex-
ulted in the triumphant refurrection of the Second;
and the grand old harp which bewailed the
fuccefles of the baleful ferpent, yielded hope and
rapture as he ftruck in the promife of the woman's
conquering Seed.   Thus he came, the predeftined
poet of Paradife, to "juftify the ways of God to
man."   And, remembering thefe features of his
life and character,—this threefold preparation of
nature, grace, and knowledge, for his great work,
—we may now read with admiration and approval
the noble introduction of his theme, and his bold
but not unwarranted invocation of the Divine
Spirit :—

> " Of man's firft difobedience, and the fruit
>   Of that forbidden tree whofe mortal tafte
>   Brought death into the world, and all our woe,
>   With lofs of Eden, till one greater Man
>   Reftore us, and regain the blifsful feat,
>   Sing, heavenly mufe, that on the fecret top
>   Of Oreb or of Sinai didft infpire
>   That fhepherd who firft taught the chofen feed
>   In the beginning how the heavens and earth
>   Rofe out of chaos : or if Sion hill
>   Delight thee more, and Siloa's brook that flow'd
>   Faft by the oracle of God ; I thence
>   Invoke thy aid to my adventurous fong,
>   That with no middle flight intends to foar
>   Above the Aonian mount, while it purfues
>   Things unattempted yet in profe or rhyme.

And chiefly Thou, O Spirit, that doſt prefer
Before all temples the upright heart and pure,
Inſtruct me, for Thou know'ſt: Thou from the firſt
Waſt preſent, and, with mighty wings outſpread,
Dove-like ſat'ſt brooding on the vaſt abyſs,
And mad'ſt it pregnant : what in me is dark,
Illumine ; what is low, raiſe and ſupport ;
That to the height of this great argument
I may aſſert Eternal Providence,
And juſtify the ways of God to man."

In this fine exordium, which contains the moral
epitome of the whole poem, may be ſeen alſo ſome
of the chief characteriſtic beauties of Milton's
ſtyle. For example, note the union of ſimplicity
and power in theſe lines. There is a directneſs
in the author's ſtatement of his ſubject, that engages our ſobereſt attention ; and the propoſition
is not at firſt far removed from the language of
ſerious proſe. Yet ſuch is the ſkilful conſtruction
of the verſe, and ſo appropriate to his theme the
elevation of the poet's manner, that we ſoon feel
ſenſibly the undulating pinions of the riſing muſe,
and know that we are borne into a higher
element. Still, there is no aſſumption of poetic
phraſe ; and the exerciſed prerogative of verſe is
ſcarcely felt. The meaſure is, as it were, abſorbed
into the matter : it is the medium only of great,
pure thoughts ; and ſo has no attribute or quality
of its own, but thoſe only of the thoughts which
it embodies. The lines flow on, in rhythmical
cadences, it is true, but emphaſized and varied
and divided more by the immediate requirements
of the ſentiment than according to a formal ſylla-
bic code. Next to the harmoniſing genius of the

poet, this refult is due to the judgment with
which he made felection of the blank-verfe meafure
for his purpofe. We cannot fuppofe that in rhymed
couplets he would have furpaffed the degree of
power, grace, and flexibility, attained by Dryden
and Pope; yet their productions read like ftudied
profefforial lectures, prepared by a fkilful mafter in
verfe. Indeed, the heroic couplet—upon whofe
two mechanical wings none ever ventured to
" afcend the higheft heaven of invention" without
fuffering the fate of Icarus—is as inferior to the
blank-verfe meafure as an inftrument limited, hard,
intractable, to another of unbounded compafs and
infinite expreffion, capable of the fineft gradations
of found, and limited only by the genius of its mafter. Such is the inftrument which Milton chofe,
fo far at leaft as regards its fubjection to his art.
In volume, breadth, and harmony, his magnificent
numbers feemed to iffue from a full-toned organ,
refounding through the earth as through cathedral
aifles and cloiftered walks, filling the vaulted arch,
and making the whole temple vocal with praife.

For a full confideration of the *action* and the
characters of Milton's poem, and a confequent defence of its claim to epic dignity and honour, we
muft refer the reader to Addifon's admirable papers
on *Paradife Loft*, originally publifhed in *The Specta-
tor*, and often reprinted, as in the edition of the
poem now before us. To abridge his obfervations would be only incurring a too imminent rifk
of weakening a powerful argument, with the cer-
tainty of traducing a moft lucid and beautiful com-

pofition. To fay fo much in fo little as he has done, would be next to impoffible; to fay it as well, would be to tranfcribe his own words. The latter courfe, which is the moft defirable, is happily the leaft neceffary; as a criticifm fo famous has become proportionately eafy of accefs. We fhall merely remark, then, on thefe particular points, that Addifon feems fully to have eftablifhed that all thofe excellencies in Homer, which are, from their nature, effential to heroic poetry,—whether of invention, conftruction, character, or verfification,—have their worthy counterpart in the *Paradife Loft;* and that, where a marked difference appears, it is commonly demanded by the wide difference of the fubjects, and often iffues in a contraft favourable to the Chriftian bard. For this refult of a comparifon between the two, which may be affirmed equally in favour of Milton's poem as a whole and in parts, one confident in the genius of our author and the legitimacy of his theme would be fully prepared; for the adequate treatment of a fubject which involves the Creation, Fall, and Reftoration of mankind,—which allows the introduction of the angelic rebellion, by way of epifode,—which has fiends for its confpirators, chaos for its highway, paradife for its garden, heaven for its court, angels for its minifters, and eternity for its iffues,—might well outweigh the vaunted " tale of Troy divine," involving merely the abduction of a Spartan woman, the rage of an infuriated Greek, and the fack of a Trojan city, all long fince loft in the overwhelming wave of time, and perifhing

utterly where they firſt appeared.   Prize the Iliad
as we may, and ſuffer ourſelves to be hurried along
its impetuous tide of beauties as we do, we cannot
forget that it is our lower, ſenſuous, ſelfiſh, and
unhallowed nature that is gratified the moſt; that
the ideal of the poet's heroiſm, and the object of
our unreaſoning admiration, is carnal, and not
moral; that it exhibits paſſion glorified, and brute
energy extolled, and revenge made ſacred, rather
than duty paramount, and ſelf renounced, and love
triumphant.   We tire of demi-gods, whoſe thews
and ſinews only prove them ſuch, and whoſe phyſical greatneſs is redeemed from contempt only by
the proportioned ſtrength of their hatred, pride,
and luſt, making them objects yet more of abhor-
rence than diſdain.   We long for creatures living
under ſome great moral law; for heroes perſiſting
againſt all diſcouragement in obedience to authority,
or not too proud to feel remorſe where their virtue
has ſuffered defeat.   The Iliad as little ſatisfies the
purer intellect and ſpiritual aſpirations of the Chriſtian reader, as the boy's " game of ſoldiers" can
ſuffice to pleaſe during the reſtleſs and inquiring
period of youth, or throughout the nobler years of
maturity and wiſdom.   It is the primer of moral
life, though the perfection of early art ; a picture,
duly preſerved and valued, of our world in its
bright, wilful, wayward infancy, which now hangs
in the nineteenth century of the Chriſtian era for
our occaſional glance of curioſity and intereſt; in
which we trace the natural rudiments of life, and
mark the rude expreſſion of inſtinctive feelings

which have long fince received fyftematic education and moral control. It is therefore that the undertaking of Milton was fo fuperior in importance.
Though we fhould grant that Homer in no way
failed in regard to qualifications for his tafk, and
was equal in genius to Milton himfelf, we cannot
wonder that the poem of the latter fhould take a
higher place ; that an audience " fit though few,"
but enlarging with the fpread of Chriftian fentiment and pure morality, fhould derive a higher
pleafure from its elevated character; and that it
fhould become the acknowledged ftandard of what
is great in poetic ftyle, and of what is true in individual tafte.

But, notwithftanding this high general eftimate
of the *Paradife Loft*, we **muft** admit that the author does not always furmount the great difficulties of his fubject with equal eafe or with uniform
fuccefs. The relations of the celeftial and infernal worlds with our own mixed race and material
planet rendered the choice of appropriate imagery
and juft analogy a matter of perplexity and hazard ;
while the neceffity of limiting poetic invention to
a plan confiftent with revealed truth, and in harmony with Chriftian fentiment, taxed to the utmoft the judgment and the genius which it was
ultimately to reward **with** proportionate renown.
What learning and tafte could do to obviate thefe
difadvantages, and reconcile thefe contrarieties, was
done by Milton. But enough is difcoverable in the
poem, both of imperfection and incongruity, to
fhow **that his** high theme involved ferious poetic

drawbacks ; that, although for the moſt part congenial to his grave and ſoaring ſpirit, it ſometimes
bore him beyond the regions of human ſympathy
and diſtinct conception.   Thus, in the firſt two
books, juſtly eſteemed among the fineſt of the
poem, the author treats of matters ſo entirely
foreign to our experience, and ſo imperfectly conceived by our earthly imaginations, that all his great
ſkill can accompliſh is to make us for a time forget the groſs materialiſm of his infernal regions, and
the parliamentary logic of his ſatanic council. For
what is Pandemonium, after all, but a chamber of
debate, reared for the princes of hell ? And though,
with conſummate art, our poet has made it riſe up
complete as by ſpiritual magic, and proportioned
its gloom and vaſtneſs to the tarniſhed grandeur of
the angelic rebels, we ſee that it is modelled on the
material principle : we know that it has extenſion,
though unmeaſured ; and ſeats, though they be
thrones ; and lamps, though they need neither trim-
ming nor attendance.   So of the debate itſelf.   It
is kindred to earthly parliaments : the ſpeakers follow and ſucceed each other ; anſwer or evade foregoing arguments ; are impatient, ſarcaſtic, ſophiſtical, and out of order, like their human prototypes.
So of the perſonal adjuncts of Satan : they diſ-
tinguiſh his royalty and pre-eminence by phyſical
ſuperiority ; and he is armed like one of Homer's
heroes.   It is true that this embodiment of ſpiritual
enmity, this material clothing for an ineffable conflict, is in great part finely managed :—

> " His ponderous fhield,
> Ethereal temper, maffy, large, and round,
> Behind him caft : the broad circumference
> Hung on his fhoulders like the moon."

Here the poet is indeed meeting his mighty fubject more than half-way, and fo leffening the fearful dif-tance betwixt the feen and unfeen worlds : but a certain incongruity remains ; and when he adds,—

> " His fpear—to equal which the talleft pine
> Hewn on Norwegian hills, to be the maft
> Of fome great ammiral, were but a wand—
> He walk'd with, to fupport uneafy fteps
> Over the burning marle,"—

we become confcious, after a moment's reflection, of the unhappy neceffity which could urge our poet to fuggeft the greatnefs of a fallen feraph by defcribing the magnitude of his walking-ftick. This may appear an unfair expreffion to employ ; but the idea is precifely that of our author. Its abfurdity is ftrictly due to the real difadvantage which Milton himfelf was unable to obviate ; and, the oftener thefe paffages of his poem are perufed, the more diftinctly is that difadvantage felt. What analogy the whole field of nature could fupply, and what appropriatenefs of expreffion the ftores of language offered, and what varieties of cadence and rhythm the profody and tafte of a cunning ear and cultivated mind could furnifh, were not awant-ing in our author : for thefe have confpired to pre-ferve the moft arduous part of his moft arduous undertaking from fudden failure and abfolute bur-lefque. And if Milton could do no more than this, (and, when reporting of celeftial and infernal coun-cils, we dare not fay he has done more,) the fact

is furely fufficient to warn from fuch dangerous
ground all men lefs richly gifted or lefs thoroughly
prepared.

The fixth book of Paradife Loft ftrikingly exemplifies both the difadvantage juft mentioned, and
the comparative fuccefs with which it has been encountered.   It is entirely occupied with a record
of that conflict in which the higheft of created
fpirits contended againft the arms of omnipotence, and ftrove on the edge of perdition to fcale
the throne of Deity.   The narrative is fuppofed to
be related by the archangel Raphael to our father
Adam.   On one fide of the engagement are
Michael and Gabriel, leading the choice celeftial
cohorts ; and, on the other, Satan with his revolted
angels ; and the utter difcomfiture of the rebels is
only achieved by Meffiah, coming in his Father's
might.   To put this brief but pregnant argument
in detail, and yet lofe none of its impreffive and even
awful character, would feem to tafk the powers of
fome eye-witneffing feraph, ftriking his harp of
gold, and rehearfing in the ear of heaven that ancient and celeftial epos.   Were it about to be attempted by man for the firft time, how earneftly
fhould we diffuade ! what fruit of folly fhould we
deprecate !   But it is the praife of Milton that here
he has incurred no cenfure ; for, not to fail in fuch
a tafk is greatly to fucceed.   In fome degree he reconciles us to that terreftrial analogy, inadequate
though it be, which in the opening books reminds
us of the grofs materials which every painter of the
inferno muft employ, that through our corporal fenfe

he may reach our more fpiritual imagination. Indeed, the method is undoubtedly legitimate, though
one of extreme difficulty. Whatfoever is unfeen
or unknown, provided we have fome clear intellectual conception of it, may be illuftrated by
fome vifible counterpart, or fet forth in fome
human analogy. Our compound nature infures
this. Our experience unites the two worlds of
material and immaterial things ; and the poet
caufes the one to correfpond entirely to the other.
The ftrife of the " embattled feraphim" does not
utterly tranfcend his powers ; but it taxes them to
the utmoft, and demands them in fulnefs and perfection. The reader may hear Milton himfelf, as
he acknowledges the weaknefs of a mortal's tongue,
and yet labours with the theme of angels. The
paffage which relates the encounter of Satan and
the archangel Michael is an exemplification of the
mingled merit and defect afcribed to the fupernatural portions of the poem.

In fuch lines we have fome intimation of the
arduous nature of the poet's tafk, and feel perhaps
fome mifgivings as to his real competence and
power. But, as he advances, he appears to triumph over every difficulty. We foon become
confcious that he is rifing " to the height of his
great argument." He is at length mafter of his
theme, moulding it by the fervour of his genius
into fymmetrical and glowing beauty. The approach of Meffiah to decide the battle, which
threatens to uproot the foundations of heaven, is
defcribed with aftonifhing majefty and power, and

G

founds in our ears like the voice of another prophet, charged with the announcement of a new apocalypfe. But the vifion is retrofpective, and the voice thrills backward paft the morning ftars. Our bard has caught the fpirit of Ezekiel, and fo makes bold with his grand imagery, and reflects into primæval eras a portion of his magnificent prophecy. Nothing furely can be finer, either in conception, meafure, or language, than the deliberate, folitary, overwhelming inroad of Meffiah among the banded rebels.

> " So fpake the Son, and into terror changed
>   His countenance, too fevere to be beheld,
>   And full of wrath bent on His enemies.
>   At once the Four fpread out their ftarry wings
>   With dreadful fhade contiguous, and the orbs
>   Of His fierce chariot roll'd, as with the found
>   Of torrent floods, or of a numerous hoft.
>   He on His impious foes right onward drove,
>   Gloomy as night; under His burning wheels
>   The fteadfaft empyrean fhook throughout,
>   All but the throne itfelf of God.   Full foon
>   Among them He arrived; in His right hand
>   Grafping ten thoufand thunders, which He fent
>   Before Him, fuch as in their fouls infix'd
>   Plagues: they, aftonifh'd, all refiftance loft,
>   All courage; down their idle weapons dropt:
>   O'er fhields and helms and helmed heads He rode
>   Of thrones and mighty feraphim proftrate,
>   That wifh'd the mountains now might be again
>   Thrown on them, as a fhelter from His ire.
>   Nor lefs on either fide tempeftuous fell
>   His arrows, from the fourfold-vifaged Four,
>   Diftinct with eyes, and from the living wheels,
>   Diftinct alike with multitude of eyes;
>   One fpirit in them ruled, and every eye
>   Glared lightning, and fhot forth pernicious fire
>   Among the' accurft, that wither'd all their ftrength,
>   And of their wonted vigour left them drain'd,
>   Exhaufted, fpiritlefs, afflicted, fallen."

Of the allegory of Sin and Death, in the fecond book, we entertain an almoft unmixed admiration. It is faid, indeed, that allegorical figures fhould have been held inadmiffible by our author, as interfering with the more definite impreffion of his infernal characters, and as being too fhadowy to encounter the perfonal hoftility of Satan, though himfelf a fpirit. But thefe theoretical objections (to which the fineft inftances of allegory are open) vanifh under the influence of the poet's power, when we fee depictured the ftrange refemblance of thefe mighty combatants before hell-gates. They are of undoubted kin : Sin has Satan for her parent, and is the inceftuous mother of his offspring, Death ; and here truth and allegory are fo exquifitely blended, that no revulfion is experienced from a confufion of nature, but only a fenfe of awe, in prefence of the deformity, malignity, and hate of this triumvirate of terrors. Was ever fight more monftrous or confounding than that of Satan and his ghaftly fon ? Was ever fo inconceivable a duel pictured by fo realizing a pen ?

> " So fpake the grifly Terror, and in fhape,
> So fpeaking and fo threatening, grew tenfold
> More dreadful and deform. On the other fide,
> Incenfed with indignation, Satan ftood,
> Unterrified, and like a comet burn'd
> That fires the length of Ophiuchus huge
> In the arctic fky, and from his horrid hair
> Shakes peftilence and war."

We never read this or kindred paffages in our author without exulting in the power of language, and the range of a poet's art. The pencil of the

grandeſt painter muſt fail here.   What would be
the Titanic figures of Michael Angelo, or the
vaſty darkneſs of Martin, in compariſon with this
ſuggeſted and portentous viſion,—thrown, not
upon the feeble retina of the eye, but upon the
kindling and growing imagination, capable of receiving, in undiminiſhed length and fervour, the
image of Satan when he ſo ſtood " unterrified, and
like a comet burn'd."   The whole remainder of
this book, to the moment when the arch-fiend—
labouring through chaos, paved only with the
rugged and diſordered elements—iſſues to a ſight
of the new creation he is ſeeking, is a continued
illuſtration of this remark concerning the power of
language, and abundantly teſtifies to our author's
ſkill in its employment.

But the fineſt beauties of this " divine poem"
are yet to be remarked.   Theſe conſiſt in the hu-
manities, which are the features moſt diſtinguiſhed
in every great poetic work, be it ſacred or profane.
Every true poet, even when his flight is for the
moſt part ethereal, derives (like Antæus) freſh
ſtrength and vigour from the touch of his native
earth.   We have elſewhere endeavoured to ſhow
that invention in the creative ſenſe is not the poet's
attribute, but only in the ſenſe of combination ;
and that nature is the original of his profoundeſt
work of art.   From this it might readily be inferred,
if it were not daily ſeen to be the caſe, that imitation is with him moſt perfect where obſervation is
moſt conſtant and complete ; that human life and
character yield finer ſubjects for his pencil than an-

gelic creatures, and terreftrial lake and mountain
more tempting landfcape than that garden which
is watered by the river of life. The facred epic of
Milton furnifhes a ftriking illuftration of this truth.
Its grandeur is not, after all, its true greatnefs : its
ftrength and beauty and fublimity are manifefted
in human love and frailty and affliction, rather than
in feraphic ardours and unfullied joy. The hero
in whom is concentred all its potent intereft is
Adam, worthy to be the father of our race, and for
whom we feel a filial fentiment of love, awed into
higher reverence by its long defcent. The partner of his ftupendous fortunes both heightens and
attracts that intereft into her own lovely character,
—which is ftill an undivided intereft, as in the
moon we fee only the reflected glory of the fun.

The manner in which our firft parents are reprefented by Milton is extremely fine ; and equally
fo in their ftate of innocence, of temptation, and
of guilt. So well to paint them in their firft eftate
is the more admirable, as it was the more difficult ;
for it was but too likely that an attempt to delin-
eate the perfection of Paradife fhould end in feeble
generalifation and utter want of character. Yet
individuality is ftamped upon their human perfection. In Adam we have all the grace and gene-
rofity of chivalry, without its boaftful language and
impracticable aims ; and all the weight of knowledge and wifdom, without its partiality or pride.
He is ftrong without infolence, ardent without intemperance, and elevated without ambition. He
is the foremoft as well as the firft of men, the head

as well as the author of us all.   Fairer than Ab-
falom, more royal than Auguftus, more beneficent
than Alfred,—in him are gathered up all the
nobleft virtues of his nobleft fons.   But his qualities and honours are real and not conventional, abfolute and not comparative, and neither fullied by
infirmities nor clouded by error.   The character
of Eve is, perhaps, the moft lovely conception of
woman that was ever embodied by the poet's art.
She is the counterpart and confort of Adam—bone
of his bone, and flefh of his flefh ; the complement
of his nature, and the crown of his exiftence. Made
for him by the Almighty's hand, fhe was the complete fulfilment of his defires and wants ; drawn
from him as the cloud is from the bofom of the
ocean, fhe yearned towards him as the river hurries to its primal fource.   The exquifite contraft,
and the no lefs perfect correfpondence, of this noble
pair, are beautifully fuftained throughout.   Their
love is the acknowledged pattern-paffion of all fucceeding generations : founded on efteem, growing
through admiration, cemented by gratitude, and
fubfifting in confidence and joy.

The firft acquaintance and union of this noble
pair, as rehearfed in Eve's delightful reminifcence,
and in language fo modeft, conjugal, and true, is
probably the moft charming paffage in the whole
poem.   Its great beauty can hardly fail to imprefs
the moft carelefs reader : it appeals alike to the
fimpleft heart and the moft cultured imagination.
Of fimilar merit and ftill higher intereft is the
fpeech of Eve on waking from her prompted dream,

in which the fhadow of impending **evil is feen for**
a moment to darken and difturb her yet pure foul,
and then, in the light of Adam's confolation, paffes
away as the fhadow of a **cloud** over the re-fmiling
meadow. To the dream of Eve there is, **however,**
this objection,—that, as it could not but be received
as a folemn warning of the danger awaiting our
parents from the temptation of evil fpirits, fo it
greatly aggravates the crime of their fubfequent difobedience. Indeed, that Eve, forewarned, fhould
yet put faith in the flattering promife of the ferpent, fuggefts the idea that fome moral taint had
been communicated by the dream itfelf; that **the**
foul whifpers of the demon " fquatting at **her ear**"
had engendered a fatal tendency to fin, or left fome
unholy fpell upon her imagination that weakened
her refiftance of **evil, if it** did not **injure her per-**
ception of truth and goodnefs.

The circumftances of the Fall, including its
more immediate confequences, are fet forth by
Milton with much judgment and tafte. He invents
but few particulars which are not more or lefs fuggefted by the Scripture hiftory, and none that are
not confiftent with it. The fubject being undertaken, the dramatic action of his poem demanded
fome fuller details of our parents' fin than was furnifhed by the language of infpiration; and **thefe,**
we think, he has imagined and defcribed in a manner open to the leaft poffible objection. With **a**
juft appreciation of the object and **means of art, he**
has felicitoufly avoided involving himfelf in theological difficulties, and lawfully availed himfelf of

that meafure of poetic licence which the general language of Scripture allowed, and the human intereft of his poem required. But the Bible remains, throughout, both his authority and his model. The whole narrative of the temptation and fall has a fcriptural air. Adam is identical with the patriarch of our race, of whom Mofes writes in terms fo fimple and dignified. Eve is the mother of us all, and the collateral mate of Adam. If Milton has fomewhat harfhly reprefented the fatal weaknefs of the woman, he has not extenuated the more wilful guilt of the man. If the character of Adam is tinctured with fome of our author's proper felf, and that of Eve embodies his own opinion of female excellence and frailty, we cannot but acknowledge that his ideals were noble and engaging, and worthy to be fet on high as the reprefentatives of our race. The ninth book of Paradife Loft, in which the crifis of human hiftory is recorded, abounds in paffages of intereft and fkilful delineation. We have noble mufic and manly wifdom in almoft every line. It might be profitably read and difcuffed, verfe by verfe; or read with conftant paufes and occafional repetition : for, like all true poetry, its light is in itfelf, and deliberate re-perufal will manifeft it more and more. The immediate effects of the Fall upon our firft parents, —their carnal intemperance, mutual reproach, and angry recriminations,—are in ftrict keeping both with the Mofaic record and the known depravity of our nature ; while they are made ftrictly to fubferve the artiftical purpofes of the poet. Well

may the miserable Adam, late the friend and
favourite of God, but feeling now the ruinous disobedience to have corrupted and degraded his whole
being, exclaim in anguish,—

> " How shall I behold the face
> Henceforth of God or angel, erst with joy
> And rapture so oft beheld ?   Those heavenly shapes
> Will dazzle now this earthly with their blaze
> Insufferably bright.   O might I here
> In solitude live savage ; in some glade
> Obscured, where highest woods, impenetrable
> To star or sun-light, spread their umbrage broad
> And brown as evening !   Cover me, ye pines !
> Ye cedars, with innumerable boughs
> Hide me, where I may never see them more !"

From this point the poem advances steadily in interest and beauty to the end.   In the tenth book
the altercation of our parents is renewed, and its
features are more characteristically marked.   The
angry invectives of Adam alternate with generous
compassion for the grief of his unhappy partner.
His impatience of her folly is contrasted with her
meek submission to a lot of shame and sorrow.   We
regret, with him, the curiosity and pride which
lured Eve into disobedience ; but we admire in her
the patient love and fortitude still witnessed in her
daughters, and gratefully acknowledge that woman
has abundantly cheered the desolation which in a
subordinate degree is due to her.   In the next and
penultimate book the archangel Michael is com-
missioned to drive out the disobedient pair from the
garden of God's own planting.   His announcement of that duty strikes them with despair and
grief :—

" He added not ; for Adam at the news
  Heart-ftruck with chilling gripe of forrow ftood,
  That all his fenfes bound : Eve, who unfeen
  Yet all had heard, with audible lament
  Difcover'd foon the place of her retire.
  ' O unexpected ftroke, worfe than of death !
  Muft I then leave thee, Paradife ? thus leave
  Thee, native foil ! thefe happy walks and fhades
  Fit haunt for gods ? where I had hope to fpend,
  Quiet though fad, the refpite of that day
  That muft be mortal to us both. O flowers,
  That never will in other climate grow,
  My early vifitation, and my laft
  At even, which I bred up with tender hand
  From the firft opening bud, and gave ye names !
  Who now fhall rear ye to the fun, or rank
  Your tribes, and water from the ambrofial fount ?
  Thee, laftly, nuptial bower ! by me adorn'd
  With what to fight or fmell was fweet ! from thee
  How fhall I part, and whither wander down
  Into a lower world ; to this obfcure
  And wild ? how fhall we breathe in other air
  Lefs pure, accuftom'd to immortal fruits ? ' "

We find it difficult to reftrain our quotations
within neceffary limits. It is the effect of this
fuperb poem that, the more we read of it, the more
we wifh to read : our ear grows accuftomed to its
fonorous meafure, and our mind rifes to the tone of
its majeftic fenfe. We have heard how Eve laments the impending expulfion ; and we muft find
room for a few lines of Adam's lamentation alfo.

" This moft afflicts me, that, departing hence,
  As from His face I fhall be hid, deprived
  His bleffed countenance. Here I could frequent
  With worfhip place by place where He vouchfafed
  Prefence Divine ; and to my fons relate,
  ' On this mount He appear'd ; under this tree
  Stood vifible ; among thefe pines His voice
  I heard ; here with Him at this fountain talk'd.'
    *   *   *   *   *

In yonder nether world where fhall I feek
His bright appearances, or footftep trace ?
For though I fled Him angry, yet, recall'd
To life prolong'd and promifed race, I now
Gladly behold though but His utmoft fkirts
Of glory, and far off His fteps adore."

Then the archangel fhows to Adam, from the higheft hill of Paradife, the future generations of the world. We have before had a retrofpective epifode, and here is a vifion of anticipation. Gabriel related the wars of the angels, and the marvels of creation : Michael now rolls back the curtain of the future ; and our prime anceftor is alternately furprifed, and awed, and comforted, as great cities, wide-fpread evils, and the long promifed Saviour, fucceffively appear. This epitome of human hiftory is full of attractions, moral and picturefque ; the whole relation by which the vifion is accompanied is fuftained with the dignity of the heroic Chriftian mufe. It extends to nearly the clofe of the laft book ; and by its fulnefs of promife we are better prepared for the rigorous fulfilment of the angel's miffion. We read with dimmed eyes, but not with defpairing hearts, of our unhappy parents, when, driven out of Paradife, they looked back and faw it " waved over by that flaming brand ;" we behold them going forrowfully into exile ; but they go " hand in hand" together, and every tear that forces itfelf into their human eyes breaks into a rainbow in the light of hope and mutual confolation.

In this great poem, as in the perfect fhield of Achilles, the total univerfe is epitomifed ; but the univerfe, as known to Milton, exceeds and enfolds that of Homer, as the ethereal fpaces envelop earth. Its twelve books comprehend, as in a zodiac, the fum and feafons of human hiftory;—removing from the fummer folftice of Divine complacency and love, to the dark and cheerlefs winter of difobedience and disfavour, but emerging toward the infinite gladnefs again. The whole of man, and the auguft miniftry of his falvation, are embodied here: his creation and benediction; the weight of his curfe, and the promife of his recovery; the unpeopled feats of the angels, and the repeopled thrones of faints; the Deity Himfelf, dividing among the Perfons of His Godhead a feveral fhare in the great drama of redemption, projected from everlafting, and crowning the eternal years.

To this comprehenfive theme our author has brought a correfponding breadth of treatment, and richnefs of decoration. The grand outlines of his fubject, which extend into three worlds, are filled with their appropriate lights and fhadows, contrafting while they blend, and harmonifed into one magnificent frefco by a miracle of art. The tapeftry which he has embroidered for no fingle nation, but for the family of Adam, glows with the colours of every clime, and ftirs with the actions of every age. He has rifled ancient learning and all fcience; exhaufted the refources of technic fkill, and moulded to his purpofe every rugged element of good; elicited a grace even from barbaric ftory, and fpoiled the pagan gods of praife and tribute due only to Jehovah whom he fung. And all thefe treafures of knowledge and power are made fubfervient to one great moral end. They revolve, indeed, on the axis of the poet's perfonal genius, but advance only in obedience to the central and attracting glory of God; and the native impulfe, fo far from hurrying him apart, fpeeds him along the orbit of his cheerful deftiny, as a planet obeys, in every hair's breadth of its journey, the ruling and reftraining influence of the fun.

An immediate tranfition from Milton to Pollok is not neceffarily an abrupt one. The differences of gait, and height, and feature, are eafily difcerned; but their inviolate office is the fame. Moreover, their identic infpiration may be faid to have derived from one to the other. The priefthood of genius is not, indeed, hereditary; but each high *flamen* of the order is wont to light his torch at a prede- ceffor's fire. We remember to have read that Cowley was firft infpired with a love of poetry by a perufal of the *Fairy Queen*,—a copy of which he chanced upon in fome old-fafhioned window- fettle. And it was when the youthful Pollok— then an humble labourer on his father's farm in Renfrewfhire—made fudden prize of the *Paradife Loft* " among fome old books, on the upper fhelf of the wall-prefs in the kitchen" at his uncle's houfe, that his innate love of all noble and beautiful things expatiated for the firft time in an imaginative work and an ideal world; and poffibly then the firft vague longings for poetical renown, and the firft dim out- lines of his future theme, arofe to animate and occupy the profound enthufiafm of his nature.

But, though the fire was communicated, the fuel was his own, and the afpiring tongue of flam e was fhaped and coloured by intrinfic genius.   Cowley is not more diftinct from **Spenfer than** Pollok is from Milton : the interval between the former two is greater, but the difference of the latter is not lefs decided.   It is difficult to perceive, in **the** metaphyfical conceits and tortuous ingenuity **of Cow**ley's poems, any indication of his love for Spenfer, —whofe affluent ftream of verfe, fparkling with inexhauftible romance, **feems** to difdain its meafured limits, and **revels** beneath the redundant imagery of its **own** fertile **banks, and then** flows onward with majeftic fweep, **a copious,** moral, and refounding fong.   It **cannot be** fo ftrictly maintained that *The Courfe of Time* awakens no **recol**lection of the *Paradife Loft;* for Urania is the mufe of both, and under her guidance each poet ventures " into the heaven of heavens."   But, withal, there is a ftriking difference as to the manner in which they fo " prefume." This difference, however, will be more properly characterized after we have illuftrated, more at large, the ftyle and purpofe of the later work

The manner in which the action of the poem opens, after a brief invocation, **is** very **bold and** ftriking. The imagination of the reader is at once feized upon, and therewith he is tranfported to a region and a period yet incalculably diftant in the future and unfeen world.   It is the poet's defign to rehearfe the general fortunes of our earth, in connection with the moral hiftory of mankind. **For** this no hill in time affords fufficient profpect :

all muft be feen in connection with the end, and
bearing the approval of God's everlafting fmile, or
the eclipfe and condemnation of His averted countenance.   Rapt upwards on the pinion of the
mufe, we find ourfelves fuddenly partaking of the
eternal calm, infinitely removed from the duft and
turmoil of this paffing fcene.

> " Long was the day, fo long expected, paft
> Of the eternal doom, that gave to each
> Of all the human race his due reward.
> The fun—earth's fun, and moon, and ftars, had ceafed
> To number feafons, days, and months, and years,
> To mortal man.   Hope was forgotten, and fear;
> And time, with all its chance and change, and fmiles
> And frequent tears, and deeds of villany
> Or righteoufnefs, once talk'd of much, as things
> Of great renown, was now but ill remember'd;
> In dim and fhadowy vifion of the paft
> Seen far remote, as country which has left
> The traveller's fpeedy ftep, retiring back
> From morn till even; and long eternity
> Had roll'd his mighty years."

The epoch and the fcene being fo magnificent,
it is fitting that the actors fhould be no lefs than
angels and beatified fpirits; and the mighty pro-
fcenium, whofe breadth is that of the New Jerufa-
lem, is accordingly fo occupied. Firft we behold
" two youthful fons of Paradife," who employ the
unmeafured hours in pure and facred converfe,
" high on the hills of immortality."   Thefe look
from time to time over the boundlefs profpect of
fpace, ready to welcome fome returning meffenger
of light, or fome creature newly perfected in virtue,
" from other worlds arrived, confirmed in good."

> " Thus viewing, one they faw, on hafty wing
> Directing towards heaven his courfe; and now,
> His flight afcending near the battlements
> And lofty hills on which they walk'd, approach'd.

For round and round, in fpacious circuit, wide,
Mountains of talleft ftature circumfcribe
The plains of Paradife, whofe tops, array'd
In uncreated radiance, feem fo pure
That nought but angel's foot, or faint's, elect
Of God, may venture there to walk.   Here oft
The fons of blifs take morn or evening paftime,
Delighted to behold ten thoufand worlds
Around their funs revolving in the vaft
External fpace, or liften the harmonies
That each to other in its motion fings.
And hence, in middle heaven remote, is feen
The mount of God in awful glory bright.
Within, no orb create of moon, or ftar,
Or fun, gives light ; for God's own countenance,
Beaming eternally, gives light to all."

The new-arrived is a ftranger from a diftant world,
who, having in his flight heavenward come fuddenly to a mountainous wall of fiery adamant,
and, entering, feen within a number of wretched
beings tortured and toffed upon a burning lake, inquires of the bleffed two what may be the juft
caufe of fo much mifery.   Thefe cannot anfwer
him ; but they call to mind " an ancient bard of
earth," who is wont to recall events that long ago
befell the human family.   To him the three repair, and liften with grave attention and growing
intereft while he recounts the hiftory of his native
fpot, the earth.   It is this narration which forms
the bulk and body of the poem, extending from the
fecond to the final book.

   Hitherto our brief quotations have not been
eminently characteriftic of our author.   His pre-
lude teaches us of things celeftial; but Milton had
fo taught us before with unexampled tafte and dignity.   It is only juftice, then, to fay that the merits

of *The Courfe of Time* are diftinct and peculiar ; and
while they muft be allowed to *range far lower* than
thofe of the *Paradife Loft*, they yet more widely
differ from them. The originality of Pollok's
genius ftrikes us in every page of his work ; and is
as vifible in his treatment of the fubject at large, as
in verfification and verbal expreffion. His poem
might be diftinguifhed as the Evangelical Epic. It
dwells rather upon the moral character of individual man, than on the external hiftory of his
race : it defcribes the varieties of folly which feparately feduced the human family in their pro-
bationary ftate : it expofes the evil heart of
unbelief, of pride, of avarice, and of fenfuality : it
depicts the humbleft and the higheft focial virtues,
and exemplifies them in charming portraitures,—
as in that of a young and dying mother : it inftances, among the providential afflictions of mankind, the mental cloud of difappointment by which
the author had himfelf been chaftened and improved. No hypocrify is left unftripped, no vanity
undetected, no lie uncontradicted. The poet in
imagination afcends to the everlafting heights of
futurity, and affumes the awful pofition of a fpirit
who has long fince left the day of doom behind,
that he may fee with undeluded eyes, and drefs in
their true colours, the bufy perfonages of earth. As
they approach him from the mafquerade of time,
each uncovers his features to the light, and hears
himfelf unflatteringly defcribed. What an epitome
of human life is here ! All that feduced men from
their duty—the vices that were plainly and groffly

H

such, and the plausible ambition which assumed to be equally allied **to virtue and to honour**; and all that obscured the truth of eternal things from the heedless sons of time; and all **the** false **distinctions and** awards that made the external aspect of society one huge disguise; the indulgences of youth, **the worldliness** of manhood, the covetousness of age; **God's** judgments graciously suspended, and man's **indifference** fatally prolonged, till Divine forbearance **became** exhausted just when human wickedness had grown most infatuated, and the defiance hurled to heaven touched the electric cloud charged with Almighty **wrath**—**these are the** moral features, and this the general catastrophe, embodied in *The Course of Time.* **From this** masterly **review of** temporal history it is difficult to choose an example, because such choice involves rejection; yet many isolated passages have become such through their superior excellence, and live vividly in the reader's memory. The character of Byron is drawn with a vigour worthy of his own amazing pencil, and with a moral truth and comprehensiveness that exceed his most admired delineations. It is a favourite passage, and well known to the young; but so highly characteristic of our author's best manner, and so admirably fitted to sustain repeated perusal, that we are tempted to transcribe a part of it once more.

" He touch'd his harp, and nations heard entranced.
 As some vast river of unfailing source,
 Rapid, exhaustless, deep, his numbers flow'd,
 And open'd new fountains in the human heart.
 Where Fancy halted, weary in her flight,

In other men, *his* freſh as morning roſe,
And ſoar'd untrodden heights, and ſeem'd at home
Where angels baſhful looked.   Others though great
Beneath their arguments ſeem'd ſtruggling, whiles
He from above deſcending ſtoop'd to touch
The loftieſt thought ; and proudly ſtoop'd, as though
It ſcarce deſerved his verſe.   With Nature's ſelf
He ſeem'd an old acquaintance, free to jeſt
At will with all her glorious majeſty.
He laid his hand upon ' the Ocean's name,'
And play'd familiar with his hoary locks ;
Stood on the Alps, ſtood on the Apennines,
And with the thunder talk'd as friend to friend ;
And wove his garland of the lightning's wing,
In ſportive twiſt—the lightning's fiery wing,
Which, as the footſteps of the dreadful God,
Marching upon the ſtorm in vengeance, ſeem'd ;   .
Then turn'd, and with the grasſhopper, who ſung
His evening ſong beneath his feet, converſed.
Suns, moons, and ſtars, and clouds, his ſiſters were ;
Rocks, mountains, meteors, ſeas, and winds, and ſtorms,
His brothers, younger brothers, whom he ſcarce
As equals deem'd.   All paſſions of all men,
The wild and tame, the gentle and ſerene ;
All thoughts, all maxims, ſacred and profane ;
All creeds, all ſeaſons, Time, Eternity ;
All that was hated and all that was dear ;
All that was hoped, all that was fear'd, by man ;
He toſſ'd about as tempeſt-wither'd leaves,
Then ſmiling look'd upon the wreck he made.

＊   ＊   ＊

The vices of mankind have ſeldom been more
truly diſcriminated, or more unſparingly expoſed,
than in the pages of this young moraliſt and poet.
By turns they are forcibly denounced and ſtrongly
ſatiriſed.   The author does not pauſe to poliſh his
well-headed arrows, ſo eager is he to launch them
at the hydra he aſſails.   With bitter ſarcaſm he
gives triple point to his invective, making it rankle
wherever it has force to reach.   This habit of de-

nunciation to which his subject led him, has not, indeed, contributed to the poetical perfection of our
author's work : on the contrary, it has marred with
its intemperate tone, and lowered by its familiar
phrafeology, and broken by its abrupt and rugged
verfification, the grace, dignity, and harmony proper to epic fong.   And here it may be well to fay
what fhould candidly be faid from this lefs favourable point of view.   It cannot be difguifed from the
reader that many blemifhes and imperfections de-
tract from the general merits of the poem.   It is
planned, as a whole, with exceeding judgment ;
but its execution is very unequal.   The paffages of
fuftained dignity and power are comparatively few,
while the poet's manner frequently degenerates into
familiarity and coarfenefs.   Familiarity of language
or illuftration is not neceffarily beneath the dignity
of epic verfe.   How fimple and beautiful are fome
of the metaphors in Dante's *Divine Comedy !* and
even thofe which have no remarkable grace to recommend them have commonly the appropriate
merit of being graphic in a high degree.   " Rapidly
as the pen writes I or O" is the comparifon by
which the Tufcan pictures, almoft to our eyes, the
fudden effect of a fcorching and deftroying flame.
The allufion is to fomething familiar, but not low ;
for the art of writing is univerfally efteemed, and
therefore the mind is not offended by reference to
its moft fimple act.   But Pollok is not always influenced by the fame good tafte.   Force and contraft he feeks at any price ; and he achieves a bold
antithefis by dropping fuddenly from the " feventh

heaven of invention" into the limbo of all low and
creeping things. On the eve of judgment he warns
the yet rejoicing fun that he fhall prefently be feen
to " fet behind eternity," but fpoils this noble image
with a feeble anti-climax,—" *For thou fhalt go to
bed to-night and ne'er awake!*" Unfortunately,
this deficiency of tafte affects fomething more than
mere metaphors and phrafes: it cafts whole paragraphs in a rhetorical rather than a poetic mould,
and exchanges the tranquil, undoubting manner of
the mufe, for the denouncing and vehement tones
of the preacher. It would appear that the author's
religious zeal urges him to this; but, rightly confidered, neither his fubject nor his purpofe demands fo great a facrifice: if one or the other did
fo, the poetic medium were improperly chofen.

The Courfe of Time is probably familiar to moft
of our readers: it is therefore unneceffary to occupy any of our limited fpace with inftances of the
author's lefs perfect ftyle. It is much more defirable to invite to a re-perufal of one of thofe better
paffages which are equally characteriftic, and yet
more frequent. Pollok was neither mifanthropi-
cal nor fanatic, but a truly Chriftian poet and philofopher; and hence, throughout his retrofpect of
time, he rejoices to remember and acknowledge
abundant fources and fcenes of happinefs, chequer-
ing the darker ground of human life with varied
fhapes of beauty, and innumerable though evanef-
cent fancies. The fifth book largely teftifies to our
author's cordial love of nature and humanity.

" Abundant and diverſified above
  All number, were the ſources of delight;
  As infinite as were the lips that drank;
  And to the pure all innocent and pure;
  The ſimpleſt ſtill to wiſeſt men the beſt.

    *   *   •

  And there were, too—Harp! lift thy voice on high,
  And run in rapid numbers o'er the face
  Of Nature's ſcenery,—and there were day
  And night, and riſing ſuns and ſetting ſuns,
  And clouds that ſeem'd like chariots of ſaints,
  By fiery courſers drawn, as brightly hued
  As if the glorious, buſhy, golden locks
  Of thouſand cherubim had been ſhorn off,
  And on the temples hung of Morn and Even:
  And there were moons and ſtars, and darkneſs ſtreak'd
  With light; and voice of tempeſt heard ſecure:
  And there were ſeaſons coming evermore,
  And going ſtill, all fair, and always new,
  With bloom, and fruit, and fields of hoary grain:
  And there were hills of flock, and groves of ſong,
  And flowery ſtreams, and garden-walks embower'd,
  Where ſide by ſide the roſe and lily bloom'd;
  And ſacred founts, wild harps, and moonlight glens,
  And foreſts vaſt, fair lawns, and lonely oaks,
  And little willows ſipping at the brook;
  Old wizard haunts and dancing ſeats of mirth;
  Gay feſtive bowers and palaces in duſt;
  Dark owlet nooks and caves and battled rocks;
  And winding valleys roof'd with pendant ſhade;
  And tall and perilous cliffs, that overlook'd
  The breadth of ocean ſleeping on his waves;
  Sounds, ſights, ſmells, taſtes, the heaven and earth, profuſe
  In endleſs ſweets, above all praiſe of ſong:
  For not to uſe alone did Providence
  Abound; but large example gave to man
  Of grace, and ornament, and ſplendour rich,
  Suited abundantly to every taſte."

The ocean is a favourite theme with poets of
every grade. But, while it has a faſcination for
all who feel the poetical tendency, it is only a
ſnare to thoſe whoſe power of comprehenſion and

expreſſion falls lamentably ſhort of their undefined longings and myſterious awe. While it ſerves to prove the maſtery of the mighty, it very plainly expoſes the weakneſs of the weak. For this reaſon we may ſafely make it the teſt of the deſcriptive and general powers of a poet; and, when we would know if he be juſtified in adventuring ſome ambitious flight of ſong, let us follow him to the ſhores of that mighty element which girdles all the earth, and liſten how he puts words to its inarticulate muſic, and evolves rich harmony from its diſcordant thunders, and interprets betwixt the God of nature and the inferior ſons of God. For the true poet the ocean is a mighty inſtrument: without the touching of his fingers, it is " full of ſound and fury, ſignifying nothing:" the chaotic waves tumble unmeaningly, till the fiat of intelligence roll over them, and then they aſſume the true eternal order, in uniſon with the muſic of the ſpheres. All great poets ſhow their maſtery here: Homer in a few grand lines, through which the deep ſea ſeems to pour itſelf; Virgil in more than one pictureſque and ſonorous paſſage; and our great dramatiſt in a brief ſtorm of poetry, in which we ſee by glimpſes the poor ſhip-boy " on the high and giddy maſt," rocked fearfully " in cradle of the rude imperious ſurge." With modern bards a yet bolder minſtrelſy has been crowned with yet more eminent ſucceſs. It is to the mighty ſea, with its reſounding ſhores and unappeaſable commotion, that Byron leads the wearied and wayward Childe, there to ſeek calmneſs for a ſeaſon from the tumult

of contending paſſions in preſence of a confuſion
and a noiſe ſo vaſt as to be awful, and there to loſe
all ſenſe of his ſorrow in oblivion of himſelf,—exulting in a conſciouſneſs of *His* only majeſty and
power who rebukes the pride of man with one unconquerable element. And it is in proſpeƈt of the
ſame (as ſeen from St. Leonard's) that the bard of
Hope re-tunes and ſtrengthens his lyre, teaching it
a not leſs dulcet but more harmonious meaſure, and
ſinging therewith, in a rapture of new health and
gladneſs, *Hail to thy face and odours, glorious Sea!*

But the ſtrain in which our author commemo-
rates the ocean is inferior to none of theſe. It is a
magnificent apoſtrophe, almoſt worthy the hallowed lips and the immortal harp of the long-ſainted
bard from whom it is ſuppoſed to break, and of the
reſurreƈtion-morning on which his triumphant
memory reviſits it. He ſeems to magnify and
glory in the thalaſſian might and muſic, juſt when
both are about to be ſuſpended for ever, and gladly
ſeizes occaſion to prolong its murmuring echo
through the eternal vaults.

" Great Ocean! too, that morning thou the call
　Of reſtitution heard'ſt, and reverently
　To the laſt trumpet's voice in ſilence liſten'd.
　Great ocean! ſtrongeſt of creation's ſons,
　Unconquerable, unrepoſed, untired,
　That roll'd the wild, profound, eternal baſs
　In Nature's anthem, and made muſic ſuch
　As pleaſed the ear of God! Original,
　Unmarr'd, unfaded work of Deity,
　And unburleſqued by mortal's puny ſkill,
　From age to age enduring and unchanged,
　Majeſtical, inimitable, vaſt,
　Loud uttering ſatire day and night on each

Succeeding race and little pompous work
Of man ! unfallen, religious, holy Sea !
Thou bow'dſt thy glorious head to none, fear'dſt none,
Heardſt none, to none didſt honour, but to God,
Thy Maker, only worthy to receive
Thy great obeiſance ! Undiſcover'd Sea !
Into thy dark, unknown, myſterious caves,
And ſecret haunts, unfathomably deep
Beyond all viſible retired, none went
And came again, to tell the wonders there.
Tremendous Sea ! what time thou lifted up
Thy waves on high, and with thy winds and ſtorms
Strange paſtime took, and ſhook thy mighty ſides
Indignantly, the pride of navies fell ;
Beyond the arm of help, unheard, unſeen,
Sunk friend and foe, with all their wealth and war ;
And on thy ſhores men of a thouſand tribes,
Polite and barbarous, trembling, ſtood amazed,
Confounded, terrified, and thought vaſt thoughts
Of ruin, boundleſſneſs, omnipotence,
Infinitude, eternity ; and thought
And wonder'd ſtill, and graſp'd, and graſp'd, and graſp'd
Again : beyond her reach, exerting all
The ſoul, to take thy great idea in,
To comprehend incomprehenſible ;
And wonder'd more, and felt their littleneſs.
Self-purifying, unpolluted Sea !
Lover unchangeable, thy faithful breaſt
For ever heaving to the lovely Moon,
That, like a ſhy and holy virgin, robed
In faintly white, walk'd nightly in the heavens,
And to thy everlaſting ſerenade
Gave gracious audience ; nor was woo'd in vain.
That morning thou, that ſlumber'd not before
Nor ſlept, great Ocean ! laid thy waves to reſt,
And huſh'd thy mighty minſtrelſy. No breath
Thy deep compoſure ſtirr'd, no fin, no oar ;
Like beauty newly dead, ſo calm, ſo ſtill,
So lovely, thou, beneath the light that fell
From angel-chariots, ſentinell'd on high,
Repoſed and liſten'd, and ſaw thy living changed,
Thy dead ariſe. Charybdis liſten'd, and Scylla ;
And ſavage Euxine on the Thracian beach
Lay motionleſs ; and every battle-ſhip
Stood ſtill ; and every ſhip of merchandiſe,
And all that ſail'd of every name, ſtood ſtill."

With this noble ftrain our extracts muft conclude.   In the Book where it occurs, as well as in
that which immediately follows, there are many
paffages of a very high ftyle of poetry.   The condition of the world, when the morning of the judgment broke over it with the light of a common
day,—the heedlefs, headlong, and unprincipled purfuits of men,—the fudden paralyfis of nature, and
the arreft made upon all the tribes and nations of
mankind,—are ranged in ftriking contraft before
us.   The little feathered fongfter fainting in middle
air, while on his harmony " perpetual filence fell,"
—and the lordly eagle dropping into the valley, " a
clod of clay,"—and the ploughman falling before
his fteers,—and the fhepherd witneffing his flock
" around him turn to duft,"—while the lion in his
den

   " Grew cold and ftiff, or in the furious chafe
    With timid fawn, that fcarcely mifs'd his paws,"—

this awful fufpenfion of the whole creation is very
vividly defcribed; and the filence of momentary
diffolution condemns with ftartling fuddennefs and
folemnity the preceding hum of bufinefs and of folly.
Not lefs impreffive is the review of the vaft and
rifen multitude who are feen to cover thickly all
the land and fea, " of every nation blent, and every
age."   Then follows the fentence of irrevocable
doom,—the approval of the righteous, and the condemnation of the wicked; fucceeded by the inftant perdition of the one, and the immediate tranflation of the other to heaven.   In thefe latter
Books the author well fuftains the accumulating

interest of his theme ; his imagery becomes grander, and his verfe more weighty ; and, as his
chariot of time nears the appointed goal, the fpokes
of its mighty wheels gleam far more vividly, and
its burning axle glows under the increafed momen-
tum and accelerated fpeed. We may inftance,
among the moft ftriking portions of the tenth and
laft Book, the defcription of the outpouring of the
Divine vengeance, commencing, "So faying, God
grew dark with utter wrath ;" and (for its poetical
merit) the deftruction of the long-guilty earth by
fire, preparatory to its renewal and re-habitation.
The hymns addreffed to the Almighty are alfo very
noble.

We are reluctant, in conclufion, to compare the
merits of Milton and Pollok. While comparifons
are proverbially odious, they are efpecially fo when
employed to depreciate the leffer of two admirable
authors, each poffeffed of diftinct and independent
merits. Points of wideft difference do not neceffarily involve inferiority in the fmalleft degree,
while they may fkilfully be made to imply it in the
greateft. To compare Milton and Pollok in this
fpirit would be a gratuitous injury to the latter,
whofe pretenfions never made fo bold a rivalry.
Yet we may be allowed to diftinguifh their characteriftic merits, if only to fhow the wide difference
in their manner and defign, and the confequent abfurdity of an unfriendly contraft. The great inferiority of Pollok's work may be admitted from
the firft. The author's true admirers never contended or thought otherwife. They confider, in-

deed, that *The Courfe of Time* has from its firft appearance, with fome brief exceptions, been unduly
depreciated by the literary world ; but they acknowledge, alfo, that many zealous perfons have
erred yet more widely, though from more pardonable motives, in extolling it as the equal of the
Paradife Loft, and the co-heir of its renown.   In
truth, no reflecting perfon could fail to obferve
that the two works are of widely different orders of
merit ; and it is more than probable that this inequality, extended to the authors, was radical as well
as adventitious, and due in a large degree to difference of native power.   But the queftion of natural
gifts is here complicated by circumftantial diverfity.
The years, the era, and the country of our authors
were unlike.   The one wrote in the eager dawn of
manhood, but under the fhadow of a cloud deftined
to ftifle all his day of life. The other poured forth
his foul in fong when his eyes had returned from
beholding the vanity of all earthly things, and his
ears had grown only the more fenfitive to the mufic
of an unfeen world.   As the buoyant energy of
youth differs from the fuftaining ftrength of riper
years, fo does the character of Pollok differ from
that of Milton.   What the redundant foliage of
June is to the golden fruit of Auguft, fuch is *The
Courfe of Time* to the *Paradife Loft*. The natural
ardour of Pollok was in the ftage of daring effort
and unlimited promife ; but the grave temperament of Milton had grown yet more rugged
through years of poverty and neglect, while his
real tendernefs found expreffion only through his

imagination, and fo modulated his verfes into trueft pathos. Pollok was not wholly unindebted to claffic lore, for he had lately been a diligent fcholar; but Milton had from earlieft boyhood drunk freely of the Caftalian fpring, had ever found it fweet and pleafant to his tafte, and conftantly returned to it with never-fatisfied delight. And this diverfity is plainly traceable in their refpective poems, influencing the choice and moulding the form throughout. *The Courfe of Time* is a bold cartoon, filled in with all the typical characters of earth, but having little or no local colouring to give warmth and harmony to the whole; the *Paradife Loft* is an imperifhable frefco, painted in vaft compartments, under the glowing light of a Syrian fun, with more than Buonarotti's power, and only lefs than Raffaelle's grace. Pollok is yet in the flufh of youth, but feels a prophetic intimation of his fate, and fo makes hafte to be famous. Milton, like the Royal Preacher, has felt the vanity of life; and, like Saul, he is at times poffeffed of an evil fpirit: yet, in emulation of the one, he has not neglected to rifle the treafures of nature and of art, to put together a temple worthy of the Lord; and, with a fkill tranfcending the fullen greatnefs of the other, he becomes his own enchanter; and, with ftrains that might almoft " create a foul under the ribs of death," he charms the evil genius from his bofom. One looks forward to the judgment, and onward to the blifs of faints made perfect; the other, equally overleaping " the flaming bounds of time and fpace," runs

backward and precipitates himfelf beyond the further wall of Paradife, and fpreads wing in the pre-
Adamite eternity.   But the contraft is almoft
endlefs.   We might fhow how one is the type of
the Chriftian, and the other of the Jewifh, era;—
how Pollok comes to us preaching the fimple and
pure morality and love of his Mafter Chrift; and
how Milton appears to our imagination in the
gorgeous trappings of the Aaronic priefthood,
fwinging in his hand a golden cenfer, and leading
the grateful litanies of every tribe.

But we muft haften to conclude. Milton's work
muft ever receive fuperior honour, but may be
deftined, notwithftanding, to a comparatively narrow circle of readers.   His theme and manner are
grave, elaborate, and ftately; his verfe, unlike the
fimpler fabric and ruder texture of the other, is a
perfect web of harmony, bright with inwoven
graces, and coftly with embroidered learning; his
matchlefs work is full of fuch poetry as none but
fpirits fomewhat kindred can enjoy, and pregnant with exquifite allufions which heighten the
imaginative feaft with the charms of refined affociation.   Many qualities and accomplifhments go to
the formation of the readers of fuch a poet; and,
therefore, when he defired to find " fit audience,"
he was aware it muft confift of " few." The fubject of Pollok's mufe is of more common and perfonal intereft, and its treatment is appropriately
fimple, inftead of laboured or recondite.   Its religious earneftnefs recommends it to many who
would not fo readily appreciate a more purely po-

etical merit. On the whole, the ftyle of the youthful author is not ill adapted to his defign and fub-
jeƈt. For a great purpofe he feized the facred lyre,
and " rolled its numbers down the tide of time."
He did fo with a fuccefs that has been too grudg-
ingly allowed by literary men ; for, abating only
the carelefs execution of many paffages, we can
fcarcely conceive anything more fuited to intereft
and imprefs the ferious reader than the copious
freedom of its languge,—level to the fimpleft ap-
prehenfion ; and the vigorous mufic of its verfe,
—melody to the moft unpraƈtifed ear.

ON THE WRITINGS OF
MR. CARLYLE.

T is a remarkable fact, that every literary **work** which has achieved a permanent **reputation,** or attained to the
pofition **of** a national claffic, is **more**
or lefs perfect in refpect of ftyle. So uniformly is
this found to **be the cafe,** that, although **many**
works are more efteemed for the wifdom of their
contents than the graces of their manner, yet we
may fafely predicate that a glaring deficiency in
point of **ftyle** would prove fatal to their permanent fuccefs. We can fcarcely, for our own
part, imagine the cafe of a manual of wifdom
which fhould be wanting in its appropriate vehicle
of form and language ; **for** great thoughts are
moulded, in return, by expreffions which they have
ferved to modulate ; and it is certain that this perfection of manner is a neceffary condition of their
univerfal acceptance and uncloying delightfulnefs.
No other quality, apart from this, ever availed to
fave the production of human wit or ingenuity from
early neglect and ultimate oblivion. Works of the
profoundeft learning, of deep natural refearch, and

of great critical fagacity, that feverally aftonifhed
contemporary minds with refults equally magnificent and valuable, have perifhed from their own
weight, not being animated and buoyed by that
fubtle fpirit from which the charm of ftyle is conftantly evolved.   Thefe authors had found nature
lavifh of materials, and fondly conceived that it
was referved for them to arrange and preferve them
for human admiration ; but they proved collectors
only, and not artifts : they failed to evoke order
out of confufion, or to vindicate the fupreme utility
of beauty.   The moment that death took them
from their cumulative work, it was liable to be
feized upon by fome more mafterly and plaftic
genius ; to be broken up, and fifted, and put
through a procefs of felection ; and then joined,
and fhaped, and moulded, and made perfect :—the
huge folio chronicles, crowded with matters vital
and indifferent, take then the claffic form of hiftory, where facts appear only in their relation to
truth, and fo become the manuals of ftatefmen and
philofophers.   Thus Tacitus and Hume furvive a
thoufand more laborious annalifts.   The latter,
indeed, is a ftriking example of the infinite perfuafivenefs of ftyle.   So apt, confiftent, and harmonious, are the ideas in his great work, and fo
lucid, pure, and varied the expreffion, that it may
henceforth defy the multiplied competition of ages.
No fruitful refearch will fuffice to difcredit it, and
no novelty of thought avail to fuperfede it.   It is
immortal by the conditions of its birth ; for it

I

affumed the body of truth when it received the foul of genius.

Let not the flovenly or eccentric writer fay fcornfully of Style, that it is the mere externalifm of thought, as unworthy of a philofopher's attention as the cut of his coat or the fhape of his hat. It is the outward and vifible fign of exactly correfponding graces. It is not drefs to the wax-figure, but form and expreffion to the ftatue. Style is one of the moft comprehenfive terms in our language; and, as applied to literature and the arts, is made to include both the harmony of thought and language, and the felicitous correfpondence of both to truth and nature. It is, therefore, as requifite that the mathematician and the moralift fhould aim at perfection in ftyle, as it is that the poet and the humorift fhould do fo; or rather it is a merit as neceffary to evince the maftery of the former as it is to fecure the triumphs of the latter. Exactitude of thought can only manifeft itfelf by precifion of language and clearnefs of expreffion; and fo a definite and axiomatic ftyle will appropriately fymbolife and embody a definite philofophy. What, then, muft we think of him who practically afferts that ordinary grammatical language is a poor and inadequate medium of his thoughts? who, not fatisfied with a fimple predicate of truth, or an intelligible ftatement of opinion, breaks out into ftrange apoftrophes, half-fentences, and fighs, which no man can rationally connect, or even feparately conftrue?

Style, therefore, is not a merely fuperficial merit;

nor can it be rejected as an unfair teft of found authorfhip and claffic compofition. If a humorift is happy in his portraiture of character, it is that felicity of delineation that makes his compofition elegant, and not the mere choice of appropriate phrafeology and illuftration; for thefe latter are fuggefted by the former, and have perhaps little to recommend them but their fimplicity and truth. If a poet is indeed the mafter of his theme, language will be to him as potter's clay, and the completed poem will prove the faultlefs image of his fancy. If the moralift or philofopher is really diftinct and confident in his ideas, his words will be only the pure medium of thofe ideas, and the reader will fenfibly enjoy the prefence of his author's mind. Failing to exprefs himfelf in this clear, proper, unfuperfluous manner, there is a hitch fomewhere in our author's greatnefs. Wanting this ferene, oracular, and perfect fpeech, he muft not hope to have a liftening world for his audience, or to entrance pofterity by an undying voice. Lefs than wife, let him be content to learn : not yet perfect, let him continue to improve. The " prophets" of mankind muft not come from Babel, ftammering difcordant tongues. If " nature" has indeed commiffioned them, they will employ her one true language, known to all her children.

We have been led into thefe remarks by an attempt to account for the eccentricities of Mr. Carlyle's more recent and characteriftic work; and we regret to fay that the conclufion juft arrived at bears ftrongly againft the pretentious

claims of thofe very fingular productions. We
fhould blame Mr. Carlyle even more, if we
efteemed his genius fomewhat higher. But the
grofs abfurdity of his ftyle is, we fufpect, not fo
much his fault as his misfortune. His wanton defiance of grammar and of tafte is not a mere wilful
abufe of power, but rather a pitiable exhibition of
weaknefs. Let it be juft fuppofed that Mr. Carlyle may have—as he is conftantly affirming or in-
finuating—fome grand fpecific for the improvement of mankind. But ordinary language is inadequate for its expreffion, and he breaks out into
one of the unknown tongues. It would feem, then,
Mr. Carlyle poffeffes ideas not only profoundly
good and ufeful—for fuch were thofe of Bacon and
Locke—but incommunicable alfo. The language
of daily life might indeed fuffice to convey the vulgar truths of his great predeceffors. Their lips
might drop maxims of fimpleft wifdom " as faft as
the Arabian trees their medicinal gum." With
them their readers may ftill have intelligent enjoyment, as not wholly deftitute of the fame
reafon and affections. But to prefume to underftand Mr. Carlyle would be making ourfelves too
much his equals, if it did not even give us the advantage over him. Let us, then, be content to
wonder. Too much familiarity breeds contempt ;
and if we knew him better, is it certain we fhould
efteem or truft him more ? It is well that we
fhould not be undeceived ; let us live in hope if we
die in defpair ; let us repeat his oracular words time
after time, and guefs them in our own favour, and

delude ourfelves to the laft. Shall we, forfooth, prefume to know more than our mafter ?

The works to which thefe obfervations apply range in refpect of number to fome ten or dozen volumes, publifhed at fhort intervals during the laft twenty years. To many of our readers they will probably be more or lefs familiar ; but to a greater number the author and his works are known, it may be, only by repute. It is defirable, therefore, that we fhould firft mention fome of the publications by name ; and afterwards illuftrate their character, and juftify our animadverfions, by one or two examples, felected with due fairnefs, but neceffary brevity. Let us ftate at once that our chief object is not to challenge Mr. Carlyle's literary reputation, or to deny his literary merits. If we deplore the popular character of the one, and fpeak in qualified and meafured terms of the other, it is that we may the better accomplifh the ulterior purpofe we have in view, by fhowing that, if the public accept of this falfe teacher as their prophet, it is not becaufe they are pardonably mif- led by a fubtle and confummate genius. With this object in view, we have thought it right to de- vote a preliminary fection to Mr. Carlyle's literary character, and afterwards to examine his preten- fions as a focial and religious philofopher.

In a chronological retrofpect of Mr. Carlyle's writings, the order of time is coincident with that of merit ; and on this head we may be expected to enlarge. But the moft ufeful part of a critic's office, and therefore the moft important, is monitory and corrective. Were it otherwife, we might find a good deal to fay in Mr. Carlyle's praife, even to the exclufion of all cenfure, from difinclination and want of fpace. As it is, while maintaining the error and expofing the danger of his unqualified admirers, we will not fail to mention thofe better qualities to which other pens have done more than ample juftice. Why fhould we deny that which is patent to all the literary world, which alone mitigates the folly of its praife, and which gives efpecial emphafis to our note of warning and reproof?

The earlieft and beft works of Mr. Carlyle appeared in the departments of biography and criticifm : his *Life of Schiller* remains a favourable fpecimen of the former; and the collection entitled *Mifcellanies*, in four volumes, and confifting chiefly of his contributions to the *Edinburgh* and *Foreign Quarterly Reviews*, furnifh fpecimens of his genius for the latter. With thefe productions we may clafs—as making together the lift of thofe exercifes of his pen which may be excepted from the general animadverfions we feel bound to make —his nervous and beautiful tranflation of the *Wilhelm Meifter*, and his right earneft introduction to, and able editing of, *Cromwell's Letters*, at a comparatively recent period. In all thefe works there is a degree of merit and originality which no reader will be difpofed to queftion or reluctant to acknowledge. Their tone is for the moft part healthy and mafculine ; and if fome of the author's views, incidentally introduced, are exceptionable or extreme, the treatment of his fubject is, in the main, correct as well as masterly; its outline, bold, definite, and true; and its colouring, alternately vivid, picturesque, and quaint. The critical *Miscellanies* may be named as most to our taste and judgment,—the work in which we think the author has evinced the truest power, and found the real bent of his discursive genius, which is critical rather than didactic, and descriptive more than philosophical. His papers on the German authors, Wieland, Goethe, Schiller, and Richter; on the Scotchmen, Burns and Walter Scott; on the English, Johnson, and his much-gifted, much-despised biographer; on Mirabeau, Voltaire, and Diderot; are specimens of intellectual portrait-painting, differing widely indeed from the weak water-colours of too many literary artists, and dashed rather with the breadth of Raeburn than finished with the studied elegance of Lawrence. This talent of graphic portraiture is perhaps the most remarkable gift of our author; and, aided by marvellous chiaro'scuro and strong scenical effects, it finds almost boundless indulgence in his work on the *French Revolution*, which we have hesitated to class among his better writings, (notwithstanding its evidence of rare ability,) both because of its ethical unsoundness and its impertinent obscurities of style. Mr. Carlyle entitles it *a History*; but it is no such thing. Any gentleman of respectable business habits, average intelligence, and moderate leisure, who should repair to this work for a consecutive and clear account of the great Revolution in France, fraught with its own unmistakable les-

fons of philofophy, would become fadly bewildered
at the very outfet.   The riddle of the fphinx, pro-
pofed in Ethiopic, or written in hieroglyphics,
would be nothing to the threatening problems of
that ftrange wild book.   Let the initiated few be-
laud it as they may, and fpeak of its occult and rare
philofophy ; true hiftory is written fo that he who
runs may read ; true learning is fimple as well as
fublime in its refults ; true wifdom communicates
the lore of genius in the language of a child.   To
thofe by whom the fubject has been previoufly
maftered, Mr. Carlyle's eccentric volumes will
have a certain intereft,—to fome of thefe, a perfect
fafcination.   But there is no rational coherence,
after all ; or none that is fufficiently apparent.
And already " art is long, and time is fleeting ;" if
we perplex and lengthen out the one, do we not
virtually wafte our little portion of the other ?
Thofe, therefore, who fpeak of this work as a
model of the true hiftoric ftyle, know not what
they fay.   It is a commentary, and not a hiftory ;
a feries of fitful fketches, not an example of ferene
art ; a panorama—painted in lurid hues, and exhibited by torch-light—of the fearful reign of
terror, moft like that ancient one of anarchy and
chaos.

From the period of this laft publication it was
that the erratic ftyle of Mr. Carlyle became aggravated and confirmed.   This was evidently to be
traced to his undifcriminating love of German letters and philofophy, and efpecially of the latter ; for
the former, feparately confidered, is at leaft too pure

and claffical, in its beft examples, to be chargeable with Mr. Carlyle's obfcure and unequal mode of fpeech. The lucid profe of Goethe is rather the reproachful contraft, than the juftifying model, of his admirer : it is the perfect medium of the author's thoughts, like a fheet of fine plate-glafs, through which the bright and moving objects of nature are beheld, and which interpofes only an air of ferenity and diftance ; while the language of Mr. Carlyle refembles too much a pane of knotted, blue, unequal glafs, giving to all things a cerulean or prifmatic hue, and diftorting them into all unreal fhapes. From Jean Paul Richter he has evidently copied much, and imbibed more. But this was furely an unfortunate ftandard to fet up, and entirely unworthy of an original mind. What is natural and characteriftic of the German Richter, who could write no otherwife, is offenfive and unpardonable in the Anglo-Scotchman, trained in clearer modes of thought, and capable of purer fpeech. The truth is, as we fhall fhortly fee, that our author had confounded two things which fhould ever be kept diftinct ; and in their turn they have confounded him. He proclaimed the banns of German art and German Metaphyfics ; or at leaft he attempted to accomplifh the unnatural union. Not content with being a critic of the grand Teutonic poetry, he afpired at the fame moment of time to be an expofitor of German myftical philofophy. Either, fingly confidered, was a tafk worthy of his powers, though the former was more congenial to his ftyle of thought and composition. But, if both were to be undertaken, they at least demanded a separate, distinct, and serious treatment. Mr. Carlyle seemed to think otherwise; and the attempt to give philosophic views of nature, man, and GOD, in a fictitious framework, and a disconnected, light, irreverent manner, resulted in a work entitled *Sartor Resartus, or the Life and Opinions of Herr Teufelsdrökh.* This compound of profanity and jargon is a **fair** specimen of our author's ethical and literary merits, as seen in all his recent and characteristic works; and therefore we **shall take the** trouble of examining it **more** nearly than it otherwise **deserves.** Afterwards we **will** look **into our** author's **book** on *Heroes and Hero Worship*; and there probably we shall find a more undisguised acknowledgment of the two great principles of his audacious **system,** manifesting themselves in an idolatry essentially pagan, and a pantheism virtually godless.

Dulness is by no means a common fault with Mr. Carlyle. His genius is too brilliant to fail of attracting even the careless reader, and withal so erratic that our sense of admiration is prolonged by that of growing wonder, not to say alarm. We follow him at first with praise on our lip, and expectation in our hearts; and, when we have ceased to admire and trust **him, a** certain powerful curiosity compels **us to follow** his mysterious flight; and when we can no longer trace his whereabouts, **we** stand lost in wonder **at** the blue flame in which he disappeared. Ever verging toward some quar-

ter of the higheſt heaven, we ſtill hope to paſs with
him into more ſacred precincts ; and when he falls
ſuddenly plumb down through the inane, there is
a myſtery in that exit by which we are halfwith-
drawn from diſappointment and diſguſt.

But dull and irkſome Mr. Carlyle often is, if you
will only let him play out his play ; and the reaſon
of this is obvious on a moment's reflection : *for
only what we intelligently enjoy can we permanently
attend to and admire.* The greateſt philoſopher
will obſerve the ſtars all night, and only grieve
when the " gariſh day" drowns all their ſolemn
beauty, and the " work-day world" begins to clamour down their ethereal muſic. But who that is
paſt childhood will not weary of a diſplay of fire-
works, prolonged and repeated through all the
patient night, till every beautiful device has become
worn down to a ſkeleton of wood and wire, and
the memory of each bright and ruſhing rocket is
loſt in the ſenſe of its black and ſulphurous recoil ?
In ſome ſuch manner as this have we been alternately attracted and repelled ; ſucceſſively charmed,
ſurpriſed, and diſappointed ; but ultimately and
thoroughly wearied and perplexed ; by Mr. Carlyle's firſt eſſay in tranſcendental art-philoſophy.
It is entitled, *Sartor Reſartus : the Life and
Opinions of Herr Teufelſdröckh. In Three Books.*
It is elſewhere termed by its author *The Philoſophy
of Clothes,* and conſiſts of fragments of the obſcure
hiſtory, and ſpecimens of the ponderous work, of
a learned German Profeſſor. But this imputed
origin is evidently fictitious ; the editor and author

are not only fimilar, but identical; the book is properly lettered on the back, what it emphatically is throughout, " Carlyle's Sartor Refartus." His paternity is audible in every page, where he fings wild lullabies to his odd-featured child, mixed up with quaint denials: it betrays itfelf, moreover, in his every movement, gefture and grimace. Herr Teufelfdröckh is as hiftorical a character as Diedrich Knickerbocker; but we cannot fay that *The Philofophy of Clothes* is either as intelligible or as delightful as the famous *Hiftory of New-York.* Both, indeed,—the high-Dutchman and the low, —are in turn the fource and fubject of rare fatiric humour; but that of Diedrich is genuine, broad, unmixed, and loveable; while Teufelfdröckh is himfelf a very evident "unreality" or " fham,"— a hollow mafk, provided with a fettled, erudite, mechanic fmile, to difguife the painful nature of thofe profane and unprofitable fpeculations of which it is made the mouth-piece.   In brief, Mr. Irving's fictitious hiftory is a model of its kind; and its perfect ftyle is the refult both of the confcious legitimacy of his plan, and of the rare felicity and balance of his powers; while Mr. Carlyle ftumbles in the rugged path of his pfeudo-biography, and juftly fears that when he moft fuccefffully tranfports or puzzles us, he moft plainly fhows the hero and the author to be identical; and fo, haftening to ridicule or qualify the philofophic rant of the one, we are left wholly confounded as to the real fentiments of the other.

But it may, perhaps, be faid, we do injuftice to

Mr. Carlyle by comparing him with an author fo
different as Mr. Irving; that, the object of the
latter being the amufement of his readers only, he
is left free to attend to the graces of ftyle, as he is
more dependent upon thefe; while the purpofe of
the former is other and far higher, aiming to blend
improvement with delight, and to initiate us into
fome of the profoundeft myfteries of nature by lift-
ing a corner of the veil which divides the world of
matter from the world of fpirit. Juft fo: fomething like this we believe to be our author's great
defign; he defires to pafs through all external
fhows, which are to nature what clothing is to
man, and to lay his hand upon the naked heart of
God's great univerfe, and to repeat in our attentive ears the burden of its " healthful mufic."
But, before we commend his temerity, we muft
learn of his fuccefs. Since he attempts fo much
more than the author to whom reference has been
made, if his fuccefs be only equal, the refult will be
of far greater power and value. But to the refult
we muft appeal, and not to the attempt alone; and
therefore it was that we conceived no injuftice
would be done to him by comparing his elaborate
work with Mr. Irving's humbler effay, which in
fome points it refembles; for, wherein it differs, it
might be expected to excel. That fuch is not the
cafe, we have deliberately proved for ourfelves;
and our wifh is that we could, with reafonable brevity, furnifh the means of conviction to our readers.
But it is impoffible to convey any adequate notion
of this book, the *Sartor Refartus*, by means of ab-

ftract or fynopfis; and this, alfo, for the old reafon,
—it is mainly unintelligible. As a rational being
foon wearies of the moft agreeable jargon, fo it is
impoffible to carry away the fubftance or meaning
which it never had. Neither the beauties nor the
abfurdities of our author are properly transferable
or tranflatable. To appreciate a gorgeous pile of
clouds, you muft fee them *in extenfo* for yourfelf:
we cannot fhake down fome few folds by way of
fpecimen. Their beauty confifts in their fantaftic
variety of fhape; their long-drawn filaments of
vapour; their mountain-ridges that run down half
the zodiac, and their volcanic peaks that tower to
the meridian; their unfubftantial vaftnefs, ever
moving, and ever breaking into ineftimable numbers; their infinite gradations of light and colour,
following the wake of day in picturefque confufion,
and melting each into the other; their endlefs
imagery of all things actual, poffible, and conceivable; their fudden apparition; their filence, fwift-
nefs, and evanefcence; the boundlefs field of their
mufter, and the unimaginable fplendour of their
march. It is in a cloud-land fomewhat refembling
this, that the genius of Mr. Carlyle revels and dif-
ports itfelf, weaving his fineft works out of mifts
and exhalation, and breaking up the rainbow (as
though jealous of the beauty which refults from
law) that he may fling its colours to enrich the
dragon and chameleon of his fiery web. We have
truths here; but not maftered, and not marfhalled:
and fo in their order—or rather in their turn—
they difappear, and leave our minds fo far unoc-

cupied. And thus, at the end of our author's performance, we find no pofition to which we have
advanced ; we are ftill gazing into cloud-land, and
there feems a hurrying over the blue fpaces ; but
the laft fquadron of that brilliant army is as ineffec-
tive as the firft ; their banners are neither tarnifhed
by duft and ftrife, nor crowned with victory and
laurel ; they pafs idly over the parade-ground of
the fky, and the blue fpaces are left vacant as before.

Now, from all this we want the reader to judge
how difficult it muft be to give a plain ftatement or
abridgment of the work before us ; or to put in fy-
noptical form any fentiments or views of Mr. Carlyle which he has chofen to collect and print together, as though forming a confiftent and intelligible whole. And it is the difficulty of felection,
fpringing from the fame caufe, which has hitherto
prevented us from allowing our author to fpeak for
himfelf, and lead us, we fear, into a rather tedious
attempt to characterize the ftyle and tenor of his
book. We muft now, however, redeem our
promife, and juftify our defcription, by an extract
from the volume itfelf, referving fome general obfervations upon its whole fpirit and tendency. We
choofe, with all fairnefs, a paffage in our author's
beft manner, which fhows, fo far as a fingle extract
can, the peculiar afpirations by which he is poffeffed—rather than infpired. It is taken from the
feventh chapter of the firft book, entitled, *The
World out of Clothes* ; and, like the reft of the
moft daring part of the volume, which is full of in-

terrogatories, fuggeftions, and crudities, is adroitly fpoken through his *alias* the philofopher.

" *With men of a fpeculative* **turn**, *(writes Teufelf-dröckh,) there come feafons,* **meditative,** *fweet, yet awful, hours, when in wonder and* **fear** *you afk yourfelf that unanfwerable queftion,* " *Who* am I ;" *the thing that can fay* " *I*" (das Wefen das fich Ich nennt ?) *The world, with its loud trafficking,* **re-***tires into* **the** *diftance; and through the paper-hang-ings, and ftone-walls,* **and** *thick-plied tiffues of com-merce and polity, and all the* **living** *and lifelefs in-teguments (of fociety and a body) wherewith your exiftence is furrounded,—the fight reaches forth into the* **void deep,** *and you are alone with the univerfe, and filently commune* **with** *it, as one myfterious pre-fence* **with** *another. . .* **Who** *am I?* *What* **is** *this* me ? *A voice, a motion, an appearance ;—fome embodied vifualifed idea in the eternal mind?* Cogito, ergo fum. *Alas,* **poor** *cogitator, this takes* **us** *but a little way.* **Sure** *enough I am ; and lately was not ; but whence?* **How** *?* **Whereto** *? The anfwer lies around, written in all colours and motions, uttered in all tones of jubilee and* **wail,** *in thoufand-figured, thoufand-voiced, harmonious* **nature** *; but where is the cunning eye* **and ear** *to whom that God-written apocalypfe will yield* **articulate** *meaning?* *We fit as in a* **boundlefs** *phantafmagoria and dream-grotto : boundlefs,* **for the fainteft ftar,** *the remoteft century, lies not even* **nearer the verge thereof:** *founds and many-coloured* **vifions** *flit round our fenfe ; but Him, the unflumbering,* **whofe** *work both dream and* *dreamer are, we see not; except in rare half-waking moments, suspect not.* Creation, *says one, lies before us like a glorious rainbow; but the sun that made it lies behind us, hidden from us.* Then, in that *strange dream, how we clutch at shadows as if they were substances; and sleep deepest while fancying ourselves most awake!* Which of your philosophical *systems is other than a dream-theorem; a nett quotient, confidently given out, where divisor and dividend are both unknown?* What are all your national wars, with *their* Moscow *retreats, and sanguinary, hate-filled revolutions, but the somnambulism of uneasy sleepers?* This dreaming, this *somnambulism, is what we on earth call "life;" wherein the most, indeed, undoubtingly wander, as if they knew right hand from left; yet they only are wise who know they know nothing.* . . . Pity that *all metaphysics had hitherto proved so inexpressibly unproductive!* The riddle of man's *being is still like the sphinx's secret; a riddle that he cannot read, and for ignorance of which he suffers death, the worst death, a spiritual.* What are your axioms, *and categories, and systems, and aphorisms?* Words, *words.* High *air-castles are cunningly built of words, the words well bedded also in good logic mortar, wherein, however, no knowledge will come to lodge. The whole is greater than the part: how exceedingly true! Nature abhors a vacuum: how exceedingly false and calumnious! Again, nothing can act but where it is: with all my heart; only, WHERE is it? Be not the slave of words; is not the distant, the dead, while I love it, and long for it, and mourn for it, here in the genuine sense as truly as the floor I stand on?* But *that same* WHERE, *with its brother* WHEN, *are from the first the master-colours of our dream-grotto;* say, rather, the canvas *(the warp and woof thereof)* whereon all our dreams *and life-visions are painted.* Nevertheless has not a *deeper* **meditation** *taught certain* of every *climate and* **age** *that the* WHERE *and the* WHEN, *so mysteriously inseparable from our thoughts, are* **but** *superficial, terrestrial adhesions to thought; that the Seer may discern* **them** *where they mount up out of the celestial* EVERYWHERE *and* FOR-EVER? *have* **not all** *nations conceived* their **God** *as omnipresent and* **eternal;** *as existing in a universal* HERE, *an everlasting* NOW? *Think* **well, thou** *wilt* **find that** *space* **is** *but a* **mode** *of our human sense, so* **likewise** *time; there is no space and no* **time;** WE *are—we know not what; light-sparkles floating in the æther of Deity!"*

Here, then, **we** have our author's philosophy, epitomised **by himself.** He begins with spurning the Cartesian stand-point, *Cogito, ergo sum,* professedly as a basis far too narrow, but really as one unnecessarily solid; for **how** can the firmness of reason serve him who is **about to** take such a metaphysical flight? **Yet, to do Mr.** Carlyle justice, he is here **more** explicit than usual. His philosophical principles **are tolerably well expressed** in the passage **above quoted;** and though **he has** contrived to **say as much in a** page as he could hardly **perhaps** establish in a volume, yet it is an agreeable

change to be able to underſtand his meaning. To
accept his theory is, of courſe, another matter, and
one that is much more difficult. That theory demands no elaborate refutation at our hands. Even
if diſpoſed to diſpute the ſteps (or leaps) by which
he hurriedly arrives at the concluſion, " there is no
ſpace and no time," *we* have too little left of either
to ſpend that little in defending the reality of both.
Our chief concern is with the problem of being,
which he ſo boldly undertakes to ſolve ; and we
prefer to judge of his ſucceſs by the reſult attained.
We will repeat that reſult in his own words ; he
ſhall anſwer the momentous queſtion ; and then
let the reader judge how far the philoſophy of Mr.
Carlyle is likely to ſupply or ſuperſede the more vulgar truths of religion. Hear him ! " We are—
we know not what ;—light-ſparkles floating in the
æther of Deity !" Of courſe, the latter clauſe is
utterly unmeaning, if we regard the former as a
true confeſſion. But that confeſſion is full of ſigni-
ficance. When Mr. Carlyle is led to own his
darkneſs, how thick and palpable muſt that darkneſs be ! Well may he lament that metaphyſics
ſhould prove " ſo inexpreſſibly unproductive !"*

---

* The judicious reader will obſerve that our remarks are
intended, not ſo much to depreciate the value of metaphyſical ſcience (if ſcience it be), as to ſhow how miſerably it
is miſapplied by our author ; and how totally inadequate it
is at all times either to explain the origin and nature of our
being, or to ſupply, from a conſideration of its ſuppoſed
character and deſtiny, the moral rule of life to our ſpecies.
As with our ordinary duties, ſo alſo with thoſe of a more
ſtrictly religious character : both are apprehended by the
moral ſenſe, availing itſelf of every preſent light ; and as we

But is this really all? Is there no paſſage in Mr. Carlyle's volume **more** definite and ſatisfactory than **this**? **So far as** we can judge, there is abſolutely none. In his own emphatic phraſe, the whole is a " weltering chaos." Inſtead of ſolving the riddle of exiſtence, he repeats it time after time with every doleful emphaſis, and turns it up-ſide down—that we may not loſe its **meaning** through treating it with too much reverence. **We** read on, without advancing; and go further, only to fare worſe. Sometimes the title of a chapter promiſes much, **and then we are** certain to be diſappointed moſt; **till at laſt the** repeated evil works **its own** cure, and a brilliant heading, like the ſtarry nucleus of a comet, prepares us for a **cloudy** and attenuated tail. At one time we ſee written, *The Everlaſting No*, and wonder what deeper or what wider vacuum has been diſcovered by this prince of negative philoſophers; but it proves only to be a labelled ſpecimen of his great gaping univerſe. With ſome faint hope we come upon another chapter, and read, *The Everlaſting Yea*; but, after **the** moſt intent liſtening, the noiſy oracle is found **to have** confuſed, **but** not informed the mind.

---

do not pauſe in the performance **of the** relative duties of life till each **is** proved obligatory **by a complete** ſyſtem of ethics whoſe authority ſhould **admit of no poſſible** doubt—for then life itſelf **muſt ceaſe ere a theory of** life could be univerſally agreed upon; ſo, **in matters of** religion, **we are** led firſt to acknowledge **the being and** word of God, **and** then the reaſonableneſs of our faith is increaſingly manifeſted by the correſpondence of natural and revealed truth, and of our experience, to the relation inſtinctively aſſumed.

Many high-sounding phrases, as " sanctuary of sorrow," or " divine depth of sorrow," come unexplained upon us ; and many scriptural precepts, as,
" Love not pleasure—love God," " Whatsoever
thy hand findeth to do, do it with thy might," are
thrown in our path ; but to enjoy—or even rightly
to appreciate—them, we must shut our eyes to
Mr. Carlyle's " dream-grotto," and remember the
fulness of evangelic truth which is stored up in the
briefest line of inspiration.   Love God !   This is
indeed " the Everlasting Yea ;" for it is the primal
law of our creation, and the ultimate perfection of
saint and angel.   Truth is truth, even upon the
lips of presumption.   But what does the precept
mean, in the mind of Mr. Carlyle ? Is it with him
anything but a time-honoured phrase, hallowed by
the unsuspecting faith of eighteen centuries, and
embodying, in a superstitious formula, the vague
longings of a hundred million hearts ? We fear
not.   Belshazzar drank wine with his princes, his
wives and his concubines, out of the consecrated
vessels of the temple : *they drank wine, and praised
the gods of gold, and of silver, of brass, of iron, of
wood, and of stone*.   And in like manner the sym-
bols of a yet purer faith, the language and precepts of the same holy and jealous God, are dis-
honoured and profaned in our own day, if with less
insolence of manner, yet with only the more profound contempt, by men who call upon His name
in one breath and question His existence in another,
and who dare to distribute His incommunicable attributes as the property of trees and stones,

deifying if not adoring the infenfate forms of nature. *

The next work of Mr. Carlyle, confifting of fix lectures on *Heroes and Hero Worfhip*, is entertaining enough ; and, what is more, it poffeffes one good pervading thought.   Finding a grain of gold, he has hammered it out into two hundred leaves. To glorify the fons of genius is one of the literary tendencies of the age ; but Mr. Carlyle's book was the firft to fix the features of the popular heroic, and to furnifh a brief gallery of heroes, each in his place and order.   We fay advifedly " the popular heroic;" for Mr. Carlyle's notion of heroifm is not effentially different from the vulgar one, of which the chief element is extraordinary power.   To this, indeed, is due the ftriking intereft with which our author's pencil has invefted the fubject ; for he has drawn the popular idol in a picturefque and commanding attitude.   We admit, moreover, that fome of his views are conceived with hiftorical accuracy, though treated with poetical expreffion ; and there is very much of the volume which is even profoundly true, and commends itfelf no lefs

* It would be eafy to juftify this ftrong condemnation by a feries of extracts, whether of whole paffages or fingle phrafes.   Yet, if we had fpace and time at our command for this purpofe, the refult would be lefs convincing to the reader than a perfonal acquaintance with the writings themfelves ; for our author's tone is fceptical throughout, and can only be defended from the charge of grofs profanity by the frank avowal of unbelief.   That avowal is not made ; on the contrary, the armoury of Scripture is pillaged for a traitor's purpofe, but in the guife of an adherent to the facred caufe.   Yet Mr. Carlyle is the great eulogift of fincerity, the denouncer of all hypocrify and " cant !"

to the judgment than the fympathies of men. But, after all, we are compelled to fay that this dangerous topic is very dangeroufly handled. Pictorially, Mr. Carlyle's characters are well and ftrongly marked ; but, ethically, they are not difcriminated, the true from the falfe. Courage, earneftnefs, fuccefs, thefe are the qualities our author delights to recognize and honour. But thefe are furely the groffer attributes of greatnefs, correfponding only to mufcular fuperiority or a larger flow of fpirits. Is there no ftandard of true greatnefs apart from its more vifible actions and effects ? The political agitator is then more heroic than the filent and felf-denying comforter,—the bronze-headed form of the ufurper more noble than the patient face of the uncomplaining martyr. Accordingly, we find Mr. Carlyle making little diftinction in his heroes befide their feveral degrees of earneftnefs and power. Force of character, quite independently of its direction, is the virtue he almoft exclufively admires. Grant this notion of a hero to be juft, and then—however little we may thereafter value fuch a character—we muft allow that it here receives ample juftice. Thus, for example, throughout his portraiture of Luther, we fee that the fturdy nature of the man has made him a favourite ; not the purity of his motives, nor the unwavering confidence of his mind, nor even the facred juftice of his caufe. We feel that by a fimilar treatment the names of Dominic and of Attila might be ennobled. The character of Luther is, notwithftanding, ably delineated in this book ; and the following paſſage will ſerve to ſhow how the profound humanity of the **German Reformer** is appreciated by the ſympathy of genius :—

" *At the ſame time, they err greatly who imagine that this man's courage was ferocity,—mere coarſe diſobedient obſtinacy and ſavagery, as many do. **Far** from that. There **may** be an abſence of fear which ariſes from the abſence of thought or affeǝ̌ion, from the preſence of hatred and ſtupid fury. **We do not value the** courage **of the** tiger highly. With **Luther it was far** otherwiſe; **no accuſation could** be more unjuſt **than this of mere ferocious** violence brought againſt him. **A moſt gentle heart withal,** full of pity and love, as indeed the truly valiant **heart ever** is. **The** tiger, **before a** ſtronger foe, flies : **the tiger** is not what we **call** valiant, only fierce and cruel. **I** know few things more touching than thoſe ſoft breathings of affeǝ̌ion, ſoft as a child's **or a mother's,** in this great wild heart of Luther. So honeſt, unadulterated with any cant, homely rude in their utterance, pure as water welling from the rock. . . . . . **Once he** looks out **from** his ſolitary ' Patmos,' the **Wartburg, in** the middle of the night : the great vault of immenſity, long **flights of** clouds ſailing through it,—dumb, gaunt, huge,—who ſupports all that? ' None ever ſaw the pillars of it; yet it is ſupported.' **God** ſupports it. **We** muſt know that God is great, **that God** is good, and truſt where we cannot ſee. Returning home from Leipſic once, he **is** ſtruck by the beauty of the harveſt fields. How it ſtands, that golden yellow corn, on its fair taper ſtem,* *its golden head bent, all rich and waving* **there,—** *the meek earth, at God's kind bidding, has produced* **it once** *again; the bread of man!* **In** *the garden* **at** *Wittenberg, one evening* **at** *sunset, a little bird has perched for the night. That little bird, says Luther; above it are the stars and deep heaven of worlds; yet it* **has folded** *its little wings; gone trustfully to rest* **there** *as in its* **home: the** *maker of it has given* **it too a home!** **Neither are** *mirthful turns* **wanting :** *there* **is** *a great free human heart in this* **man.** **The** *common speech of him has a rugged noblenefs, idiomatic, exprefjive, genuine; gleams here and there with beautiful poetic tints. One feels him to be a great brother-man."*

This is true of Luther, **as it is true** of a thoufand other noble natures. **But we** have no hint of " the greateft greatnefs of the man ;" for that was peculiar to himfelf, **as it was** exprefsly beftowed for the accomplifhment of an extraordinary work. Therefore Luther was not well chofen as the type of **Mr.** Carlyle's hero ; but he feems determined to confound things fpiritual with things natural, and to attribute the effects of both to the operation of one uniform dynamic agency. The great error of the book feems to be this exaltation of a certain blind **and** irrefpective FORCE. If might *is* right, then indeed we muft acknowledge with him the greatnefs alike of Burns and Luther, of Napoleon and Knox. Nay, **if** there be no evil but weaknefs, and if determination is of itfelf heroic, and if fuccefs fufficiently proclaims divinity, then muft we accept the whole feries of demi-gods in his pantheon, " from Norfe Odin to Englifh Samuel Johnfon, from the Divine Founder of Chriftianity to the withered Pontiff of Encyclopædifm." But the reader may inquire, What is the truth or value of a fyftem which claffes thefe together, confounding good and evil, and not even diftinguifhing between human and divine ? We cannot tell. We only know that, if an indomitable will or wide dominion is their bond of union, the awful group may be fitly completed by another member,—by Satan, that arch-hero. To that powerful prince has been juftly afcribed the virtue here made common to them all. It is he whom the " purged ear" of the poet heard exclaim, *To be weak is to be miferable ;* and from this fentiment arofe that famous refolu-tion,—was it not heroic in the firft degree ?—*Evil, be thou my good !*

But we have not yet done with the fubject of hero-worfhip. It is too ftrongly characteriftic of Mr. Carlyle's moft injurious writings, and too pro-minent a development of the prevailing atheifm, to be difmiffed without a more radical expofure. Moreover, we have no wifh to evade the difficul ties of our tafk by confining ourfelves to the lan-guage of cenfure ; and there are fome paffages in Mr. Carlyle's book which are really fo plaufible in themfelves, (while they are at the fame time abfolutely fearful in their confequences,) that many a fincerely honeft reader would doubt his own candour if he did not at once admit their force. The copy before us has apparently fallen into the hands of fuch a reader; and we find its pages marked here and there with an approving pencil. The following is a paffage fo approved. It occurs in Mr. Carlyle's account of the genus " Prophet," which, of courfe, is a natural production, though of rather high clafs and character :—

" *We have chofen Mahomet, not as the moft eminent Prophet, but as the one we are freeft to fpeak of. He is by no means the trueft of Prophets; but I do efteem him a true one. Farther, as there is no danger of us becoming any of us Mahometans, I mean to fay all the good of him I juftly can. It is the way to get at his fecret : let us try to underftand what he meant with the world; what the world meant and means with him will then be a more anfwerable queftion. One current hypothefis about Mahomet, that he was a fcheming impoftor, a falfehood incarnate, that his is a mere mafs of quackery and fatuity begins really to be now untenable to any one. The lies which well-meaning zeal has heaped round this man are difgraceful to ourfelves only. When Pococke inquired of Grotius where the proof was of that ftory of the pigeon trained to pick peas from Mahomet's ear, and pafs. for an angel dictating to him; Grotius anfwered that there was no proof! It is really time to difmifs all that. The word this man fpoke has been the life-guidance now of one hundred and eighty millions of men thefe twelve hundred years. Thefe hundred and eighty millions were made by God as well as we. A greater number of God's creatures believe in Mahomet's word at* *this hour than in **any word whatever**. Are we to suppose that it was **a miserable** piece of spiritual legerdemain,—this **which so many** creatures of the almighty have lived and died **by**?   **I, for my part**, cannot form any such supposition.   I will believe most things sooner than that.   One would be entirely at **a loss what to** think of this world, **if quackery** so grew **and** were sanctioned here."*

And **this it** is which perpetually triumphs over Mr. Carlyle, and which occasionally staggers the mind of his benevolent **reader.   Is** it possible that **vast numbers of our race should follow** and embrace a hollow lie ? **or, if so, is not** so popular a delusion something more genuine, **more admirable,** even more true, than the naked verities **which** attract only our purest affections, and satisfy our highest reason ?   In matters of religion this writer affects the large majority. In matters of philosophy, we suppose, he would hesitate to apply this very dignified test of truth, or it would tell sadly against his hero-worship : Galileo must then have been pronounced an obstinate old heretic to assert the **motion** of the earth, when all the world besides, who had eyes as well as he, declared that they saw nothing of the kind.   This interesting corollary is however kept wholly out of sight.   Truth is important in matters of science ; but with respect to religion we are all so many children, and one nursery-**story** is as good as another—be it taken from the annals of England or of fairy-land.   Enough if the little creatures are persuaded and amused, diverted from all prefent mifchief, and deluded into a romantic paft or future.

The way in which Mr. Carlyle has been led to accept every form of religious error as not wholly or chiefly untrue,—as *fubjectively right* even when *objectively* **wrong**,—it is not difficult to trace. In his philofophy, evil is but a circumftance; goodnefs is the very effence of man's nature, as of all elfe. Men, indeed, may be deceived by their own fenfes and reafon,—as were thofe zealots who imprifoned Galileo; but the moft brutal maffes of mankind are never mifled by their paffions, or degraded by the object of their love and worfhip. The human heart is fo pure, fo prone to good, that Mr. Carlyle can truft it to any amount! If he would know, therefore, what is worthy of peculiar reverence, and of as much belief as a philofopher of his fchool may condefcend to, he has only to obferve the direction of vaft maffes of our fpecies, and follow in their wake—at leaft with his approving eyes: for, of courfe, fo catholic a philofopher cannot join himfelf to any fingle band of worfhippers. They will lead him (in contemplation) to an altar and a god fufficient and appropriate for the time, and only to be fuperfeded by fome later development of the religion of nature. It matters not greatly what is to be worfhipped—an angel, or an onion; a gracious, or a malignant being; God, in fpirit and in truth, or the devil, with obfcene and cruel rites. Human nature is fo lovely a thing, if left to wander at its own fweet will!

In this way Mr. Carlyle is driven to extol the

idolatrous practices which he cannot confiftently condemn. Setting out with the doctrine of the natural purity and rectitude of the human heart, he muft hold himfelf ready to accept its every manifeftation as a type of innate beauty and virtue. The tendency of our uncorrupted inftincts is furely towards the great and good Divinity from which we have our being. As water finds its own level, and as the rivers haften to the fea, does not the creature, by an invariable law, tend ever to the Creator? So he reafons, *à priori*; and the refult is a theory of harmony throughout the univerfe of God. Unfortunately, if he fhould reverfe the procefs, and argue from effect to caufe, will he find the fame pure fource operating as the fountain of hiftory and life? What *is* the God that is fo varioufly worfhipped? Do the obfcene rights of Indian mythology celebrate a God of purity? or the bloody hecatombs of Mexican or Druid worfhip give fatisfaction to a God of mercy? Are we led ftraightway to adoration of the Divine unity, by the contemplation of ten thoufand deities? Do we recognize the Divine effence in perifhable wood or ftone, the Divine glory in images of His meaneft creatures, or in monfters compounded by the moft loathfome imagination of man? Not only are human aberrations, however various, all laid forfooth along the fingle path of rectitude, but human contradictions are charged full with the Divine confiftency. Our author can prove that all forms of religion are effentially right, however oppofed in fpirit and expreffion to each other; but

it is only by demonſtrating that none can poſſibly be
wrong. At preſent he has only affirmed as much:
we wait with ſome curioſity for the demonſtration.

The Chriſtian philoſopher is, happily, at no loſs
to account for the idolatry which he both admits
and laments. All the phenomena of human nature,
and eſpecially thoſe ariſing from the confuſion of
good and evil, are explicable in the light of Scripture truth: at leaſt, that confuſion, as witneſſed in
the world, receives much light, if not a full ſolution, from the book which has preſerved to us
the ſacred hiſtory of mankind. In this matter
reaſon is eminently the handmaid of revelation.
The more thoroughly we appreciate the continual aſpirations of mankind after ſome ideal
good, the more readily do we admit the truth
of that record which affirms that God made man
in His own image: the more deeply we experience,
and the more widely we obſerve, the deceitfulneſs,
the hatred, and the cruelty of the human heart, the
more willingly ſhould we embrace that book
which ſo emphatically declares, " The heart is deceitful above all things, and deſperately wicked."
Hiſtory is intelligible only in the light of the bible :
the bloodieſt as well as the beſt mythology bears
witneſs to the religion of Chriſt. " They have
forſaken Me, the fountain of living waters, and
hewed them out ciſterns, broken ciſterns, that can
hold no water." The whole ſad ſtory of humanity,
with all its innumerable forms of crime and folly,
is epitomiſed in that one text. It is God's lamentation over the departure of His favourite race.

They have left Him; and whither fhall they go? Live independently they cannot. They were not made for themfelves. They have wandered boldly from the Fountain of all authority as well as happinefs, only to fuffer an infatiable thirft both of worfhip and delight.

Let us confider for a moment the cafe of the Arabian Prophet,—fo peculiar in itfelf, and fo plaufible in our author's ftatement. Now, let it be affumed that Mahomet has often been mifreprefented and maligned; that he had certain commanding moral qualities as well as intellectual gifts; that he was not, in the vulgar fenfe of the word, an impoftor, fince it may be held that no man ever impofed a new creed on mankind till he had firft impofed it on himfelf; and hypocrify is but a fubordinate—we had almoft faid an unconfcious—element in the forces of fanaticifm. But we fubmit that the fpread of his tenets is out of all proportion to his individual powers. We muft look for the fecret of his fuccefs rather in the character and circumftances of the Arabian people, than in the perfonal greatnefs of their prophet. Indeed, it is the common error of Mr. Carlyle and his fellow-worfhippers to magnify individual human agency till it is fomething god-like, and then to render it an undue homage. They forget "what great effects from trivial caufes fpring." They know it is certain that mighty confequences muft proceed from *adequate* caufes; but the river rolling through the plain is not all due to the rill efcaping through a cleft of the mountain. It is fed by neighbouring rivulets, and augmented by the winter-rains; the higher table-land is fecretly but furely drained for its increafe; and a thoufand independent fprings find glad fellowfhip and a fwifter courfe in its community of waves. And fuch is the hiftory of Iflamifm in relation to the influence of its Prophet. Mahomet was but a fuperior type of his own followers, not the feminal author of that race. It is probable that his character was deeply infcribed upon his little fect; and it has grown vaftly in the lapfe of ages, as a name carved upon a ftripling oak enlarges from year to year; only (in each cafe) what has been gained in magnitude is loft in diftinctnefs and in depth. We are not partial to that fpirit of modern criticifm which delights in turning the remote into the mythical, and explaining the literal by the fymbolical; nor do we wifh to fee it applied to the ftory of Mahomet. Fable and fact, like wheat and tares, are too intimately blended in that field of time for any but the angel of the judgment to difcriminate. But the records are too contradictory, too extraordinary, too parabolical for us to accept them as literal truth. What feems to us extravagance may be thought indeed only common juftice to the Prophet's memory, and profitable reading to his genuine difciples; but the oriental hiftorian muft be felt rather than underftood by us. His language of flowers defies tranflation; and if its odorous beauty embalms a character that muft otherwife have decayed like that of common mortals, we fhall not err too far in admiring that which proclaims, if not the real worth of the deceafed, yet the love and reverence of his kindred. And here another confideration meets us. As with the facts of the Prophet's hiftory, fo alfo with the moral character of his actions : if we cannot difcriminate the former, how fhall we rightly eftimate the latter ? The great Judge only can apply the ftandard in every individual cafe ; but with the Arabian leader the rule is widely different from that which will condemn an Englifh profeffing Chriftian, or even an enlightened Englifh deift. It is not pretended, even by the moft uncompromifing champions of our faith, that Mahomet and his followers will be arraigned in one indictment, and involved in one wholefale fentence. We believe, with Mr. Carlyle that " condemnable idolatry is *infincere* idolatry ;" but we believe, further, that *all* idolatry is infincere. Who can find out God to perfection ? Truly none. But what human foul was ever fully fatisfied with lefs than God ? Finite in himfelf, man belongs to the Infinite. Having no plummet that can found immenfity, all leffer waters are too fhallow for his foul ; and where his plummet ftrikes he dare not wholly venture. Perhaps not the dulleft favage who has made the wooden god which he believes in, does heartily believe in the god which he has made. Better than this, that he fhould be his own divinity—though then how forely muft he feel the need of another and a higher, if only to fave him from a tyranny at once fo impotent and fo ruinous —from the domination of a creature fo weak and wicked as himfelf.

Fully to counteract the whole of the evil fug-geftions infufed into this work, would require a fyftematic expofure of undue length. A falfehood may be infinuated in a line, which can only be thoroughly difproved and difplaced by a compre-henfive ftatement of the truth, and this, to be ex-clufive of error, muft be broad as well as funda-mental. The pantheiftic theories of Mr. Carlyle, which are more properly crudities in him, affume a fhape more worthy of the name in other writers of the fame fchool; for even Parker and Newman, with all their vague and wordy fentiments, pretend to a fcientific method, and fo frankly fubmit their doctrines to a due examination; and if, after all, they prove in part unintelligible and for the reft un-tenable, we muft refpect the apparent fincerity of the men, while we fternly condemn the rafhnefs and prefumption of the teachers. It is to authors like thefe, therefore, that we muft repair for a text, when propofing to difcufs the philofophy of the "Catholic Series." Mr. Carlyle is an author *fui generis*, who only ufes the new eclecticifm as a fit-ting framework for his panorama of all great human movements; whether puritan, or thug, or fanf-culotte; in fhort, it is only as an author, deter-mined at all cofts to be effective, that he finds fuitable material and variety in fo very "catholic" a creed.

We cannot leave this part of our fubject without one further remark. The ravings of *Hero-worfhip* fitly fupplement the impious doubts of *Teufelf-dröch.* Idolatry is the refuge of man's heart from

the horrors of pure atheifm ; and in this curfe both
favage and philofopher are equally involved. The
one abandons his offspring to fome bloody tyrant
deified as Moloch ; the other burns incenfe at the
hardly lefs bloody fhrine of Napoleon the Great.
No fooner is the fountain of living water dif-
paraged and deferted, under the idea that a wife
and well-ordered mind fhould never thirft for any
good external or fuperior to itfelf, than our wife
man is feen ftealthily drinking at fome foul human
cefs-pool, or hewing out fyftem-cifterns of his own,
" broken cifterns," collecting every earth-polluted
ftream, but retaining only its fediment and flime.
And thus God vindicates His truth, even in the
cafe of thofe who continue to outrage and deny
His claims. When their proud hearts refufe to
bow before the Majefty of heaven and earth, faying, " Who is God, that we fhould fear Him ?"
He caufes them to lick the very duft from off His
feet.

We haften to a brief confideration of Mr. Carlyle's laft work, and the more gladly, as it promifes
to exemplify the fruits of his teaching in the life
and death of a difciple. But one word by the way,
if only to indicate with the ftricteft brevity the
tone and character of two intermediate publications. Thefe are called refpectively *Paft and Prefent* and *Latter-Day Pamphlets.* They are apparently intended to perpetuate Mr. Carlyle's focial
and political opinions,—which they promife to do
much as the Egyptians preferved their dead, dif-

figuring with powerful drugs and spices, difguifing in a thoufand tortuous linen-folds, and hiding in dark narrow chambers under a huge pyramid of ftones. This is Mr. Carlyle's method of prefenting his embodied philofophy to the admiration of mankind ; and in thefe circumftances it is naturally a matter of fome little difficulty to do ample juftice in our reprefentation. So fuccefsfully are his thoughts difguifed and mummified, that, even if we could fucceed in removing fufficient of the cumbrous ftone-heap where they lie entombed, to admit a ray of common day-light, we fear that their fymmetry and complexion would prove any-thing but charming to the eye of modern tafte. In fhort, thefe pyramids of hard words are likely to remain the inexplicable monument of their buil-der's folly, juft ferving to remind the world of that fpecies of pompous oblivion which is fometimes achieved, by the wild genius of men like Jacob Bœhme, for doctrines which are not commonly dead, or fimply corrupt, but heavily fealed down in their moft difmal grave, and fetid with a rank and complicated odour.

Let us pick one ancient rag out of this leffer pyramid, called *Paft and Prefent;* holding it, never-thelefs, at a wholefome diftance, and letting hea-ven's bleffed air blow in between. It is the old maxim, *Laborare eft orare,*—"To labour is to pray: work is fufficient worfhip." If the book urges anything, it is the neceffity, the dignity, the virtue of labour. This idea is certainly not a new one. In fome fhape or other it is as common to be met with as bits of broken glafs. But, put into Mr. Carlyle's kaleidofcope, it is aftonifhing how pretty and how bright the notion is; into how many novel forms it flides with every movement of the fingers,—always, indeed, with the fame fhowy colours, but ever varying its fantaftic pattern. The folly of this deception is apparent to the leaft reflecting and confcientious mind. To labour is *not* to pray. We may ufe God's materials, and yet deny His right and title to them; we may co-operate, for our own ends, with certain of His eftablifhed laws, and yet ignore His power and prefence in them. *Shall a man rob God?* Yet men do it every day; appropriating His means, and fruftrating His pur- pofe; feeking their own aggrandifement rather than His glory. Mr. Carlyle's philofophy is not very deep if it does not teach him that labour, con- fidered *per fe*, is of no moral value, but only as it is an appropriate or appointed means to a lawful and noble end. True it is that induftry is an obligation of our prefent ftate, fo linked with the economy of human life, that we profit or fuffer, in certain eftablifhed degrees, according as our efforts are well or ill directed and fuftained. But this act, or this feries of acts, has no element of wor- fhip in it. We cannot pretend to Divine favour by obedience in fome points to the law originally written in our natures, but now well-nigh oblite- rated through fin; we dare not even come into the Divine prefence with no other offering than the fruit of our labour. This prefumptuous error is

as old as Cain, who alfo dared practically to affert
that to work with his hands was fufficiently to
worfhip God, and who offered the fruits of the
earth cultivated by him as a fatisfactory acknowledgment of fealty and fubordination. But God
rejected his offering with difpleafure ; for this was,
in effect, to appeal to the law, which frowned
fteadily and with awful threatening upon the un-
bloody facrifice of Cain. And *now*, as *then*, it is
only as all our works are begun, continued, and
ended in HIM, " the Propitiation," by whom we
find accefs and favour, that they are in any wife
acceptable to God. Prefented in any other name,
the moft ponderous offering of induftry or genius
that we may roll upwards toward His throne will
only recoil in infinite mifchief and condemnation
on our fouls.*

The *Latter-Day Pamphlets,* in their collected
fhape, form perhaps the moft extraordinary production of the age. A book fo entirely and obfti-
nately unintelligible was, probably, never written ;

---

* If Mr. Carlyle were not fo great a philofopher, and
too highly flattered to adopt readily the teaching of a meek
and pious fpirit, he might learn whence the true fanctity of
labour is derived, from the lips of good George Herbert :—

> " Teach me, my God and King,
>   In all things Thee to fee,
> And what I do in anything
>   To do it as for Thee.

> * * *

> " A fervant with this claufe
>   Makes drudgery divine :
> Who fweeps a room as for Thy laws,
>   Makes that and the action fine."

and certainly one at the fame time fo original and amufing was never read. Of courfe, we do not intend to fay that its words and fentences are feparately void of meaning, or wholly incapable of conftruction: but this we do deliberately affirm, that *on no one of the many fubjects* which Mr. Carlyle's pen here glances upon, or plays around, *do we find any direct or deliberate expreffion of opinion, theoretical or practical,* deduced as a focial truth, or urged as a political neceffity; nor have we any the flighteft idea of Mr. Carlyle's remedy, or clafs or feries of remedies, for the great and many evils of fociety;—evils which, according to our author, are not merely attendant upon the working of our focial and political fyftem, but incorporated with its very effence, and lying at the root of all civilized inftitutions. Effrontery and inconfiftency are ftamped in brazen characters on every page of this grofs libel. The induftry and earneftnefs that were, as we have feen, "the be-all and the end-all" of his moral code, are here of no avail to propitiate his wrath at what he deems their mad and ruinous mifdirection, but only ferve to aggravate the fpafm of his rage. Talk of offending "the Divine filences!" (as our precious author fo indignantly does)—furely never were the filent energies and patient fufferings and human virtues of our toiling race fo impudently outraged and infulted as by this loud torrent of invective. No one clafs is fpared from his catalogue of nuifances that "offend the fun," and "cry out for burial." All is rottennefs and diforder in the focial fabric;

all is speedily falling back to chaos. With marvellous inconsistency, the man who sees such grace
and goodness in every form of human worship—
though its incense be the fume of passion and its
rites the solemnization of cruelty and lust—sees
only gilded vice and unmitigated folly in every
walk and institution of civilized life! Falling
from the mad prophetic rant of his former works,
he is here exhibited, not as the *Cassandra*, but the
Thersites, of the age; standing, in turn, over every
silent group of labourers in this earnest century
and most earnest country, and voiding his unwhole-
some abuse equally over all. In these pages every
time-honoured virtue that adorns humanity meets
with indignant denial or scornful depreciation.
Philanthropy is maudlin, and benevolence is weak-
ness, and industry is avarice, and statesmanship is
trickery, and liberty a chimera, and religion cant!
England is especially the target of Mr. Carlyle's
scorn: the British constitution is the choicest
specimen of folly which the sun beholds in all this
great "museum of absurdities." Indeed, almost
the only preference of a positive kind which may
be distinctly gathered from this book, made up as
it is for the most part of inexplicable hatreds and
dislikes, is the author's hearty preference of a good,
strong, iron despotism to the most elaborate and
well-balanced constitutional government. Nothing seems to irritate him so much as the words
" emancipation," " enfranchisement," " liberty,"
" voluntary principle." Prison-visiting and me-
lioration very evidently disgust him; and as to

flavery, fo cordial is his regret for the decadence of that ancient inftitution, that he feems to emulate the zeal of poor Bofwell, who declared that to abolifh the flave trade would be to " fhut the gates of mercy on mankind !"

Such are Mr. Carlyle's views of fociety, as at prefent conftituted. But the moft difcouraging circumftance is the abfence of any fpecific or remedy. We are pretty frequently told, indeed, that unlefs we fpeedily adopt another method, and chime in with the eternal laws, we muft look out for fomething dreadful ; and the very leaft that would feem likely to befall us, (but we hope it is only his ftrong way of fpeaking,) is a fudden chaos, or univerfal limbo. We are warned, frequently enough, that it will not do to go about mending and tinkering the unhappy manners of the age ; for *it* is fo rotten, and *we* are fuch bunglers, that we fhall infallibly make more holes than we can ftop. We muft begin *de novo*, and ftart right this time, and keep fo too, or we fhall prefently be overtaken by—we really dare not tell the reader what, partly becaufe it is fo alarming in Mr. Carlyle's language, and partly becaufe we do not exactly underftand the nature of the danger, after all. It is juft poffible that matters are not fo bad as we had begun to fear. And, indeed, the moft agreeable feeling which we have known to refult from a perufal of thefe *Latter-Day Pamphlets*, is when, clofing them with a painful but confufed impreffion of the hopelefs ftate of England,—its mammon-worfhip, follies, and hypocri-

fies,—we turn to the bufinefs and intercourfe of
life, and find fo many encouraging features in fociety; fo many noble tendencies, active and benevolent; and fo large an amount of private virtue
and individual piety, contributing to the general
order and fuccefs, and multiplying, on all hands,
the fum of human happinefs. The change is fomething like that which might be experienced in
turning from the wards of an hofpital in Bedlam,
to the green fields of the hufbandman, or the glorious forum of public life and affairs.

But it is moft important to know the nature and
extent of Mr. Carlyle's influence in the religious
or ferious world, and efpecially among thofe ardent
fpirits who are ready to follow the moft daring
leader into the fpiritual myfteries of our nature.
His focial views are not likely to have great weight
with practical men till they fhall be more clearly
defined, and by this means better underftood. But
it is not thus with regard to his religious fpeculations: for, ftrange enough, men do not extend the
neceffity of that practical wifdom to the perfonal
affairs of the foul, which they fail not to recognize
in matters of merely temporal concern. In the
latter cafe, a man foon becomes convinced that, if
he look not after his own bufinefs, he cannot fhare
the general profperity, though he admire and appreciate it never fo much. But how many are
there who indulge an intemperate curiofity as to the
nature of the human fpirit,—its origin, and effence,
and character, and deftiny,—who yet feel no paramount intereft in the fafety of their own! Of GOD,

too, they have a certain ftrange defire to know much that muft remain unknown till we can "fee Him as He is:" but to feek a preparation for that transforming vifion—by afcertaining His favour, and their perfonal relationfhip to **Him, and feeking** firft a renewal of, and then a perpetual **growth in,** His image and likenefs—feems never to **occur to** them as the firft as well as the higheft **point for** their confideration, the chief and only wifdom **of** every individual foul of man.   It is to this clafs of minds **that** the writings of Mr. Carlyle are efpe-cially alluring. **Wandering after a** forbidden know-**ledge, and fcarcely expecting to be** made certain or fatisfied, they do **not quarrel with the** unfatisfactory nature of his excurfions **into** the myfteries of being, dazzling, but unproductive, as they are.   **Reverf-**ing the divinely-appointed order, they neglect to tafte firft of the tree of life, and foon find the bit-ter fruit of that other tree to be the knowledge of their own mortality and mifery, and the oblivion **of all** divine and faving truth.

The laft publication of Mr. Carlyle, as we have already intimated, is the *Life of John Sterling.* Of **this** affecting ftory we have no heart to fpeak in much detail ; and we are glad to entertain a rea-fonable perfuafion that the reader of thefe pages is more or lefs acquainted with its fubject, at leaft through the medium of literary notices and extracts. To thofe, however, by whom he may be unknown **or** unremembered, we would briefly fay—John Sterling was a young man of great literary promife, **and** confiderable though defultory performance ;

contributing papers of varied merit, firſt to the
"Athenæum," afterwards to "Blackwood's Magazine," and occaſionally to one or other of the
" Quarterly Reviews."   Having an ardent deſire
to do good, and feeling a growing inclination to
theological ſtudies and miniſterial purſuits, he ac-
ceded to the propoſal of his friend Archdeacon
Hare, took holy orders, and became curate in the
pariſh of Hertſmonceaux. After a brief ſervice of
eight months, he was compelled by failing health
to relinquiſh the ſacred functions ; and for the remainder of his melancholy days did little more
than bear manfully the burden of a waſting life,
and dream fitfully the dreams of an unſound ambition, and wander, a well-nigh hopeleſs invalid, in
purſuit of milder air and mitigated pain, to Madeira
and to Rome, and finally to Ventnor in the Iſle
of Wight, where, on the 18th of September, 1844,
" all thoſe ſtruggles and ſtrenuous often-foiled endeavours of eight-and-thirty years lay huſhed in
death."

But why do we ſpeak of Sterling's premature
decline as conſiſting of melancholy days, and his
whole life as an affecting ſtory? Afflictions, though
in themſelves grievous, may be welcomed as ſalu-
tary diſcipline, and even prized for the ſtronger
conſolations they induce. The valley of the ſhadow
of death is not always or altogether dark : the Divine ſmile may diſſipate its central gloom, and the
ſhining city beyond may indicate its glorious termination.   Nor does the language of the biographer,
when he refers to " thoſe ſtruggles, and ſtrenuous

often-foiled endeavours," of neceſſity imply a lamentable or unhappy frame of mind. A warfare that is ſtill a conſcious triumph, or a race that gives increaſed aſſurance of ſucceſs, is already crowned with a virtual anticipation of reward; it partakes of the bleſſedneſs of final victory, as well as of the wearineſs of preſent ſtrife: nay, this little wearineſs is loſt in that profound bleſſedneſs, as the exulting ſoul ſubjects and colours all the leſſer man. It is not, therefore, the ſuffering believer, nor the diſabled Miniſter, that we preſume to pity. The champion of the truth may be diſmounted by providence, but he can only be overcome by ſin; and when be may no longer lead on the aggreſſive ranks, and neither advance nor witneſs their full or final triumph, ſo long as he holds faſt the ſhield of faith, his perſonal ſafety is ſecured as by a ſevenfold ægis; and the general victory of the church may well be truſted by him to its great Deliverer and Head.

In juſtice to Mr. Carlyle, we muſt remark that Sterling's deflection from the path of orthodoxy and the ſimplicity of faith ſeems to have commenced before their perſonal acquaintance with each other; and in juſtice to Sterling himſelf, we muſt heſitate to admit that he ever wholly abandoned or thoroughly miſtruſted thoſe great ſcriptural truths which he had early imbibed. It is not, we think, for any fellow creature to ſay whether, or when, or in what degree, he *knowingly* ſuffered himſelf to be deceived by the ſpeciouſneſs of carnal reaſon, and henceforth found no clue out of the

tangled labyrinth of nature. His powers were
brilliant and active. There is evidence in his
writings of much acutenefs ; and a certain ready
productivenefs was alfo characteriftic of his fertile
and well-cultivated mind. But of wifdom—which
has been happily defined by a living author as *that
exercife of the underſtanding into which the heart
enters*—he feems to have had but little ſhare ; and
hence his life, defpite a certain moral bias, and the
affluence of an intellect fparkling, if not profound,
appears to have had no commanding moral purpofe, and to have borne no practical or correfponding fruit.   We gather, from a careful perufal both
of Mr. Hare's account of his friend, and Mr. Carlyle's more elaborate biography, that a habit of unprofitable fpeculation had early gained upon the
mind of young Sterling ; and to us it is no lefs
apparent that this fubjective tendency of his, this
morbid introverfion of the mental eye into the
myfteries of his own nature, and this curious prying into the fprings of public faith, while dangerous
to the moft philofophic and religious mind, if unduly or exclufively indulged, were particularly fo
in his cafe.   And here, may we venture on a
remark of general application ?   Being eftablifhed
in a faith to which all natural and moral things
bear evidence, and the beft teftimony of which is
lodged in the innermoft confcioufnefs of the fpirit,
—with what fhow of *wifdom* does a man abandon
or begin to doubt the facts and verities of Scripture,
merely upon the application of certain arbitrary
principles of criticifm, which feem only to difcredit

in one way what has been fo frequently attacked in fo many, yet fuccefsfully in none? That philofophy muft be clear and mafterly indeed which would reafon the fun out of the heavens, and difprove alike the noon-tide heat, and vernal green, and fummer bloom. It will hardly do to point to fome remaining patch of fnow, or fome unfruitful fpace of earth. A Chriftian has all the materials of a juft and comprehenfive faith, while he can never obtain more than a fraction of the materials due to a confiftent fcepticifm; fo that the moral evidences of Chriftianity, while they are fufceptible of almoft endlefs illuftration from the fide of nature and reafon, cannot poffibly receive therefrom any general or abiding injury; and much lefs are they in danger of being fuperfeded thereby. While it is competent to us to go on to *demonftrate* the Chriftian's faith, the vaft majority of believers are content to *feel* its truth, with fuch corroboration only as the experience and obfervation of every day fupply. "Man's firft word," fays Archdeacon Hare, " is *Yes* ; his fecond, *No* ; his third and laft, Yes; and, while the bulk of men ftop fhort at the firft, very few attain to the third." Poor Sterling feems to have preffed into the fecond ftage without ftrength to traverfe all its rugged breadth; but, though he never attained to the laft perfection of belief, where the philofopher and faint are found to be identical, there is fome reafon to hope that by a gracious influence he was led to retrace his fteps, to linger near—and quietly pafs over into—the firft happy paths of a fimple and fatisfying faith.

If the rationaliftic philofophy was fo highly injurious to the peace of Sterling, Thomas Carlyle
was not more fortunately chofen to be his " guide,
philofopher, and friend." We would not exaggerate the influence of the latter upon the former,
which was probably lefs than the reader of Mr.
Carlyle's biography would be led to fuppofe. Sterling always fought the battle of orthodox Chriftianity againft the irregular darts of that ftrange
Teutonic genius ; and this both in public and private, with the pen as well as with the tongue. But
though many of thefe fiery darts were repelled,
fome evidently remained to fret his fpirit to the
laft, even if not permitted to prove mortal to his
fpiritual health. He was ftrongly fafcinated by
the energy, the boldnefs, and the eloquent unreafon of his friend ; and, though he hefitated to call
him mafter, he could not wholly refift the authority of his mind. It is melancholy to think how
pernicious was that unequal friendfhip to the feebler
of the twain. Sometimes he feems to wifh to
throw off the galling yoke from his fpirit ; but perfonal and intellectual ties difcouraged this moral
enfranchifement. That Sterling never *did* wholly
break through this bondage, is evident from his
laft letter to our author, written only a month before his death. How could Mr. Carlyle dare to
print a meffage fo burdened with reproach,—reproach more dreadful, becaufe half-unconfcious
and wholly uncomplaining? " For the firft time
for many months," fays Sterling, " it feems poffible
to fend you a few words, merely, however, for

M

remembrance and farewell. On higher matters there is nothing to fay. I tread the common road into the great darknefs, without any thought of fear, and with very much of hope. With regard to You and Me, I cannot begin to write ; having nothing for it but to keep fhut the lid of thofe fecrets with all the iron weights that are in my power. Towards me it is ftill more true than towards England, that no man has been and done like you. Heaven blefs you ! If I can lend a hand when THERE, that will not be wanting. It is all very ftrange ; but not one hundredth part fo fad as it feems to the ftanders-by."

Thus does this dying man adopt the language of Deifm, in deference to the fcoffing mafter of his mind ; while it is evident that the light of nature by which alone he dares to write, is only as a fepulchral lamp, " making night hideous," and the prepared grave difmal beyond expreffion. " *I tread the common road into the great darknefs!*" If we had been perufing the life of fome heathen of good renown, whofe lot had fallen in a gentile land, ages before " life and immortality were brought to light by the gofpel," this would ftill have been a melancholy clofe. Even then, we muft have dropped a tear for mortal mifery un-relieved by any certain hope, and courageoufly enduring what it was fo helplefs to remove ; and fighed *Alas!* for that poor philofophy which could not draw the earneft of immortality from the deep well of human confcioufnefs, or truft the fparkling promife as it rofe. But this is a picture of fome-

thing infinitely worfe,—a confummation e ven
more frightful in its filence than that of the poor
ftudent, led to the twelfth hour of his laft day of
liberty, impiety, and pleafure, who finds his lamp
expiring in deep fobs of light, and fupernatural
noifes gradually invading all the air. So with
poor Sterling, but that he would not be known
(at leaft by one mocking fpirit) either to complain
or tremble. Life's bufinefs has been idly done in
idle fpeculations on its myfteries ; and now there
is neither comfort in the paft nor affurance for the
infinite future. And what is the return or confolation offered by Mr. Carlyle for a facrifice fo
unfpeakable as this, made by his young difciple?
He amufes himfelf by drawing the life of his
feeble friend, for fuch he evidently holds him to
have been ; makes it as artiftic as poffible, arrang-
ing his chief figure in the moft interefting of atti-
tudes, fupported by back-ground and acceffories
of the moft attractive kind. His zeal and admiration for the " hero" of his work is (as ufual)
quite fubordinate to his intereft in the work itfelf.
Not, perhaps, that he loves Sterling lefs, but that
he values Carlyle more. His genius deigns to
fhine upon him only as the fun upon a fatellite,
and that merely upon the hither fide, where he
fees himfelf reflected. His pity often borders on
contempt ; and he feems to difmifs the book into
the world with the air of a man who has done well
with a very poor fubject, and made a miferable
human fcarecrow into a very tolerable clothes-
horfe to receive his own tawdry finery.

We have feen that the end, as exhibited in Mr.
Carlyle's pages, is very full of gloom ; but in Mr.
Hare's account it affumes a more cheering afpect.
The evening before his death, John Sterling wrote
thefe lines in pencil, and gave them to his fifter.
Why they were fuppreffed in Mr. Carlyle's narrative, will fufficiently appear from the verfes themfelves, which would hardly have contributed to the
impreffion he was defirous of leaving on the
reader's mind.

> " Could we but hear all nature's voice,
>   From glowworm up to fun,
> 'Twould fpeak with one concordant voice,
> ' *Thy will*, O GOD *! be done.*'

> " But hark, a fadder, mightier prayer,
>   From all men's hearts that live :—
> ' *Thy will be done in earth and* **heaven**,
>   *And Thou my fins forgive !*' "

Thus, in a few pencilled lines, we have fome
recantation of poor Sterling's errors,—fome acknowledgment of the two great truths of natural
and revealed religion.   Thefe he, perhaps, never
quite relinquifhed, though Mr. Carlyle would lead
us to imply as much.   The mafter and difciple
were then divided in fentiment, before they were
divorced by death.   The mafter ftill teaches the
independence of nature, and the abfurdity of " a
perfonal God ;" but the pupil afferts *the authority
of the* CREATOR, *and the fubmiffion of every
creature.*   The mafter ftill affirms the purity and
rectitude of man's inner heart, maintaining that all
deviations from truth and goodnefs have an external origin in oppofition to internal teaching ; but

the pupil gathers only this humiliating truth from human error,—*the need*, to wit, *of Divine forgiveneſs.* Probably Mr. Carlyle would ſneer at the crowning weakneſs of his friend, always " wanting in due ſtrength." For ourſelves, we are thankful for this additional teſtimony to the wretchedneſs of unbelief, and the truth of Chriſtianity.

Of Mr. Carlyle we have little more to ſay. The reader is now enabled to judge, with ſome accuracy, both of his talent and of his teaching. We commenced by bringing his vaunted literary excellence to the ſingle but ſufficient teſt of ſtyle ; and though our ſpace did not admit of ſuch quotations as might be neceſſary to convince the unacquainted of his grand deficiency in this particular, we confidently appeal even to his admirers, if we have not fairly charaſteriſed his ſtyle, and that without exaggeration. Of courſe thoſe who blindly admire and follow him will aſſert this to be his higheſt merit, and ſay that when he differs from other eminent examples of ſtyle he therein far ſurpaſſes them, and ſerves to deteſt their weakneſs and incompetence. Thus an American enthuſiaſt triumphantly contraſts our author's love of paradox and ſcorn of grammar with " the inanities of Addiſon." Contraſt indeed ! As there is no accounting for taſtes, we ſhould perhaps be thankful for the exhibition of one which, if unaccountable, is not unamuſing. We may ſuppoſe this critic to have a private opinion that day-light is very inſipid compared with gas in chandeliers ; and we ſhall know that we have met with him once more when we hear convulfions quoted as a proof of ftrength. Afterwards, we attempted, under many difficulties, to afcertain the drift of Mr. Carlyle's philofophy ; but as this was not to be appreciated on any but tranfcendental principles, and even fuch as it is, has never been definitely ftated by our author, we fear that we failed to convey the fatif-faction which we did not receive ; and perhaps fomething of the kind may account for our author's failure alfo.   One trial more remained.   Accord-ingly, we fought to afcertain the practical value of Mr. Carlyle's teaching by reference to the career and character of one of his difciples.   This was the more feafible, as the life of fuch difciple was prepared to our hands by the mafter himfelf: fo we opened the life of John Sterling.   We found him beginning life full of promife and accomplifh-ment : we left him on the couch of death, cur-tained by a more than mortal cloud of doubt and forrow, which his enfeebled hand could only partially draw back.   What light fell on that death-bed came *not* from the lamp of Mr. Carlyle's philofophy, but from beyond it, making it yet more pale and fickly.

But is not Mr. Carlyle a writer of extraordinary genius ?   It appears to us that he is not.   But the fubject of "genius," with the nature and limita-tions of its merit, is one upon which we may hope to find fome future opportunity of fpeaking at greater length, and with fuller fatisfaction.   A recent French critic—writing in the *Revue des Deux Mondes*—maintains that Mr. Carlyle is the greateſt thinker our country has produced in modern times. We can only ſay that, as it ſeems to us, he thinks to very little purpoſe. We adviſe the reader, when next he meets an ardent admirer of our author's writings, to requeſt a ſtatement of a few definite points for which thoſe writings are to be valued, and eſpecially of the particular truths therein announced or illuſtrated. The poet may claim to be heard in his own rhythmic and choſen language ; but the philoſopher whoſe doctrines or precepts admit of no abridgment or laconic ſtatement, muſt permit us to doubt of their exactitude or truth. If Mr. Carlyle is the greateſt thinker of our times, alas for the country of Bacon and of Butler. Nay, we have, in that caſe, ſadly degenerated from the dialectic genius of the time of Hume ; for, however ſophiſtical were the arguments of that philoſopher, ſtill they *were* arguments, carefully addreſſed to reaſonable men, and thus frankly offering the opportunity of refutation, which has ſince been freely accepted and made good. But Mr. Carlyle offers no ſuch opportunity, and deſerves no ſuch praiſe. It has been remarked (with reference, we believe, to the ſtyle of Gibbon) that it is impoſſible to refute a ſneer ; and a ſimilar reflection is conſtantly riſing in the mind of the reader of Mr. Carlyle's productions. He has a fatal aptitude for word-painting—a gift invaluable to the writer of poetic fiction, who can thus put as it were a ſpirit into inanimate objects of nature. We could name a popular author who has this

faculty in perfection, and whofe peculiar praife it
is that he rarely or never abufes it to faften a falfe
impreffion on the mind, by conveying a profound
untruth in the guife of a fuperficial analogy.   But
Mr. Carlyle is conftantly offending in this manner,
till the mind of his reader, if not enflaved by his
great fhow of power, revolts againft fuch unfair-
nefs.   What does he mean, for inftance, in repre-
fenting the Chriftian Minifter as "weltering" under
a heap of "Hebrew old clothes?"   The real object of the author is to imprefs the unguarded reader
with his own particular notion, that Chriftianity is
virtually effete, and fhould in all reafon become
obfolete alfo.   The manner of conveying this impreffion is very fubtle.   "Hebrew old clothes,"—
as though he objected only to a Judaifing or merely
formal worfhip: but then it is applied in the cafe
of a Proteftant clergyman; and thus the reader is
almoft involuntarily led, by the dexterous ufe of
this analogy of fancied refemblance, to defpife every
approach to a defined belief in the character and
commandments of God, and to an orderly celebra-
tion of His worfhip and fervice.   And this is the
manner in which our "philofopher" affumes the
great point at iffue between him and the believer!—
thus fcornfully rejecting, as ufelefs and worn-out,
that catholic Chriftianity which is found to be
adapted alike to every age, and clime, and circumftance of man; which fupplies and harmonifes the
principles both of public and of private virtue; and
which exalts and bleffes the individual, while it
advances and ennobles the whole fpecies.

The pre-eminent moral of Mr. Carlyle's literary hiftory we take to be this : Every effort after forbidden or unprofitable knowledge is rewarded only by increafed confufion and uncertainty, and induces rather a weaknefs than an improvement of the intellectual and moral powers. To feek, without affiftance from Revelation, an acquaintance with the myfterious future, is only to infure our ftumbling even in the prefent life. A too curious prying into " the fecret things," which belong only to God, is ever followed by a departure from thofe fteps of practical truth which already put us in the direction and under the influence of our true and higheft deftiny, and which would ultimately, in another ftate of exiftence, lead us into the very heart of the myftery itfelf. All finite creatures are fubject to the conditions of law, and among thefe is *gradation* as a condition of advance ; yet in virtue of our fpiritual relation to the Divine Being and the invifible world, we are allowed to anticipate, even now, much of that final ftate to which we are deftined. But this fpiritual nature is alfo under a law ; and it has pleafed the Father of our fouls to make implicit reliance on His word, and ready acceptance of the terms of His favour, the conditions of our initiation into all truth,—into a living, vivifying ftate of knowledge, which is as real as it is comprehenfive, and which, even in its earlieft ftage, is the beginning of eternal life. Thus practically fecured from all moral error, and thus faithfully promifed a perfection both of fpiritual and intellectual good, it is no part of true wifdom to

suffer metaphyfical reafonings—the vapours arifing
from a grofs and earthly region, to becloud the immediate vifions of the foul; **or** to permit the imperfect and partial fenfes to overcrow **the** immortal
fpirit, which alone is able to apprehend the powers
of the world to come. To expect **that** there
fhould be no myftery is to make God **our fellow,**
and eternity an infinitely dreary day. **To admit**
that there is and muft be fuch, is to acknowledge
the being of Him who dwelleth in THE LIGHT
WHICH NO MAN CAN APPROACH UNTO, WHOM NO
MAN HATH SEEN OR **CAN SEE.** Let us trace Him
reverently where His fteps **are** clearly feen, and
acknowledge that the leaft **of His** works, vifible
and ufeful in our moft humble **and** daily concerns,
is linked in the chain of His adminiftration with
the higheft that takes hold upon His throne, and
anchors the univerfe to His faithfulnefs and power.
And when we have no anfwer or explanation to
give; when fome awful providence thunders the
judgment of its miffion, and only whifpers its myfterious mercy; when evil feems to profper by a
law, and the great counter-law is left to operate
unfeen; let us then encourage the filence of a
ferene but active faith, or only **take** up the confident language of the poet :—

"So He ordain'd, whofe way is in **the** fea,
    His path amidft great waters, and **His** fteps
    Unknown;—whofe judgments are a mighty deep,
    Where plummet of archangel's intellect
    Could never yet find foundings, but from age
    To age let down, drawn up, then thrown again
    With lengthened line and added weight, ftill fails;
    And ftill the **cry** in **heaven** is, ' O THE DEPTH ! ' "

TENDENCIES OF MODERN POETRY.

THE publication of thefe **two volumes,*** within the fpace of the laft few months, prefents an opportunity of which we gladly avail ourfelves, and fo proceed at **once** to offer fome brief remarks upon the **leading** characteriftics of modern poetry. **The whole** of this wide fubject **could** not, indeed, **be difcourfed** upon from **fo limited a text;** but **for exhibiting** the **more** prominent **features and marked** tendencies **of poetry in the prefent day, we could** not, perhaps, have felected better illuftrations than thofe which come moft recently to hand. Of thofe features and tendencies they furnifh, it is true, **exaggerated types; but for this reafon** they are

---

* *Balder*, by the Author of " The Roman ;" and *Poems*, by Alexander Smith. In revifing this **article,** and one or two others in the prefent **volume, the** author has made no attempt **to** obliterate the traces of their original purpofe and pofition. If the leffons they contain fhould find no application in the future, the papers will at leaft, and all the fooner, acquire hiftorical fignificance,—ferve to regifter one important phafe **or crifis of modern** Englifh literature, and to fhow that **the public journalift was not** unfaithful to his truft.

only the more adapted to our prefent purpofe, as a
public leffon is illuftrated beft by examples in high
relief.

It is neceffary, perhaps, to obviate the mere
fufpicion of narrownefs or prejudice. In art we
profefs our taftes to be fufficiently eclectic. We
are not of thofe who, from a natural or acquired
bias towards one clafs of poetry, would deny the
name to every compofition of another fchool.
The charm of this great art, as of its greater prototype, is its wonderful variety. It has fomething
for every tafte and every mood; it breathes fucceffively the airs of every feafon, and touches by
turns the fimpleft bofom and moft cultivated mind.
And if it be true,—as we believe it is,—that its
great mafters have the fuffrages of every clafs, and
attract the humbleft to find fome natural charm
in thofe human features, whofe deeper and divine
fignificance makes the higheft to return, and
ponder, and gain frefh intelligence, with every
further contemplation, it is alfo true that there is
another order, whofe office is more limited, but
not lefs authentic. Seldom, indeed, is the gift of
genius thus univerfal in its power; far more frequently is it thus circumfcribed and fpecial. A
Madonna of Raphael,—all can fee beauty there;
peafant as well as prince, and Proteftant as well
as Catholic; not only maid and mother, with their
myfterious fympathy, but boy and man, and all
who have ever found or felt fome natural ftrain of
love. But where is the connoiffeur who has
traced all the magic of its art, and exhaufted all

the treafures of its truth and tendernefs,—who has
perufed it thoroughly, is fatisfied completely, and
is content to look upon it for the laft time ?   A
play of Shakefpeare,—this is patent to every fchool-
boy ; it is hiftory for the million, a repertory for
every mafquerader, a world for every humorift, a
manual for every ftatefman, a text-book for every
moralift.   But where is the fcholar or critic who
has pointed out every beauty, and fupplied the
final glofs, and learnt the whole leffon ?   Honour
then to Shakefpeare and this chofen few !   Thefe
are the High Priefts of Nature, who minifter at the
great altar in the open fervice of the temple.   But
there are humbler oratories embayed within its
folemn aifles, and there the pilgrims from every
region may hear words of comfort, each in his
own dialect ; and the priefts themfelves drink fym-
pathizing words from each other's lips.   There
are Poets who need Poets for an audience,—who
have fed their imagination upon the felecteft images
and daintieft thoughts ; and men of coarfer mould
can have no fympathy with thefe.   There are
others, who have brought learning to enrich their
art, and whofe elaborate compofitions are fo
many pieces of embroidered tapeftry, bright with
traditionary fplendours, and moving with heroic
life.   Honour then to Collins and to Gray !   All are
welcome who are fervants faithful both to virtue
and to man, and who make Truth and Beauty
the handmaids who unveil the face of Nature.   In
this fpirit we gladly recognize the mufe of Keats,
with its fenfuous delight in every natural object,

and its almoſt pagan reverence for the dumb old deities of Greece,—and the genius of Shelley, ſoaring, like his own ſkylark, "higher yet, and higher," and ſhedding from illuſtrious wings the whitenefs of ideal beauty on everything beneath.

Neither do we deny that true poetry may, in ſome faint degree, reflect the ſpirit of the age which gives it birth. Of ſome ſpecies,—ſuch as ſatire, comedy, and the like,—it is the peculiar function ſo to do ; and for many of the more ſerious kinds, it is no neceſſary detraction, that they indicate, with more or leſs diſtinctnefs, the character of the times in which the author lived. Poetry of the beſt deſcription will often take ſomething of its form and temper from popular and paſſing influences, from the force of national and temporary circumſtances : for, though individual genius is the fire in which it is raiſed to its white heat, the preſent age is yet the anvil on which it is beaten into ſhape. This is chiefly true of poetry of a peculiar kind, moſtly popular in its character, and always lyrical in its expreſſion : of that which is higheſt and beſt, the moſt artiſtic and elaborate, we may confidently ſay that it is eſſentially independent of current tendencies,—that a ſpirit of utilitarian progreſs, if allowed to interfere, will more frequently deteriorate than exalt it ; and an age of metaphyſical inquiry ſerve rather to confound its pure æſthetic genius, than to yield it a truer or nobler theory of life.

As there is much error prevalent on this point, and as that error is, as it ſeems to us, a principal caufe of the failure of many poems of undoubted genius in our day, we may, perhaps, **be allowed to** examine it more fully. We are perfuaded that the ill-conftruction and feeble execution of thefe works are, in great meafure, due **to** unfound notions **of** poetic art ; while only **from** the obfervance of its genuine principles **can moral truth, and every** minor excellence, refult.

That poetry fhould, according to **the** language of our **great dramatift**, " fhow the very age and body of **the times, its** form and preffure," is, indeed, a **maxim of** fome value to the artift of every clafs ; **but it** is frequently repeated in our ears by thofe who forget to interpret it in the light of that great mafter's practice, and who both miftake its **mean- ing, and exaggerate its importance.**

Firft, they miftake **its meaning.** It fignifies,— at leaft in **its application to the art under review, of** which precifely it was not firft fpoken,—not that poetry of fet purpofe **muft, but** that poetry of the right ftamp ever **will,** reflect the lineaments of *the age, not of the poet himfelf, but of that imagined in the poet's fable.* It dictates, not the choice of **fubject, which** is left abfolutely free, but the fidelity of imitation, which is ftrictly and primarily demanded by æfthetic law. Is **the** time we live **in full of** earneft inquiry, practical reform, philan- **thropic** effort, and focial improvement ? **Thefe,** then, will more or lefs appear in all works, even of the epic clafs, whofe fcene and era are expreffly identical **with ours ;** but thefe **works** moftly take **the fhape of the profe novel.** They will fome-

times, alfo, condenfe themfelves in verfe, and find
warm utterance in thofe brief and popular lyrics by
which a nation or a clafs gives expreffion to its
tranfitory throes. But we are fpeaking now of
poems which, by their elaboration or their length,
evidently make pretenfions to the higheft rank of
art; and the method of true art is not altered by
the genius of an age. Its appeals are made from
one individual mind to another, and not from the
individual to a collective people. It advocates no
meafure of reform, however preffing or defirable;
it occupies itfelf with no fingle branch of induftry
or fcience, however ufeful; it does not even,
without manifeft deterioration and failure, rehearfe
the crude and difordered fancies of any fingle mind,
however gifted, and though it be the poet's own.
The nature of art is effentially objective and con-
ftructive. A poem, like a painting, is ftrictly a
compofition, whofe materials—felected almoft in
whatfoever place you will—are faithfully combined
by the æfthetic faculty,—a faculty that is neither
wholly intellectual nor wholly moral, that acts in
great meafure like inftinct, but needs the co-opera-
tion of fcience and intelligence.

But, fecondly, our critics exaggerate the importance of this maxim, even when underftood in
their own limited and leffer fenfe. Poetry depends
far more on the effential than the accidental; on
the permanent than the temporary; on man himfelf
than national coftume or political conditions.
For this reafon it is that no poem worthy of the
name can ever grow dim with age, but is frefh

through all time. No man fpeaks fo fincerely to his fellow-man as the poet; none is fo free from the affectations and falfehoods which divide one clafs in fociety from another, and make one generation almoft ftrange to that which follows; no one, therefore, is fo widely recognized, fo welcome in every neighbourhood, fo fecure againft the changing fafhions and confounding dialects of time. The beft, and even the moft popular, poems in the world are thofe which are leaft fhaped or coloured by the fpirit of the author's age. If the ancients ftill move and delight us, it is not that we have much in common with pagan Greece or Rome, either focially or politically confidered; for by contraft in thefe particulars we are yet more divided from them than by centuries of time. It is as men beholding the fame fun, feeling the fame wants, and fuffering the fame changes. We may ceafe to wonder then that the ballads recited in their halls, and the dramas which held breathlefs their affembled cities, are ftill frequent on our lips, and often prefent to our minds. If pleafing to the young or to the old once,—as the Iliad or the Odyffey,—why not to youth or to experience now? If grateful to the inftinct of filial piety once,—as the Antigone of Sophocles,—why not to filial piety in our day alfo? That thefe are not even more popular among us is only becaufe, with all their force of truth, they are not true enough,—not fimply, fully, and profoundly fo. They are Greek to a fault, as well as human to a miracle. Something of artifice ftiffens the march of their otherwife confummate art ; the brooding fhadow of one great national belief obfcures much of the delicate tracery of life ; the demands of one grand action admit too feldom of a fweet and natural relief. Hence the defective fympathy exifting between this age of readers and that age of poets ; hence the need of culture and knowledge on the part of the former, before they can thoroughly enjoy the lofty creations of the latter. Something, indeed, of this is chargeable on the great difference, even of perfonal character, which the influence of our northern civilization, and efpecially of the new and better religion, has wrought upon mankind in modern times ; but ftill more, we fufpect, is due to the lefs perfect fympathies of the poet,—for Sophocles is not the rival of Shakefpeare. For fome of the higheft purpofes of art, the ancients were fufficiently related to men in every age to bequeath examples of abiding intereft ; and, in the main, we have reafon to congratulate ourfelves on the actual legacy we enjoy ; and certainly it does not forbid our admiration and wonder. Even our purer faith does not neceffarily exclude our fympathy ; all the nobler fentiments of natural religion—and poetry *as an art* would perhaps do well to concern itfelf with thefe alone—are to be met with in the bards of every country ; wifdom and beauty find an oriental drefs in Sadi and Ferdoufi, a claffic one in Sophocles and Homer, and in either drefs we may welcome both. If we know how to keep poetry in its proper place, and expect from it only its legitimate effects, we fhall not hefitate to profit and delight ourſelves by Virgil as ſecurely as by Milton ; if we are ſo fooliſh as to draw our higheſt principles therefrom, we ſhall only err too far in either caſe.

But if the poet is indeed thus independent, and reſtrained neither to his own locality nor era, it is certain he will uſe this liberty, and for the moſt part fix his choice upon a diſtant or ſomewhat unfamiliar ſcene. The reaſons for this are obvious and irreſiſtible. In the firſt place, he is more likely to apprehend the limits of his ſubject, to recognize its genuine features, and to ſketch the whole more freely, when he beholds it from a certain elevation,—from ſome height where no prejudices can obſcure, and no diſtractions interrupt, his clear and calm obſervance,—where ſerene impartial art may exerciſe its functions undiſturbed. But there is another conſideration hardly leſs important. Above all things it is neceſſary that poetry ſhould pleaſe ; and that it may ultimately and profoundly pleaſe, it muſt firſt and eaſily attract. To this end, nothing is more likely to contribute than ſome novelty of external features, tending to ſtimulate our languid curioſity, and leading us, perhaps unawares, into a deeper ſympathy with all that is of more real and abiding intereſt. True it is that what is moſt eſſential in poetry, is that which touches us moſt nearly, and is promptly recognized and felt as true ; but everything which diſtinguiſhes it as an art, which raiſes it above the level of ordinary proſe literature and learning, is traceable to ſome form of pleaſure, senfuous or intellectual, as, for inftance, to our delight in imitation, melody, or grouping. It is idle to object that a great poet fhould have a higher purpofe than to pleafe; enough for us to know, that to pleafe by means of its legitimate refources is the firft condition of his art, and for him to underftand that he can no more difpenfe with the lighter charm of novelty, than with the incorporated graces of harmonious verfe.

We hope the relevance of thefe remarks will foon be more obvious to the reader. Much of the defectivenefs of recent poetry arifes, as we think, from a difregard of thefe firft principles. Its faults, indeed, are both many and various, affecting ftyle and fentiment as well as plan : but this deliberate weaknefs of defign is doubtlefs a radical and primary defect; and this vague and vain attempt to give voice and utterance to the ftruggling forces of the age, brings a difturbing influence into the young poet's mind ; while the effect of both together is to deny to his production that intereft which arifes from a definite purpofe and an united action, attended, as thefe commonly are, by a due variety of character, and a fober and fubordinated ufe of language.   The books now claiming our attention will ferve to illuftrate this degenerate tendency ; but, before turning particularly to them, we may briefly refer to two living authors who have fet a contrary example, and proved both the foundnefs and fuccefs of their canons of art,— Henry Taylor, in " Philip Van Artevelde," and Walter Landor, in his " Hellenics." Do we want poems more beautiful—can we find any more genuine—than thefe? Neither of them is faturated with what is called " the fpirit of the age ;" we do not know that they are even biaffed by it ; perhaps the ftudent of a hundred years hence could not learn the period of their production by internal evidence. Yet few authors of the prefent day are fo certain to fulfil their century, few volumes of our teeming prefs more likely to be ftudied and perufed in the future. Both works are acceptable to the healthieft and pureft modern tafte ; for though the fubject is mediæval in the one cafe, and claffical in the other, they are the productions, not of antiquarians, but of poets.

But ours is not the argument of limitation or undue control; and we gladly admit that, if the poet is not reftricted to the prefent, neither is he excluded from it. The Mufe that has the wings of the morning may fold them above our noifieft cities, and gracefully alight in the forum or the market-place. The influence of the prefent Laureate has not always been for good upon his followers ; for they have caught his tone, but lack his pure infight and almoft perfect tafte. Yet it feems to us that, in the poems of Tennyfon himfelf, both thefe conditions—which refpect the tranfitory and the abiding, and find an element of this in a chaos of that—are fulfilled in a remarkable degree. He draws his infpiration from the native well of his own fancy, and yet fings from his height of place in the middle of the nineteenth century. His genius is affected, but not overborne,

by the tumultuous fpirit of the times, by the triumphs of material fcience, or the conflicts of the
public foul.   Hence the fweetnefs, as well as the
fubtlety, of his verfe, the clearnefs of his ideas, and
the eafe of his expreffion.   The doubt of other
men he feems to pity, rather than to fhare.   As a
poet, he knows that enough of the beautiful and
the good remains for him, enough of the lafting
and the true ; and therefore he glances only into
the dark vortex of fcepticifm, and " drops a melodious tear," and in another moment he is foaring
upward and away : refting now on Ida, he re-
modulates the plaint of the deferted Œnone,
henceforth immortal as love and grief can make it ;
and now, alighting on the pillar of St. Simeon
Stylites, he rehearfes the fearful leffons of afcetic
virtue.   From this true conception of his art, and
this faithfulnefs to the univerfal and abiding above
the merely local and tranfient, it is due that the
writings of the Poet-Laureate harmonize with the
ftandard poetry of all times, and take their place
at once as claffic pieces.   For choicenefs of imagery
and allufion, for mufical fweetnefs of intonation,
and for that intellectual quality which is power
and eafe and affluence at once, the poems of Tennyfon may worthily compare with the minor
poetry of Milton.   Each is a mafter of lyrical expreffion, and fings from his own deep, human
heart, as independent both of age and country.
And yet we dare not fay that there is no indication
that thefe poets lived at different periods ; only
that indication, which is pofitive in the cafe of

Tennyſon, is merely negative in that of Milton.
Milton ſeems to ſing for recreation,—to unbend
his ſterner genius in ſome light exerciſe of imagination or fancy ; and ſo he borrows ſomething of
the ſpirit of pagan poetry, the more thoroughly to
maſk the age of puritaniſm from his own regard.
In Tennyſon, under much the ſame conditions of
facile grace and exquiſite alluſion, we have
glimpſes of a mind that forecaſts the fortunes of
his race, whoſe thoughts are all thrown forward
" by the progreſs of the ſuns," and, like penſive
ſhadows, dapple the ſunny future ; but his ſpirit is
cheerful throughout, and full of hope, if not evinc-
ing the confidence of faith ; and, in his ſweet wild
muſic, we no longer hear "anceſtral voices pro-
pheſying war," but a chorus—diſtant, yet jubilant,
faint as echo, yet rounded and harmonious as the
ſpheres—celebrating the age of peace and happineſs,—

> " And one far-off divine event,
>   To which the whole creation moves."

We muſt not any longer defer the promiſed introduction of our two young poets, but forthwith
preſent them to the reader. When he has made
their acquaintance, our previous obſervations on the
art which they profeſs may recur to him as having
a diſtinct bearing on our eſtimate of their practice
and ſucceſs.

The principal poem in Mr. Smith's volume, entitled, " A Life Drama," and that of " Balder," by
the author of " The Roman," are elaborate produc-

tions of the fame fchool of poetry ; and it is, therefore, no caufe for wonder, nor even ground of complaint, that they have much in common.   Their
originality is fufficiently marked and diftinguifhed,
and their poetical merits—though in each cafe
graphic and pictorial—are not fo fimilar as to be
eafily confounded.   The bond of their union, as
ufual in all fects or fchools of poetry, is rather in
that which is adventitious than effential,—in what
is doubtful t hanin what commands our admiration
and efteem ; and this being the cafe, we fhall not
wonder to find a great refemblance in the external
form of their refpective poems.

Each of thefe works is remarkable as having the
length of an epic, the form of a drama, and the
nature of a rhapfody. It has, indeed, a beginning,
and fomewhere (if you can find it) a middle, and,
in the long run (if you have only patience) an end ;
but, in the fenfe of Ariftotle, it has none of thefe.
There is abfolutely nothing to prevent you rever-
fing the order of the fcenes, except it be a
fuperftitious notion, that the author *muft* have had
a reafon for difpofing them as they are at prefent
found.   By this oriental ftyle of reading, you will
lofe none of its vivid paffages, and may fave yourfelf fome general difappointment.   Indeed, it is
very likely you will find it improve as you proceed
from that point, as to us it grew ferioufly worfe
while we proceeded from the other.

In each cafe, alfo, a poet is hero as well as
author. This is highly characteriftic of the poetical
fraternity in our day. It is evident that the modern

bard efteems no ordinary theme deferving of his
fong; and fo he turns to glorify himfelf, and worfhip his own art by way of exercifing it. His
rhapfody is all about genius,—its forrows, ecftacies,
divinity, and might; what it can do if it only
pleafes, and what it fcorns to do for fo miferable
an audience as humanity can furnifh. No longer
holding "the mirror up to Nature," he fits and
turns it fairly on himfelf, and finds trace of thunder
in every fcar, and demon-beauty in every fantaftic
lock; the blue of his eye fuggefts (to him) the
unutterable depths of heaven, and in the curl of
his lip he reads and practifes contempt for a paltry
world of profe.

It is eafy to find paffages in both of thefe performances which may juftify the character we have
afcribed to them. The real difficulty is to meet
with a page in which Poefy, or Fame, or Genius is
not extolled or invoked in good fet terms; though
fometimes this unfortunate paffion—for evidently
it is not reciprocated—finds a natural relief in
equally extreme abufe, after the true lovers' fafhion.
Walter (in the " Life Drama" of Mr. Smith) exclaims, with his ufual aptitude of comparifon,—

" I love thee, Poefy! Thou art a rock;
  I, a weak wave, would break on thee, and die!
         *   *   *   *
  O Fame! Fame! Fame! next grandeft word to God!"

And foon afterwards he breaks into prophecy, and
in this manner our author contrives, with charming innocence and *naïveté*, to foretell his own appearance :—

" My Friend ! a Poet muſt ere long ariſe,
  And with a royal ſong ſun-crown this age,
  As a ſaint's head is with a glory crown'd ;
  One who ſhall hallow poetry to God,
  And to its own high uſe, for poetry is
  The grandeſt chariot wherein King-thoughts ride ;
  One who ſhall fervent graſp the ſword of ſong,
  As a ſtern ſwordſman graſps his keeneſt blade,
  To find the quickeſt paſſage to the heart.
  A mighty Poet, whom this age ſhall chooſe
  To be its ſpokeſman to all coming times."

How far Walter, or his author, is likely to " hallow
poetry to God," or be our " ſpokeſman to all
coming times," we ſhall ſee by-and-bye. In the
meanwhile let us hear how the poet of " Balder"
apoſtrophizes *his* little matter (of nine thouſand
lines).

            " O thou firſt, laſt work !
Thou tardy-growing oak that art to be
My club of war, my ſtaff, my ſceptre ! Thou
Haſt well-nigh gain'd thy height. My early-plann'd,
Long-meditate, and ſlowly-written epic !
Turning thy leaves, dear labour of my life,
Almoſt I ſeem to turn my life in thee.
Thy many books, my many votive years,
And thy full pages number'd with my days.
I could look back on all that I have built,
As on ſome Memphian monument, wherein
The Kings do lie in glory, every one
Each in his houſe, and forward to thy blank,
Fair future, as one gazes into depths
Of necromantic cryſtal, and beholds
The heavens come down."

The adoption of ſuch ſuſpicious heroes as theſe
bodes no good to any laboured or ambitious poem.
If epic, it will be without incident, and full of
reverie ; if a drama, the choice ſpirit will have all
the ſpeaking to himſelf, and the ſcene lack action,

character, and iſſue. There may, indeed, be found room for much ingenious deſcription, *à propos* to anything or nothing; for a poetical hero may ſurely exerciſe a double licence,—his author's, and his own. Then, all the bits and fragments that our poet has ever written, in every conceivable mood and tenſe, may be fitly uſed up here. Theſe are the conveniences of ſuch a plan; but they ſtop chiefly with the author's part, and do not much befriend the reader. Many little poems do not make a great one; ſtill leſs do ſeveral fragments make a whole. An epic poem is not manufactured like a quilt; nor do the pieces emptied, whether in diſguſt or admiration, from a young man's portfolio, fall, as by magic, into the true dramatic mould.

But ſkill and judgment of the higheſt order have often failed in coping with difficulties which our young authors boldly add to thoſe which lie naturally in their way. So confident are they of their own powers, and ſo certain to attain the goal of fame, that they put hurdles on the courſe, and take a five-barred gate in pure bravado. Their choice of ſubjects in theſe performances are inſtances in proof of this unlucky confidence. We do not think the poetic character very ſuitable for expreſs delineation by poetic art, even as a matter of occaſional choice, and when one true genius ſeeks thus to re-animate another. In a brief monody an intereſt of the kind may poſſibly be ſuſtained, but hardly in a poem of more artiſtic form. We cannot think that even Goethe has wholly ſucceeded in his

dramatic rendering of the life of Taſſo. Byron's
"Lament" is more to our liking, becauſe it is leſs
both in pretenſion and extent. But in the caſe of
the authors before us, there is far leſs promiſe of
ſucceſs. Their heroes—Walter in the one caſe,
and Balder in the other—have not the *preſtige* of
acknowledged genius ; they have no grand aſſocia-
tions to call up, nor any fadeleſs laurels to diſplay
upon their brows. Of courſe, then, they muſt approve their claims to the character in the work
where they appear, which muſt at once eſtabliſh
the author and the hero. Now, both Mr. Smith
and his anonymous brother have evidently felt this
obligation ; but we almoſt deſpair of conveying to
the reader any adequate idea of the great efforts,
and greater ſacrifices, they make in order to obtain
the character and praiſe of genius. It is clear that
they deſign to give us the quinteſſence of the
genuine article. Nothing that might for a moment
be taken, by thoſe who hear it read, for ſimple
proſe, or recognized as the thought and language of
daily life, is ſuffered upon their pages for a moment.
It is one unmitigated ſtream of genius,—we ſuppoſe,—that ſcorns all rule, as any river of ſpirit will
overflow its bounds.

The "Life-Drama" of Mr. Smith is underſtood
to be the work of a very young man ; and, therefore, we are not without hope that he may yet live
to ſhow that friendly reproof has not been loſt
upon him. In entertaining ſuch a hope, of courſe
we acknowledge the reality of his poetic gifts,
which, indeed, are not inconſiderable. His poem

is moftly free from metaphyfical obfcurities ; and
ifolated pictures of great beauty meet you on every
page.   He has great eafe, as well as force of language : though limited in range, his pencil is extremely vivid in expreffion.   Here is a famous
character, drawn in three lines :—

> " Befide that well I read the mighty bard,
>   Who clad himfelf with beauty, genius, wealth ;
>   Then flung himfelf on his own paffion-pyre,
>   And was confumed."

Surely that comparifon is very fine.   Another
fpecimen of his power, though tinged with his own
peculiar extravagance, is the following, addreffed
to an infant :—

> " O thou bright thing, frefh from the hand of God !
>   The motions of thy dancing limbs are fwayed
>   By the unceafing mufic of thy being !
>   Nearer I feem to God when looking on thee.
>   'Tis ages fince He made his youngeft ftar :
>   His hand was on thee, as 't were yefterday,
>   Thou later Revelation !   Silver ftream,
>   Breaking with laughter from the lake divine
>   Whence all things flow !   O bright and finging babe !
>   What wilt thou be hereafter ?"

This, we fay, is a favourable example of our
author's manner ; but even in thefe lines we may
trace that extravagance of language which is one
of his prevailing faults. If we were to quote much
more, the reader would foon difcover his other
prominent defect, namely, a fatal poverty of ideas.
The poem lacks fubftance, form, and truth ; and,
in fpite of the brilliance of certain parts, it is moft
unfatisfactory as a whole.   To the young and
ardent it muft neceffarily convey a falfe impreffion

of life ; to the experienced and right-minded it brings only wearinefs and impatience. The hero is a poet, who knows nothing of mankind or fociety, and only the worft part of himfelf. He talks as familiarly of fun, and moon, and ftars, and mountains, as if they were his neareft neighbours ; but of his actual neighbour—of man, in his fober fphere of action, with chaftened affections, and reafonable hopes, and cheerful courfe of duties ; of man, in his varied relationfhips and trials, as yielding to or maftering his own fortunes—he knows or tells us abfolutely nothing. Hence his inceffant ufe of ftars, and clouds, and feas, and crifped fmiles ; for ignorance inftinctively cowers down behind extravagance. Not without reafon does Walter fay, "I love the ftars too much." Even when he condefcends to any terreftrial objects, they are always the largeft and moft gaudy of their kind. His garden teems with paffion-flowers ; his aviary is ftocked with birds of paradife. He makes love in the moft fumptuous manner poffible. There is nothing valuable or extenfive which is not at his lady's fervice : of all his (promifed) prefents, a kingdom is about the pooreft and moft common-place. He is perfectly enamoured of a lazy life, and would fill up the hours with endlefs love and maundering. He is not afhamed to fay,—

> " O let me live
> To love, and flufh, and thrill—or let me die !"

Well, this Walter is the deliberately chofen " hero" of Mr. Smith ; not felected as a warning,

but prefented as a model and example of what he
holds to be the higheft type of man,—the poet,
deftined " to fun-crown this age." We hardly fee
how the author can avoid the imputation of Walter's fentiments ; at any rate, he is refponfible for
the general character, as fixed and approved by
the action of the poem. Mr. Smith cannot fafely
plead the laws and licence of dramatic poetry ; for
by thefe he is condemned. The work is, indeed,
formally, though not virtually, dramatic ; and as
all that Walter fays or does is unrefuted in the
courfe of the action, and uncontrafted by any
nobler character, the evident moral is, that this
precious hero is the favourite of poet as well as
providence. His end is very edifying. Walter
the feducer has a tranfient paffion, or rather paffage, of remorfe, induced, no doubt, by the recollection that he has fome fine things to fay in that
character ; and then, fuddenly brightening up, he
coolly determines to make a handfome figure in the
world yet, and afterwards, leaving it with contempt,
go as by right to heaven. Only hear him !—

" I'll reft myfelf, O World, awhile on thee,
    And, half in earneft, half in jeft, I'll cut
    My name upon thee, pafs the arch of Death,
    Then on a ftair of ftars go up to God."

This is not indeed the actual finale of the piece ;
but nothing afterwards occurs to alter our impreffion of the whole. Two friends of Walter meet,
and fpeak of his poem as " a hit ;" they tell us,
moreover, that it was " done at a dafh." All this
very naturally confirms our impreffion that the

author and the hero are identical; and, if fo, we muft fay that Mr. Smith has very cleverly antici-pated the popular effect of that ftyle of poetry in which he has indulged. In a later fcene Walter meets with the injured Violet, whom he had de-ferted, and profeffes fuddenly to be cured of all his evil and romantic habits, and turned to conftancy in love, and duty in the ordinary affairs of life. There is nothing to make this converfion probable or permanent. What we muft regard as the moft hopeful fign of improvement is the flighting way in which he can endure to mention his favourite ftars : he is brought to admit,—

> " A ftar's a cold thing to a human heart,
> And love is better than their radiance."

We gladly pardon the defective grammar, in con-fideration of the fentiment, which indicates at leaft fome meafure of returning reafon.

Let us turn for a moment to the other volume before us. Who, then, and what, is " Balder ?" Balder is not the divinity of Scandinavian mytho-logy,—the Apollo of the North,—Balder the Beautiful. Neither is he a perfonification of the poetic character. We are afraid he is an Englifh poet, who has taken to gloomy and unhealthy ways. The only other perfonage in the drama — excepting a Doctor Paul, who appears but twice— is Amy, the poet's wife. Between thefe two the long difcourfes of the poem are fuftained, though in very unequal proportions. Balder has the firft words and the laft to himfelf, and a very unreafon-

MODERN POETRY. 193

there is comparatively little. The poet foliloquizes
in his ftudy; and when we are fuppofed (not
without reafon) to have had enough of his diftem-
pered thoughts, we find a fmall relief in hearing
" through the door the voice of Amy," which is
frequently mournful and melodious in the higheft
degree. We are not certain if we rightly apprehend
the prominent idea which difturbs the reft of Balder, and makes him fo unfociable a being; but it
would feem that, having totally loft his relifh for
the affairs and fatisfactions of life, he has begun to
entertain a morbid and infane defire to behold the
face of Death. Death comes and takes the place
of his babe; but this touches not him fo much as
Amy; and as the babe lay on the bofom of his
wife, this is a dread exchange and awful fellowfhip
for her. The plaints of Amy, if occurring in a
piece of more dramatic and realizing power, would
be affecting in a high degree. From this point we
do not thoroughly underftand the author's drift,
but fufpect that Balder would have more intimate
relations with the grim and fpectral foe. His wife
falls ill; Balder threatens to murder Doctor Paul,
if he do not cure her; and yet—ftill unfatisfied and
craving—he contemplates her flaughter by his own
hand; but whether moved by fome profound
reafon which he holds equal to a repeal of the for-
bidding ftatute, or urged by fate and irrefiftible impulfe, is not clear. An opportunity is given for
the accomplifhment of his defign by the intrufion
of Amy into his ftudy, during his momentary

o

abfence, with the purpofe of awaiting his return. Balder enters, and takes up a fcroll : it is the MS. of his great poem. He addreffes it in terms expreffive of his hopes and admiration ; and when he has got through only a page and a half of choice comparifons, in which his fondnefs likens it to all mute but mighty things, his wife makes herfelf and her mifery known, and flings the ufurping parchment out of the window into the moat. Then follows a fcene of paffion and unreafon which in itfelf is very beautiful and mafterly. The lady's madnefs throws her into a fwoon ; and in that unconfcious ftate her hufband is intent on killing her, when the fcene fuddenly clofes. So ends this ftrange volume ; but not fo the work ; for this is only the firft portion ; and whether tithe or moiety who fhall tell ?

The following lines, forming part of a long eulogy prepared by Balder for his victim, Amy, will put the reader in poffeffion of the manner which prevails through the entire volume ; it contains, in brief, almoft all the charaCteriftic blemifhes and beauties of our author's ftyle :—

" So the world bleffed her ; and another world,
Like fpheres of cloud that inter-penetrate
Till each is either, met and mixed with this.
And fo the angel Earth that bears her Heaven
About her, fo that wherefoe'er in fpace
Her footftep ftayeth, we look up, and fay
That Heaven is there—SHE moved, and made all times
And feafons equal ; trode the mortal life
Immortally, and with her human tears
Bedewed the everlafting, till the Paft
And Future lapfed into a golden Now
For ever beft. She was much like the moon

Seen in the day-time, that by day receives
Like joy with us, but when our night is dark,
Lit by the changeless fun we cannot fee,
Shineth no lefs. And fhe was like the moon
Becaufe the beams that brightened her paffed o'er
Our dark heads, and we knew them not for light
Till they came back from hers; and fhe was like
The moon, that wherefoe'er appeared her wane
Or crefcent, was no lofs or gain in her,
But in the changed beholder. I, who faw
Her conftant countenance, and had its orb
Still full on me, with whom fhe rofe and fet,
Knew fhe had no lunation. In herfelf
The elements of holinefs were merged
In white completion, and all graces did
The part of each. To man or Deity
Her finlefs life had nought whereof to give
Of worfe or better, for fhe was to God
As a fmile to a face. Ah, God of Beauty!
Where in this lifelefs picture my poor hand
Hath done her wrong, forgive; fhe was Thy fmile,—
How could I paint her? That I dared effay
Her image, and am innocent, I plead
Refiftlefs intuition, which believes
Where knowledge fails, and powerlefs to divine
Or to confound, ftill calls the face and fmile
Not one, but twain, and contradicts the fenfe
Material, which, beholding her, beholds
Effence, not Effluence, nor Thine, but Thee."

The faults of this elaborate defcription—which
is only the fummary or concluding part of one far
more extenfive—are radical and pervading. It is
extravagant in the extreme; and yet, after all, what
qualities that really command love and efteem,
are told us of this lady? It is only a tranfcendental doll that the poet has dreffed up in mift and
moonbeam, without one human feature to attract
our regard or engage our confidence. Perhaps,
innocence—the innocence native to unfullied
creatures—is the charm intended to prevail

throughout the picture.   Not to urge that this is falfe to nature, and far beyond the range of our belief and fympathy, the author manifeftly fails in the embodiment of his fair ideal.   Not in fuch ethereal graces did Milton clothe the Eve of Para- dife,—not fo dangeroufly did he venture to con- found her effence with that of the Divine and Per- fect Being; yet, in that lovely portraiture, we have all that is womanly, and true, and pure,— humanity idealized by the perfection of its feveral qualities, and feminine affection and devotion fub- fifting in the lovelieft of human moulds.   But this picture of the poet's Amy is furely moft unreal; we can form no conception of fuch a being as he labours to depict ; it is fo fhadowy that the moon, intended to inveft it only, ftreams fairly through it ; and, at the firft light of day,—the firft dawn of re- flection,—it melts infenfibly off, and we have not the fainteft notion left us of this unearthly beauty. Yet, as we are bound to believe that Amy was everything to her enamoured poet, what muft we think of her deliberate and barbarous murder at his hands ?   Surely, no doubt fhould have been allowed to reft upon our minds of the nature and ftrength of motive leading to this diabolic purpofe.

Of the final and prefiding moral of this un- finifhed poem we cannot pretend to fpeak ; but the tendency of the part before us we do not hefi- tate both to judge and condemn.   Apart from the outrageous action with which it feems to conclude, —the effect of which is fo fubordinate that we omit it from our calculation,—there is more than enough to fatisfy us, that no time can be lefs profitably fpent than that devoted to its perufal. Many of its faults originate, no doubt, in that defective ftructure to which our introductory remarks had reference; but we muft point them out now, in the particular fhape which they affume, as grofs faults of exaggeration and difproportion, both in ftyle and fentiment.

The ftyle of " Balder" may be pronounced equally remarkable for beauties and defects; but it muft be underftood that its beauties are limited to the minor qualities of expreffion and illuftration, while the larger attributes of ftyle, deftined to harmonize and order and fubordinate the parts, are almoft wholly wanting. It is frequently obfcure as well as gorgeous, feemingly written with great facility, and certainly read with a fluent eafe which makes the fearch for meaning, however neceffary, quite impracticable. Once launched upon a tide of verfe fo affluent and fparkling, the reader is foon carried out of his own, if not his author's depth; and, hopelefs of regaining his feet, refigns himfelf to float away while all the willowy and monotonous banks glide by. The effect of this kind of poetry upon the mind is very fingular. Having no earthly intereft, it has, neverthelefs, a certain charm for the bewildered fenfe. Abounding far more in brilliant imagery than diftinct ideas, the reader is aftonifhed by the opulence of language and the endlefs fucceffion of pictures prefented, often with great vividnefs, to the mind. This excefs and total infubordination of imagery is characteriſtic of the ſchool of rhapſodiſts and dreamers. Sometimes one feeble circumſtance or thought—and that not ariſing out of any incident in the poem—is treated to a train of ten or even twenty ſimiles, each far outſhining its poor antecedent, which, of courſe, is quite forgotten long before the laſt illuſtration has appeared and vaniſhed. Sometimes this poetry is metaphyſical, and ſometimes it is eminently ſenſuous; or rather it is each by turns, as the thought and illuſtration ſucceſſively predominate. The thread upon which much of the delicate and ſplendid imagery of " Balder" is ſtrung, is a peculiar and morbid ſtrain of ſpeculation, ariſing in the moody poet's mind. This pſychological condition, and its curious phenomena, are not eaſily deſcribed by a pen ſo blunt as ours, but may be found in all their ſtrange and intricate proportions in the poet's endleſs reverie. The following lines have more or leſs reſemblance to many hundred others, dictated by this ſame *queſtionable* ſpirit :—

> " Am I one and every one,
> Either and all ? The innumerable race
> My Paſt ; theſe myriad-faced men my hours ?
> What ! have I fill'd the earth, and knew it not ?
> Why not ? How other ? Am I not immortal ?
> And if immortal now, immortal then ;
> And if immortal then, exiſtent now ;
> But where ? Thou living, moving neighbour, Man,
> Art thou my former ſelf,—me and not me ?
> Did I begin, and ſhall I end ? Was I
> The firſt, and ſhall I one day, as the laſt,
> Stand in the front of the long file of man,
> And, looking back, behold it winding out,
> Far through the unſearch'd void, and meaſuring time
> Upon eternity, and know myſelf

> Sufficient, and that, like a comet, I
> Pafs'd through my heaven, and fill'd it ?"

We admit that the metaphyfical idea embodied in thefe lines is expreffed in a highly poetical manner; and perhaps it is not more, but lefs, abfurd in fuch a drefs than its cuftomary ftyle of fober profe. Yet a little of this kind of writing is enough; and we become naturally impatient when it is found to prevail through fo large a quantity of verfe, and in a form of compofition where it was leaft to be expected.

Turning to a later part of the volume, we find Balder thus pompoufly witneffing to the vanity of human life :—

> " I have tried all philofophies; I know
>   The height and depth of fcience; I have dug
>   The embalmed truth of Karnak, and have fail'd
>   Tigris and Ganges to the facred fource
>   Of eaftern wifdom; I have lived a life
>   Of noble means to noble ends; and here
>   I turn to the four winds, and fay, ' In vain,
>   In vain, in vain, in vain!' "

Surely we ought to be made to fee more diftinctly how the ufe of " noble means to noble ends" were fo entirely fruitlefs; throughout the prefent work no fuch ends or means are employed or fought by Balder. Befides, it is very eafy, but not equally artiftic, for an author to affert, in fo many words, the vaft learning and experience of his hero, when of this, alfo, wholly wanting to be affured by fome collateral evidence :—otherwife we are treated only to a truifm, the echo which every human heart awakes to the preacher's " vanity of vanities." In the cafe of Balder,—dreamer as he is,—fo large a range of learning and experience is juft what we are moft difpofed to doubt. He feems to have enervated his foul, and anticipated the voice of " vanity," by abftracting himfelf from all the wholefome influences of daily life and common duty.   To idle on the grafs in his *beau-idéal* of an earthly Paradife; to do a day's work would evidently fill him with fatigue and difguft, if the bare notion of it did not caufe his feeble nature to collapfe. He cries (like Walter) in the fpirit of this luxurious philofophy,—

> " Alas! that one
> Should ufe the days of fummer but to live,
> And breathe but as the needful element
> The ftrange fuperfluous glory of the air!
> Nor rather ftand apart in awe befide
> The untouch'd Time, and faying o'er and o'er
> In love and wonder, ' Thefe are fummer days.' "

And fo this precious fentiment is made the frequent burden of his fong, and more or lefs precifely its mufical refrain; for our bard is found flighting to the laft

> " The untouch'd Time, and faying o'er and o'er
> In love and wonder, ' Thefe are happy days.' "

We prefume it is not neceffary to occupy more time or fpace by further extracts from this poem. It is clear that neither nature nor humanity is fairly reprefented in the pages of " Balder." For the one you have the colour without the compofi-tion of Turner; the bright, headlong, and dif-ordered rack of clouds, but not the delicate and

truthful line of coaſt. For the other you have the
vivid palette of the pre-Raphaelite, but not his
faithful and pathetic pencil. To the laſt-named
ſchool of art the poem bears ſome ſtriking points
of reſemblance ; but, on examination, we ſhall
find more of contraſt than coincidence in theſe
artiſtic ſchools. Both are obſervant of the delicate
and the minute in nature, and full of exquiſite by-
play ; but the pre-Raphaelite is a realiſt, and the
modern poet an ideal rhapſodiſt ; the one truſts to
find due ſentiment and moral reſult from an almoſt
literal exhibition of the truth ; the other dreams
his dream of metaphyſical and wildeſt beauty, and
then rifles nature for images of like power, like
majeſty, like evaneſcence, or like grace. We
ſhould leſs regret the ſtructural defects of this
poem, if it abounded in aphoriſms of ſubſtantial
worth. When our great poet drew the character
of a man moſt worldly-wiſe, he put into his mouth
an involuntary tribute to virtue, that is in admirable
keeping and full of moral truth. The counſel of
Polonius to his ſon is ſummed up in one brief
maxim :—

> " To thine own ſelf be true,
> And it muſt follow, as the night the day,
> Thou canſt not then be falſe to any man."

How well does this expreſs the linked order of the
moral virtues !—the ſocial not only conſiſtent with,
but included in, the perſonal, and both ſo intimately
joined, that to do higheſt juſtice to yourſelf, is alſo
to fulfil the laws of brotherhood and duty to your
neighbour. Our author, among all his brilliant

fayings, finds no opportunity of teaching fuch a truth. In the " Night Thoughts" of Dr. Young, there are a thoufand inftances of the value of this fecondary element of poetry, and the more valuable in that work, becaufe the primary artiftic element is wanting.   But nothing of the kind rewards the reader of this ftrange farrago.

In taking leave of Mr. Smith and his companion, we hope that none who have gone with us thus far together, can miftake the real grounds of cenfure upon which we have proceeded.   If we have fome-times fpoken lightly of their defects, it is not becaufe we under-rate the ferious mifchief of fuch productions.   If many features expofe them to flight and ridicule, their fpirit and tendency make them obnoxious alfo to our juft reproof.   Our readers have had fome means of judging of the freedom, bordering upon profanity, with which they make light ufe of the name and character of God ; but this is done to an extent which our few extracts could not adequately fhow.   On the lower grounds of art their condemnation is as ftrictly merited.

The author of " Balder" is the more deferving of reproof, though perhaps only the lefs likely to profit by it, becaufe it is his fecond work and moft deliberate choice.   Yet talents fo high as thofe which this author poffeffes, were not given to be fquandered in intemperate fancies, which, while they enervate the recklefs poffeffor, can only de-prave the fine imagination and relax the moral tone of rifing manhood.   The youth of England,

if they are to meet manfully the duties of their
future life, muſt be hardy in their intellectual paſtime as well as in their holiday ſports; for the
one is as neceſſary to their mental and moral health,
as the other to their phyſical maturity.   To ſteep
their minds in poetry like that which we have
turned from, is about as wiſe as to ſpend their ſum-
mer evenings, and make their nightly bed, in a
ſteaming hot-houſe, only for the privilege of re-
poſing under the leaves of ſome huge exotic. How
much better to follow the muſe of Scott over
breezy heath and mountain fell ; to watch the
feaſt in Brankſome Hall, or purſue the flying ſtag
as he ſeeks " the wild heaths of Uum-Var !" It is
the faſhion, we know, to decry the poetic achievements of Sir Walter Scott, to ſtyle them (what,
indeed, they are) mere verſified romances : and
we may admit that many of his contemporaries,
as Campbell, Rogers, and Coleridge, ſtruck loftier
muſic from their lyres, and warbled a ſweeter and
a rarer ſong.   But let the new generation of poets
beware how they puſh the ſtrain too far, and give
us ſo much that is intenſely poetical (as they intend
it); and eſpecially how they permit the expreſ-
ſional parts of poetry to overlay its more ſubſtantial elements.   The ſure effect of this will be to
drive us back to the homelier but healthier ſtan-
dards, and among the reſt to the plain but nervous
minſtrelſy of Scott, with its ſimple melody and
vivid freſhneſs, its hearty ſympathy with external
nature, and its ſkilful blending of the familiar and
romantic.

POPULAR CRITICISM.

THE ſpirit which preſides over compoſition of the pureſt ſort, is known by
the name of *taſte;* the choice and
order of language in which it finds
expreſſion, is denominated *ſtyle.* Is the former
ever a ſuperfluous gift? Is the latter a merely
ſuperficial quality? Theſe inquiries we propoſe to
anſwer, firſt by a direct, and then by a more explicit, negative.

There is the cloſeſt poſſible relation and interaction between the form and ſubſtance of literary
works; and the lighteſt graces of a given production will be found rather characteriſtic than independent of its eſſential merits. In ſtyle we have,
therefore, an indication as well as an inſtrument of
truth. It is a teſt of the competence, fidelity, and
triumph of an author,—at leaſt, within certain
obvious limits,—as well as a guarantee of his legitimate influence in the world of mind. Even
the ſlighteſt product of literary taſte, however frail
and indefinable its graces may appear, is not to be

too lightly rated ; for if thefe graces fhould be
clofely analyfed and obferved, it will be found that
the appofite and the truthful are their prevailing
elements, and the fource alike of their beauty,
character, and moral worth.

It may furprife fome readers to fpeak of the
moral worth of mere works of tafte ; it will furprife them yet more to affert the immoral tendency
of productions groffly deficient in this quality. It
feems, indeed, to be very generally unfufpected,
that weak, prefumptuous, and foolifh writings, and
fuch as are loaded with fpurious ornament, or filled
with falfe conclufions, are actually demoralizing in
their effects upon fociety ; that they gradually, but
furely, deprave the moral fenfe, as well as darken
the underftanding ; that too frequently they are
the fource of error and confufion, in regard to fome
of the authoritative doctrines and duties of our
fphere. Yet, as a fact, the alliance of falfe tafte
and unfixed principles is very notable in the popular literature of our day. Efpecially is this to be
obferved in the tendency to indulge in factitious
fentiment, or in bold, unwarranted, and profane
analogies,—in the difpofition to remove ancient
landmarks, and to confound important diftinctions.
In thefe refpects the caufe of virtue and religion is
often ferioufly betrayed by its profeffed fervants.
While infidelity—at leaft in fome quarters—is
fmitten with a fatal love of truth, with a fpirit of
candour, diligence, and ftrict inquiry ; and is thus
induced to bring its monftrous features to the light,
and fcare thereby both wife and fimple from its

embrace; irreligion, on the other hand, is foftered and encouraged by loofe ftatements and florid pictures proceeding from the hands of nominally Chriftian men. It is well that we fhould underftand the real danger of our literature; that, namely, wherein its worft character begins, and which is moft fwift, though moft infidious, in its advances. There is little to be dreaded from the purfuits of fcientific men, foberly and fairly conducted, nor from their conclufions, duly weighed and openly ftated, even when thefe men may be fufpected of no love for truth beyond its material manifeftations. But much evil is to be apprehended, and, indeed, is daily witneffed, from loofe and paffionate appeals to the imagination and affections; from a ftyle which never deviates from the falfe heroic pitch, leaping from one pit of bathos to another; from a criticifm which runs riot among follies it was invented to reftrain, which knows neither difcrimination nor temper, which deals out hafty and wholefale meafures of admiration and difguft, which confounds human genius with divine infpiration, and brackets the all-unequal names of holy Prophets and profane and faithlefs poets.

The evils we affert and deplore may commonly be traced (as will prefently be fhown) to glaring incapacity and prefumption in the clafs of writers we refer to; but they are ferioufly aggravated by want of common faithfulnefs and care in the difcharge of ferious duties. The lack of diligent fidelity is productive of great mifchief in any calling in which man may engage. Even a fingle fault is never isolated in its character, but is propagated in a thousand sad results. The neglect of any duty, the moft private and perfonal,—the committal of a wrong in any fphere, the moft limited and tempo-rary,—is fraught with evils which reach far beyond both our eftimation and control ; and only that the providence and grace of God are continually counteracting this fatal pronenefs of evil to extend and multiply itfelf, we fhould fee fuch effects fpringing up from our daily acts of thoughtleffnefs, frivolity, and pride, as we now affociate only with crimes of the blackeft hue. But evil is not lefs manifeftly evil becaufe of this benignant law. Its effects ftill extend themfelves to the third and fourth generation. The fpoken lie, the momen-tary fneer, are neither flight nor tranfient in their influence ; they re-appear and are re-echoed upon the lips of children's children. But in written books falfehood has a charter and dominion ftill more hoftile to the interefts and authority of truth. And literary falfehood is pernicious, not in propor-tion to its magnitude or malice, but to its unfuf-pected character, to its alliance with the femblance of fome, and the reality of other, virtues, to its appeal to the vain imaginations and idle prejudices of the reader. Beginning in the thoughtlefs mif-ufe of words, it may end in the confufion of all moral truth. The fteps of this declenfion may be diftinctly traced. Extravagant affertion always involves fome departure from ftrict rectitude, as well as from the rules of tafte. Unwarrantable praife or cenfure is mifleading from a fimilar excefs.

Even the mifemployment of a word may ferioufly affect the judgment of a reader in reference to fome important principle ; may confound diftinctions neceffary to be duly kept in view, or infenfibly create a prejudice the moft lafting and unjuft. It will, therefore, commonly happen, that the lofs of time incurred, and the vacuity or diffipation of mind induced, will be among the lighteft evils of inferior literature ; falfe opinions and fatal preferences are heedlefly engendered ; the habit of intellectual and moral difcipline is loft in the craving after pernicious ftimulus ; and an unconquerable diftafte for chafte and thoughtful compofition cuts off the very hope of future elevation or improvement. And hence we may learn the value, above all natural gifts and all external acquirements, of that careful, diligent, and confcientious fpirit of authorfhip which loves truth for its own fake,—truth in fubftance, in tone, in detail, in the lighteft word,—and fees no merit in the moft ingenious and attractive paradox.

The theme opened up to us by thefe reflections is of no fmall extent ; but, in the few pages allotted to this article, we can deal with it only in one department. We fhall proceed to fpeak, then, of the moft prevalent and injurious of thefe exifting evils. Some nuifances there are which cry out for immediate abatement, and this is one of them. We hold that both the manifeft deterioration of the public tafte, and the threatening confufion of moral truth, are mainly due to the example and encouragement of our popular critics and fine writers; and of thefe the moft notorious offender is Mr. George Gilfillan.

Many reafons concur to fix our choice upon the writings of this gentleman, and to juftify the free handling we propofe to give them. The popularity of their author we naturally infer, both from the frequency with which his name is quoted in the provincial newfpapers, and the fact that one of his works has been encouraged into a third feries, and another into a third edition. This popularity among a large clafs of readers involves no fmall amount of influence, and no light meafure of refponfibility. But Mr. Gilfillan has a further claim upon our attention. In the pages of no other living writer, at leaft of equal reputation, could we find fo many prime examples of fo many literary faults. He reprefents very fairly and fully one confiderable fection of the prefs, with its coarfe attractions and many blemifhes and imperfections; and we are not furprifed to learn from himfelf, that he contributes largely to four or five of the popular ferials of the day. He will, no doubt, be flattered to learn that traces of his " dafhing" hand are very vifible on their pages; for there he leaves his mark in unmiftakable characters.

We do not fcruple at the utmoft freedom in dealing with the public character of Mr. Gilfillan. His own practice would releafe us from any great reftraint of delicacy, and, indeed, would juftify us in a degree of licence which we decline to ufe. To the judgment of a ftrict and candid criticifm, he is particularly open. He cannot plead youth

in bar of juſt ſeverity, ſince we learn from his own
pages that it is full twenty years ſince he attained
the age of manhood. He cannot plead inexperience, ſince he is a voluminous and inceſſant
writer; and the volume now before us is a third
ſeries of literary verdicts deliberately collected and
re-iſſued to the world. He cannot plead modeſty
of pretenſion, or a deſire to ſhun the obſervation
of the public; for the ſame volume exhibits him
in the character of a judge, claiming a wide and
comprehenſive juriſdiction,—a critic of men and
affairs as well as of books and authors,—a critic of
critics, challenging the judgments of ſuch men as
Macaulay and Hallam, and approving or condemn-
ing, by his own ſtandard, the weights and meaſures
long current in the world of criticiſm.

Conſidering our own poſition, we are not likely
to ſet up too high a ſtandard of critical excellence,
or to demand perfection from Mr. Gilfillan in the
exerciſe of the functions he has aſſumed. We
have no idea, for inſtance, that the talents of a
critic muſt needs emulate the genius of his author;
and, indeed, this is one of the very grounds of our
complaint againſt Mr. Gilfillan. Under an exaggerated notion of the ſympathy exiſting between
a genial critic and a great orator or poet, he
abſolutely ſeems to run a race with them, and to
diſpute their prize. This is not a mere occaſional
ſally of our critic; it is very deliberately defended,
as well as uniformly practiſed, by him. He
actually ſays, in ſo many words, " Every criticiſm
on a true poem ſhould be itſelf a poem." We

shall prefently fee what ftrange follies he is betrayed into by thefe fudden and unchecked im-
pulfes of admiration.

We may afk, in paffing, what is the value of
this "genial criticifm?" Surely, as criticifm, it is
of the leaft poffible fignificance or value. There
are cafes, it is readily granted, in which the abfence of a certain fympathy with the loftieft mood
and the moft delicate fancies of genius, is a dif-
qualification for the critical office, at leaft in fo far
as thefe cafes are concerned. But every critic is
not called, nor is any frequently, to give a public
eftimate of thefe high and peculiar monuments of
greatnefs; and even when this qualification is
plainly defiderated, the judgment pronounced will
not greatly err, if formed according to recognized
and important principles. An example may ferve
to make our meaning clear. Dr. Johnfon furnifhes, in his own character, a ftriking inftance of
defective fympathy; but his writings are no lefs
ftriking fpecimens of mafterly criticifm. He had
no very delicate perception of the refined and
beautiful,—no ear for the moft delicious fnatches
of poetic mufic. His limited tafte permitted him
only partially to appreciate the airy fancies of a
Collins, or the fuperb imagination of a Gray. The
elements of Milton's minor poetry were too fubtle,
and their combination too exquifite, to fenfibly
affect his groffer organization, or find an index of
fufficient delicacy in that coloffal mind. Yet even
to thefe he did no pofitive injuftice; of fome of
them he has faid finer things than their moft paf-

fionate admirers.   In all the other countlefs fubjects fubmitted to his difcriminating power, he
ftands confeffedly the firft of critics.   And why
fo ?   Simply becaufe the moft neceffary and
valuable qualities of the critic were poffeffed by
him in plenitude and perfection.   For thefe qualities, be it remembered, are not rightly concerned
with the rareft individual beauties of authorfhip.
When an orator or poet " fnatches a grace beyond
the reach of art," the critic may duly point it out,
and, if need be, defend this occafional exercife of
the prerogative of genius ; but to the *art* his duty
is for the moft part properly reftricted, and under
its generous laws he is to fee the products of the
individual mind moft happily fubdued.

The character and fphere of true criticifm will
be better underftood, if we remember that it is deductive in its origin, and difciplinary in its application.   It is *deductive* in its origin.   The higheft critics
the world has yet feen—from Ariftotle down to
Addifon and Johnfon—have all deduced the rules
of compofition, and framed its feveral ftandards,
rather from the examples of the poets than from
neceffary and abftract laws.   What the grammarian
does for ordinary language, that the critic performs
in refpect to the more exalted language of the
mufe.   Ariftotle himfelf is the fervant rather than
the Procruftean tyrant of the fons of genius ; for
thefe are a fountain of law unto themfelves ; and it
was the humbler duty of the Stagyrite to tranflate
the art of Homer into axioms and rules of fcience,
and to publifh them as the authorized grammar of

poetry thenceforth. And if any demur to this re-
ftriction, and complain that the chartered rights of
genius are fo confined or forfeited, we beg them to
confider that the grammar of poetry is not only
taken from the mafters of fong themfelves, and is
therefore fubftantially and perpetually correct, but
that, like other grammars, it is capable of large ad-
ditions and improvements from time to time; that,
as frefh examples of the language of the mufe are
fuggefted and given off by the deeper and wider
experience of humanity, the vocabulary and theory
of the critic alfo will expand, and find new illuftrations to widen and confirm its ancient laws. So
we find it in the hiftory of literature : criticifm has
followed in the wake of the advancing arts, if at a
becoming diftance, yet with equal fteps. The
great principles of criticifm, like thofe of univerfal
grammar, are the fame in every tongue, and are
applicable through all time to works in poetry,
eloquence, hiftory, or the fine arts ; and if it required the genius of an Ariftotle to formulate thefe
principles in the beginning, it is competent to a
Wilfon or a Dallas to carry them further towards
perfection, and give to his *theoria* nobler degrees
of beauty, majefty, and ftrength.

But for all practical purpofes, criticifm muft be
confidered as one of the applied arts ; and, in this
character, its action is ftrictly *difciplinary.* To
conferve the purity of language, and maintain the
dignity of letters ; to reftrain the exceffes of youthful genius, and to point out the models of trueft
excellence ; to fupply the defects, and counteract

the biafes of **partial education ;** to encourage noble
effort ; to reprove unworthy affectation ; to warn
againft the indulgence of a luxuriant fancy, and to
cherifh the exercife of fober thought as the bafis of
every genuine performance,—thefe are, in brief,
the duties to be confcientioufly **fulfilled.** For their
adequate difcharge is demanded, no **doubt,** fome
natural advantage,—fomething akin to that **excel-**
lence which the critic is to promote and keep ever
before him ; for how fhall he venture publicly to
approve and crown what he does not confcioufly
or well appreciate ? But the qualities moft effential **are** good judgment and **cultivated** tafte,—a
power of difcrimination which **refides in** a ftrong
native underftanding, **when** developed by careful
exercife, and furnifhed with confiderable knowledge. We would not overftate the accomplifhments neceffary for the due performance of literary
cenforfhip in this age of vaft literary productivenefs.
Happily **they** are not many, nor, for the moft part,
fuch as **may not,** with diligence, be almoft in-
definitely improved. They are nearly all included
in a loving intimacy with the elder mafters of com-
pofition, combined with a readinefs to greet the
ancient **law in** its neweft manifeftation, and to recognize both variety and degrees of excellence in
the kingdom **of** mind. Perhaps only the felf-
affertion of ignorance and intolerance are abfolute
difqualifications. **Our** profeffional critics form
now a large and influential body ; but they have
no legiflative function. They are fimply an
organized police, bound to maintain order and

decorum in the republic of letters ; or, at the moft, they are its magiftrates, fet " for the punifhment of evil-doers, and the praife of them that do well." It is not neceffary for them to difcufs the merits of the laws which they adminifter ; it is ftill more unfeemly to promulge and act upon *impromptu* canons of their own.

The leffon we would draw from thefe confiderations fhall be very fimply ftated. While the pofitive merits of a critic may be of almoft any quality and degree, there are certain negative ones which are indifpenfable. It is the leaft we can expect from a literary cenfor, that he fhould not himfelf infringe the literary proprieties. If he do not fenfibly elevate, he muft not actually corrupt, the public tafte. Any wanton experiments upon language, any unfeemly affectation or difplay, any indulgence of tawdry rhetoric or foolifh extravagance of tone, is not only a dereliction of private duty, but a betrayal of the public intereft. Above all, or next only to that honefty of intention which we will affume to influence, in fome meafure, the moft thoughtlefs and incapable, it is neceffary that no infirmity of temper fhould interfere with the deliberate mood of juftice, or fubftitute the language of coarfe perfonal invective for that of critical difpleafure.

Now all thefe blemifhes are very prominent in the pages of Mr. Gilfillan. In effect, if not in intention, he is a corrupter and a mifleader of youth. He is not free from faults of language which would difgrace the themes of a third-clafs school-boy. His ſtyle is always looſe, and very often turgid; epithets the leaſt appropriate are choſen only for their ſuppoſed effectiveneſs, and yoked together without parity or propriety of any kind. His raſhneſs hurries him into aſſertions of the wildeſt nature, and his freedom borders cloſely upon profanity. And, as if theſe were ſo many virtues which make our author impatient of infe-rior merit, and give to him an unuſual licence in the language of reproach, he ſcolds in good ſet terms, and in a ſtyle which lacks only diſcrimination and decency to make it poſitively ſevere.

The characteriſtic laſt mentioned ſhall be firſt exemplified. Mr. Neale, a clergyman of the Church of England, with ſtrong Anglican preju-dices, undertakes to alter and adapt the " Pilgrim's Progreſs " for the uſe of children in the Engliſh Church. The deſign was fooliſh in the extreme, but not diſhoneſt. Neither the fame nor the in-fluence of Bunyan is at this time of day at the mercy of either Jeſuit or Tractarian. His book is ſo thoroughly imbued with the ſpirit of a true evangeliſt, that it defies perverſion. The editor of ſome particular reprint may mar its literary beauties, and even injure its ſcriptural ſimplicity; but the " improver " muſt be anſwerable for this diſtortion, and enough of the original will doubt-leſs remain to outweigh and counteract its faults. We dare not ſay the attempt was really diſhoneſt, becauſe conſcientious men have frequently felt juſtified in exerciſing a ſimilar liberty, though, as we think, generally with much higher wiſdom and

far truer tafte.   In noticing this book, Mr. Gilfillan lofes all difcretion, when perhaps he required
it moft.   A judicious eftimate of the folly involved
in the defign, and committed in the execution, of
this book, with a firm and appropriate reproof
adminiftered to the prefumptuous editor, would
have been a very feafonable fervice to the reading
world, and not unlikely to deter other zealots from a
like offence.   But there is no element of perfuafion in the ftyle which Mr. Gilfillan has adopted.
We have as little tafte for Mr. Neale's improvement of Bunyan as Mr. Gilfillan himfelf ; but why
fhould our critic fubftitute perfonal abufe for definite expofure ?   There is, furely, no more wit than
charity in his exclamation : " O, J. M. Neale !
thou miferable ninny, and bigot of the firft magnitude !"   Such a pitiful want of temper was never
aggravated by fuch a plentiful lack of tafte.   Even
the hafte and warmth of compofition can never
juftify the ufe of fuch unworthy language ; but
what muft we think of the judgment which deliberately transfers it from the fwift oblivion of a
popular Scottifh ferial to the region of ferene and
fettled literature ?   If Mr. Gilfillan could have
fhown his author to be a ninny and a bigot, he
might have kept clean lips, and fpared to infult
the criminal whom it was his duty only to convict.

   This is not an occafional fault of Mr. Gilfillan.
None of his faults, indeed, are fo.   They are repeated with tirefome iteration ; and there is as
little variety in his actual blemifhes as in his intended beauties.   So thickly do thefe abufive epithets

occur in Mr. Gilfillan's **pages,** that we grow
accuſtomed, if not reconciled, to them.   But
ſometimes a background of charming delicacy brings
out this favourite figure into ſtrong relief.   On the
very page, for inſtance, where he rebukes a northern
journaliſt for calling the late Mr. Hazlitt " an aſs,"
he pronounces a certain living **critic, whom he**
points out by no uncertain name, to be an " ape
of the firſt magnitude !"

When Mr. Gilfillan's page is unuſually free
from theſe rhetorical diſplays, we are admitted to
a glimpſe of his ordinary **ſtyle,** forming the back-
ground of theſe ſtriking **pictures.**   This level compoſition, as it comparatively is, **may be** fairly deſcribed as frivolous in **ſubſtance, and very looſe** and
feeble in expreſſion.   What makes this **wretched**
manufacture more contemptible, is the contraſted
dignity of his pretended theme.   We have, **for**
example, a ſeries of papers under the title of " A
Conſtellation of Sacred Authors."   It is rather,
however, as ſacred *orators* that Mr. Gilfillan treats
Chalmers, and Hall, and Irving, although, by
ſelecting this method, he is able to furniſh only
ſecond-hand deſcriptions.   It is queſtionable, we
have always thought, how far the characteriſtic
and comparative merits of great pulpit celebrities,
even when they have departed from us, may be
canvaſſed with advantage and propriety.   But it is
certain that **Mr.** Gilfillan's treatment of theſe
ſubjects is open to the ſtrongeſt objections.   His
lighteſt fault is trivial goſſiping, which can have
no rational bearing on the theme propoſed.   A

fober eftimate of the minifterial gifts of the orator,
and of the peculiar manner of their development
and exercife, is the moft removed from the range
of our critic's power; but it is alfo that which he
is leaft defirous to fupply. The paper on " Robert
Hall" may be inftanced as in ftriking contraft
with the dignity and power of that great man's
genius; it is weak and unworthy to the laft degree.
Of the truth of this cenfure we will enable the
reader to judge for himfelf. After affuring us that
the effay is meant as a " calm and comprehenfive
view" of Mr. Hall's " real characteriftics, both in
point of merit, of fault, and of fimple deficiency,"
our critic proceeds in the manner following :—

" *We labour, like all critics who have never
feen their author, under confiderable difadvantages.
' Knowledge is power.' Still more, craving Lord
Bacon's pardon, vifion is power. Cæfar faid a
fimilar thing when he wrote, '* Vidi, vici.*' To fee
is to conquer, if you happen to have the faculty of
clear, full, conclufive fight. In other cafes, the fight
of a man whom you mifappreciate, and, though you
have eyes, cannot fee, is a curfe to your conception of
his charaEter. You look at him through a mift of
prejudice which difcolours his vifage, and even, when
it exaggerates, diftorts his ftature. Far otherwife
with the prepared, yet unprepoffeffed, look of intelligent love.*"

Very curious is the jumble of ideas in this fhort
paffage. No man accuftomed to accuracy of

thought or language could have fo hopelefsly confounded ordinary fight with mental appreciation.
And then, what an improvement of Lord Bacon's
apophthegm ! what an interpretation of Cæfar's
famous boaft ! That Mr. Gilfillan fhould pronounce " the look of intelligent love" to be " prepared," yet at the fame time " unprepofleffed," is
an attempt at exquifite refinement which we
cannot recommend him to repeat : his *forte* is
quite in the oppofite direction. After a full page
of this material, in which our critic's entanglement
is every moment frightfully increafed, a fudden
effort brings him to his immediate theme ; and the
character of Robert Hall is fet forth in this edifying manner :—

" *We have met with fome of thofe who have feen
and heard him talk and preach, and their accounts
have coincided in this,—that he was more powerful
in the parlour than in the pulpit. He was more at
eafe in the former. He had his pipe in his mouth,
his tea-pot befide him, eager ears liftening to catch
his every whifper, bright eyes raining influence on
him; and under thefe various excitements he was
fure to fhine. His fpirits rofe, his wit flafhed, his
keen and pointed fentences thickened, and his audience
began to imagine him a Baptift Burke or a Johnfon
Redivivus, and to wifh that Bofwell were to undergo
a refurrection too. In thefe evening parties he
appeared, we fufpect, to greater advantage than in
the mornings, when Minifters from all quarters
called to fee the lion of Leicefter, and tried to tempt*

him to roar by such questions as, 'Whether do you think, Mr. Hall, Cicero or Demosthenes the greater orator?' 'Was Burke the author of Junius?' 'Whether is Bentham or Wilberforce the leading spirit of the age?' &c. &c. How Hall kept his gravity or his temper under such a fire of queries, not to speak of the smoke of the half-putrid incense amid which it came forth, we cannot tell. He was, however, although a vehement and irritable, a very polite, man; and, like Dr. Johnson, he 'loved to fold his legs, and have his talk out.' Many of his visitors, too, were really distinguished men, and were sure, when they returned home, to circulate his repartees, and spread abroad his fame. Hence, even in the forenoons, he sometimes said brilliant things, many of which have been diligently collected by the late excellent Dr. Balmer and others, and are to be found in his Memoirs."

We have no space for further extract of this sort; but we can assure the reader that there is nothing better than this foolish and unprofitable gossip in Mr. Gilfillan's " clear and comprehensive view" of Robert Hall. Equally void of useful knowledge and just discrimination are the essays on Dr. Chalmers and Edward Irving. They only derive the most transient interest from the misappropriation of these great names, which run the greatest risk of disenchantment from such popular degradation and abuse. Let the reader turn to the flippant article on Dr. Winter Hamilton, and then he may be prepared for the qualifications of a critic who could write, and print, and publiſh, and re-publiſh an eſtimate of miniſterial character, commencing in the loweſt pot-houſe ſtyle.

We cannot pretend to challenge all the queſtionable verdicts of this book, nor to point out a tithe of its literary faults; and having little hope of Mr. Gilfillan's improvement, we ſhall glance at ſome of his more prominent peculiarities rather with a view to the reader's profit than his own. If we ſhould not be able to preſerve throughout a tone of ſerious remonſtrance, the fault will not be ours; and, in the end, we will endeavour to make ſome amends by eliciting the moral of the whole.

Let us inſtance, in the firſt place, our author's ſtyle of panegyric. Marked though it is by conſiderable novelty and boldneſs, we cannot bring ourſelves to reliſh it. Always profuſe, it is often ſtrangely miſapplied, and much too frequently profane. Other critics think it needful to give praiſe in detail, meaſure, and proportion; but Mr. Gilfillan finds it more convenient to throw it by the lump, and often it falls upon the wrong perſon, and always it alights with damaging effect. Modeſt, reputable men, who naturally ſhrink from being forced into compariſon with famous, lofty, and even ſacred worthies, may well fear to attract the admiration of our author. Mr. Iſaac Taylor is here pronounced " a Chriſtian Coloſſus;" Edward Irving, a " Titan among Titans, a Boanerges among the Sons of Thunder." When the latter preaches in the Caledonian chapel, " it is Iſaiah or Ezekiel over again, uttering their ſtern yet

muſical and poetic burdens." The imagery and
language of the former is nothing leſs than " barbaric pearl and gold." " Bulwer has made out
his claim to be the Milton of noveliſts." Diſraeli
" bears a ſtriking reſemblance to Bonaparte."
The poem of " Balder" is " a wilderneſs of
thought,—a ſea of towering imagery and paſſion."
There is much more of the ſame diſcriminating
kind, as we ſhall preſently diſcover. In the meantime we are ſpared the trouble of characterizing
this ſtyle of panegyric by our author himſelf, who,
in two or three ſentences of this volume, gene-
rouſly gives us the key to all the reſt. Thus we
read, (on page 237,) " Falſe or ignorant panegyric
is eaſily detected. *It is clumſy, careleſs, and fulſome ;*
it often praiſes writers for qualities they poſſeſs **not***,*
or it ſingles out their faults for beauties, or, by **over-**
doing, overleaps itſelf, **and falls on the other ſide***."*
This is ſaid by our author **without a** remorſeful
twinge,—with all the oblivious calmneſs of a lucid
interval.

But Mr. Gilfillan tells us, " he is nothing if
not critical." Unfortunately he cannot qualify
his wholeſale adulation without ſtultifying himſelf.
In one little ſentence he will ſnatch back all the
laboured and pompous praiſe he has beſtowed,
and ſlap the receiver's face into the bargain. Thus,
after having encouraged one of our young poets
with outrageous eulogy, he quietly lodges this
little ſtone in the other pocket : " Many of his
paſſages would be greatly improved by leaving out
every third line." If this cenſure be honeſt, what

muſt be the value of the praiſe that went before ?
The faɛt, of courſe, is, that the poet did not merit
either one or the other; and we hope he may be
able to deſpiſe them both.

Of epithet and expletive there is no lack in
Mr. Gilfillan's page. Indeed, it is here more
plentiful than choice, and more prominent by far
than pleaſing. It would be very idle, however, to
regret the abſence of that meaſured nice propriety
of phraſe—the warp of language fixing the woof
of thought—which is the inwoven and enduring
charm of every literary fabric. It is far more
natural, under the circumſtances, to wiſh that our
critic's ſingle epithets were a trifle more appropriate, and that their combinations did not utterly
defy appreciation. We can only afford to give a
ſolitary ſpecimen of this peculiarity : it muſt therefore be one of the compound kind, and uſeful as
a Chineſe puzzle on a winter's evening. Who,
then, but Mr. Gilfillan could have found terms to
praiſe " the *glowingly acute, gorgeouſly clear*, and
dazzlingly deep criticiſms of poor Hazlitt ?" The
reader who derives from this deſcription any definite idea of Mr. Hazlitt's literary charaɛter, is
worth knowing; and we ſhould be proud to make
his acquaintance.

The language of illuſtration and metaphor forms
a ſtill larger element in our author's compoſition.
Perhaps his particular admirers—and poſſibly the
hero himſelf, in an unguarded moment of ſelf-
dalliance—would ſay his ſtrength reſides in theſe
abundant flowers of ſpeech, as Samſon's in his

profuſe and curling locks. We do him then peculiar juſtice in pointing attention to a number of
theſe tropes.

So incongruous are our author's figures—ſo
frequently and unaccountably changed in the courſe
of a ſingle ſentence—that when a really juſt reflection eſcapes him, it is either diſtorted or deſ-
troyed by the very language intended to give it
force. The following is a ſtriking inſtance of this
fault :—

" *For too often we believe that high genius is a
myſtery and a terror to itſelf; that it communicates
with the demoniac mines of ſulphur as well as the
divine ſources; and that only God's grace can determine to which of theſe it is to be permanently connected; and that* only the ſtern alembic of death
can ſettle the queſtion, to which it has on the whole
turned, whether it has really been the radiant angel
or the diſguiſed fiend."

We are puzzled to conceive how an author ſo
practiſed as Mr. Gilfillan could have deliberately
written the laſt clauſe of this ſentence ; though
indeed we have no occaſion to be ſurpriſed at
anything of the ſort. The " ſtern alembic" is
poſitively a new idea. Yet it is not difficult to
match the foregoing extract by applying to the
ſame ſource :—

" *If Mr. Maſſey comes* (*as we truſt he ſhall*) *to
a true belief, it will corroborate him for every trial*

and every fad internal and external experience ; **and**
he will ftand like **an Atlas** above the ruins of a
world,—calm, firm, penfive, but preffing forwards
and looking on high."

The allufion to Atlas is here peculiarly unfortunate, **as** that mythological perfonage is fuppofed
to have ftood *below* a world which **was** *not* in ruins,
and in an attitude quite inconfiftent with " looking
on high ;" and even 'were it otherwife, the pofition of " ftanding, calm and firm," fomewhat
militates againft the notion of his " preffing forwards." A fimile is commonly employed to affift
our realization of fome thought ; but it is no wonder that the very oppofite effect attends one fo ill
chofen as the above.   Indeed, we muft abfolutely
forget it, before we can appreciate the literal
meaning of our author.   The reflection is good ;
but the figure is a nuifance and a blot.   The fame
remark applies to the following :—

" *Byron* **was** *miferable* *becaufe he felt himfelf an
orphan, a* funbeam cut off from HIS fource, *without
hope and without God in the world.*"

Any one but Mr. Gilfillan would infallibly have
put his pen through the middle claufe of this hafty
and ill-confidered fentence : **though** ftill trite, it
would have been at leaft tolerable.   But it never
occurs to our author, **that** a miferable funbeam,
deftitute of hope and of God, is a very abfurd and
incongruous idea ; and he gathers it accordingly
into his book of **many** beauties.

Our readers will probably be gratified to hear
Mr. Gilfillan's "judgment" on Milton and Shakefpeare. The oracular volume from which we
have already learnt fo much, is not filent here.
Of Milton, indeed, we have no formal or deliberate
eftimate ; but his genius, character, and works,
are made to do various duty in ifolated fentences
throughout the book, furnifhing eafy ready-made
comparifons of intellectual and moral greatnefs.
In thefe allufive paffages all the diftinctive features
of the poet's character are very innocently forgotten,
and prophecies delivered by divine infpiration are
coupled with poems fuggefted only by human
fancy. Thus, in the paper on Æfchylus, we read
of " yet loftier regions, fuch as Job, Ifaiah, and
the Paradife Loft." Between this latter work
and the Prometheus, we have an elaborate parallel,
of which, however, it will probably fuffice to quote
the following fentences :—

" *It was comparatively eafy for Æfchylus to enlift
our fympathies for Prometheus, if once he were reprefented good and injured. But firft to reprefent
Satan as guilty ; again to wring a confeffion of this
from his own lips ; and yet, thirdly, to teach us to
admire, refpect, pity, and almoft love him all the
while, was a problem which only a Milton was able
either to ftate or to folve.*"

If this was Milton's problem,—to make us refpect and almoft love the Prince of Darknefs,—he
has, in our opinion, very happily failed : were it

otherwife, our refpect for the author would be inverfely proportioned to that which his hero was permitted to infpire. But Mr. Gilfillan has fallen into a curious miftake. He has evidently in this, and apparently in fome other points, confounded the Satan of Milton's poem with the Satan of Mr. Robert Montgomery,—two characters that are effentially different. The Satan of Mr. Montgomery exhibits fuch candour, penitence, and fcorn of evil habits, that it is impoffible *not* to " refpect and almoft love him."

From the clofing article of this interefting volume, we felect a paffage on " the poet of all time." It may fitly pair off with that juft quoted on his great fucceffor :—

" *Shakefpeare's wit and humour are bound to-gether in general by the amiable band of good-nature. What a contraft to Swift! He loathes; Shake-fpeare, at the worft, hates. His is the flavering and ferocious ire of a maniac; Shakefpeare's, that of a man. Swift broods, like their fhadow, over the feftering fores and the moral ulcers of mankind; Shakefpeare touches them with a ray of poetry, which beautifies if it cannot heal. ' Gulliver' is the day-book of a fiend; ' Timon' is the magnificent outbreak of an injured angel. His wit, how fertile, quick, forgetive! Congreve and Sheridan are poor and forced in the comparifon. How long they ufed to fit hatching fome clever conceit! and what a cackling they made when it had chipped the fhell! Shake-fpeare threw forth a Mercutio or a Falftaff at once,*

*each embodying in himself a world of laughter, and
there an end. His humour, how broad, rich, subtle,
powerful, and full of genius and geniality it is!
Why, Bardolph's red nose eclipses all the dramatic
characters that have succeeded. Ancient Piftol
himself shoots down the whole of the Farquhars,
Wycherleys, Sheridans, Goldsmiths, and Colmans put
together. Dogberry is the prince of donkeys, past,
present, and to come. When shall we ever have such
another tinker as Christopher Sly? Sir Andrew
Aguecheek! the very name makes you quake with
laughter. And, like a vast sirloin of English roast
beef, rich and dripping, lies along the mighty Falstaff,
with humour oozing out of every corner and cranny
of his vast corporation."*

If the reader thinks that one perufal will fuffice
for the full appreciation of this paffage, we affure
him he is much miftaken. The effect of a fingle
reading is only to confound ; but a repetition will
infallibly add wonder to his confufion, till, loft in
fucceffive objects of amazement, confufion once
more takes the place of wonder. Collecting our
fcattered fenfes, we may now attempt to point out
fome of the curiofities of this paragraph of errors.
Not one fentence of the whole is left undiftin-
guifhed either by obfcurity, abfurdity, or falfehood.
Relatives are hopelefsly divided from their antece-
dents ; words chofen for their force, and mutually
confronted, are made to exchange meanings, and
fo become ridiculous by emphafis ; while figures
the moft incongruous are recklefsly mixed up with

facts the moſt literal. **We** are not ſurpriſed to read
of " the ſlavering and ferocious ire of a maniac ; "
but quite new to us is " that **of** a man." We had
ſuppoſed that loathing was ſometimes pardonable,
and hatred never ; but it ſeems that **while Swift**
loathes, Shakeſpeare " *only* hates." The inſtinctive ſenſibility of virtue is given **to the gloomy**
Iriſh Dean ; the radical and unamiable **vice is**
charged upon our "winſome Willie." In his choice
of ſimiles our critic is equally felicitous. Swift
broods over an ulcer like **its** ſhadow ! but Shakeſpeare beautifies it by **a ray of poetry** ! We do not
expect—and hardly wiſh—to ſee the match for
that compariſon. Its **effect is to make** us incon-
tinently ſhut **our eyes and hold our breath.** The
remaining curioſities of this paſſage **rather puzzle**
than ſurpriſe us. Why is Gulliver a " book," and
Timon only an " outbreak ? " Then, immediately
following, whoſe " wit " is ſo " forgetive ? " And,
not to be too troubleſome, what *is* " forgetive
wit ? " Perhaps it is that ſort which makes Ancient Piſtol " *ſhoot* down" the whole **of** the
Farquhars, Wycherleys, &c. The verdict upon
honeſt Dogberry moſt readers will diſpute, thinking **the** author has waived too readily his own pretenſions. Only the coarſe compariſon of Falſtaff
has the tame diſtinction of being literal and obvious
without abſurdity.

A critic like our author **is** naturally ſevere upon
his imbecile contemporaries. When Mr. Hallam
diſcourſes about poetry, **Mr.** Gilfillan is " reminded
of a blind man diſcourſing on the rainbow;" and

complacently remarks, " The power of criticizing
is as completely denied him as is a fixth fenfe ; and
worfe, he is not confcious of the want." In
another precious morfel, we learn that " Hallam is
feldom unduly minute, never unfair, and rarely one-
fided : his want is fimply that of the warm infight
which ' loofens the bands of the Orions' of poetry,
and gives a fwift folution to all its fplendid problems."
The misfortune of Mr. Hallam is, that he does
not belong to the " impulfive" fchool of criticifm ;
our author, therefore, writes him down "mechanical." His paper on Ariofto is pronounced " cold
and creeping ;" and here we may remark, that
Mr. Gilfillan evidently employs thefe words as
fynonymous and interchangeable. If you are clear
you are fo cold ! If temperate, you muft needs
be very tame. The truth is, Mr. Gilfillan has
acquired a morbid love for the errors of genius ;
and this paffion hurries him fo far, that not only
does he defend and juftify the groffeft blemifhes
he can difcover, but very confiftently carries his
principles into practice, and makes a merit of
imitating the " glorious faults" of our great writers.

We fhould be very forry to vindicate the literary
character of Henry Hallam from the cenfures of
George Gilfillan. It is not yet come to that. In
one fhort fentence,—" He has far too much tact
and knowledge to commit any grofs blunders,"—
our critic himfelf fays more for his author than we
could venture to fay for our critic. The reader
will probably take our word for it, that Mr. Hal-

lam's paper on the " Paradife Loft" contains no fuch *morceau* as that with which we have prefented him from Mr. Gilfillan's page.

If Mr. Hallam is held thus lightly in our author's judgment and efteem, the writings of Mr. Macaulay appear to excite only his utmoft anger and difdain. There is fomething about them which he can neither forget nor forgive. Often trampled down by his fcorn, they are fure prefently to rife in his face, and irritate him beyond endurance. This reftlefs and recurring enmity is, perhaps, not difficult to be underftood. The very exiftence of fuch a critic as Mr. Macaulay—not to mention his popularity and influence—is a perpetual offence to fuch a writer as Mr. Gilfillan ; a filent, but fignificant, reproach. Our author feels that " his genius is rebuked" by the mafter of a ftyle diftinguifhed for accuracy, eafe, and fulnefs, at once fo dignified and fo correct ; and more efpecially as he is unable to taunt the Effayift with facrificing beauty to correctnefs, or with being cold, uninterefting, or conventional, in deference to literary orthodoxy. No doubt it is very irritating to obferve, beyond the poffibility of doubt or of denial, that a writer fo eminently " correct" is, at the fame time, very far removed from " creeping." To be judicious, temperate, and truftworthy, yet neither voted dull, nor abandoned by the younger fpirits, nor fhelved in a dufty corner of the reference-library ; to be ornate, as well as accurate, in compofition ; to infpire enthufiafm, yet bear the ftricteft fcrutiny ; to fuffer the reſtraints of grammar and propriety, yet achieve a proud, and even popular, ſucceſs,—all this is unpardonable vice in Mr. Macaulay, and more than Mr. Gilfillan can well bear. Our author wonders that ſuch "abject traſh" (theſe are his words) ſhould "gain unchallenged acceptance, and require his humble pen to daſh it into expoſure and contempt." And "daſh it" accordingly he does. In the firſt place, we are invited to the rehearſal of a literary parallel, inſtituted by our critic, between the characters of Burke and Macaulay. We need hardly ſay, that this compariſon is not more odious than gratuitous. Some points of it are true, but not pertinent; while much the greater part is both impertinent and untrue. The following ſentences are too characteriſtic, at leaſt of their inditer, to be paſſed unquoted :—

"*Burke's digreſſions are thoſe of uncontrollable power, wantoning in its ſtrength; Macaulay's are thoſe of deliberate purpoſe and elaborate effort, to relieve and make its byways increaſe the intereſt of his highways. Burke's moſt memorable things are ſtrong, ſimple ſentences of wiſdom, or epithets, each carrying a queſtion on its point, or burning coals from his flaming genius; Macaulay's are chiefly happy illuſtrations, or verbal antitheſes, or clever alliterations. Macaulay often ſeems, and, we believe, is, ſincere, but he is never in earneſt; Burke, on all higher queſtions, becomes a ' burning one,'—earneſt to the brink of frenzy. . . . . Macaulay's literary enthuſiaſm has now a far and formal air,*

*it feems an old cloak of college-days worn threadbare ;
Burke's has about it a frefh and glorious glofs,—it is
the ever renewed fkin of his fpirit.   Macaulay lies
fnugly and fweetly in the penfold of a party ; Burke
is ever and anon burfting it to fragments.   Macaulay's moral indignation is too* **laboured and anti-
thetical** *to be very profound;* **Burke's makes** *his
heart palpitate, his hand clench, and his face kindle,
like that of Mofes as he came down from the
Mount.*"

Referving our remark **on** this irreverent climax,
let us call **the** attention **of the reader to** the claufe
we have diftinguifhed by **Roman type.**   When he
has fully appreciated the pretty thought that **the**
" fkin" of Mr. Burke's " fpirit" was periodically
caft, like a ferpent's flough, we have another comparifon to offer to the admirers of that ftatefman, alfo
drawn from natural hiftory, and alfo fuggefted by
the pleafant fancy of our author.   It is only a little
farther on in the volume, that Mr. Burke is defcribed as " a mental camelopard," for the fingular
reafon, that " he was patient as a camel, and as a
leopard fwift and richly fpotted."   Mr. Gilfillan
feemingly forgets, or poffibly is not aware, that the
camelopard is not a hybrid, deriving its qualities
from thefe two creatures, though his name happens
to be a compound of theirs.   The moft charitable
of natural hiftorians never afcribed patience to the
giraffe : even with reference to the camel, it is a
long exploded fuperftition, which doubtlefs was
originally due to the fact that, like ourfelves, he

ſtands in great need of that paſſive virtue, and has
abundant opportunities for bringing it to perfection.

This depreciatory parallel—for ſuch we ſuppoſe
it was intended to be—may be accepted as a
ſpecimen of Mr. Gilfillan's ſkill in a form of compoſition to which he is peculiarly partial.   We are
treated in this volume to no leſs than three in
honour of Edmund Burke,—to wit, Burke and
Macaulay, Burke and Johnſon, and Burke and
Brougham; the latter thrown off *impromptu*, and
included in a parentheſis of half a page.   Indeed,
Burke has the honour of attracting the moſt
dangerous regards of Mr. Gilfillan, who never
ſpeaks of that great man without enthuſiaſm of the
moſt rapturous and incoherent ſort. This is a very
curious and inſtructive fact ; it ſhows, not only
that love may exiſt with infinite diſparity, but that
the deepeſt admiration is not neceſſarily transforming in its character.   Our author warmly admires
the works of Edmund Burke, and writes himſelf
like—George Gilfillan.

With the organ of compariſon ſo ſtrongly developed, our critic is hardly fair in laying to Mr.
Macaulay's charge an undue fondneſs for antitheſis
and point.   It is only too evident, that he ſpares
no pains to attain the ſame dexterity, with what
ſucceſs might eaſily be ſhown. If we were inclined to follow the example of theſe authorities,
—and perhaps it is our turn,—there could not
poſſibly preſent itſelf a more favourable occaſion.
One critic handled by another, and both compared

by a third,—there is fomething unufual at leaft in
that. But we muft decline the tempting invitation,
not becaufe it is a little abfurd, as well as ungene-
rous, " to compare great things with fmall ;" for the
epic poets do it without reproach ;—but the points
of contraft exifting between the literary characters
of Mr. Macaulay and our author are too numerous,
as well as too obvious, for our rehearfal.   There
is, indeed, a more fummary method of comparifon,
in which fome characteriftic beauty or defect is made
inclufive and decifive of all the others.   Thus we
might mutually oppofe the chief faults of thefe
contending parties.   The great fault of Mr. Macaulay's ftyle is its pofitive uniformity of excellence.
Unlike every author that we know befides, Homer
himfelf included, he never nods.   So unflagging
his genius, fo fleeplefs his activity, fo prompt his
memory, fo available his learning, that the reader
gains no moment of repofe, till attention, fafcinated
fo long, fuddenly fails, and the mind runs fairly off
to find relief.   Invited to an intellectual repaft,
we have fumptuous viands in great variety and
matchlefs profufion fet before us; but one luxury
fucceeds another with fuch rapidity, that tafte has
barely time for perfect fatisfaction, and we fuddenly
quit the ftill groaning table to avoid the evils of
excefs.   This fplendid profufion is, in fome fenfe,
a fault as well as a misfortune ; for literature intended to anfwer human needs, fhould be more
nearly adapted to the character and powers of
human nature.   But we fubmit, that it is a very
different fault which Mr. Gilfillan commits, and a

very different misfortune which his readers fuffer. On his part, too, there is a ceafelefs profufion ; but it is of words inftead of thoughts, of colours inftead of images ; of errors, inanities, and abfurdities ; of great truths miferably garbled, and doubtful ones intolerably mouthed. For the mental repaft which he ferves up he has evidently rifled richer tables, gathered a mifcellaneous heap of odds and ends, fwept them into his own difh, added a copious ftream of frothy rhetoric, and whipped the whole into a towering fyllabub. Indulgence in fuch a compound can only be attended by naufea or inflation.

As it will ferve to bring us to the moft important part of our fubject, we muft take fome further freedom with Mr. Macaulay's name, while we briefly mention another exploit of our author. Mr. Gilfillan cannot reft till he has broken a lance with his "rival" in the critical arena. Challenging Mr. Macaulay's eftimate of Lord Bacon's genius and philofophy, he charges the reviewer with facrificing the character of Plato, in order the more pointedly to honour the great Englifh fage. Having picked this " pretty quarrel,"—we cannot but admire his boldnefs,—our critic at once proceeds to reconftruct the parallel, and give Plato the better half of each *antithefis.* Had our fpace permitted, we fhould have been glad to offer thefe rival compofitions to the reader in collateral columns. As this is not convenient, fo neither is it quite neceffary to an underftanding of their refpective merits. A fingle fentence, chofen in all fairnefs from either eftimate, will fuffice to indicate the character of both :—" The philofophy of Plato," fays Mr. Macaulay, "began in words, and ended in words. The philofophy of Bacon began in obfervation, and ended in acts." See now how Mr. Gilfillan turns the tables :—" Bacon cured corns, and Plato heals confciences !" It is too late to afk the reader to decide between thefe two ; for he has already done fo. If both critics facrifice a fhare of truth to the love of verbal antithefis, it is only Mr. Gilfillan who outrages tafte and judgment for the fake of a paltry alliteration. If Mr. Macaulay has fomewhat underrated the influence of Plato in the world, he has at leaft done noble juftice to the fruitful philofophy of the Englifh fage : but our author has ingenioufly contrived to wrong both worthies ; for, dealing only in extremes, he muft needs thruft them one upon either horn of his critical dilemma, and the victim of his adulation is, as ufual, the one moft deeply wronged. Moft deeply wronged, we fay, becaufe the mind revolts from an afcription of divine and faving power, even to the moft illuftrious of the heathen, and is, therefore, apt to become intolerant of his juft pretenfions.

If we trouble ourfelves or our readers further with Mr. Gilfillan's opinions upon Plato, it is only becaufe fomething more is involved than a point of literary tafte. We commenced by afferting the intimate connection between juft criticifm and moral truth, between trafhy and unworthy literature and falfehood of the moft dangerous fort. Not willing to beat the air, and have no profit for our pains, we fixed the charge of public deterioration upon a writer of no fmall pretenfions; and that charge we are bound by every proper **motive to** make good.

Mr. Gilfillan's Quixotic championfhip of Plato urges him into groffly exaggerated ftatements, both of the elevation of that philofopher's doctrine, and of the extent and value of his influence on mankind. Chriftianity is reprefented as the mere fulfilment of Platonifm: the heathen fage is placed but little lower than Chrift, and generally on a par with the Apoftle John. We are gravely informed that a combination of the philofophy of Plato, and the divine teaching and working of Jefus confti- tutes the only theology deferving the name; and that Plato's harveft lay in "the flow yield of fouls." The only apology for this language of a Chriftian minifter is a pitiful one at beft. The real meaning and tendency of the expreffions ufed are probably unfufpected by the author himfelf. He writes with an eager love of antithefis and difplay, in which all other confiderations are merged and loft. It is ufelefs, then, for this and other reafons, to point out to Mr. Gilfillan wherein confifts the error, fo vital andpervading, which disfigures his comparative eftimate of Chriftianity and Platonifm. He does not need to be told the truth, and he is incapable of improving by its repetition. It is not from a pofitive ignorance of the diftinction which it behoved him to maintain, that he has written thus defectively; but from a total incapacity of

keeping that diftinction clearly before him, and of
expreffing it in adequate and proper terms. This
is apparent from the fingular fact that, in this very
volume, the author profeffes the higheft admiration
for Mr. Henry Rogers' noble effay on Plato, and
actually quotes the beautiful paragraph in which
the character of Socrates—the model of Platonic
virtue—is fo ftrikingly contrafted with that of our
Redeemer. Thus it fortunately happens, that the
fame blundering indifcretion which threatens to
produce fo much mifchief, provides, in fome
meafure, for its own correction and rebuke.

But this is not the only inftance in which Mr.
Gilfillan is betrayed, by his befetting genius, into
deluding and unwarrantable language. If the
danger is fometimes fmall, it is only becaufe the
abfurdity is too great, or the obfcurity too denfe.
Thus, in the following fentences, the mind is rather
fhocked by the appearance of evil, than affaulted
by actual untruth. "A new poet, like a new
planet, is another proof of the continued exiftence
of the creative energy of the Father of fpirits. He
is a new meffenger and mediator between the Infinite and the race of man." The firft fentence is
nothing but a high-founding truifm ; for that only
is predicated of poet and planet, which is equally
true of oyfter and pebble. If the latter fentence
could be proved to mean anything, it would probably appear as an offence againft religion ; fo we
cling to the perfuafion of its inanity, left we fhould
be obliged to condemn it as blafphemous and profane. In like manner, when Mr. Gilfillan de-

clares that "the ftars are the developments of God's Own Head," we feel a momentary revulfion, but refuse to attribute the expreffion to any deliberate or confcious want of reverence for the Divine Majefty. It is fimply the natural refult of fo much ambition, hurry, taftelefineſs, and incapacity. But we did feel, and we do, ftrong indignation and difguſt on meeting the paffage in which our author compares the face of Mr. Burke, after fpeaking in the Houfe of Commons, to the countenance of Mofes as it fhone with reflected glory, after forty days' communion with his Maker. Anything more reprehenfible than this, conceived in worfe tafte, or uttered in more wanton defiance of propriety and truth, could not readily be found beyond the limits of the book in which it is contained. Within thofe limits it is only too often and too nearly approached.

But Mr. Gilfillan has alfo come forward as a critic of facred literature; and this circumftance calls for a few obfervations on "The Bards of the Bible," a work already praifed and popular.

As compared with that which we have juft put down, this volume is agreeable and meritorious, free from many of the author's more glaring faults, and of fufficient intereft to gratify a refpectable and numerous clafs. The fubject is itfelf fo great and inexhauftible, that he muft be a forry writer indeed who cannot turn it to advantage. To one who commands a fluent pen, and who is moreover unchecked by the fpirit of reverence,—yes, even for the mere book-maker,—what a quarry is furnifhed in the Chriftian **Bible** ! Its grand old ftories of patriarchal life, its fublime charaéters, its gorgeous fcenery, its human pathos and divine wifdom, its dignity, variety, and univerfality; and thefe all coloured and endeared by the affociations of dawning intelligence and early **childhood,** form a body of material, the rudeft index of which muft needs outvie in intereft the moft finifhed fpecimens of human art. As eaftern peafants build their rude huts from the ruins of Baalbec, fo do fuch authors conftruét their literary edifices,—woful in their difproportions, and clumfy **in their** poor contrivances, but very coftly **in** their material of cedar and gold, of porphyry and **brafs ; and** here a fculptured image, not quite effaced, and there a pillar or an altar, not yet overthrown, are more than enough to rivet the attention and reward the fearch.

The faults of this book, we fay, are not fo glaring as thofe of the author's "Third Gallery of Portraits ;" but they are fubftantially the fame in charaéter, however fubdued in tone and modified in form. There is the fame lack of precifion, difcrimination, and fobriety ; the fame taftelefs and tirefome ftrain upon the imagination of the reader. The work throughout is vague in its portraitures, unworthy in its allufions, and irreverent in its treatment. It is in the preface to this volume that our author **enunciates the** maxim already quoted, " Every true criticifm on a genuine poem is itfelf a poem." Accordingly the author pro-

duces a rhapſody when he imagines he is writing a
critique. Trying his predeceſſors by his own
warm ſtandard, he finds them cold and tame.
Lowth is only " elegant ;" he " never riſes to the
height of his great argument." His criticiſm wants
" ſubtlety, power, and abandonment." (Surely a
critic is the only ſpecies of judge who was ever
impeached for this deficiency,—this fatal want of
" abandonment.") But Herder, it ſeems, " was a
man of another ſpirit ; and his report of the good
land of Hebrew poetry, compared to Lowth's, is
that of Caleb or Joſhua to that of the other Jewiſh
ſpies." One would naturally ſuppoſe, from the
alluſion of this paſſage, that Biſhop Lowth ſpoke
in moſt diſparaging terms of " the good land of
Hebrew poetry ;" but our author probably means
that he lived long and familiarly in that " good
land," explored all its vineyards, taſted all its
variety of fruits, and gathered more than one rich
ſpecimen,—which, indeed, is true.

It muſt be granted that Mr. Gilfillan is a critic
of a very different ſtamp to Biſhop Lowth. His
notion of poetry is ſo looſe and general, that he
ſeems to hold that whatever is good in literature is
poetical. Thus with him all the Bible is true
poetry, and one bard not eſſentially diſtinguiſhed
from another. We have poetry of the New
Teſtament as well as of the Old ; and it is with
evident reluctance that our author excepts from
the ſame category the argumentative writings of
St. Paul. In all this Mr. Gilfillan gives evidence

of much good feeling **and** many devout affociations ; but none of any peculiar fitnefs for the
office whofe functions he has affumed.

While the plan of this work is thus radically
faulty, the ftyle and fpirit of **its** execution confpire
to make it really pernicious. **When he** meets with a
chapter infcribed " The Poetry of the Pentateuch,"
the phrafe is fufficiently doubtful to make the
reader paufe, or hold himfelf ready for further **in-**
timations of the author's meaning.   In what fenfe
is the Pentateuch **to be** efteemed as fo much
poetry? Knowing Mr. Gilfillan's peculiar man-
ner, we are able **to acquit him of** doubting the
authenticity and truth **of the Mofaic** record ; but
the curfory **reader of his volume may** not **be**
equally prepared. **He finds** a frequent tranfition
from fome high-founding praife of Hebrew King
or Prophet to a modern and perhaps not much
refpected name.   In point of tafte, this is an obvious blemifh, **as** nothing but difenchantment can
refult.   Thefe allufions are feldom warranted by
any real propriety, and never fanctioned by any
evident advantage ; they are gratuitous folecifms
in a work where a certain dignity of tone is demanded by the elevation of its theme.   We could
fpare our author **many** of his grander flights, to
efcape the humiliation and danger of his fudden
and perilous defcents ; **for danger** of a certain
kind there is.   **The diftinctive** infpiration of the
facred bards is not, indeed, denied ; but they are
forceduncceremonioufly into profane company, and
compared at random with modern and even living

authors; till the reader is apt to fuppofe them all of one guild. It is of no ufe to affert a diftinction in one place, and then lofe fight of it in every other. Why fhould the names of Shelley and Coleridge and Byron,—of " Lalla Rookh" and Macaulay's " Lays,"—of " Macbeth," " Feftus," and the " Pilgrim's Progrefs," fo frequently appear on pages profeffedly devoted to the Bards of the Bible ? Serving no purpofe of ufeful illuftration, their introduction is at beft a grave impertinence and an oftentatious folly.

It is time to bring thefe ftrictures to a clofe ; but it remains for us to notice, by anticipation, a remonftrance to which they may poffibly expofe ourfelves. We have faid much about our author's faults, but what of his real merits ? Are they ab-folutely *nil*, or we fo injurious as to fupprefs them ? Let us own that fomething might have been in-genioufly arrayed upon the other fide. A book may be pofitively worfe than worthlefs, and yet not abfolutely void of merit. As there is no popular fallacy which does not take rife from fome partial or defective view of truth, fo, perhaps, never was there a literary reputation earned without talent of fome kind or other. This talent may be folitary, and fo ufelefs ; perverted, and fo mif-chievous ; out of all proportion, a deformity, an excrefcence ; but fomething there will be to ex-tenuate, if not to juftify, the public folly. If a writer chance to be the reverfe of faftidious, he may run on at almoft any length upon any given fubject. If he be, moreover, a perfon of vivid

imagination, he can hardly fail to give off some
striking things, struck out in the impetuosity of
his headlong course.   Mr. Gilfillan is an author
of this kind.   He has imagination, though it
be not elevated or enlarged, not cultivated or
enriched, not trained by intellectual habits, or
subordinated to the rule of judgment.   It is a
somewhat distempered imagination, too soon excited, and too far indulged.   Our author's thoughts
are therefore only fine by accident.   His similes
are generally audacious failures ; but occasionally
they are of striking excellence, and, like a fortunate rebellion, justify themselves by their success.
When he says of John Sterling, " His mental
struggles, though severe, were not of that earth-
quaking kind which shook the soul of Arnold, and
drove Sartor howling through the Everlasting No,
like a lion caught in a forest fire ; " there is a splen-
dour about this final image which makes us wish
it were not so awkwardly introduced.   Still better,
because not so encumbered, is his description of
the policy and power of Russia, as " *the silent con-*
spiracy of ages,—cold, vast, quietly progressive, as a
glacier gathering round an Alpine valley."   These
images, we say, are fine ; and they are so because
of their striking aptitude and truth ; and a few
more of the same kind might, doubtless, be gathered from this author's publications.   But to
what good end ?   It is certainly not desirable to
encourage the use of Mr. Gilfillan's pen on the
wide, and high, and solemn, and important themes
of which he is enamoured, for the sake of giving

full fcope to the indulgence of this gift of doubtful value ; and to themes of humbler character and leffer moment he will hardly be perfuaded. If any confideration could induce Mr. Gilfillan to forget, for fome fhort time, the great men of the world,—to leave the Mirabeaus and Miltons on their craggy heights ; if he would lay afide all books, and watch the world of men and nature with calmer eyes, and never write a line fuggefted by one already written,—we fhould yet have hopes of him. But we fear he is too far gone in his love of power to defcend from his dictatorial eminence ; and we cannot flatter his pretenfions to occupy the throne of univerfal criticifm. While he is making his pompous awards in every conceivable direction, we point to the evidence juft given as in very ridiculous contraft. He has in truth no fingle qualification for the office of a critic, either of facred or profane literature, and, in affuming the one after the other, he has only added prefumption to incompetence, and irreverence to prefumption.

ALFRED TENNYSON.

E have in Mr. Tennyſon the pureſt ſpecimen of the poetic character which the laſt half-century has produced; and this we ſay in entire remembrance of the great poetic lights by which that period has been illuſtrated and adorned. It may be premature to fix the relative poſition of a ſtar ſo recently appearing in the literary firmament; but the purity and ſplendour of its ray are not to be miſtaken. If the caſe be ſo; if (to purſue the metaphor a little longer) an orb of ſong be really before us; the art-critic may do well to put by his opera-glaſs as quite unſerviceable, ſince the teleſcope itſelf will only ſerve to ſeparate it in its ſphere, and aſſiſt us in defining its relative poſition. The glaſs of criticiſm may detect a meteor or falſe light of any kind; but it cannot augment the glory of a ſtar. In other words, a great poet is at nearly equal diſtance from us all. Taſte, ſcience, and the niceſt obſervation do but imperfectly appreciate what the naked ſenſe enables all men to enjoy. Of courſe, this is no reaſon why the lofty ſphere of Mr.

Tennyſon ſhould be tacitly aſſumed by us ; and it will preſently appear that, while we deem it futile to offer direct proofs of his poetic rank, we are yet ready to aſſign ſome reaſons for that very favourable eſtimate which we have formed and expreſſed.

Since a new poet is not unfrequently announced, it is time that we ſhould learn to take the term in an accommodated ſenſe, or otherwiſe to qualify unreaſonable hopes. This we may beſt do by remembering all the virtues which that title promiſes, and all the honours which it properly confers. By ſo doing we ſhall be more juſt to the new aſpirant ; we ſhall bear in mind how many are the chances againſt his being either now, or in the future, a worthy heir of fame, and feel neither diſappointment nor contempt becauſe his young deſerts fail far below the ſtandard of poetic greatneſs. Have any of us well obſerved how high that ſtandard is ? While poetic feeling is by no means an uncommon element in human nature, and poetic power is not the leaſt frequent of natural endowments, a great poet is, perhaps, the rareſt of all human characters. Perfection, indeed, is not to be expected in this earthly ſtate, while humanity is ſubject to ſo many drawbacks and infirmities ; but poſitive excellence is more frequently achieved in any intellectual ſphere than that of poetry. This is due chiefly to the fact, that it is not an intellectual ſphere alone, —that for the art and myſtery of ſong is demanded a combination of natural gifts, and moral qualities, and concurrent circumſtances, ſuch as no other exerciſe of genius calls for ; while theſe conditions

are as delicate in their nature as they are impera-
tive in their obligation ; and the world, which is
fo conftantly miniftering to them on the one hand,
is as conftantly militating againft them on the
other.

The natural endowments of the poet are primary and indifpenfable ; for thefe fupply the very
bafis of his character.　The large brain, or univerfal organ, fufceptive of all the affections, and
apprehenfive of all the truths of humanity,—in
this gift are included all the reft.　It would be
unprofitable, if no worfe, to go further in this direction, except, perhaps, to fuggeft that fome faculty,
anfwering to the *ideality* of the phrenologifts, is
the arch and crown of all the others, is the medium
by which they all communicate, and *in* which they
all inofculate and end. This may form the original
diftinction of poetic genius ; but otherwife it may
be faid to confift in a certain fulnefs and harmony
of all the faculties, which ferve to infure a rare and
unerring infight into nature, ufing that term in the
moft comprehenfive fenfe.　The brain, the mind,
the character of a great poet, is *totus, teres, atque
rotundus.*

It is true, then,—an old truth ever new,—that
the poet is born and not made.　But let us not
therefore judge that his deftiny is accomplifhed, or
his crown fure. Baffled, wearied, or diverted from
his courfe, he may never reach the goal for which
Dame Nature has equipped him.　He may be
born a poet, and die a philofopher ; he may be born
a great poet, and die an obfcure one !　This para-

dox is not inexplicable, is not hard to be underftood. The truth is, that to live the life poetic,
to nourifh all its affections, to develope all its
powers, and fo eventually to anfwer all its miffion,
is at once a great trial of conftancy, and the teft
of fuperior fortune. The pofitive attributes of the
poetic character are, we repeat, primary and indifpenfable; but thefe are of themfelves inadequate,
and may altogether fail in conferring, by their own
inherent force, either the confummate minftrelfy
or the immortal guerdon. Hence many perfons
of poetic mark and promife, whofe energies have
afterwards found fcope and exercife in other fpheres,
have not been able to fuftain the poetic character
in all its breadth, fimplicity, and power. Born
under the fmile of all the mufes, they have finally
attached themfelves to one. Feeling the ftirrings
of the prophetic genius, they have allowed the fpirit
of the world to break in upon them, and loft its
facred mood. From deliberate choice or gradual
inclination, at the fuggeftion of duty or from the
violence of circumftances, the poet has often fold
his vaft inheritance, and bought a field; given up
his intereft in the beauties of a world, and centered
it upon fome fmall productive province; exchanged,
it may be, divination for fcience, and art for criticifm. Nor fhould we wonder at this circumftance.
There is nothing more eafy than this procefs of
deterioration; for fuch it is, though not always to
be deplored. The poet, as belonging to the order
of a natural priefthood, fhould be devoted and fet
apart to his fpecial office. He muft go in and out

among mankind, sustain all its relations, experience all its sorrows, have share in all its delights ; but he must gather up the skirts of his " singing robes," as he passes through the forum and the market, as he mingles with the crowd of partisans and worldlings, as he loiters in the halls of industry and science. He must contract no dust or stain of any class. He must be in the world, but not of the world ; may indulge its partialities, but must have no share in its prejudices ; may love his country much, but must love his species more. Knowledge he must have ; but it must not be labelled or laid up in artificial forms. What he gains as a *savan* he must enjoy like a child, that he may employ it like a poet. Now, against this mood of wise simplicity, of earnest but catholic delight, a thousand influences array themselves,—poverty with its cares, business with its distractions, and pleasure with its strong allurements. The best qualities of the poet's nature may prove his most besetting snares. His keen love of approbation may lead him to seek the praise of a frivolous society, or a superficial age. His love of knowledge may divert him into partial studies ; his love of beauty betray him into luxurious and fatal ease. Or all these may act together, and dissipate the mind, and degrade the moral sense, until he makes shipwreck both of happiness and fame ; foundering, like some rich merchantman, ill-manned but costly-freighted, the victim of too much treasure and unequal seamanship.

But this is not all. The conditions necessary

for the production of a poet of the firſt order, are beſet with peculiar difficulties in a **period of advanced** civilization and high literary attainments. All that is valuable in a poet's education is the fruit of his individual effort, **of** ſevere but generous ſelf-culture ; and hence it follows, that he has more to loſe than gain **by the mechanical aids** to knowledge, by the eager **ſpirit of reſearch, by** the varied and ceaſeleſs **acquiſitions of an era like** our own. It **was not always ſo. In** the world's nonage he **enjoyed a** liberty dearer than aught beſide ; and in ſinging from his own full heart and mind, in celebrating, without model, dictation, or reſtraint of any kind, heroic deeds, ſtrange fortunes, pure love, and ſimple faith, he rehearſed all the powers **of** language, and anticipated **all** the reſources **of** invention. Hence that **miracle of art, that epitome** of literature, which **bears the name of Homer.** Hence **the fulneſs,** clearneſs, and authority of Shakeſpeare's **muſe. And** becauſe this freedom **was** gradually **invaded by** the advance of ſcience, or enfeebled **by** preſcriptive laws, we have to lament the poor **imitative** notes of the poetry of the laſt century, and **the** "uncertain ſound" delivered from the ſilver trumpet of the preſent.

It is true that the generation which has only lately paſſed away had juſt cauſe to glory in its bards. If no "bright particular ſtar" burns ſolitary in that quarter of the hemiſphere, we may ſee there a conſtellation of lights, diſſimilar in radiance and of different magnitudes, but ſoftly blending all their aſſociated **glories.** Much fine and genuine poetry illuftrated the regency and reign of George the Fourth. Yet the deteriorating influences we have enumerated may eafily be traced in the productions of that period ; and even when they have allowed fome compofitions to come forth pure and uninjured, they have ftill operated with certain effect in preventing the full development, or in marring the grand fimplicity, of the poet's character. We repeat, this is not always to be regretted ; other forms of literature have often profited by this deviation or perverfion ; but the fact at leaft may be clearly afcertained by a brief reference to our poetic kalendar.

Of all the modern poets, Campbell and Rogers have made fureft work for immortality. Whatever is effential and permanent in poetry of the ancient claffic type, has been beautifully adapted by the Englifh mufe of Rogers. In Campbell, there is frequently fomething of a more meretricious character ; but many of his lyrics have the true bardic fpirit and the ftrong Saxon voice ; and his ftory of Gertrude and her fortunes in the wildernefs of the Savannah, while it breathes an Arcadian fweetnefs of its own, is invefted with a thoufand graces which confer a perdurable beauty. But neither of thefe authors is the great commanding poet of his age ; and ftill lefs can this be faid of any of their celebrated contemporaries. Scott revived with eminent fuccefs the foul of border minftrelfy ; but his hearty, healthful verfe had neither the concentration nor the pitch of poetry ; it pleafed rather from the romance and frefhnefs of

his theme, than becaufe of its general truth or deep
fignificance. Byron, even in his beft productions,
evinced a fatal lack of comprehenfivenefs, a deficient eye for form, and an excefs of fentiment **not**
often of the pureft fort. His intenfe egotifm **un-**
fitted him for doing juftice to other and more
noble types of character ; **while a** great egotift **is**
never a great **poet, unlefs** (like Milton or Dante)
he is **alfo the greateft** and foremoft man of his age.
He **wanted the moral** far more than the intellectual
qualities **of** greatnefs ; and had no right conception
of the beauty, dignity, and power of virtue. Incapable of exercifing the higheft functions of the
poet, he might probably have become the firft
fatirift of his day. The mufe of Shelley was the
apotheofis of philofophy. Liftening to his **fong, it**
feemed that the foul of **Plato was paffing mourn-**
fully over an æolian lyre, **and a beautiful** abftraction
—**call** it wifdom, liberty, **or** virtue—rofe in fupernatural fplendour, **and** vanifhed among the ftars.
The genius **of** Moore was mufical rather than
poetic : **he** delighted and excelled in melody, but
always failed **in** profound or harmonious combinations. Fancy **he** had, and feeling in a moderate
degree ; but **in** imagination he was almoft totally
deficient. His ftyle was artificial,—his tafte for
the beautiful, limited, conventional, and factitious.
Neither the Englifh **heart** nor the Englifh head
could find fatisfaction in his minftrelfy ; and even
his fweeteft fongs lofe more than half their charms
when divorced from the melodious airs which
animated them **at the** firft, and gave to them the

principle of life. **Southey was** a lefs popular but far more genuine poet. **Indeed,** all the gifts, and nearly all the graces, of his **art** were prefent with him ; and this he has evinced by the tafte, variety, and invention of his numerous verfe. But he ftudied man too little, and books **far** too **exclufively.** The frefhnefs and the freedom of **the poetic cha-** racter were loft in his fcholarly feclufion: he taxed his powerful mind with continual efforts of re-pro- duction ; and the genius that was at firft only difturbed became finally overlaid. His thirft of knowledge **joined with the exigencies** of daily life **to draw** him **from communion with the mufe ;** and inftead of **the greateft poet of the age, he will be** henceforth **known as the nobleft and pureft of its** men of letters. Far different moral **caufes led to** no very different iffue **the** marvellous powers of Coleridge. With the fineft ear, the moft delicate fancy, and the moft fuperb imagination of any poet **of** that famous period, **he left** the dial that ftands within **the** poet's garden to peer behind the **clock-** work of **the** univerfe, and grew bewildered in pre- fence **of the vaft** machinery, and fell ftunned and voicelefs **before** the awful proceffion of **its** wheels. He exchanged poetic fynthefis for metaphyfical analyfis ; gathered fome fragments of the under- working law, **but** relinquifhed **all the** fmiling appanage of **nature.** The **world** ftill waited for its poet. Many thought **he had** already come in the perfon **of** William Wordfworth, whofe pre- tenfions were defpifed or overlooked, only becaufe of the ftudied plainnefs of his appeal. Yet thofe pretenſions were at leaſt ſufficiently advanced, if not haughtily preferred or royally ſupported. He eſſayed all the varieties of his art, from ballad meaſures to epic lengths ; but he had not eminent ſuccefs in more than two. Excepting only ſome fifty of his ſonnets and a few noble odes, there is nothing in his volumes which the world could not well ſpare. His ballads are not ſo much ſimple as naked, not ſo much homely as proſaic. His " Ex-curſion " is tedious, verboſe, metaphyſical ; ela-borate in manner, and not ſtinted in dimenſions, it is quite wanting in conſtruꞓtive art ; it is indefi-nite in its purpoſe, and inconcluſive as a whole. There is little difficulty in pointing out this author's chief defeꞓt. He had the poet's mind, but not the poet's manner ; he had ſomething of the artiſt's taſteful eye, but little of the artiſt's ſkilful hand. His touch was often feeble, heſitating, ineffeꞓtual ; and ſeldom did he inform the piꞓture with a pleaſ-ing or a perfeꞓt grace. The philoſophical element is too manifeſt and too predominant in all his works. A ſage he was ; but no crowned poet, no magician. He had the lore of Proſpero, his gravity, and his dignity ; but no wand was in his hand, and no Ariel at his beck.

From each of the authors we have named, many beautiful poems have been received into the antho-logy of England ; but who is by emphaſis THE POET? We find ſomething to admire in the " works " of every one ; but where is the maſter that lifts up all the powers of our hearts and minds together, and makes nature to dance in concert

s

with the foul at the mere hearing of his voice?
The Chriftabel of Coleridge, the O'Connor's
Child of Campbell, the Adonais and Ode to the
Sky-Lark of poor unhappy Shelley, Moore's tender
Melodies, and Wordfworth's noble Sonnets,—
thefe are choice pieces in our claffical repertory,
and we can only fpare them from our fide becaufe
they are already graven in our hearts. But fomething of higher note, of rarer excellence, is yet a-
wanting ; and while the world yet waits, breathlefs
with expectation, a **clear** high voice is heard advancing on the ear, and **the** poet's advent is unmif-
takeably announced **in the character** of his fore-
runner.

" The rain **had fallen, the Poet arofe,**
　　He pafs'd by the town, **and out of** the ftreet,
　A light wind blew from the gates of the fun,
　　And **waves** of fhadow went over the wheat,
　And he fat him down in a lonely place,
　　And chanted a melody loud and fweet,
　That made the **wild fwan paufe** in her cloud,
　　And the lark **drop down** at his feet.

" The fwallow ftopt **as he hunted** the bee,
　　The fnake flipt **under a** fpray,
　The wild hawk ftood with the down on his **beak,**
　　And ftared with his foot on the prey.
　And the nightingale thought, ' I have fung many fongs,
　　But never a one fo gay;
　For he fings of what the world **will be,**
　　When the years have died away.' "

　It is not our intention to **enter** minutely into
the character and merits of Mr. Tennyfon's poetry.
Prefuming that our author's publications **are** more
or lefs familiar to the reader, we fhall briefly indicate the qualities **which** feem to juftify in fome

degree the praife of his admirers, and give to him
a high and independent place among the Englifh
poets. To this courfe we are certainly moved by
no fpirit of partifanfhip ; and we may equally dif-
claim that feeling of exclufive preference which is
fo apt to warp the judgment and corrupt the tafte.
Our fympathies (as the reader probably by this time
knows) are not deeply engaged in favour of the
fubjective fchool of poetry, with which Mr. Tennyfon is commonly, but not quite fairly, identified ;
yet it is only juft that the diftinction fhould be
made, and clearly marked, between what is genuine
and original in the prefent claimant, and what is
meretricious and extravagant in his younger rivals.
There is fome danger of the former fharing in the
condemnation of the latter; and fo an injuftice
may be done to one of the moft gifted of his race
and order. Yet it is furely idle to confound the
merits and pofition of Mr. Tennyfon with thofe of
certain imitators and enthufiafts. His poems are
too well conceived, his thoughts too harmonioufly
ordered, to allow anything but reckleffnefs or incapacity fo far to misjudge his real character. He
has no relation to what has been defignated " the
fpafmodic fchool of poetry," excepting that his
genius has quickened into unequal emulation the
poetic inftinct of far inferior men ; and in thefe
cafes it was only natural that the external features
of his poetry fhould be moft clofely followed, and
carried to " wafteful and ridiculous excefs." Hence
his frequent but felicitous ufe of flowers, for the
fubordinate purpofes of fentiment and imagery,

is mere purpofelefs profufion in the pages of fome of our younger poets ; and what in him is but an occafional voice of wonder, or of doubt, becomes in them an intolerable fenfe of moral confufion, and a monotonous wail of mifanthropic grief.

But your orthodox man of tafte will reject the claims of Mr. Tennyfon, as ftoutly as thofe of his moft extravagant contemporaries. His delight is in the fatires and the epitaphs of Pope. He calls eafily to memory, and repeats, with proudeft emphafis, the opening lines of " The Traveller," and triumphantly inquires, " Do you want finer poetry than that ? " He believes alfo in Shakefpeare ; and though it is perhaps twenty years fince he read much of the great mafter's volume, you may truft him for correct quotation, as he illuftrates fome pafling incident, fome trait of character, fome point of cafuiftry, by noble apophthegm or golden rule of life. Yet it may be obferved, that if his love of Shakefpeare is unmeafured, his appreciation is fomewhat limited. The poet is for him a clear-eyed, mellow-voiced, and genial man of the world, a fhrewd obferver, a pleafant fatirift, a merry wit. He heartily enjoys the Shakefpearian comedy ; but gives the hiftory and tragedy, the fentiment and forrow, quite a fecond place ; puts " As you like it " before " The Tempeft," and quotes more frequently the fayings of Polonius than thofe of Hamlet. Our orthodox man of tafte is not to be defpifed. For thefe ftrong preferences we rather honour than condemn him. What he admires, is genuine, is admirable ; whoever elfe is found in

judgment, he at leaſt is ſo. Nor do we ſay that
the Laureate of the preſent day will ever take rank
with the univerſal favourites, the claſſics of all
time. But orthodoxy is apt to be literal and harſh,
as well as found ; and when it charges obſcurity,
exceſs, and wantonneſs upon the poetic meaſures
of Mr. Tennyſon, it is quite poſſible that the deficiency and fault may not reſt wholly with the
poet. Handel is the grand *maeſtro;* yet is there
no muſic in the wild and wailing ſymphonies of
Beethoven? Goethe is the great ſage; yet is
there no wiſdom, ſhimmering like innumerable
glowworms, in the foreſt of Jean Paul's quaint
fancy and invention? Gainſborough and Rey-
nolds are the glory of the Britiſh ſchool ; but is no
ſentiment to be found in the fertile grace of Stoth-
ard, no freſhneſs in the homely paſtorals of Con-
ſtable? It is the higheſt-mounted man who ſees
the fartheſt ; and that is the trueſt taſte which
comprehends the wideſt kingdom and the moſt
numerous ſubjects in its impartial range. But
beſides this neceſſary power of catholic appreciation of all that is genuine in literature or art, another conſideration ſhould repreſs excluſive judgments. The writings of Pope and Goldſmith, and
even thoſe of Shakeſpeare, form no ſufficient teſt
of the reader's love of poetry ; for a man of comparative dulneſs may find amuſement in the mere
letter of theſe compoſitions. It is quite another
thing to find pleaſure in Spenſer's " Fairy Queen,"
or Milton's " Comus," or, of later date, in the fine
fragments of young Keats, beautiful as Elgin

marbles.   This is indeed to give evidence of deep
poetic feeling ; and it is juft the ear and fancy
which are fo arrefted, that will find, as we believe,
a fatisfaction, not inferior, but ftill deeper and more
complete, in the productions of the prefent Laureate.

Mr. Tennyfon has been thought to owe much
to the philofophic mufe of Wordfworth ; but we
cannot trace the debt.   The only likenefs we can
difcern between thefe authors, is in the devotion
of their lives to the attainment of poetic excellence.
Becaufe of this fuftained and rare devotion, in
which they equally fecured fome pure advantages,
and exercifed their powers with fulleft freedom,
we may all the more fairly eftimate the relative
refults.   One grand particular may be felected as,
in fome degree, inclufive of all the reft ; and fignificant, if not decifive, of their refpective merit.
The difference in the ftyle or manner of thefe two
poets is ftriking, and, at the fame time, characteriftic of more effential differences.   Wordfworth's
thoughts are often beautiful and juft ; and being,
moreover, elaborately fet in meafured verfe and
ftudied phrafe, there is a certain dignity about the
whole, which challenges the praife of poetry.   Yet
we feel, fometimes painfully, the fubfervience of
the fpirit to the letter of poetic truth, of the
æfthetic to the rational appreciation of external
things, and mark too clearly the deliberate coinage
and patent artifice of all his words and lines.
Poetry is with him the felected medium of his
thoughts, not the fpontaneous language of infpired

lips. It is very different with Mr. Tennyson.
The bees of Hybla have swarmed about his mouth
in infancy,—a marvellous ease and sweetness are
found in all his utterance. He does not assume
the language of poetry; he rather realizes the story
of the royal fairy whose words were all pure pearls.
He puts a poetic thought in poetic phrase naturally, necessarily, as every action of a prince speaks
of high breeding and habitual power. But this is
not all. If this were his chief merit, if poetic
phrase were allowed to stand in place of profounder
qualities of truth, then the palm should justly be
awarded to the sage of Rydal. Better a rhythmical
philosophy than a shallow poetry. Better the
labouring, mournful, doubtful voice of Nature crying after God, and a discord tortured out of the
" still sad music of humanity," than the procession
of inane and glittering fancies, catching, like
bubbles, the nearest light, and then bursting from
sheer tenuity and emptiness. But is it so with the
muse of Alfred Tennyson? His beauties of language and poetic phrase are not the set purpose,
but the pure redundancies, of his genius; and yet
they are not so far redundant but that they are
made to serve the chief design,—to give collateral
light, to touch, and tone, and harmonize the whole
picture. Underlying all that wealth and beauty
of expression, that play of fancy, that sparkling
evanescent foam of imagery, the author's main
design, like the strong current of a calm summer
sea, carries his reader forward almost imperceptibly;
and so lulling are the sights and measures which

falute him,—fo idle the green, white, crefting, and
relapfing waves, fo motionlefs the thin, pure, dappled fleeces of the upper fky,—that he can hardly
perfuade himfelf that he is drifted towards fome
grand conclufion, towards fome ifland of rare
lovelinefs and regenerating clime, towards fome
new continent of boundlefs treafure and dominion.
Yet fo it is. In all the poems of our author there
is more than meets the eye of the imagination, and
more than the delighted ear can well appreciate.
The moral is profoundly felt, the leffon is received
at once into the heart; but not lefs clearly are we
taught, not lefs certainly are we raifed into a region
of elevated truths. From a higher point we furvey
a wider field, bounded by a more diftant, but ftill
beautiful, horizon. From a " peak in Darien,"
from fome rare ftand-point of this poor and
" ignorant prefent," we catch glimpfes of the tide-
lefs and boundlefs Pacific of ideal truth, and feel
how profound is that divine faying, that only " the
things which are unfeen are eternal."

This union, or rather this interfufion, of
thought and language; this wonderful co-ordina-
tion of detail and defign, of final purpofe and fubordinate expreffion; this fubtle incorporation of
the fpirit of poetry, by which the groffer medium
is fublimed, and the diviner effence projected into
form; is eminently feen in our author's poem of
" The Two Voices." In that fine dialogue, a
troubled foul maintains a controverfy with his evil
monitor: in what ftyle and temper, and with what
ultimate fuccefs, a few quotations may fuffice to
fhow.

" **Again** the voice fpake unto me,
  '**Thou** art fo fteep'd in mifery,
  Surely 'twere better not to be.

" ' **Thine** anguifh will not let thee fleep,
  Nor **any** train of reafon keep:
  Thou canft not think, but thou wilt weep.'

" I faid, ' The years **with change** advance;
  If I make dark **my countenance,**
  I fhut my life from happier chance.

" ' Some turn this ficknefs yet **may** take,
  Even yet.' But he: ' **What drug** can make
  A wither'd palfy ceafe to fhake ?'

" I wept, ' Though I fhould die, I know
  That **all** about the thorn will blow
  In tufts of rofy-tinted fnow;

" ' And men, through novel fpheres of thought,
  Still moving after truths long fought,
  Will learn new things **when I** am not.'

" ' Yet,' faid **the fecret voice,** ' fome time
  Sooner or later, will grey prime
  Make **thy grafs** hoar with early rime.

" ' Not lefs fwift fouls that yearn for light,
  Rapt after heaven's ftarry **flight,**
  Would fweep the tracks of day and night.

" ' Not lefs the bee would range her cells,
  The **furzy prickle fire the dells,**
  The foxglove clufter dappled bells.'

" I faid that ' all the years invent;
  Each **month is various to prefent**
  The world with fome development.

" ' Were this **not well,** to bide mine hour,
  Though watching from **a** ruin'd tower,
  How grows the day of human power ?'

" ' The **higheft**-mounted mind,' he faid,
  ' Still fees the facred morning fpread
  The filent fummit over head.

" ' Will **thirty** feafons render plain
  Thofe **lonely** lights that ftill remain
  Juft breaking over land and main ?

"'Or make that morn, from his cold crown
And cryſtal ſilence creeping down,
Flood with full daylight glebe and town?

"'Forerun thy peers, thy time, and let
Thy feet, millenniums hence, be ſet
In midſt of knowledge dream'd not yet.

"'Thou haſt not gain'd a real height,
Nor art thou nearer to the light,
Becauſe the ſcale is infinite.'"

Maſtering a ſtrong reluctance, we paſs by many
beautiful verſes of this poem; and, further on, we
read:—

"'O dull one-ſided voice,' ſaid I,
'Wilt thou make everything a lie,
To flatter me that I may die?

"'I know that age to age ſucceeds,
Blowing a noiſe of tongues and deeds,
A duſt of ſyſtems and of creeds.

"'I cannot hide that ſome have ſtriven,
Achieving calm, to whom was given
The joy that mixes man with heaven:

"'Who, rowing hard againſt the ſtream,
Saw diſtant gates of Eden gleam,
And did not dream it was a dream;

"'But heard, by ſecret tranſport led,
Even in the charnels of the dead,
The murmur of the fountain-head—

"'Which did accompliſh their deſire,
Bore and forbore, and did not tire,
Like Stephen, an unquench'd fire:

"'He heeded not reviling tones,
Nor fold his heart to idle moans,
Though curſed, and ſcorn'd, and bruiſed with ſtones:

"'But looking upward, full of grace,
He pray'd, and from a happy place,
God's glory ſmote him in the face.'"

However the general tenor of our author's philofophy be judged,—and on that topic we referve a few remarks,—there can be little doubt of its highly poetical character ; and the verfes we have tranfcribed are fufficient to fuftain what we have juft preferred as the peculiar praife of Mr. Tenny-fon. All he writes is poetry : it may be of more or lefs diftinguifhed merit, and more or lefs obvious in its truth and **beauty** ; but in every mood of his mind, in all the tones and meafures of his fong, the poet's office is fuftained, and the poetic func-tion purely exercifed. We have no logic chopped into longs and fhorts ; no dull, pert argument, dreffed up in figured robes, in which it naturally, **but** abfurdly, ftumbles at almoft every ftep. In the midft of a bufy, learned, enterprifing age, **our** author has efcaped its deadening and deteriorating influences, and is as pure a minftrel as any trou-badour of the age of **chivalry.**

Before quitting this poem of " The Two Voices," which fo happily exemplifies our author's poetic ftyle, it may be allowed to carry us ftill for-ward in our eftimate ; for it is not more beautiful in parts, than it is complete and perfect as a whole. There is great truth to nature, and a fine moral leffon, embodied in the concluding verfes. In his mental ftruggles the tempted fufferer has, in each inftance, manfully repelled the fuggeftions of " The Voice ;" but his triumph is not complete, his cure is not effected, without affiftance from the external world. A morbid introverfion of the mind, an eager, but unhallowed, curiofity, had evidently fown the firft feeds of doubt, and given occafion to the tempter of his foul; and the evil one had him, as it were, at difadvantage on his own ground, fo long as the conteft was maintained wholly from within. A new arena muft be chofen; frefher and healthier influences muft be allowed to invigorate and fecond nature; action muft confirm the feeble dictates of his reafon, and wideft obfervation correct the partial *data* of fecluded thought, and bring the whole being into accordance with the world of nature and the arrangements of Providence :—

> " I ceafed, and fat as one forlorn.
>   Then faid the voice in quiet fcorn,
>   ' Behold, it is the Sabbath morn !'
>
> " And I arofe, and I releafed
>   The cafement, and the light increafed
>   With frefhnefs in the dawning eaft.
>
> " Like foften'd airs that blowing fteal
>   When woods begin to uncongeal,
>   The fweet church-bells began to peal.
>
> " On to God's houfe the people preft :
>   Paffing the place where each muft reft,
>   Each enter'd like a welcome gueft.
>
> " One walk'd between his wife and child
>   With meafured foot-fall firm and mild,
>   And now and then he gravely fmiled.
>
> " The prudent partner of his blood
>   Lean'd on him, faithful, gentle, good,
>   Wearing the rofe of womanhood.
>
> " And in their double love fecure,
>   The little maiden walk'd demure,
>   Pacing with downward eyelids pure.
>
> " Thefe three made unity fo fweet,
>   My frozen heart began to beat,
>   Remembering its ancient heat.

"I bleſt them, and they wander'd on:
I ſpoke, but anſwer came there none:
The dull and bitter voice was gone.

"A ſecond voice was at mine ear,
A little whiſper ſilver-clear,
A murmur, 'Be of better cheer.'

"As from ſome bliſsful neighbourhood,
A notice faintly underſtood,
'I ſee the end, and know the good.'

"A little hint to ſolace woe,
A hint, a whiſper breathing low,
'I may not ſpeak of what I know.'

"Like an Æolian harp that wakes
No certain air, but overtakes
Far thought with muſic which it makes:

"Such ſeem'd the whiſper at my ſide:
'What is 't thou knoweſt, ſweet voice,' I cried.
'A hidden hope,' the voice replied:

"So heavenly-toned that in that hour
From out my ſullen heart a power
Broke, like the rainbow from the ſhower,

"To feel, although no tongue can prove,
That every cloud that ſpreads above,
And veileth love, itſelf is love."

In "The Palace of Art," and "The Viſion of
Sin," the ſame fine vein of moral poetry ſubſiſts.
But the moſt popular and perfect of our author's
compoſitions do not preſent the moral element ſo
diſtinctively: in theſe it is merely held in ſolution,
while in thoſe it is caſt down as a bright precipitate.
The poet is generally ſucceſsful in both theſe
ſtyles of compoſition. What an air of truth, and
health, and happineſs, breathes in his Engliſh
idyls!—in "Dora" and "The Gardener's Daughter," and that exquiſite bucolic, "The Talking
Oak." But the genius of our poet, like the genius

of his age, is effentially lyrical. The lighteft of individual fancies, and the graveft of prophetic burthens, flow from him in eafy, and abundant, and pellucid fong. In " The Princefs" we have both thefe elements—idyllic fweetnefs and lyrical perfection—well exemplified, and linked together by a fable of infinite delicacy and grace. The poem is " a Medley," for the age is fuch ; and all its various qualities and features are reprefented in its pages ; and efpecially are they fketched in its fantaftic prologue with a touch fo light, fo faithful, fo poetical, that it appears rather the effect of magic than of art. Again : what freedom of defign and execution in the ftory of thofe wilful beauties ! what images of feminine lovelinefs ! what diffolv- ing views of wayward and capricious paffion ! what final glimpfes into the heart and oratory of true womanhood ! But the fineft meafures of this poem are diftinct and feparable. Its fongs and idyls are incomparably beautiful ; and now haunt the foul with a fenfe of its own myftery and im- mortality, and now "lap it in foft Lydian airs." Who that has read can ever forget the " fmall, fweet idyl," beginning, " Come down, O maid ! from yonder fhepherd height ?" Too well known, alfo, is the famous Bugle Song to admit of its quo- tation ; but the echo of it remains upon the ear, and wanders through the mind and heart, and grows only the more diftinct as it faints in utter finenefs.

In the poem of *In Memoriam,* the admirers of our author recognize the fulfilment of his

higheſt promiſes, and the culmination of all his brilliant powers. Others point to it in vindication of
their former coldneſs and miſtruſt, as ſtrongly confirming the charges of obſcurity, exaggeration, and
myſticiſm. One thing, at leaſt, is clear : this
poem is intenſely characteriſtic of the author ; if it
owes much to the fineſt qualities of his genius, it
indicates ſomething alſo of his prevailing fault.
The reader will remember that this memorial
poem is compoſed of a ſeries of ſmaller poems, or
ſtrophes, written under the influence, more or leſs
remote, of grief for the loſs of a dear and moſt ac-
compliſhed friend, and finally depoſited—a handful
of violets, a chaplet of *immortelles*—upon a long-
cold grave. The character of this rare tribute of
love and admiration is quite unique. Compoſed
at different times, and under different moods of
mind, it varies in the perſonal pathos of its grief.
Mourning the early loſs of a much-gifted friend,
the poet's genius prompts him to ſpeculation ; and
he glances, with wondering, awed, yet not un-
ſteady gaze, into the myſtery of life, the deſtiny of
man. In this attitude of brooding thought—in
its intenſely ſubjective character—lie both the
ſtrength and weakneſs of this poem, its value as a
rare and precious ſtudy, its iſolation from the popular ſympathy and taſte. Here again we have that
happy fuſion of ſentiment and language, and that
interaction of thought, and muſic, and expreſſion,
which give ſo great a charm to all our author's
poetry. Theſe harmonies are, with many readers,
the chief merit of *In Memoriam* ; but perhaps

its moſt faſcinating **quality is** that which borders
cloſely upon the obſcure,—**which** ſuggeſts to the
ſoul, rather than ſpeaks **to the** mind, and affords
dim intimations of ſomething " more than meets
the ear." The ſpeculations of the poet have given
riſe to great ſuſpicions of his faith ; and ſome have
charged a pantheiſtical tendency upon the whole
production. We do not wonder at the grave
ſuſpicions ; but the concluſion of the author's
pantheiſm ſeems to us unfounded. We have no
decided recognition of revealed and ſaving truth,
nor any indication **of that** clear and perfect confidence which **the goſpel confers on** the believer ;
but faith in **God, in** His perſonal character, in His
overruling, but myſterious, **providence,** and **even**
in His gracious purpoſes through Chriſt, does appear in our author's pages, and comes to relieve
his gloomieſt doubts. He recoils from the con-
cluſions of learned infidels, and from the cold
ſpectre which they worſhip under the name of
" Nature."

—————————" And he, ſhall he,

" Man, her laſt work, who ſeem'd ſo fair,
  Such ſplendid purpoſe in his eyes,
  Who roll'd the pſalm to wintry ſkies,
Who built him fanes of fruitleſs prayer ;

" Who truſted God was love **indeed,**
  And love Creation's final **law ;**—
  Though **Nature, red in tooth** and claw
With ravin, ſhriek'd againſt his creed ;

" Who loved, **who ſuffer'd** countleſs ills,
  Who battled **for the** True, the Juſt,—
  Be blown about the deſert duſt,
Or ſeal'd within the iron hills ?

" No more ?   A monſter then, a dream,
    A diſcord ; dragons of the prime,
    That tare each other in their ſlime,
  Were mellow muſic match'd with him.

" O, life as futile, then, as frail !
    O for Thy voice to ſoothe and bleſs !
    What hope of anſwer, or redreſs ?
  Behind the veil, behind the veil."

Little ſpace is left to us to ſpeak of Mr. Tennyſon's laſt production : but the work is in every-
body's hands, our contemporaries have diſcuſſed at
large its beauties and defects, and, after the general views we have preſented of what ſeems to us
the character of our author's poetry, few words
will ſuffice to ſhow in what manner we eſtimate
the new effort of his muſe. The poem of "*Maud*,"
which was expected with too great eagerneſs, has
been naturally received with too little candour and
allowance.   This is the tax an author pays for
his own great reputation. We not only expect ſtill better things of him than he has yet
achieved, but his work muſt be of a certain pre-
conceived deſcription, and his triumph univerſal
as well as eminent.   He muſt pleaſe all, and each
in his own way.   If his later ſtyle reſemble the
former, he is ſaid to be wearing himſelf out ; if it
conſiderably differ, he is loſing himſelf in a wrong
direction.   Now the poem before us, though long
enough to give the leading title to a volume of
minor pieces, makes no extraordinary pretenſions,
and challenges no eſpecial admiration. It is no
allegory of the war on the one hand, and no epic
illuſtration on the other. It is the dithyrambic of

a thwarted and embittered **youth**, degraded by the
evils **of** a peftilent and bloated peace.   This fubject was probably felected as affording occafion for
exhibiting the focial ufes of a war like that in which
we are engaged,—an object, **no** doubt, primary in
the defign of the poet, but made fecondary and incidental **only** in his poem.   We **are** not **altogether**
pleafed **with the** choice which Mr. Tennyfon
has made.   In truth, the poem is not eminently
pleafing as a whole ; it lacks that clearnefs, fymmetry, and ferene expreffion, which are the laft
perfection of the artift.   **Yet our juft** confidence
in Mr. Tennyfon **makes us diffident in** this conclufion ; and **fure we are that repeated** ftudy of
his poem **has greatly leffened the** diffatisfaction
which a firft perufal left upon our minds.   **Some**
readers mifs painfully the wonted eafe and fmooth-
nefs of our author's poetry : but an ear fo cunning
as this mafter's is not eafily betrayed ; and under
his moft rugged lines will be found a full current
of harmonious mufic, fuch as no dulcet meafures
can pretend to.   The fecret of this verfification—
of its novelty, abruptnefs, and feeming harfhnefs—
is its profound and exquifite adaptation to the mind
as well as to the ear : it reconciles the voice of
paffion, the moods of waywardnefs and fear, with
the fupreme demands of art ; it is reprefentative
poetry in the loweft as well as in the higheft fenfe.
Take, for example, the firft ftrophe of the poem.
We have feen thefe ftanzas quoted as a mere bur-
lefque of poetry.   Read them again,—read them
aloud ; and it cannot fail to be perceived that the

choice of accentual, rather than of pure metrical, effect was moft felicitous. Say, if you pleafe, our author has turned a column of police reports into poetry. Yet, poetry it furely is, and that of a very noble kind. Every word is effective ; every accent falls in the critical place and time ; every line is graphic and fonorous in the laft degree. The paffage reads like a public indictment, and, rifing into a declaration of war, feems to clofe with the blaft of a trumpet.

The remaining beauties of this poem are acknowledged and felt by all. There is no need to quote, much lefs to vindicate, the inimitable fong beginning, " Come into the garden, Maud." It is the exuberant paffion of a true and earneft heart, unfolding in an atmofphere of balmieft oriental fancies, and efflorefcing into rich and odorous beauty—fo fweet that the fenfe aches at it, fo delicate that no pencil can define it, fo fimple that a child may fall in love with it, fo fubtle that no philofophy can analyfe it, fo marvellous that all muft be content to ponder and enjoy it. But this queen-lyric is only fuperior, and not folitary, in its beauty. It overpeers a band of rival graces. Only lefs charming than the invocation we have referred to is the ftrain commencing, " Go not, happy day, from the fhining fields ;" but it is to the other as the primrofe to the rofe. In the penultimate ftrophe of the poem we have a ftill higher triumph of poetic genius in the delineation of a difordered mind. Nothing is more certain in fact, and nothing more difficult to realize in art, than the " method" which is involved even in utter " madnefs." It is a teft worthy of the powers of Shakefpeare himfelf; and few befides have paffed it undegraded. Yet Mr. Tennyfon muft be numbered with the few, fo admirable is the manner in which gleams of memory, and glimpfes of the truth, are made to break through the lowering clouds of paffion and unreafon.

Of the minor poems which compofe the latter half of this volume, the fineft is the " Ode," firft publifhed on occafion of the Great Duke's burial. To fay that it is worthy of the author, and equal to the theme is high, but not unmerited praife. It is martial mufic, keen, clear, or duly muffled, reftraining its exulting note in prefence of the grave, and that one Foe, unconquered and unevaded. " The Brook" is an idyl of the kind in which Mr. Tennyfon has always fuch fuccefs ; and the lines fuggefted by " The Daify," fo different from thofe of Montgomery and Burns which bear the fame title, are written in the author's characteriftic manner, and have an independent beauty of their own.

NOCTES AMBROSIANÆ.

THE same man in different circumstances, and what then? Postpone his birth, translate his home, alter his social grade, and, in all outward things, reverse his fortune; will his character be developed into the same substantial form? Can the imagination re-adjust the features of a life in any new position? To do so would be a matter of the highest difficulty, but perhaps it is not quite impossible. Yet, if we endeavour to estimate the results of this hypothetical combination, our conclusion must remain unverified: it is only a conjecture at the best. With persons of ordinary stamp, who accept their destiny as infants receive their breath and children daily bread, it is easy to conceive how little alteration would be made in their lot by their birth happening in other lands or earlier ages. To know the habits of such age or country is to know the quality and tenor of their lives. A postman of the present day may not have been a letter-carrier in the period of the Commonwealth; but, so far as his lot depended on himself, it would not have ranged much higher. But what if Cromwell had been the fon of fome modern Barclay? Would he have followed the genius of command to the borders of revolution, or been content with the parliamentary pofition, fay, of Sir Fowell Buxton, taken arms againft the accurfed Slave-trade, and crowned his reputation in our own day by a fingle-handed conteft with public abufes of every kind and fhape? Alas! there is none in whom we can recognize the re-animated foul of Cromwell. And then, Alfred, the Saxon Monarch,—fuppofe him to have been born in a humbler fphere, but a brighter age, emerging from the middle clafs on this fide of the ftruggling millennium of the modern world, inftead of fhining at the moment of its grim beginning. Shall we ftyle him author, politician, or profperous merchant? He might have been one or all: he would have been eminent for large views in fome department of national or focial policy: he muft have commanded the refpect and admiration of all wife men in the fphere felected by his will and illuftrated by his genius and refource.

We know not if thefe fpeculations may feem to the reader plaufible, or otherwife. But there is one ancient character for whom we have no diffi-culty in finding a modern reprefentative; and this we do fet forth with greater confidence. Suppofe that one of thofe yellow-haired and lawlefs fea-kings, who difturbed the Heptarchy, and fang the wild fongs of Scandinavia as they failed in queft of plunder or in pure love of conqueft and renown; who ftood only in fear of Thor, the Thunder-god, and gave conftant praife and worfhip to Balder,

the blue-eyed deity of love and mufic,—fuppofe
the deftiny of fuch an one poftponed to our well-
regulated age, and his firft breath drawn in modern
Edinburgh, inftead of his laft figh breathed in defiance on the fhore of the ftormy Hebrides ; how
then fhall all his powers, phyfical and moral, develope and attach themfelves ? It feems to us that
fuch a phenomenon has really occurred. The
ftrong, fierce, generous Viking wakes to unfeafon-
able life at the dawning of the nineteenth century.
He brings with him all the adventurous daring of
a pirate's nature, in union with all the paffionate
affections of a poet's heart. He grows up to the
royal ftature of humanity, his yellow hair falling
in untamed profufion about his maffive brows.
He leaps a diftance fo gigantic that the lowland
carle ftares in metaphyfical aftonifhment. With
equal eafe he will knock down a bullock, or drink
drown a baillie. His mirth is more uproarious than
the laughter which fhakes Olympus ; his wifdom
and ferenity more mellow than the fun which fets
behind the hills of Morven. There is no due
outlet for his active enterprife, and fo his bufy
mind goes out after all knowledge,—lifts itfelf up
on the wings of poefy, and darts forth its eagle
vifion into the cloudland of philofophy. Untrained
as a marauder, he becomes terrible as a critic.
Denied the murderous club of his forefathers, he
feizes eagerly upon a trenchant weapon of offence,
—fince caught up into heaven, and known as the
conftellation of *The Crutch*,—and becomes henceforth the terror of all feeble poets and conceited

cockneys, and tyrant over all the foes of Tory-
dom.

In this fketch of the character of the late Profeffor Wilfon we have briefly indicated the
ftrength, variety, and affluence of his natural gifts;
and we have no doubt that when we are furnifhed
with a detailed narrative of his life and feveral performances, it will more than juftify our fummary
defcription. But the reader is not called upon to
wait for fuch a proof. It was as the " Chriftopher
North" of Blackwood's Magazine that Profeffor
Wilfon earned his fplendid reputation ; and the
fulnefs and maturity of his athletic powers were
all put forth in the compofition of the *Noctes
Ambrofianæ,* now before us. In thefe admirable
papers the man as well as the author, the humourift as well as the philofopher, the citizen as well as
the moralift, appears in the utmoft freedom of undrefs, and from them, more truly perhaps than
from any circumftantial memoir, may be drawn
the faireft eftimate of his character, opinions, and
career.

Some of our readers may remember the time,
—now thirty years gone by,—when thefe papers
began to attract the attention of the public ; and
we ourfelves can recall the pleafure which (ten
years later) the laft few numbers of the feries,
then juft brought to a triumphant conclufion, produced in our minds, in that opening ftage of
youth when the love of reading is a paffion the
moft eager and predominant. But many will require to be told, and others to be reminded, that
the *Noctes Ambrofianæ* affume to be the record of

convivial mirth and rational diſcourſe occurring at certain imaginary ſuppers, under the roof of one Ambroſe, in the city of Edinburgh. The principal interlocutors are three,—Chriſtopher North, Editor of Blackwood's Magazine ; Hogg, the Ettrick Shepherd ; and Timothy Tickler, a gentleman of the old ſchool, ſtanding ſix feet four in his ſtocking feet. None of theſe characters are purely imaginary ; yet as they appear in the work before us, in eminent relief and due proportion, they are all the maſterly creations of Profeſſor Wilſon.

Tickler is ſuppoſed to adumbrate, in certain perſonal traits, the character of Robert Sym, the author's maternal uncle, who, as the editor informs us, " died in 1844, at the age of ninety-four, having retained to the laſt the full poſſeſſion of his faculties, and enjoyed uninterrupted good health to within a very few years of his deceaſe." He was formerly a writer to the Signet, but retired from buſineſs at the commencement of the preſent century. He does not appear to have been a literary character, in the ſtricter ſenſe of the phraſe, and had no further connection with Blackwood's Magazine than that ariſing from an intereſt in its ſucceſs, and a friendſhip with its chief contributors. We may readily conclude with Mr. Ferrier, that the Tickler of the *Noctes* is almoſt entirely a creature of the imagination, or, at leaſt, a faint but noble outline worthily filled in. In the figure of Chriſtopher North, the author has ſketched himſelf,—not ſtrictly in his own character and perſon, and not in his profeſſorial robes, but

in his editorial capacity, as feated in the chair of
" Maga," and fwaying the critical fceptre in the
northern capital. We recognize the likenefs as
conditionally true. In fome notable particulars
the Chriftopher North of " Maga " and the *Noɛ̃es*
differs from the Profeffor Wilfon of private life.
The former is a gouty old bachelor, hobbling by
the aid of his memorable crutch; the latter was
then in the prime of life, and the proud father of
a happy family. The former gives himfelf dictatorial airs, and fpeaks fometimes as one " flown
with infolence and wine;" the latter was generous,
candid, affectionate, and juft. But the difference
ends in thefe few affectations, and fome others of
a kindred fort. The boundlefs animal fpirits, the
glorious invective, the fparkling wit, the ripe and
ready wifdom, of the " old man eloquent," are all
characteriftic of the great Profeffor. Through his
pleafant mafk we fee the features of the firft profe-
poet of the age, beaming with benignity and kindling
with a mild intelligence; and it adds a zeft to the
reader's pleafure to know, that, although dear Chriftopher acts rather as moderator than leader in thefe
mirthful *foirées*, yet he is not merely the prefiding
genius of the fcene, but the Profpero of all this
brilliant mafquerade, at whofe fole bidding thefe
philofophic revels rife and fall as by enchantment.

But the Mercurius, or chief fpeaker, of thefe
convivial meetings is the Ettrick Shepherd. Here,
too, we have a real character, of genuine but
limited proportions; but we fee it expanded to
the meafure of ideal greatnefs, ftamped with a

broader and far deeper individuality, and fuſtained throughout with wonderful ſuccefs. James Hogg, the poet of Mount Benger, ſupplied the hint of this delightful character ; and the homely, genial, joyous temperament of his original is never loſt ſight of in our author's fine delineation. But the Shepherd of the *Noctes* is virtually a new creation.

"*Out of very ſlender materials,*" *ſays the pre-ſent editor,* "*an ideal infinitely greater and more real, and more original, than the prototype from which it was drawn, has been bodied forth. Bear-ing in mind that theſe dialogues are converſations on men and manners, life and literature, we may con-fidently affirm that nowhere within the compaſs of that ſpecies of compoſition is there to be found a character at all comparable to this one in richneſs and readineſs of reſource. In wiſdom the Shepherd equals the Socrates of Plato ; in humour he ſur-paſſes the Falſtaff of Shakeſpeare. Clear and prompt, he might have ſtood up againſt Dr. Johnſon in cloſe and peremptory argument ; fertile and copious, he might have rivalled Burke in amplitude of declama-tion ; while his opulent imaginative powers of comi-cal deſcription inveſt all that he utters either with a picture∫que vividneſs or graphic quaintneſs pecu-liarly his own.*"—Preface, p. xvii.

So far Mr. Ferrier. If we cannot quite ſub-ſcribe to the whole of this eulogium, it is only becauſe we think the writer has confounded the total effect of theſe matchleſs dialogues, and put all to the account of him who is certainly their brighteſt ornament. It is evident that even dramatic conſiſtency would exclude the Shepherd-poet from rivalling the united powers of Plato, Shakeſpeare, and Johnſon; and if the qualities of theſe great authors be ſuggeſted, as we grant they are, by the richneſs, ſtrength, variety, and beauty of the dialogues, it is to be conſidered that the whole triumvirate contribute to the general effeƈt, which, ſtriƈtly ſpeaking, muſt be imputed to the Protean genius of the author. But the Shepherd is, nevertheleſs, pre-eminent in theſe colloquial diſplays; an infinite amount of poetry and humour is made to flow from his lips as from a fountain; both North and Tickler delight to draw him forth, and liſten to his *naïve* and ſhrewd philoſophy. In the ſeventeenth number of the *Noƈtes* he riſes into a truly Socratic ſtrain, which almoſt mars, by its exceſs of elevated thought, the harmony of his rare but more homely powers, eſpecially when he is found quoting Greek with the appropriateneſs and eaſe of a well-furniſhed ſcholar; and this ſcene, in conjunƈtion with numerous others, would almoſt juſtify the com-prehenſive charaƈter aſſigned him by the editor.

Such are the chief perſonages who meet at theſe *ſympoſia*; and nothing is more admirable than the manner in which their charaƈters are developed and ſuſtained. For dramatic power, for freedom, force, and copiouſneſs of language and illuſtration, theſe papers have no parallel in ancient or modern literature. Lucian is tame, and Landor inſuffer-

ably ftiff, in comparifon with the author of thefe
Scottifh revels. The poffibilities of genius, under
the influence of high animal fpirits, were never,
hitherto, fo fully manifefted. Nothing could exceed the realizing power which fets the fcene, the
company, fo vividly before the reader; which
makes his ear ring with the boifterous mirth, or
drink in the fteady, flowing, interrupted, and re-
current ftream of converfation; which fimulates
the effect of feftive indulgence, and from imaginary
viands diftils an intellectual wine, bright with the
pureft and moft fparkling hues of wit, and rich
with humour the moft genial and exalting.

We grant it would not be eafy, in the brief
fpace allotted to this paper, to prove by mere
quotation how merited is all the praife we have
beftowed. The very nature of the work pre-
cludes the poffibility of doing fo. The characteriftic of the *Noctes* is not an unufual polifh in difcourfe, nor even a critical fagacity both uniform
and profound: it is rather the combination of endlefs variety with perpetual frefhnefs,—the alterna-
tion of a brilliant fancy, glancing upon a thoufand
objects, and fometimes rifing into a triumphant
ftrain of natural defcription, with the tranquil fall
of fober converfation, varied only by the quainteft
humour, the flyeft fatire, the pleafanteft exaggeration, and the " wee bit" Scottifh fong, trolled
forth by the firft of Shepherds in the moft unctuous and expreffive of all paftoral dialects. It is
obvious that no " fample " can convey an adequate
idea of dialogues fo varied and fo difcurfive. It

may afford fome **notion of their ftrength and** flavour, but none **of** their **freedom,** affluence, or **range.** If chofen for its unufual power and beauty, a world of characteriftic excellence is then excluded : if of average and more level qualities, it **muft** fuffer by removal from the place in which it fpontaneoufly occurred, and acquire, by **reafon of** its being formally and feparately introduced, **a** triviality and weaknefs which do not attach **to it** in its original connection. It is fo in other and **graver** works **befide** the prefent. A page from Bofwell's Life of **Johnfon would** poorly reprefent the intellectual vigour **and fagacity** of that **true man ;** for many of **Johnfon's recorded** fayings are trivial or falfe **in fubftance, as** others are harfh and unadvifed **in fpirit** and expreffion ; **and it is** only our perfuafion of his moral worth and general wifdom which imparts a prevailing intereft to the whole. Befides and above the literary merit of his converfations, are their hiftoric value and their dramatic charm. The impreffion of a moment is left for all the ages ; and we fee a giant's cafual footftep, perhaps awkward and awry, made on the fand of time, and hardened into rock. So the intereft of Bofwell's work is mainly biographical ; as an imperfonal collection of aphorifms it would be fadly imperfect, and fubject to **a** thoufand challenges. It muft **be owned, however,** that a work of imagination like the prefent exifts under fomewhat different conditions. Having little or nothing of hiftoric value, it depends chiefly on dramatic intereft and propriety. The author prefents us with an original compofition rather than a veritable record, and it behoves him therefore to put a due fignificance into its lighteft parts : as we have not the fatisfaction always arifing from the *vrai*, we may juftly claim a fuftained prefentment of the *vraifemblable*. We bring Profeffor Wilfon to this teft in prefenting the following paffage, which very fairly exhibits the ordinary texture of thefe dialogues, and nothing more :—

" Tickler.—*Among the many ufeful difcoveries of this age, none more fo, my dear Hogg, than that poets are a fet of very abfurd inhabitants of this earth. The fimple faết of their prefuming to have a language of their own, fhould have difhed them centuries ago. A pretty kind of language, to be fure, it was ; and, confcious themfelves of its abfurdity, they palmed it upon the Mufes, and juftified their own ufe of it on the plea of infpiration !*

" North.—*Till, in courfe of time, an honeft man of the name of Wordfworth was born, who had too much integrity to fubmit to the law of their lingo, and, to the anger and aftonifhment of the order, began to fpeak in good, found, fober, intelligible profe. Then was a revolution. All who adhered to the ancient régime, became, in a few years, utterly incomprehenfible, and were coughed down by the public. On the other hand, all thofe who adopted the new theory, obferved that they were merely accommodating themfelves to the language of their brethren of mankind.*

" Tickler.—*Then the pig came fnorting out of*

the poke, and it appeared that no *such thing as poetry,
effentially diftinct from profe, could exift.* True,
that there are *fome old women* and *children who
rhyme, but the breed will foon be* extinct, *and a poet
in Scotland will be* as *fcarce as* a *capercailzie.*

" North.—*Since the* extinction, therefore, *of
Englifh poetry, there has been a wide extenfion of
the legitimate province of profe. People who have
got any genius, find that they may traverfe it as they
will,* on foot, on horfeback, or in chariot.

" Tickler.—*A Pegafus with wings always
feemed to me a filly and inefficient quadruped. A
horfe was never made to fly on feathers, but to gal-
lop on hoofs. You deftroy the idea of his peculiar
powers the moment* you clap pinions *to his fhoulder,
and make him* paw the clouds.

" North.—*Certainly. How poor the image of*—

  ' Heaven's warrior-horfe, beneath his fiery form,
     Paws the light clouds, and gallops on the ftorm,'—

to one *of Wellington's Aide-de-Camps,* on an *Englifh hunter, charging his way through the French
Cuiraffiers, to order up the Scotch Greys againft the
Old Guards moving on to redeem the difaftrous day
of Waterloo!*

" Tickler.—*Poetry, therefore, being by univerfal
confent exploded, all men, and women, and children
are at liberty to ufe what ftyle they choofe, provided
that* it be in the form of profe. *Cram it full of
imagery as an egg* is full of meat. *If* caller, *down
it will go,* and the reader *be grateful for his
breakfaft.* Pour it out *fimple, like whey, or milk
and water, and a fwallow will be found enamoured

of the liquid murmur. Let it gurgle forth, rich and racy, like a haggis, and there are stomachs that will not scun her. Fat paragraphs will be bolted like bacon; and, as he puts a period to the existence of a lofty climax, the reader will exclaim, ' O, the roast beef of Old England! and O, the English roast beef!'

" North.—*Well said, Tickler : that prose composition should always be a plain uncondimented dish, is a dogma no longer endurable. Henceforth I shall show, not only favour, but praise, to all prose books that contain any meaning, however small ; whereas I shall use all vampers like the great American shrike, commemorated in last number, who sticks small singing birds on sharp pointed thorns, and leaves them sticking there in the sunshine, a rueful, if not a saving, spectacle to the choristers of the grove.*"

In this exaltation of prose literature there is, of course, some pleasant exaggeration ; and the shepherd is allowed to step in immediately with a hearty vindication of the ancient supremacy of song. But there is a measure of seriousness in these colloquial *dicta,* and the practice of Christopher North strongly corroborates his assertion of the range and capabilities of prose composition. Much, indeed, of the literature of modern times might be adduced in favour of the same opinion ; but the works of Professor Wilson are the most striking evidences in its behalf, and none more so than the treasury of wit and humour, of pathos and

pictorial effects, with which we are now concerned.
It is no exaggeration to fay, that the profe paftorals
of the Ettrick Shepherd, fcattered in prodigal profufion throughout thefe animated pages, have more
of the power and fpirit of poetry than all the paftorals which were ever fafhioned into verfe. They
have the firft frefh bloom of nature on them, and
breathe the fweet free air of meadow and of mountain fide. Henceforth the plains of Sicily are not
more claffical than Altrive and the banks of Yarrow. But the Shepherd's powers are not limited
to the poetry of natural objects and of country life.
A fhrewd obferver of men and manners, he is
mafter of every variety of character and incident,
and, with the aid of his facile tongue, embalms
them in the unctuous dialect of Scotland. Not
emulating the literary converfations of North and
Tickler, he fhoots ahead of them by virtue of his
buoyant genius, and feizes upon the merits of a
thoufand glancing topics; is at home and paramount in every country fport, and makes the landfcape glide ghoftly by, as he defcribes a fkating
feat from Yarrow into Edinburgh; has trueft
fympathy for the moral beauty of old age, and
fpeaks of it with loving lips, while, in the perfon of
Madame Genlis, he finds a revolting contraft, and
brings out the picture of a fuperannuated French
coquette, with a fkilful, rapid, and unfparing hand;
divines character by the countenance with inftinctive readinefs, and reads the figns of hypocrify and
gluttony, as well as thofe of benevolence and virtue, with marvellous precifion; rehearfes, with

equal power, the day-dreams of his fancy and the
night-mare ftill haunting his excited recollection,
and raifes the gambler's " hell," like an earthly
pandemonium, fo vividly before the reader's eye
that innocence itfelf muft realize its truth. In
fhort, we fee a homely dialect, made fo plaftic,
copious, and extenfile, in the hands of genius,
that it anfwers every poffible demand, and feconds
the defcriptive powers which make incurfions into
every region, both of nature and of art,—from the
gorgeous fummer of a Highland loch, to the faded
and fulfome tapeftry of an ancient hackney-coach.
In the *Noctes Ambrofianæ* the reader may affure
himfelf that this is but a feeble underftatement of
the truth ; but too many extracts would be neceffary to give a competent idea of the whole production. For this purpofe, we fhould need to tranfcribe, *inter alia*, the firft part of the third number
of the *Noctes*, and the feventeenth number entire.
The former would exhibit Tickler in his character
of fportfman among the Highland lochs ; the
latter would prefent the Shepherd's character
complete, from the richeft vein of practical
humour to the higheft and fereneft flight of meditative genius. But another fcene would be ftill
wanting to a juft appreciation of the whole. Thefe
famous interlocutors fhould be heard difcourfing
on fome topic of focial or moral intereft, of a
mixed perfonal and literary character. Of this
kind is the converfation of North and the Shepherd on the domeftic rupture of Lord and Lady
Byron, occurring at the clofe of the fecond

volume. It is full of a fine humanity, and breathes the profoundeſt wiſdom of the heart. Between the ſpeakers almoſt every view of the cafe is ſuggeſted, and the claims of charity and juſtice nicely weighed.

We muſt not put aſide this brilliant and original production without briefly examining a few objections to which it is apparently open. Some of them, we think, are founded in juſtice and propriety. The work is not without grave defects and blemiſhes, though deſerving that praiſe of general truth and literary merit, which has been ſo liberally awarded. The occaſional unfairneſs and inaccuracy of ſome of its political and perſonal ſtrictures may be referred partly to its peculiar plan, and partly to the circumſtances of its production. The editor truly deſcribes it as "a wilderneſs of rejoicing fancies,"—and brambles as well as wild flowers are encountered in its devious and romantic paths. The freedom and undreſs in which the characters appear at theſe re-unions is, at leaſt, as patent as the racineſs of their convivial humour, or the ſplendour of their poetic flights. It could hardly fail to happen that, in a compoſition of this kind, written with extraordinary ſpeed, and adapted to the occaſions of a monthly journal, there ſhould be traces both of haſty judgment and tranſient but unworthy feeling. Effuſions ſo copious and ſo unpremeditated may be expected to evince the author's human weakneſs, as well as to manifeſt his extraordinary powers; and ſuch is actually the cafe. Scattered

through thefe pages are many obfervations, criti-
cifms, and conclufions, which moft readers will
not hefitate to reject as crude, or doubtful, or un-
tenable. Even on literary fubjects,—where the
author is moft found and catholic,—fome partialities are eafily difcerned to be the unconfcious
fource of critical delinquencies, as when a very
indifferent copy of verfes by Delta is pronounced
"beautiful," while the poetry of Southey is capti-
oufly diffected and fcornfully contemned. The
coarfenefs which is frequently and intimately
blended with the humour of thefe volumes is ftill
more to be regretted; for we know of no procefs
of excifion by which it could have been removed
by editorial hands, without deftruction of their
characteriftic merits. Neither are the author's
religious fentiments, or the allufions and defcrip-
tions bearing upon facred topics, in which his
characters indulge, quite unexceptionable, or in
the pureft tafte. The moral tone of the work we
hold, indeed, to be found and Chriftian in the
main. Revelation is never for an inftant doubted
or depreciated; and religion is ever recognized as
the fource of our moft ennobling fentiments. But
we are not quite pleafed with the tone in which
the Shepherd is made to fpeak of profeffing Chriftian people. We give up to his graphic ridicule
the features of the hypocrite and the fenfualift;
we do not find much fault with his defcription of
the fleeping congregation at the kirk; but why
are all the moft unbecoming vanities and indulgences here charged upon "religious ladies,"

while the worldly young **lady is reprefented as the** very emblem of cheerful innocence and truth, beaming with natural piety **the** moft amiable and refrefhing? It is charitable to fuggeft that dramatic confiftency extorted this grave afperfion and delufive theory; for they are quite in keeping with the Shepherd's favourite fentiment, that poetry is true religion.

But objections may be felt to certain features of thefe volumes, which are yet not infufceptible of a legitimate ground of defence; and thofe we fhall confider, **and this we fhall** propofe, with all franknefs and **fincerity.**

There is one feature of the *Noctes Ambrofianæ* for which the fober reader fhould be **fpecially prepared**; namely, the great devotion, both practical and theoretical, which the members feem **conftantly** paying to the pleafures of the table. **The** Shepherd and his companions **do not** hefitate to interrupt the moft entertaining theme, or fineft fentiment, with a greedy anticipation of the fupper; and when **it comes,** there is evidently nothing lacking. **By** fudden transformation is then **prefented** the feaft in feafon and the flowing bowl. The critical difcourfe, the moral cenfure, the eloquent appreciation of the charms of nature, ceafe on their lips, and are fucceeded by the well-drawn merits of a **Scotch** haggis, and **the** heart-felt praife of punch. The converfation **is** retained only as an intellectual condiment by thefe devoted men. Hearty as gourmands, **yet** delicate as epicures, they quicken the zeft of appetite by the indulgence of a learned fancy, and heighten the relifh of moft fumptuous viands by the flavour of choice Attic falt. Prefently, as the night advances, a boifterous mirth fucceeds to the quiet interchange of plea-fantry and wit; and North—the ftately and the fage—is not unfrequently fupported in unvenerable plight to the coach or couch awaiting him. From a picture fo undignified as this fome readers will be apt to turn with very natural diflike; they may even haftily pronounce it to be of pernicious and immoral tendency. But we fubmit that thefe imaginary revels muft be wholly mifconftrued be-fore they can be totally condemned. To our minds there is a fine Shakefpearian humour in thefe fcenes, which gives them the immunity of fhadowy art-creations, fo that they evade, by their buoyant unreality, the weight of ferious rebuke. We fee that all this animal excefs is purely fuppo-fititious; and though the humour which conceives it may fail by repetition, (as indeed it does,) we muft not forget the origin and fphere of that con-ception. There is here no call for the verdict of a committee of the Temperance Society; for the whole proceeding is removed beyond the limits of their practical commiffion, removed even beyond the limits of " this vifible diurnal fphere," into the region of imaginative art. The moft temperate of us all would hefitate to ground a ferious charge of gluttony againft Charles Lamb, fimply upon his unctuous praife of young roaft-pig (for which difh it is very poffible the author had no actual preference); and it would be equally unjuft, or,

rather, equally ridiculous, to condemn altogether
the imaginary revels which, in the prefent inftance,
fupply the occafion of fo much agreeable and
" large difcourfe."

The fame confideration will ferve greatly to
modify another queftionable feature of thefe dialogues. Written at a time of great political
activity, and infpired, as we have feen, by the
higheft energy of animal fpirits, they abound in
freedom of remark too often bordering upon perfonal abufe. But fome critics have exaggerated,
we think, both the number and character of thefe
injurious paffages. With one or two exceptions,
the abufe of North is not perfonal, in the offenfive
fenfe of that term. His invective is generally a
matter of pure humour, and no more indicates
malice or uncharitablenefs, than his delightful
felf-glorification betokens a degrading vanity. The
genius of exaggeration feems to infpire the whole
tirade. It is the practice of an able archer on an
indifferent target; and though he plucks his keen-
headed arrows out of the vocabulary of ridicule
and fcorn, and launches them with equal force and
truth of aim, it is not that he may wound the
apple of the eye before him, but rather that he
may empty the quiver of his own excited genius.
Even when Chriftopher is in a really fplenetic
mood, and fpeaks with downright injuftice of
fome contemporary book or author, it adds fomething to the dramatic charm of thefe *fympofia ;*
and, after all, there is not much harm done : the

well-read reader ſtill judges for himſelf of merits which are evidently diſparaged from accidental and temporary feeling, and remembers that the convivial chair is not the ſeat of meaſured and impartial juſtice.

NEW POEMS OF BROWNING AND
LANDOR.

E prefume that moft readers of the
prefent day, and our own among the
number, have had the theory of poetry
fufficiently difcuffed before them. The
fubject has not been confined to feparate effays on
" Poetics;" for hardly is a fingle paper written to
introduce fome recent book of verfes, but the
critic launches into generalities of the moft impofing kind, in which much that is true is very
fafely ventured on, and perhaps fomething that is
new is rather modeftly propounded. If there is
no great harm in this practice, there is certainly a
limit to its propriety and ufefulnefs. An introduction of the kind referred to is not decifive of
the author's merits, even when it feems to bear
moft fairly on them; for fo ample is the fphere
and theory of poetry, and fo great the ingenuity
of our critical brethren, that a very partial ftatement may be invefted with the air of a moft complete one, and judgment given on the authority of
minor canons without fufpicion raifed of a larger
and more equitable rule. For the purpofes of

juftice, then, the practice is at leaft a doubtful, if
not a dangerous, one. The fcope for entertainment which it furnifhes is more confiderable ;
but at the fame time nothing is fo liable to degenerate into tedioufnefs as any line of general remark,
which neceffarily involves fo large an amount of
repetitions and commonplaces. For thefe reafons,
which both define and urge the claims of a due
economy of time and fpace, we fhall proceed at
once to open our poetic budget.

The firft author on our lift tempts us to extend
the depreciatory obfervations already made. With
Mr. Browning before us we are ftrongly difpofed
to doubt the utility, not merely of prelufive canons,
but of direct and fpecial criticifm. So far as the
authors themfelves are concerned, and efpecially
thofe belonging to the minftrel tribe, it is likely
that our office might ceafe without material lofs
or detriment. Poets of the higheft ftamp are
their own fevereft cenfors ; thofe of the fecond
grade are commonly unalterable, the flaves of their
own idiofyncrafy ; while bards of the loweft order
are too wilful to admit, or too feeble to profit by,
either precept or reproof. Mr. Browning belongs
to the fecond clafs, which is even more hopelefs
than the laft. Mediocrity of poetic merit may be
corrected by judicious criticifm, and improved up
to a certain point ; but the native eccentricity of
genius is not to be reduced to a more perfect
fphere. The defects of Mr. Browning's poetry
are as characteriftic as its beauties : indeed, the
former in fome degree depend upon the latter, and

by this time, at leaft, they are practically infepar-
able. We muft then accept our author for what
he is, and wafte no time in fruitlefs lamentations
or advice. The energy of higheft genius works
itfelf clear of all befetments, till both character
and fame are "rounded as a ftar;" but no external
influence is appreciable in this refult. We think
it very doubtful now, if the genius of Mr. Browning will iffue from its nebulous retreat, and orb
itfelf diftinctly in our literary heaven : but certainly
no terreftrial power can operate upon him to that
end. In his cafe, therefore, and in thofe of fome
others who alfo are more or lefs confirmed in their
poetic character, we fhall confult only the pleafure
and improvement of our readers : we fhall ftrictly
obferve and illuftrate the phenomena as they arife
before us, and make no reflections but fuch as
fall directly from the mirror we hold up.

The earlieft fruits of Mr. Browning's mufe—if
we except the poem of " Sordello," which the
author appears to have repudiated, and which
fhould not therefore be taken into account—were
publifhed, in feries, under the fymbolic name of
" Bells and Pomegranates," and confift of dramas
and dramatic lyrics. His new poems differ very
flightly in form, and ftill lefs in character, from
thefe productions. The volumes entitled " Men
and Women" confift entirely of lyrical mono-
logues, about fifty in number. If the title of the
firft work was fomewhat far-fetched and fantaftical,
that of the fecond is much too literal to be appropriate. There is mufic and perfume—recondite

mufic and exotic perfume—in the one; but how
limited and exceptional is the human nature of
the other!

We have already intimated that Mr. Browning
is fo confirmed in his poetic ways, as to be far
beyond the reach of falutary difcipline. He may
be held up as a warning, and in fome few points
commended as an example; but we have no idea
that he is capable of profiting even by ftri&ures
which his own candid judgment may bow to and
admit. His lateft publication has fatisfied our
minds of this fa&. The new poems of Mr.
Browning are only fo many new examples of his
peculiar ftyle,—a ftyle ftill harfh, in fpite of intimations of a hidden mufic, and ftill obfcure, in
fpite of occafional gleams of happieft meaning.
They fhow no improvement in the way of genial
growth, but only fome advance of technic fkill.
They are effufions which have hardened in the
mould of a definite and curious intelle&,—not
fruits which have ripened on the living vine of
genius. It happens always in fuch cafes that any
eccentricity of ftyle becomes more marked, and
any defe&ive vifion more contra&ed; and it is
ftrikingly fo in the inftance now before us, where
the author's mannerifm is more prominent and
gratuitous than ever. In this refpe& the poetry
of Mr. Browning is dire&ly oppofed to that of
Mr. Tennyfon. While the genius of the latter
is mellowing year by year, the mufe of the former
becomes only more perverfe. The fpirit of
poetry is an eminently plaftic power,—the only

certain agent of poetical expreffion ; and in fofter-
ing this expanfive fpirit, which is to works of art
what the vital power is in the organic world, Mr.
Tennyfon has caufed his genius to efflorefce fo
freely and fpontaneoufly, that the crude hufk has
fallen more and more away,—his early faults of
language have ceafed infenfibly, and his verfe has
gradually become the pure tranfparent medium of
his thoughts.   Mr. Browning has not fo rid himfelf of his befetting faults.   We do not forget that
the ftyle of art he practifes is wholly different,
that his range and object are expreffly limited.
Very unequal are thefe two, in depth and compafs,
as well as in tone and colour.   The one is daily
getting farther out to fea, takes deeper foundings
and frefh obfervations ; while the other rocks idly
in the fame Italian bay, and levels his glafs at the
fame few quaint and liftlefs figures on the beach.
But independently of this effential difference, we
would point attention to the fact, that the inferior
poet is alfo the inferior artift ; that, while the expreffion of the one always finds entrance, and is
felt within the foul, the other not feldom fails in
his humbler appeal to the underftanding and
æfthetic fenfe.   It may be difficult—or, indeed,
impoffible—to give the full meaning of Mr. Tennyfon's language in any other terms ; but this is only
becaufe true poetry has no equivalent ; we are
borne along with it notwithftanding,—it does not
leave us where we were, but carries us whitherfo-
ever it will.   But Mr. Browning is a lover of the
picturefque, a ftudent of men, and a fketcher of

character and coftume ; and it behoves him to be at leaft fo far literal and intelligible, that we may appreciate the object he draws from the fame pofition which he occupies. Now, our charge is, that he is not thus literal and intelligible ; and this brings us to the queftion which fo many afk themfelves,—Mr. Browning is acknowledged for fo clever a man, that they are afhamed to afk their neighbours,—How is it that Mr. Browning's poetry is fo hard to read, fo very difficult to underftand ?

The admirers of our author would probably tell us that he writes only for the cultivated few, and that poetry of that ftamp is never obvious to the popular mind, or relifhed by the popular tafte. If we reply, that this is not true of the moft eminent, and point to Homer and Shakefpeare, they will fay, that they are content to fee him in a lower feat, and fignificantly point to Milton and to Gray. Yet the reference is rather plaufible than juft. Milton wrote two hundred years ago, when the Englifh language was ftill unmoulded and unfixed ; yet if the " Comus" or " L'Allegro" be not very widely appreciated, the reafon is not to be found in its obfcurity, to which charge, indeed, it is not ftrictly liable. Its elevation of thought, and delicacy of treatment, are remarkable ; and thefe remove it from the fympathy and tafte of vulgar readers ; but its meanings are direct and clear. No doubt its claffical allufions make fome demand upon the reader's previous knowledge ; but without fuch knowledge it is fufficiently pleafing and intelligible even upon one perufal. But no fuch knowledge avails to the underftanding of Mr. Browning's mufe, without repeated application and fevereft ftudy. Even an acquaintance with the localities and life of modern Italy may be added to his previous ftock, and he fhall ftill be in the dark as to the fignificance and drift of the author's poem; he may ftill puzzle himfelf over " A Toccata of Galuppi's,"—while the title itfelf is enough to frighten or perplex the untravelled reader. One perufal of that fingular performance will hardly gratify the moft attentive mind; and a perfon of only average poetic tafte will have fmall inducement to venture on a fecond. It muft be owned that the poem is fadly wanting in clearnefs and directnefs. Even thofe who are fain to admire becaufe they are content to ftudy it, and who fancy they difcern and feel fomething of its fine impreffive moral, are not thoroughly affured that they enter into the author's fpirit, or rightly eftimate the fentiment and meaning of his verfes. To fome —and not a few—the poem will be writ in hieroglyphic fymbols; and the fault is not wholly in themfelves,—the poet's ftyle and language is unwarrantably broken and obfcure. The fact is, that Mr. Browning is too proud for anything. He difdains to take a little pains to put the reader at a fimilar advantage with himfelf,—to give a preparatory ftatement which may help to make his fubfequent effufion plain and logical. He fcorns the good old ftyle of beginning at the beginning. He ftarts from any point and fpeaks in any tenfe he pleafes; is never fimple or literal for a moment;

leaves out (or out of fight) a link here and another there of that which forms the inevitable chain of truth, making a hint or a word fupply its place; and, if you fail to comprehend the whole, is apparently fatisfied that he knows better, and has the advantage of you there. He abandons himfelf to a train of vivid affociations, and brings out fome features of them with remarkable effect; but he gives you no clue whereby to follow him throughout.

It is this harfhnefs, which of courfe is real, and this obfcurity, which is chiefly fuperficial, that will always render Mr. Browning's poetry unpopular, becaufe they interfere with its eafy and complete enjoyment. But we can readily believe that his fmall circle of admirers are very ardent in their admiration, and almoft unmeafured in their praife. In the firft place, we value an appreciation arrived at only after fome expenditure of time and ftudy. And then the ear, the mind, become gradually attuned to the new modes of thought and fpeech. But there is fomething more than this. Both the merits and defects of Mr. Browning's poetry are fuch as belong to a peculiar fchool of art; and the mafters in every fchool have the power of roufing the enthufiafm of kindred minds; they gather round them a band of attached difciples, and are followed by the plaudits of delighted connoiffeurs. This is more feldom noticed in our poets than in the fifter art of painting; and, indeed, the poems of Mr. Browning find an almoft perfect analogy in the pictures of a certain modern fchool. Our author refembles the pre-Raffaelites both in choice

of fubject and in ftyle of treatment. He has the
fame vivid and realizing touch, and the fame love
of exquifite detail. Like them he has a ftrong
averfion to all that is conventional in the language
of his art, and like them, alfo, is liable to be mif-
apprehended and decried. His very fidelity to
nature, expreffed with fo much novelty and boldnefs, incurs the charge of eccentricity and herefy.
The traditions of his art are lefs to him than the
impreffion of his own fenfes, and the fkill of his
own right hand. But, as a poet, he muft count
upon lefs general admiration than his brother artift.
If even truth of colour is not fully eftimated by the
uneducated fenfe, and the pre-Raffaelite muft firft
furprife before thoroughly convincing and delight-
ing us, much more the independent ufe of language. We muft know the right force of words
before we feel them ; and then only are we prepared to recognize the completer meafures of poetic
truth, which Coleridge has defined to be *the beft
words in the beft order*. We fay then, of Mr.
Browning, that although any reader may be warranted in faying what he is not,—a great poet ; yet
only an accomplifhed few are able to judge of his
peculiar meafures, and pronounce him what he is
—an original and graphic artift. He is fairly open
to rebuke, and liable, befides, to general neglect ;
but no thoughtful perfon will defpife either his
talents or attainments.

The reader of his volumes will notice the large
fhare of attention which Mr. Browning has beftowed on the pictures and painters of the Italian

fchools. They are all very chara&teriftic fketches ;
and as they are for the moft part in our author's
better manner, we fhould have willingly transferred
a fpecimen to our pages,—fuch as " Andrea del
Sarto, called the Faultlefs Painter,"—but their
length forbids. The fame obje&ion refts againft
our introdu&ion to the reader of " Bifhop Blou-
gram's Apology." The verfes fo entitled embody
the after-dinner talk of a dignitary of the Romifh
Church, who, for the edification of a fceptical companion, endeavours to fhow that a certain amount
of faith is expedient to the wife, and that no larger
meafure is pra&icable in the conditions under
which we live. He compares our life to a voyage
in which all our available fpace is a narrow "cabin,"
whofe limits exclude all but the moft neceflary and
convenient articles. In fhort, this worthy Prelate
advocates a moft comfortable compromife between
the rival claims of the gofpel and the world.
Utterly falfe as fuch cafuiftry muft be, it is here
moft pleafantly and ably argued. But more to
our judgment, if not to our tafte, as well as more
convenient for the purpofe of extra&ion, is the following little poem, called " Tranfcendentalifm : a
Poem in Twelve Books." It reads in fome parts
like our author's own defence.

> " Stop playing, poet ! may a brother fpeak ?
>   'T is you fpeak, that's your error ! Song's our art ;
>   Whereas you pleafe to fpeak thefe naked thoughts,
>   Inftead of dreffing them in fights and founds :
>   —Fine thoughts, good thoughts, thoughts fit to treafure
>   up !
> But why fuch long prolufion and difplay,

Such turning and adjuftment of the harp,
And taking it upon the breaft at length,
Only to fpeak dry words acrofs its ftrings?
Stark naked thought is in requeft enough—
Speak profe, and holloa it till Europe hears!
The fix-foot Swifs-tube, traced about with bark,
Which helps the hunter's voice from Alp to Alp—
Exchange our harp for that—who hinders you?
—But here's your fault: grown men want thought you
    think ;—
Thought's what they mean by verfe, and feek in verfe:
Boys feek for images in melody,
Men muft have reafon—fo you aim at men.
Quite otherwife! Objects throng our youth, 'tis true;
We fee and hear, and do not wonder much.
If you could tell us what they mean, indeed!
As Swedifh Bœhme never cared for plants,
Until it happ'd, in walking in the fields,
He noticed all at once the plants could fpeak;
Many turn'd with loofen'd tongue to talk with him:
That day the daify had an eye indeed,—
Colloquized with the cowflip on fuch themes!
We find them extant yet in Jacob's profe.
But by the time youth fteps a ftage or two,
While reading profe in that tough book he wrote,
(Collating and emendating the fame,
And fettling on the fenfe moft to our mind,)
We fhut the clafps, and find life's fummer paft.
Then, who helps men, pray, to repair our lofs?
Another Bœhme with a tougher book
And fubtler meanings of what rofes fay—
Or fome ftout Mage like him of Halberftadt,
John, who made things Bœhme wrote thoughts about?
He with a *look you!* vents a brace of rhymes,
And in them breaks the fudden rofe herfelf,
Over us, under, round us every fide;
Nay, in and out the tables and the chairs,
And mufty volumes,—Bœhme's book and all,—
Buries us with a glory young once more,
Pouring heaven into this fhort houfe of life.
—So come, the harp back to your heart again!
You are a poem though your poem's naught.
The beft of all you did before, believe,
Was your own boy's face over the fine chords
Bent, following the cherub at the top
That points to God with his pair'd half-moon wings."

We hardly know if these lines serve more to
vindicate or to condemn the author's practice. No
doubt a few more readings would improve our in-
sight; but our present impression is only faint, and
so far not favourable to Mr. Browning's own performance. He avoids the error, indeed, of giving
us " stark naked thoughts ;" but most honest men
will find his verse as " tough" as Jacob Bœhme's
celestial prose. We leave the matter to occupy
the reader's leisurely consideration ; and pass on to
one of plainer speech.

A few words will suffice to introduce the new
production of Walter Savage Landor. In the
penultimate issue of this vigorous writer,—still
vigorous on the verge of fourscore years,—we
gratefully accepted what were proffered as the
" Last Fruits off an Old Tree," and which, by their
flavour and abundance, testified to the continued
soundness of the stock. We have now more " last
fruit;" and its flavour is still of the fine sort, though
it may lack something of its wonted fulness and
body.

In " Antony and Octavius" Mr. Landor has
done a bold thing. He has never, indeed, been
wanting in courage and independence of the
haughtiest kind ; and in the magic circle which his
genius has described and peopled, he has not hesitated to evoke the spirits of the most mighty dead,
—to re-animate the tongues of Plato and of
Cicero ; to make Dante, and Petrarca, and Spen-
ser discourse high wisdom, and pour out their ten-

dereft complaint; **to fhow us** Milton in his blind old **age,** and Shakefpeare in the affluent promife of his youth. With **what** wonderful fuccefs he has done all this, the **reader of** his works **need not be told.** But **in the flender book** before **us he appears not** as **the** delineator, **but** as the rival, of Shakefpeare; **not as** one who ventured to imagine the tenor of his youth, **but as** one who dares to challenge comparifon **with** the works of his manhood. Of courfe, Mr. Landor repudiates the thought of rivalry fo bold as this :—

"*Few,*" *fays he, "have obtained the privilege of entering Shakefpeare's garden, and of feeing him take turn after turn, quite alone, now nimbly, now gravely, on his broad and lofty terrace. . . . Let us never venture where he is walking, whether in deep meditation, or in buoyant fpirits. Enough is it for us to ramble and loiter in the narrower paths below, and look up at the various images which, in the prodigality of his wealth, he has placed in every quarter. . . . Before you, reader, are fome fcattered leaves gathered from under them; carefuller hands may arrange and comprefs them in a book of their own, and thus for a while preferve them, if rude children do not finger them firft, and tamper with their fragility.*"

But the fact **remains that our** author has chofen to **treat the fame fubject as Shakefpeare, and** in a dramatic form; **and** though no one will **be fo** unjuft **as to** inftitute a formal comparifon, yet neither can any difarm his memory of the brighteft affociations connected with the theme. It happens, too, that it is one of Shakefpeare's mafter-pieces which is thus recalled. How wonderfully is the poet's genius difplayed in the drama of " Antony and Cleopatra !" It feems to us the very richeft fruit of his exuberant mind, difplaying an almoft miraculous knowledge of the human heart, and an inexhauftible fund of fpirit and invention. The author does not perfonally appear, but he feems in effect to be himfelf fafcinated by the " ferpent of old Nile,"—to nurfe an enthufiafm which boldly challenges the equal admiration of the reader, and to afk triumphantly, Who can blame Antony without half coveting his luxurious lot? And what was there in the world he loft to compare with the world's paragon for whom he left it, and whofe wanton fancy he completely conquered and abforbed, kindling into heroic fervour the Epicurean paffion of her heart, like a tropic garden fet on fire by the unufual blazing of the fun? Pompeys and Cæfars the world will never be without ; but Antony could only play his part while Cleopatra lived. And fo,—who blames him ?—he melted into the cup of his love the jewel of a rare and coftly genius, and, drinking that intoxicating draught, he gladly exhaufted the utmoft fortune of the gods.

Yet, in fpite of this mafterly pre-occupation of the theme, the " Antony and Octavius " of Mr. Landor has merit and intereft of its own. After all, it is perhaps the only ground where our author

could any way bear up againſt ſuch odds; for he
is deeply imbued with the antique ſpirit, as well
as richly fraught with claſſical learning; and a
brief quotation will ſhow with what taſte and ſkill
he interprets **Plutarch** after the Shakeſpearian
manner. Octavius is already maſter in Egypt,
and to him enters gaily the young Cæſarion, ſon
of his uncle Julius.

" *Cæſarion.* Hail! hail! my couſin! Let me kiſs that hand
  So ſoft and white.   Why hold it back from me?
  I am your couſin, boy Cæſarion.
Octavius. Who taught you all this courteſy?
Cæſarion.   My heart.
  Beſide, my mother bade me wiſh you joy.
Octavius. I would myſelf receive it from her.
Cæſarion.   Come,
  Come then with me; none ſee her and are ſad.
Octavius. Then ſhe herſelf is not ſo?
Cæſarion.   Not a whit,
  Grave as ſhe looks, but ſhould be merrier ſtill.
Octavius. She may expect all bounty at our hands.
Cæſarion. Bounty! ſhe wants no bounty. Look around.
  Thoſe palaces, thoſe temples and their gods,
  And myriad prieſts within them, all are hers;
  And people bring her ſhips, and gems, and gold.
  O couſin! do you know what ſome men ſay,
  (If they do ſay it,) that your ſails, ere long,
  Will waft all theſe away?
                            I wiſh 't were true
  What elſe they talk.
Octavius. What is it?
Cæſarion.   That you come
  To carry off her alſo. She is grown
  Paler; and I have ſeen her bite her lip
  At hearing this. Ha! well I know my mother;
  She thinks it may look redder for the bite."

Thus the boy prattles; but the eye of Octavius
is upon him, and his admiration is not likely to
paſs over into love.

"*Octavius.* Agrippa, didſt thou mark that comely boy?
Agrippa. I did indeed.
Octavius.   There is, methinks, in him
     A ſomewhat not unlike our common friend.
Agrippa. Unlike! There never was ſuch ſimilar
     Expreſſion. I remember Caius Julius
     In youth, although my elder by ſome years;
     Well I remember that high-vaulted brow,
     Thoſe eyes of eagles under it, thoſe lips
     At which the Senate and the people ſtood
     Expectant for their portals to uncloſe;
     Then ſpeech, not womanly, but manly ſweet,
     Came from them, and ſhed pleaſure as the morn
     Sheds light.
Octavius.   The boy has too much confidence.
Agrippa. Not for his prototype. When he threw back
     That hair in hue like cinnamon, I thought
     I ſaw great Julius toſſing his, and warn
     The pirates he would give them their deſert.
     . . . My boy, thou gazeſt at thoſe arms hung round.
Cæfarion. I am not ſtrong enough for ſword or ſhield,
     Nor even ſo old as my ſweet mother was
     When I firſt rioted upon her knee,
     And ſeized whatever ſparkled in her hair.
     Ah! you had been delighted, had you ſeen
     The pranks ſhe pardon'd me! What gentleneſs!
     What playfulneſs!
Octavius.   Go now, Cæfarion.
Cæfarion. And had you ever ſeen my father too!
     He was as fond of her as ſhe of me,
     And often bent his thoughtful brow o'er mine
     To kiſs what ſhe had kiſs'd; then held me out
     To ſhow how he could manage the refractory;
     Then one long ſmile, one preſſure to the breaſt.
Octavius. How tedious that boy grows! lead him away,
     Aufidius! . . . There is miſchief in his mind,
     He looks ſo guileleſs."

We might, perhaps, have ſelected a more important ſcene than the above, and given the reader
a glimpſe of Mr. Landor's " Antony;" but we
wiſhed to impart ſome notion of the ſkill and
freedom of theſe claſſic dialogues; and the lover

of this fpecies of poetry will procure the little
volume itfelf. At any rate, our limits are tranf-
greffed, and we muft refrain from quoting more.
We believe the reader will admire the brief example we have given. We can affure him that
the whole twelve fcenes are of the fame complexion. After this novel and fuccefsful effort,
we fhould have no objection to receive a " Corio-
lanus " from the fame ftatuary's hand. " Corio-
lanus ! " What fubject more fuited to the haughty
genius and fharp chifel of Walter Landor ? It
would form an admirable companion to the " Antony and Octavius." Such compofitions could
enter into no foolifh and unequal rivalry with the
great dramatic mafter-pieces : they would render
homage, and not claim comparifon,—being only
ftill-life illuftrations of the mafter's living fcene.
Welcome as fuch, they might long ftand in the
avenue of Shakefpeare's fame ;—ftand filent, and
face to face, on either fide, diminifhed to all eyes
by the magnitude and glory of the place.

BOSWELL'S LETTERS.

IT was the practice of the moſt popular hiſtorian of antiquity to inſtitute comparifons betwixt certain of his rival heroes; but the biographic annals of mankind afford far more curious parallels than any which adorn the elaborate page of Plutarch. It would call for the exerciſe of fome ingenuity to find any but the moſt external features of refemblance in the lives of Agis and Cleomenes, of Sylla and Lyfander. There is more or lefs coincidence in the tenor of their fortunes or the ſtyle of their ambition; but in the minor traits of individual character, in that perfonal idiofyncrafy which combines and graduates the fubfifting elements of ſtrength and of weaknefs, of wifdom and of folly, there is no ſtriking and prevailing likenefs in any of thefe heroic pairs. The men of Plutarch are caſt in one large mould. They want that variety, and perhaps that imperfection, of character, which is requifite to furnifh inſtances either of contraſt or comparifon. Even where they differ from the general type, it is only as members of the fame family; and we detect their identity as we dif-

tinguifh the features of a Claudius or a Julius in
the heads of the twelve Cæfars. But the civilization of the Chriftian world, and efpecially of the
Teutonic and Celtic races, is marked by a bolder
individuality of genius. As modern art has opened
up the province of the picturefque, fo modern life
abounds in varied and contrafted characters; and
it is this very circumftance which makes our
biographic parallels more rare indeed, but alfo
more curious and complete. And to thefe comparifons the pleafures of contraft are not wanting;
for every point of coincidence is fraught with fome
quality of difference.

We have been led into this train of remark by
a perufal of the volume now before us, which
frequently recalls the pages of another book, and
vividly fets before the reader's mind the picture of
two choice Arcadians. The name and character
of Bofwell have, no doubt, often fuggefted thofe
of Samuel Pepys; but the publication of thefe
familiar letters makes the affociation quite infallible; for they exhibit the refemblance in its
moft ftriking form, and, at the fame time, extend
it to a thoufand particulars. We now know that the
amufing diarift of the feventeenth century revived
in the perfon of Johnfon's faithful henchman and
biographer, the jeft and wonder of the eighteenth.

The likenefs is fortuitous as well as character-
iftical. The circumftance which enables us to
complete the parallel of thefe two worthies, itfelf
fuggefts a fingular coincidence of fortune. The
pofthumous fame of Pepys and of Bofwell have

been equally affected by a fimilar accident,—an accident not favourable to the perfonal character of either, but largely conducive to the popularity of both. No wonder both are welcome to the world of readers. A giddy public is admitted into the fecret confidence of thefe choice fpirits, and finds it moft exquifite fun ; for rarely is fo thorough an expofure made of thofe lighter follies which provide the farce and interlude of human life. This fecret confidence is precifely of the moft entertaining kind,—the fulleft and the freeft poffible; confifting of incidents and thoughts which only a fool would commit to any, which no one elfe would have power or occafion to confide, and which even he will only whifper to his friend, or chuckle to himfelf. But the pen is a dangerous medium of fuch indulgences. Though folly fhould break its hour-glafs, and write only in the fcattered fand, who fhall provide that Time, which wantonly deftroys fo much, will not as wantonly preferve this little, harden the frail tablet into rock, and leave it in the mufeum of Pofterity? So at leaft it has fared with the confidence of Pepys and of Bofwell. Both were fhrewd men, and were able to hide fomething of their weakneffes from contemporary eyes; but each, forfooth, muft write himfelf down an afs. The one muft fniggle over his ticklifh delinquencies in the privacy of a journal kept in cipher; and the other muft needs confefs to an old college chum, now fettling into the fober walks of clerical and married life; and many years after the writer's death, when Pepys

is quite forgotten and Bofwell almoft forgiven, the
diary of the one is carefully deciphered, and the
letters of the other fuddenly difcovered. Of courfe
both are publifhed without fcruple or delay,—for
no man is entitled to the immunities of private
chara&ter fixty years after his death; the claims
of truth and of fociety furvive, and fuperfede mere
individual rights : our follies can find fan&tuary
only in a new-made grave ; and every record that
is fuffered to remain above ground to challenge
the curiofity of another generation, is juftly forfeit
in the intereft of mankind. Let the beaus and
goffips of our day look to it ! For our two leaky
friends the warning is fomewhat late. They have
nothing more to offer or withhold. We know
them from the loweft note to the top of their
compafs. We have made a parlour-window book
out of their "trivial fond records," and find it to
be moft exquifite fooling. We could not be more
thoroughly provided if each of us had a jefter of
his own. Certain it is that Yorick was a fool to
Samuel Pepys. He might tumble to amufe the
Majefty of unburied Denmark, barbarian as he
was ; but what is that to keeping the wide table
of Chriftendom on a roar ? No proofs of his
genius are extant ; his wit is a miferable tradition,
vouched only by a mad Prince and ftupid grave-
digger ; he died and made no fign ; he is quite
chapfallen ; the grin remains, but the joke has
long fubfided. Not fo with our incomparable
friend. The merriment we draw from him is
frefh and lively. His exit from the fcene was

only in order to a transformation. Fortune has
fent him fmartly back, and his future is a brilliant
and perpetual harlequinade. The pen with which
he " ciphered " is changed into a wand : he fmites
upon our wall with it, and old London re-appears.
It is now Whitehall—and Pepys, in the manner
as he lived, is feen to admire at the beauty of
Caftlemaine or the dancing of Monmouth ; the
Houfe of Lords—and deceitful Pepys throngs in
with the faithful Commons, ftands behind the
King's chair, and hears the merry Monarch read
from his lap a fpeech which he finds it difficult to
fpell ; Vauxhall—and it is ftill Pepys, fporting
with Knip or Mercer ; a domeftic interior—and
the fame old beau grows furious to fee his lady in
white wig, in fact " ready to burft with anger ; "
a church—and our gallant fidles up to take the
hand of a pretty lady, but retreats on finding it
armed with a pin ; a ftreet—and the worthy man
indulges an honeft blufh becaufe the nofe of his
companion is unreafonably red ! Who is not glad
to remember, that where there is any fhame there
is yet fome virtue ?

But Mr. Bofwell waits to be introduced, and
we have yet to ftate with more diftinctnefs his
claim to come into fuch pleafant company. It is
briefly this. Like Pepys he difplays about an
equal amount of talent and buffoonery in his life-
performance ; and while the firft-named quality
raifed him above the vulgar throng of men, the
latter fet him juft as much below. *Arcades ambo,*
they ftand the co-heritors of the moft equivocal

renown ; the wife man gives them an alternate
meed of admiration and contempt ; and the verieft
booby will gird at them with an inward and grateful fenfe of his fuperior parts. But what makes
the refemblance more ftriking, is the fact that both
were affected with the fame perfonal weakneffes,
to wit, the inordinate love of pleafure, and an irre-
preffible love of approbation. They both waded
in a fhallow fea of vanity,—and both were loft,
not fo much in overwhelming tides of vice, as by
their dreary diftance from the fhores of virtue.

It is of no ufe denying the ability of either.
Why fhould the world go back a hundred years to
find a coxcomb ? The fact is, that no fuch character, pure and fimple, is able to arreft and fix the
public mind. A man muft be fomething more
than a fool before he can amufe even the lighter
hours of the good and wife. Pepys was Secretary
to the Admiralty in the reigns of Charles II. and
James II, and beyond doubt he had much capacity as a man of bufinefs. There is fome hint of
his carrying retrenchment and reforms into that
department ; but it is certain that his dexterity in
keeping the public accounts was more than the
average of official life prefented. But Pepys was
not merely ufeful in affairs ; he was a patron of the
arts, and a man of fuperior culture. He made a
collection of books and pictures which to this day
teftifies to his fcholarfhip and liberal taftes.

Bofwell's reputation as a man of parts refts upon
different and better grounds. It is not from hiftory or tradition, but from his own literary works,

that we derive a knowledge of his powers. With rare exception it is cuſtomary ſtill to underrate them. We muſt not allow either the failings or the follies of this man to lead us into a diſparagement of his rare ability. Whatever may be the value of literary talents, they were poſſeſſed by Boſwell in an eminent degree. He certainly did not write one of the beſt of books becauſe he was one of the weakeſt of men, as ſome critics would have us to believe. He wrote it by virtue of peculiar gifts, and not at the prompting of a ſuperſtitious reverence, not by the aid of a feminine garrulity. His great performance derives none of its ſubſtantial merit from his folly or his vanity,—his pedantic habit of moralizing, or his inveterate love of pleaſure. Theſe, no doubt, are the moſt amuſing traits diſcovered in his familiar correſpondence; but how little could ſuch qualities contribute to a biography deſerving of the name and character and times of Johnſon ! Nor was our author particularly indebted to his opportunities. We do not underrate the great ſubject and the brilliant acceſſories which offered themſelves to his delineating pen ; but we ſay confidently that an equal occaſion had often paſſed by, either wholly unimproved, or turned to miſerably ſmall account, for want of a maſter able to appreciate and to ſeize the whole. The fact is, that Boſwell entertained from the firſt a juſt conception of the nature and method of the work he undertook; better ſtill, he realized his object with a rare felicity, carrying out his purpoſe to the laſt with equal perſeverance, fkill, and courage. His judgment and conftancy may be traced in every page of his immortal work; but fometimes it more directly challenges our attention. " I cannot," fays he, on one occafion, " allow any fragment whatever that floats in my memory, concerning the great fubject of this biography, to be loft. Though a fmall particular may appear trifling to fome, it will be relifhed by others; while every little fpark adds fomething to the general blaze; and to pleafe the true, candid, warm admirers of Johnfon, and in any degree increafe the fplendour of his reputation, I bid defiance to the fhafts of ridicule, and even of malignity." He then proceeds to relate, with becoming gravity, how the great moralift amufed himfelf one morning after breakfaft; how, being in Dr. Taylor's grounds, he ufed a long pole to force fome clumps of trees and other rubbifh over a waterfall; how at length a large dead cat baffled the toiling fage, who prefently threw down the pole to Bofwell, faying, " *Come, you fhall take it now;*" and how the faithful henchman, being " frefh," as well as faithful, " foon made the cat tumble over the cafcade." We fay, brave Bofwell as well as " frefh," and wife as well as brave! We accept with gratitude thy picture of the burly moralift, working with all his body and rolling with incomparable laughter : and the world fhall learn that thou, too, hadft fomething to achieve even when the mighty failed; that in virtue of elaftic youth and genius thou didft hurl a dead cat down the ftream, and left Ulyffes ftanding convulfed upon its bank, a picture, at the leaft, for evermore !

It is the firſt great praiſe of Boſwell that he attached himſelf to ſuch a maſter. In this fact, too, we recognize the leading paradox of his career. The more intimately we come to know the character of Boſwell,—his vanity, frivolity, and ſenſuality,—the more does the wonder of his hero-worſhip grow upon us. It is no very rare thing to meet with a Scotchman who prefers London to Edinburgh; and not unfrequently we may have ſeen a man about town afflicted with a literary turn, or haunted by way of conſcience with a reverence for moral greatneſs; but the queſtion remains, What attracted this poor butterfly and paraſite to the burly, rough-grained moraliſt and threadbare ſcholar of Fleet Street? The love of ſplendour and *éclat* which poſſeſſed the ſoul of Boſwell might have led us to think that only meretricious qualities, and only the moſt popular reputation, would have had any charm for him; but the fact is otherwiſe. To Paoli, the hero of his day, our author paid indeed aſſiduous court, and fluttered with evident delight in the beams of his glory; but his true allegiance was paid to Johnſon, and that when Johnſon was very far from reaching the commanding height of reputation which he finally attained. It is only juſt to Boſwell that this genuine life-long devotion, for ever unexplained as it may be, ſhould be ſet over againſt a multitude of his weakneſſes and follies. We accept it as the teſtimony of his better genius to the dignity of human life, and acknowledge once for all, that his appreciation of virtue, wiſdom, and fobriety, was at leaft equal to his inftinct of foppery, and his inordinate love of pleafure.

It is curious to obferve the influence of Johnfon upon the literary ftyle of his admirer. A certain elegant and lively freedom belongs to Bofwell's proper manner, but long intimacy with fo grave a moralift appears to have added both weight and point to his expreffions. He does not often follow with equal ftep the fefquipedalian march of Johnfon; but fometimes by an unufual feverity of thought, and fometimes by a felicitous condenfation or turn of language, he calls to mind the characteriftic excellence of his great mafter. Not unfrequently the fentiment and the phrafe are both to be referred to this impofing model. Thus in an able and elaborate letter addreffed to Dr. Johnfon, we find an ingenious paffage in favour of commutation of the fentence paffed upon the unhappy Dr. Dodd, founded upon the many acts of benevolence and virtue which preceded the folitary crime. " Such an inftance," he contends, " would do more to encourage goodnefs than his execution would do to deter from vice. I am not afraid of any bad confequence to fociety; for who will perfevere for a long courfe of years in a diftinguifhed difcharge of religious duties with a view to commit a forgery with impunity?" This fentence is fo truly in the mafter's ftyle that we look increduloufly to the fubfcription of the letter, and find that it is indeed Bofwell retorting the fedate reflection with its ufual turn,—as a boy may throw back upon a fountain the water he has juft abftracted from it.

Another inftance of his Johnfonian manner is to be found in the dedication of his *Account of Corfica* to General Paoli. Only liften to this ridiculous parrot, fwinging from the roof of his mafter's ftudy! "Dedications are for moft part the offerings of interefted fervility, or the effufions of partial zeal; enumerating the virtues of men in whom no virtues can be found, or predicting greatnefs to thofe who afterwards pafs their days in unambitious indolence, and die leaving no memorial of their exiftence but a dedication, in which all their merit is confeffedly future, and which time has turned into filent reproach. . . . . . He who has any experience of mankind will be cautious to whom he dedicates. Publicly to beftow praife on merit of which the public is not fenfible, or to raife flattering expectations which are never fulfilled, muft fink the character of an author, and make him appear a cringing parafite or a fond enthufiaft." The firft of thefe fentences is very clumfy; the fecond is a better imitation of Johnfon's manner: but both are fpurious, and therefore to be heartily contemned. It was a miftake in Bofwell to counterfeit that weighty ftyle. Bafe metal may pafs current in a lighter form; but what bullion merchant was ever deceived by ingots of lead or tin?

But Bofwell had literary merits of his own; and his imitation of Johnfon's manner was happily as rare as it was gratuitous. His *Journey to the Hebrides* is not lefs entertaining than his more famous biography; and though it may be faid that the fame great talker contributes here the fame

large element of intereſt and inſtruction, our author's merit is not much affected by the remark ;
for we are reminded of the high value of his
peculiar talents, and we congratulate ourſelves, not
exactly becauſe Johnſon was the companion of
our lively traveller, but on the good fortune which
made the inimitable Boſwell the companion of
Johnſon.   Other ſages may wander—and do wander—thither and otherwhere ; but the ſtory remains untold, or finds dull record and due oblivion,
like Johnſon's own account of the Hebridean tour.
Of that pair, indeed, we ſhall never meet the like,
on any road, in any chronicle ; for the Mercurial
genius, the lively obſervation, the tact, fidelity, and
devotion of a Boſwell, are neceſſary to that rare
conjunction.

It is well known that Boſwell was the butt of
all the wits ; and many men of little mark, whoſe
names he has embalmed in his great biography, no
doubt took lawful pleaſure in turning his faults to
ridicule.   It is certain, alſo, that he was not de-
ſpiſed without a cauſe.   But we contend that there
is nothing in his own publications, and eſpecially
nothing in his *Life of Johnſon*, to render him de-
ſpicable in our eyes.   His reverence for the learning, intellect, and character of that great man, led
him to yield a fooliſh and unbecoming deference,
and in the ſimplicity of his heart he told a good
ſtory to his own diſadvantage ; but theſe are traits
of genius compared with the manners of ordinary
men, who frequently pay court to a far more vulgar idol for more ſelfiſh ends, and whoſe affecta-

tion of independence is both part and proof of
their fervility, as the loweft reverence is meafured
by the height of its recoil.   Bofwell's was at leaft
no common-place toadyifm ; and if we fmile at
his relations to Johnfon, our fmile has nothing of
contempt in it.   It is therefore to his behaviour
in general fociety, and to thofe perfonal difplays
which amufed his affociates in the affembly or the
club, in the hours of poft-prandial exhilaration, or
thofe yet more ridiculous of ftate and dignity,—it
is to Bofwell under thefe conditions that we muft
look for the materials and the objeét of contempt.
Some glimpfes of the kind are attainable in the
writings of his contemporaries ; but how much
better to have his follies given under his own hand
to fome intimate and equal !   Then will he fpeak
out freely, and we fhall more diftinétly know why
the name of Bofwell has fo long been a fynonym
for fool.

The volume before us anfwers this purpofe and
defcription.   It confifts of about one hundred
letters addreffed by Bofwell to the Rev. W. J.
Temple, and forming the only remaining part of
what was probably a voluminous correfpondence ;
for the intimacy between Temple and his friend
was continued during their lives, which lafted a
period of fome threefcore years, and then terminated almoft together.   The difcovery of thefe
curious documents is thus related by the editor.

" *A few years ago a Clergyman, having occafion to
buy fome articles at the fhop of Madame Noel, at*

*Boulogne, obferved **that the paper** in which they **were** wrapped was the fragment of an Englifh letter. **Upon** infpection, a date and fome names were dif-covered; and further invefligation proved that the piece of paper in queftion was **part of a** correfpon-dence, carried on nearly a century before, **between the** biographer of **Dr.** Samuel Johnfon and his **early friend** the Rev. William Johnfon Temple. **On** making inquiry, it was afcertained that this piece of paper had been taken from a large parcel recently purchafed from a hawker, who was in the habit of paffing through Boulogne **once or twice a** year, for the purpofe **of** fupplying **the** different fhops with **paper.** Beyond this no further information could be obtained. The whole contents of **the parcel were** immediately fecured. **The** majority of **the letters** bear the London and Devon poft-marks, and are franked **by** well-known names **of** that period. Be-fides thofe written **by Bofwell,** which are here pub-lifhed, were found feveral from **Mr.** Nichols, Mr. Claxton, and other perfons alluded to **in** the following pages, as well as a few unfinifhed fermons and effays by **Mr.** Temple."—Preface.*

The queftion has of courfe been afked, Are thefe letters genuine? and it has been uniformly anfwered that they are. This affurance is not bafed upon the fimple ftatement we have juft tranfcribed. Many a fpurious document has been prefaced by a hiftory very plain and plaufible, vouched for by a learned editor, and iffued by a publifher of ftrict refpectability. Much more than thefe are requifite to eftablifh the authenticity of fuch a work in a manufacturing age like ours; but much more alfo may in this cafe be adduced. Moft readers will be quite fatisfied with the internal evidence of thefe letters. They approve themfelves by their omiffions as well as by their contents; they deal too largely in new material for a mere imitator's timid hand, and yet the whole is not more novel than characteriftic. We fee Bofwell in a gayer form; but the grub of Johnfon has only emerged into the butterfly, and flutters in the face of the Corfican hero. It is the fame parafite elated and transformed. So alfo we have Bofwell fucceffively courting, fcheming, grumbling, drinking,—abufing the great and reproaching himfelf,—full of envy, fondnefs, conceit, animal fpirits, *ennui*, and defpair. And many of thefe are new phafes of character in one who has hitherto appeared as a fort of flunkey-coxcomb, never greatly ftirred out of his own deep felf-efteem, not very ferious, and yet not quite unfteady. But it is Bofwell after all,—not ftanding befide his mafter's chair, and fcaring a blue-bottle from his mafter's wig, but efcaped down-ftairs to his other, undrefs heaven, emptying the bottle, and chucking the houfemaid under the chin. Yes, it is Bofwell below ftairs.

We muft glean from thefe letters fome of the more prominent incidents and traits. Nothing is more amufing than the effect which fome fuccefs in the beft fociety of London produces on the mind of Bofwell. It affords him an abfolute re-

velation of his own importance. " I am really," he
fays, " the *great man* now. I have David Hume
in the forenoon, and Mr. Johnfon in the afternoon,
of the fame day, vifiting me. Sir John Pringle,
Dr. Franklin, and fome more company, dined with
me to-day ; and Mr. Johnfon and General Ogle-
thorpe one day, Mr. Garrick alone another, and
David Hume and fome more *literati* another, dine
with me next week. I give admirable dinners and
good claret; and the moment I go abroad again,
which will be in a day or two, I fet up my chariot.
This is enjoying the fruits of my labours, and appearing like the friend of Paoli." This is fufficiently good, but the continuation is better,—and
mark how carelefsly thefe triumphs are introduced !
" By the by, the Earl of Pembroke and Captain
Meadows are juft fetting out for Corfica, and I
have the honour of introducing them by a letter to
the General. David Hume came on purpofe the
other day to tell me that the Duke of Bedford was
very fond of my book, and had recommended it to
the Duchefs. David is really amiable. I always regret to him his unlucky principles, and he
fmiles at my faith ; but I have a hope which he
has not, or pretends not to have. So who has the
beft of it, my reverend friend ?" Poor David, the
philofopher, is here taken at a fad difadvantage ;
and James the popinjay is making the beft of both
worlds at a great rate. No doubt " my reverend
friend" was greatly edified.

If you take Bofwell in his own fphere, and
on his own terms, he is worth any money. If you

should ever look down upon your bargain, he will
soon raise himself in the market by **a cheerful re-
hearsal** of his merits. These letters show, in a
hundred places, how thoroughly this ingenious
creature had persuaded himself of his own rare
virtue. On these occasions the Corsican General
naturally rushes to his mind, **as a sort of** unexceptionable reference. **When** his cross-grained father,
the shrewd old Laird of Auchinleck, writes with-
out a due sense of his paternal privilege, the tra-
velled youth exclaims, " How galling is it to the
friend of Paoli to be treated thus !" and then, giving
his correspondent that credit for discernment which
his father had justly forfeited, he fondly adds,
" Temple, would you not like such a son ? would
you not feel a glow of **parental joy ? I know you**
would."

The earlier portion **of the present** volume is
enlivened by the gayer sallies of our author, touching his numerous amours and flirtations. Some
of these **are** disreputable ; but most of them are
simply ridiculous. Of the former class is his passion for "a pretty, lively, black little lady,"—meaning by this description, what Pepys meant in using
similar terms, namely, a handsome brunette, and
not a nigger beauty. The affair adds little credit
to the character of Boswell ; and though not offen-
sively obtruded in the published portion of his
letters, it might perhaps have been omitted altogether **with** advantage.

Not so his courtship of the lovely Blair. This
is much too good a story to lose, and we shall treat

the reader to all the particulars we know. It is thus that our hero opens the catalogue of her attractions in a letter to his friend : " There is a young lady in the neighbourhood here who has an estate of her own, between two and three hundred a year, just eighteen, a genteel person, an agreeable face, of a good family, sensible, good-tempered, cheerful, pious. You know my grand object is the ancient family of Auchinleck,—a venerable and noble principle. How would it do to conclude an alliance with the neighbouring princess, and add her lands to our dominions ? *I should at once have a pretty little estate, a good house, and a sweet place.*" It is worthy of remark, that the summary of advantages contained in the last sentence does not include the lady,—except we suppose her to be in the house. We are then given to understand that the old Laird has been prompting his son in this direction. " My father is very fond of her ; it would make him perfectly happy : he gives me hints in this way : *I wish you had her, —no bad scheme this ; I think, a very good one.* But I will not be in a hurry ; there is plenty of time." Just so. In matters of this sort it is so easy to add temperance to prudence ! When love has its origin in " a venerable and noble principle," how calm and reasonable a thing it is !

But once embarked in any enterprise of the kind, our lover is not long wanting in enthusiasm. He presently proceeds with spirit, and soon arrives at the declamatory stage. " The lady in my neighbourhood is the finest woman I have ever

feen. I went and vifited her, and fhe was fo good
as to prevail with her mother to come to Auchinleck, where they ftayed four days, and in our romantic groves I adored her like a divinity." Then,
on a fomewhat lower key: "My father is very
defirous I fhould marry her,—all my relations, all
my neighbours, approve of it." The ftrain is
again raifed a little, but ftill it is no great things:
" She looked quite at home in the houfe of Auchinleck. Her picture would be an ornament to the
gallery. Her children would be all Bofwells and
Temples, and as fine women as thefe are excellent
men." Muft we conclude that love, like life itfelf,
is a rather mixed affair?

Nothing will fatisfy him now but making the
lady perfonally known to his friend. We have
many urgent appeals to this purpofe. " Temple,
you muft be at Auchinleck; you muft fee my
charming bride. If you cannot return in autumn,
pray refolve to take a ride now, and on pretence
of viewing the feat of your friend, view alfo the
woman who has his heart. . . . . My Signora is
indeed a wonderful creature: you fhall know all.
But again let me entreat of you to take one romantic ride, to oblige, moft effentially, your moft
cordial friend." This "romantic ride" is foon
arranged. Temple is to pay a vifit at Adamtown,
—the feat of the heirefs,—partly in the character
of ambaffador, and partly in the humbler character
of fpy. He is duly provided with an Itinerary and
" Inftructions." This extraordinary document is
ftill extant, and given in the volume which affords

us thefe particulars. **It is far** better than a ftate **paper,** and we **are tempted to** transfer it to our pages.

" Inftructions for Mr. Temple on his Tour to
Auchinleck and Adamtown.

"*He will fet out in the fly on Monday morning
and reach Glafgow by noon. Put up at Graham's,
and afk for the horfes befpoke by Mr. Bofwell.
Take tickets for the Friday's fly. Eat fome cold
victuals. Set out for Kingfwell, to which you have
good road; arrived there, get a guide to put you
through the muir to Loudoun; from thence Thomas
knows the road to Auchinleck, where the worthy
overfeer, Mr. James Bruce, will receive you. Be
cofy with him, and you will like him much; expect
but moderate entertainment, as the family is not at
home. Tuefday.—See the houfe; look at the front;
choofe your room; advife as to pavilions. Have
James Bruce to conduct you to the cab-houfe; to the
old caftle; to where I am to make the fuperb grotto;
up the river to Broomfholm; the natural bridge;
the grotto; the grotto walk down to the Gothic
bridge: anything elfe he pleafes. Wednefday.—
Breakfaft at eight; fet out at nine; Thomas will
bring you to Adamtown a little after eleven. Send
up your name; if poffible, put up your horfes there,
—they can have cut grafs; if not, Thomas will
take them to Mountain, a place a mile off, and come
back and wait at dinner. Give Mifs Blair my
letter. Salute her and her mother; afk to walk.
See the place fully; think what improvements fhould*

be made. Talk of my mare, the purse, the chocolate. Tell, you are my very old and intimate **friend.** *Praise me for my good qualities,—you know them; but talk also how odd,* **how inconstant,** *how impetuous. Ask gravely, Pray don't you imagine there is something of madness in that family? Talk of* **my** *various travels,—German princes,—Voltaire and Rousseau. Talk of my father;* **my** *strong desire to have my own house. Observe her well. See,* **how amiable!** *Judge* **if** *she would* **be** *happy with your friend. Think of me as the great man at Adamtown,—quite classical, too! Study the mother. Remember well what passes. Stay tea. At six, order horses to go to New Mills, two miles from Loudoun; but if they press you to stay all night,* **do** *it. Be a man of as much ease as possible. Consider what a romantic* **expedition** *you* **are on;** **take** *notes; perhaps you now fix me for life.* Thursday. *—Return to Glasgow from New Mills or from Adamtown. See High Church, New Church College, and particularly the paintings, and put half-a-crown into the box at the door. My friend Mr. Robert Fowles will show you all.* Friday.— *Come back in* **the** *fly. Bring your portmanteau here. We shall settle where you are to lodge. N.B. —You are to keep an exact account of your charges."*

It is just possible that something almost as ridiculous as the above may have been written gravely down; but such a composition has never publicly transpired before. Every line of it, moreover, is characteristic of the weak and worldly sinner it

proceeds from ; and, on the whole, it is hard to
fay whether it is more welcome to the humourift,
or more faddening to the graver ftudent of humanity.

Mr. Temple feems to have been well received,
and to have made a favourable impreffion upon
the " princefs " to whom he was accredited ; for
" fhe and Mrs. Blair were quite charmed with the
young parfon, with his neat black periwig and his
polite addrefs." But the caufe he fought to forward was not deftined to profper. From this
time forth no genial fun fmiled on the loves of
Auchinleck and Adamtown. The fwain wrote
duly to thank his miftrefs for the entertainment of
his friend ; but he waited long and anxioufly for
a reply. " What can be the matter ? " he exclaims to Temple. " Probably the letter you
carried has been thought ftrange, and fo diftant
from any rational fcheme, that it has been refolved
no longer to carry on fo friendly and eafy an intercourfe with me. Or what would you fay if the
formal nabob whom you faw there has ftruck in,
and fo good a bird in hand has made the heirefs
quit the uncertain profpect of catching the bird in
the bufh ? I am curious to fee how this matter
will turn out. The mare, the purfe, the chocolate, where are they now ? " Ay, indeed, where !
We fhall no doubt hear again of that " formal
nabob."

In the meantime there feems to be fome hope
for our friend ; his fun at leaft fhines out for a
feafon. He receives a moft agreeable letter from

his goddefs, explaining, apologizing, making all fo bright. He writes to his friend in the higheft fpirits. "Am I not now as well as I can be? What condefcenfion! What a defire to pleafe! She ftudies my difpofition and refolves to be cautious, &c. Adorable woman! Don't you think I had **better not write again** till I fee her?" And after an interval of fome weeks he has the happinefs to date from Adamtown. "In fhort, I am fitting in the room with my princefs, who is at this moment a finer woman than ever fhe appeared to be before." Perhaps this is becaufe the fpell of the enchanting heirefs is ftrongeft on her own *ground.* But even here his happinefs is not unqualified. He proceeds to complain of her former treatment, and to forebode troubles in the future. "At laft I am here, and our meeting has **been fuch** as you paint in your laft but one. I **have** been here one night; fhe infifted on my ftaying another. I am dreffed in green and gold. I have my chaife, in which I fit alone like Mr. Gray; and Thomas rides by me in a claret-coloured fuit with a filver-laced hat." Alas, for the unreafonablenefs and caprice of woman! Even that fplendid apparition of green and gold does not take away the lady's breath, or much affect the pulfes of her heart. "But the princefs and I have not yet made up our quarrel; fhe talks lightly of it. I am refolved to have a ferious converfation with her to-morrow morning." The interview accordingly takes place; but nothing fatisfactory refults. The ftate of the cafe appears

to be fomething like this : neither of the parties is
really in love, but one of them is fool enough to
think that he is fo, and therefore naturally becomes an amufement and a prey to the other. A
woman that is no better than a pufs, will not
hefitate to play with a heart that is no bigger than
a moufe.

We come now toward the end of this em-
broglio. For the reader's fake we fhould have
been glad if our limits had permitted the infertion
of the thirty-fourth letter of this volume,—for it
contains the beft fcene in the whole comedy,
though not the laft. Poor Bofwell, who entered
upon his part with fuch gay good humour, is now
in earneft, and has perfuaded himfelf (though only
for the moment) that the heroine before him is
really the object of his ardent affections. But the
princefs whifpers him, with a cruel mixture of
franknefs and archnefs, "I wifh I liked you as
well as I do Auchinleck!" She, too, it feems,
had caft wiftful glances over her neighbour's
fence, and hence her coquetting with a man whom
fhe probably defpifed. But we muft haften to
the clofe, which is really a very droll affair. Bofwell has met with another unfortunate fuitor of
the princefs,—apparently the "formal nabob"
aforefaid,—but one whom fhe had never encouraged ; for in this cafe there was no tempting
propinquity of two eftates. But our young laird
feels a fympathy, and foon puts him on an equal
footing in the matter of their forlorn pretenfions.
They repair to a tavern, and talk over their

grievances. " We fat till two this morning ; we gave our words, as men of honour, that we would be honeft to each other, fo that neither fhould fuffer needlefsly ; and to fatisfy ourfelves of our real fituation, we gave our words that we fhould both afk her this morning, and I fhould go firft. Could anything be better than this ?" We fhould fay, Certainly not,—but that our eye has already caught what follows. Bofwell goes for his anfwer, and he duly gets it. " ' What then,' I exclaimed, ' have I no chance ?' ' No,' faid fhe. I afked her to fay fo upon her word and honour. She fairly repeated the words. So I think, Temple, I had enough." And this time we quite agree with him.

The **nabob** goes, and fares likewife. The haughty princefs will anfwer no idle queftions about other fuitors ; but the nabob is welcome to his *No.* What becomes of the princefs does not afterwards appear. There is fome rumour of a Baronet,—but fome rumour alfo of another rupture. Perhaps fhe repented that fhe did not take the hand (and land) of the gay young Mafter of Auchinleck. That gentleman is not ferioufly hurt ; for it is a promifing fign of his recovery that he turns to his friend with this pleafant obferva- tion : " Now that all is over, I fee many faults in her which I did not fee before." Not very generous certainly ; but perhaps not quite unjuft.

We wifh to have done with this portion of Bofwell's life, and to witnefs his conduct as a

married man.   But it is not eafy to efcape from
his labyrinth of loves.   Ireland, Italy, and even
Holland, in turns fupply the emiffaries of that
tender goddefs whofe willing flave he is ; and no
fooner does he find himfelf at variance with one,
than he is in eager treaty with another.   " I am
exceedingly lucky," he writes, " in having efcaped
the infenfible Mifs B. and the furious Zelide ; for
I have now feen the fineft creature that ever was
formed, *la belle Irlandaife.*   Figure to yourfelf,
Temple,"—but the picture is at full length, and
our page is very limited.   Yet we cannot refift a
few of the notes of admiration which enfue.
" From morning to night I admired the charming
Mary Anne.   Upon my honour, I never was fo
much in love ; I never was before in a fituation
to which there was not fome objection, but here
every flower is united, and not a thorn to be
found. . . . I was allowed to walk a great deal
with Mifs —— ; I repeated my fervent paffion
to her again and again ; fhe was pleafed, and I
could fwear that her little heart beat.   I carved
the firft letter of her name on a tree : I cut off a
lock of her hair, *malè pertinax.*   She promifed not
to forget me, nor to marry a Lord before March."
But long before that time comes round, our fwain
is himfelf forfworn.   He is even once more on his
knees to the cruel princefs !   But that is not to be.

At length,—to his own relief and ours,—Bofwell indeed gets married.   His choice, if we may
call it fo, falls on his coufin, Mifs Margaret Mont-
gomerie,—a lady of few perfonal attractions, but

many higher virtues. Dr. Johnſon ſpoke with
reſpect of Mrs. Boſwell, although ſhe regarded
him with no eſpecial favour. Her huſband praiſed
her both in ſeaſon and out of ſeaſon, like a fooliſh
huſband as he was. He kept a book which he
called *Uxoriana*, in which the " good things " ſhe
uttered were preſerved.

Boſwell's marriage was, no doubt, of the greateſt
value to him. It gave him ſome intervals of pure
happineſs; it deferred the moment of his impending ruin. But no earthly bleſſing will counteract
the operation of cheriſhed and habitual vices; and
to theſe Boſwell had long been enſlaved. He
had learned, in convivial meetings, to take exceſs
of drink; and as years rolled on, the habit
ſtrengthened, and every hour of deſpondency urged
him to have freſh recourſe to the deſtructive
ſtimulus. His abſence from home, his unſettled
purſuits, his eager deſire for the notice, the company, the patronage of the great, added to the
fever of his life, and indirectly foſtered the accurſed
luſt of drink.

Early in 1789, Mrs. Boſwell fell ſeriouſly ill.
Still her huſband lingered in London,—for Scotland ſeems to have grown increaſingly diſtaſteful
to him, and he had gained the reluctant conſent of
his wife to make the family reſidence in the Engliſh
metropolis. But her increaſing malady renders
this ſtep impoſſible. It is curious to remark, in
Boſwell's letters to Temple at this period, how his
ſocial enjoyments are ſlightly daſhed with a little
ſelf-reproach. At length he breaks away from his

unworthy allurements, and goes down to witnefs the fuffering, and the patience of his wife. " How difmal, how affecting," he exclaims, " is it to me to fee my coufin, my friend, my wife, wafting before my eyes!" He returns once more to London ; and on his next fummons home arrives too late.

Perhaps the lofs of a good wife falls with the greateft feverity upon the moft unworthy hufband. He lofes the ftay of his houfe as well as the angel of his purer hours ; and miffes, under the preffure of a thoufand claims, the virtue of her vicarious excellence. And as his lofs is relatively greater, fo are his confolations pofitively fewer. Bofwell found this to be the cafe when the affliction of his wife ended in death. Truly had Johnfon pro-phefied in profpect of this event, " In lofing her you will lofe your anchor, and be toft without ftability by the waves of life." His mind became a prey to the bittereft remorfe ; and his houfe was left to him very defolate. His children claimed that care which he felt himfelf perfectly helplefs to beftow. There is fomething very felfifh in his grief,—perhaps there is in that of moft men,— but ftill it is painful to witnefs. " I cannot ex-prefs to you, Temple, what I fuffer from the lofs of my valuable wife, and the mother of my chil-dren. While fhe lived, I had no occafion almoft to think concerning my family ; every particular was thought of by her, better than I could. I am the moft helplefs of human beings ; I am in a ftate very much that of one in defpair." He re-

curs to her memory again in perplexity. " O my
friend, what would I give for one of thofe years
with my deareft coufin, friend, and wife, which
are paft ! . . . She ufed, on all occafions, to be
my comforter ; fhe, methinks, could now fuggeft
rational thoughts to me ; but where is fhe ? O
my Temple, I am miferable." It is thus that the
louder grave revenges the unreproaching patience
of our friends.

Bofwell furvived his wife fix years, dying on
the 19th of May, 1795. His career is monitory
as well as amufing. It fhows us how far mere
natural parts and literary talents may fall below
the ordinary ftandard of natural wifdom,—that
genius itfelf may incur both the taint and the difgrace of vice,—and that the bittereft lofs and
forrow which befall us are due, not to the immediate providence of God, but to the culpable im-
providence of man.

THE TERROR OF BAGDAT.

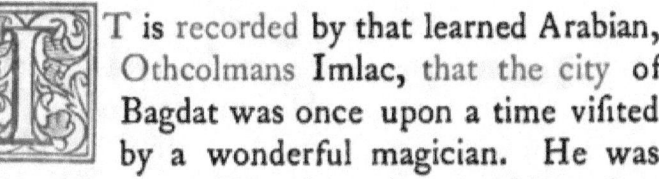

T is recorded by that learned Arabian, Othcolmans Imlac, that the city of Bagdat was once upon a time vifited by a wonderful magician. He was a venerable man with a long beard whiter than fnow; but he walked erect without the affiftance of a ftaff, as that which he conftantly carried in his right hand meafured only one foot in length, and was the inftrument of his remarkable enchantments. Soon after his arrival it became known in the city that there refided an awful power in this perfonage; that whenever it pleafed him to make the flighteft wafture of his wand in the face of any man, it caufed him in an inftant to lofe all feeling and confcioufnefs, and fo to remain virtually dead, through any period of months or years, till the action was exactly repeated and the fpell removed.

When the people heard this it brought to fome rejoicing and to others difmay. Thofe who fuffered from fevere bodily pain, or from mental torture yet more intolerable, hailed it as the promife of immediate relief; while the young, the hopeful, and the pleafure-loving, trembled at the notion of fo terrible a power over all the enjoyments of life. It was a matter of ferious inquiry, therefore, to both thefe claffes, whether the magician was of a friendly or a malicious nature ; whether likely to deaden the anguifh of the afflicted, or to rob youth of its gaiety and delight.

Prefently it was proclaimed in Bagdat that all thofe perfons who were accuftomed to invoke death for the fake of oblivion were now invited to obtain oblivion without death. Elrica, the magician, would give audience for that purpofe in a public fquare. But, in order that he might not be overwhelmed by the crowd of fuppliants, it was enjoined that the feveral claffes who fought this advantage or relief fhould come on appointed days, according to the nature of their cafes. Now it was not the moft neceffitous, or thofe in circumftances of the greateft mifery, who were invited to come on the firft day, but only that eminent few who, though bleft with every comfort of life, were known to have profeffed a philofophic indifference to its enjoyments, and a conftant readinefs and even wifh to relinquifh them. The good Elrica evidently defigned to fhow before the whole city how unconcernedly the wife man fubmits to death, or voluntarily lapfes into that unconfcioufnefs in which the horror of annihilation itfelf confifts.

The avenues to the fquare in which the magician fat were early befieged by eager crowds, but the fquare itfelf was refpectfully abandonedto that perfonage. It had been rumoured that a fmall band of philofophers were preparing to embrace the opportunity of antedating the oblivion of death. For fome time, however, no fuch party appeared; and the front ranks of the crowd were gradually urging the others back, from a fear that the magician, who was prepared with ftaff in hand, fhould waft it in their face and leave them for dead. At length two men, dreffed in long white robes, advanced through the yielding multitude, encouraging each other, and finging a cheerful fong in very feeble accents. When they faw Elrica, the magician, they paufed for a moment, and one of them feemed inclined to return; but his brother philofopher took him by the arm and led him gently forward. Then faid Elrica to them, "Hail!" And they anfwered, "Hail, mafter! But tell us," they continued, "how long fhall we lie fenfelefs and as dead before thee?" "Even till I choofe that ye fhall rife," faid Elrica; "and if I be called away from this city ye may never be reftored or raifed." Then the one that would have turned grew very pale, for the magician lifted his little ftaff; but the other invited its wafture towards himfelf, and receiving the influence full upon his face fank gently down upon the ground. Then the man who yet ftood fell trembling upon his knees, and implored that he might be fuffered to return home, which was granted by Elrica, "For," faid he, "you are not worthy to partake of his repofe."

No others prefented themfelves before the ma-

gician that day. The crowd continued to look
with increafing awe upon his face, which feemed
to grow fterner every minute ; and then they fur-
veyed with mingled admiration and pity the calm
and corpfe-like body of the philofopher, who was
prefently removed to a chamber in Elrica's houfe.

On the following day all who fuffered from extreme bodily pain were incited to feek relief at the
hands of the magician. As many in the city were
known to be fo afflicted, it was expected that a
large number would prefent themfelves in the
public fquare. And, indeed, the number was not
fmall of thofe who were borne thither on litters,
or came fupported by encouraging friends. Yet
it was obferved that whereas many had groaned
moft loudly under their torments until this time,
they now grew fuddenly mild in their complaining,
or altogether filent. Indeed, it feemed as though
the fight only of the awful Elrica had fufficed to
remove their pain ; and not a few profeffed themfelves fo far recovered as to have no occafion for
the remedy of total oblivion. Some, however,
were induced to accept of that extreme relief;
yet when on the brink of unconfcioufnefs, which
fhould have been to fuch tormented beings welcome as the gate of Paradife, the boldeft of them
were feized with a tremor, and their faces turned
white as the magician's beard. One poor fufferer,
who, peradventure had loved nature and his
fpecies more than he had wearied of a painful life,
glanced fondly, as for the laft time, at the declin-
ing fun and the human crowd, and held fo ftrongly

by the hand of a relative or friend that the fpell which fmote him fenfelefs to the ground diffolved not the paffionate clafp, and the magician was fain to unite them in one fate. For the moft part the patients, however reftlefs and talkative before, grew thoughtful and taciturn on approaching El- rica; but fome ceafed not talking to the laft. It was efpecially obferved that two women came heedleffly forward as drawn by the novelty of the fcene rather than perfonal neceffity; and they chatted together loudly and irreverently even in the prefence of the magician. But he fuddenly filenced both by waving his ftaff in the face of one; for when the other faw her companion re- duced to fuch a pitiful and abfolute filence, being indeed the fame as dead fince fhe could no longer talk, fhe turned fuddenly upon her heel and fled for her very life.

The evening being come, it was found that few only of the fufferers in the city had fubmitted to have their pain affuaged by the fufpenfion of all fenfe and confcioufnefs. Thefe few were then re- moved to the chamber of filence in the houfe of Elrica; and it was announced that any whofe minds were diftracted by misfortune or crime, and efpecially fuch as were meditating violence againft themfelves, were bidden to feek relief from the magician in the fquare. But when the day arrived, and Elrica was feated in his accuftomed place, no one ventured near him. A number of all claffes, including the wretched and the poor as well as the opulent and the gay, gathered at a diftance in the several streets converging to the square : but thefe were drawn only by curiofity and ftood repelled by fear. The very widow, newly robbed of her beloved, and whofe voice not many hours before had ftartled the dull night with cries, imploring death to return and take her alfo, now hid herfelf behind the crowd, and glanced as occafion offered at the dreaded difpenfer of oblivion. The flighteft intimation of her wearinefs of life would have caufed the multitude to fall back, and give her free accefs to his prefence ; but fhe uttered not a whifper and almoft held her breath.

At length a noife, as of fome one ftruggling, attracted all eyes to one fpot, when, the crowd dividing, two men—officers of the city—were feen hauling by the fhoulders a wretched creature, pale and bewildered, who refifted with what little might he had. But on feeing the magician he was feized with confternation and trembling, and they that dragged him hitherto henceforward carried him. Then laying him at the feet of Elrica, one of the officers faid, " Hail, mafter ! This man was found by us at daybreak in the act of felf-deftruction. Already was he ftanding on the river's edge, adjufting to his neck two heavy weights of brafs, when we feized him by the arm, and remembering your injunction we charitably fought to lead him hither. But though he feemed at firft to yield compliance, as not forry to be forced back to life, yet with difficulty have we urged him towards your prefence ; for many times did he feek to linger in the bazaars, looking covetoufly at all the wares expofed, and feeking opportunity to efcape. Then he became reftive, and behold he is now convulfed before you." As the officer ceafed fpeaking, the magician fmiled grimly at the inconfiftency of the poor wretch in throes before him; and then waving the wand in his face, exchanged the pallor of cowardice for that of death-like trance.

Now when it became known that during the ftay of Elrica none died in the city, or perifhed otherwife than by his hand, he was fhunned on every fide, as the only pretender to the ancient power of death. The fingle fear of the bridegroom in his gay proceffion was the poffible encounter of that grim old man; and the profperous merchant, who paffed a luxurious evening in recalling the ample profits of the day, or in forecafting golden ventures of the morrow, feared the intrufion of that dreaded ftep, and the fudden accefs of a fleep which fhould prove too dreamlefs and too long. The refult was a general clamour for the departure of the magician; and Elrica was efcorted through the city gates. Then all things became as before. Difeafe and death refumed their natural forms; but a great terror was lifted from the heart of the city, and though the plague from time to time ravaged it in every quarter, the mingled current of bufinefs and pleafure was never interrupted as in the time of that myfterious vifitor.